Praise for

'Classic space opera, elegantly written and beautifully plotted' GUARDIAN

'This is a hugely fun ride. It has empires crashing, civil wars, aliens, humans, scheming clans, plucky young heroes and villians fighting space battles in huge starships – what more can you ask for?' ALIEN ONLINE

'Fearsomely inventive space opera' SFX

'With THE PRAXIS, Walter Jon Williams has succeeded in creating the perfect contemporary space opera, revved up and ready to take the SF genre by force with all the artistry and panache one could ask for' ENIGMA

'Crammed full with worm holes, space ships, anti-matter bombs and all the paraphernalia of high space opera, this is a great read' THE TIMES

'Fascinating . . . this is the new space opera – done with grace and imagination' TIME OUT

'What sets THE PRAXIS apart from its more conventional kin . . . is the adroitness with which it integrates battles and disasters and species-wide politicking with the intimate, the personal, and the social. A writer who can make a formal reception, a dinner party, or a staff meeting as gripping as a fleet action is a rarity and a treasure, and that is just what we have in Williams' LOCUS

Walter Jon Williams is American, but went to school in the UK and the US. He has written SF novels since the mid-80s, and is the winner of both the Hugo and Nebula Awards. His novels include HARDWIRED, ARISTOI and METROPOLITAN. He lives in New Mexico, USA.

The Praxis

Walter Jon Williams

EARTHLIGHT

LONDON • SYDNEY • NEW YORK • TOKYO • SINGAPORE • TORONTO

www.earthlight.co.uk

First published in Great Britain by Earthlight, 2002
This edition first published by Earthlight, 2003
An imprint of Simon & Schuster UK Ltd
A Viacom Company

1 3 5 7 9 10 8 6 4 2

Simon & Schuster UK Ltd
Africa House
64–78 Kingsway
London WC2B 6AH

www.simonsays.co.uk

Simon & Schuster Australia
Sydney

A CIP catalogue record for this book is available from the British Library

ISBN 0-7434-2897-8

Typeset by Palimpsest Book Production Limited,
Polmont, Stirlingshire
Printed and bound in Great Britain by
Cox & Wyman Ltd, Reading, Berkshire

For Kathy Hedges

And with special thanks to Geoffrey Landis for wormhole physics, Steve Howe for information on the uses of antimatter, and to Tracy Clark for checking my math.

Thanks is due also to Daniel Abraham, Melinda Snodgrass, Sage Walker, Terry England, Yvonne Coats, SM Stirling, George RR Martin, Sally Gwylan, Emily Mah, Trent Zelazny, John Miller, Terry Boren, and especially to Caitlin Blasdell, without whom, etc.

All that is important is known.
The Praxis, *Preamble*.

Prologue

The Shaa was the last of its kind. It lay on a couch in the Great Refuge, the huge domed building carved out of the great granite plateau of the High City, the massive edifice from which the Shaa had once set forth to conquer their empire, from which their councils had ruled the destiny of billions, and – now – to which they came to die.

The Shaa was named Anticipation of Victory – it had been born in the early days of the Praxis, when the Shaa had commenced to plan conquests but had not yet begun them, and in the course of its long life it had personally witnessed the glories and triumphs that had followed. Other races had fallen, one by one, beneath the Shaa yoke, and on these the Shaa and its peers had imposed the uniformity of their rule.

Anticipation of Victory itself had not left the Great Refuge in centuries. It was surrounded at all times by attendants and officials, members of subject races who brought reports and requests, who transmitted its orders to the farthest reaches of its dominions. Servants washed and dressed the Shaa, maintained the vast computer network to which its nerves had been connected, and brought choice foods to cater to its diminishing appetite. Though it was never alone, not for an instant, nevertheless the Shaa was tormented by the bitter pangs of loneliness.

There was no one left to understand. No one with whom to share its memories of glory.

Memories of those early days were undiminished. The

Shaa remembered with brilliant clarity the fever that burned among its peers, the urge to bend all others, to bend the universe itself, to the perfect truth of the Praxis. It remembered the splendour of the early victories, how the primitive Naxids had been turned to the service of the Shaa, how others had then fallen, the Terrans, the Torminel, the Lai-owns, and many other races.

Yet with each conquest had come diminished expectation, a slight reduction of the fever that burned in the Shaa. Each race first had to be raised to the knowledge of their duty, cultivated with exquisite care like trees raised from seedlings, trees whose limbs had to be tied and twisted and shaped so that they would achieve perfection and union with the Praxis. And, like trees, the servitor races had to be pruned, pruned with bullets and whips and skinning knives, with the great annihilating fire of antimatter bombs, with the slow wasting of radiation and the slower, inexorable decline of starvation. The labour had been immense, the burden enormous, and the results uncertain.

If only the Shaa had more time! If they had only had a few more thousand years in which to cultivate their garden of perfection, then Anticipation of Victory could die in the certainty that its glorious task would be fulfilled.

But the Shaa hadn't the time they needed. The oldest succumbed first, their memories fading – not the old memories, which remained clear, but the newer memories which, unable to displace the old, failed to find a place in their minds.

The Shaa became unable to remember the flourishing of their own dream. They lost, not the past, but the present.

They sought artificial aids – massive computer memories that could be linked to their own nervous systems and which recorded their own lives in exquisite detail. But in time accessing these memories grew wearisome and, eventually, a painful burden no longer worth the effort.

So one by one, the great constellation of the Shaa began to wink out. The Shaa did not fear to inflict death, nor did they fear death themselves. Sad in the knowledge that they had become a burden on their own dream, they chose their own deaths, and when they died, they died with ceremony.

Anticipation of Victory was the last. It lay on its couch, among the great machines through which it searched for his memories, and it knew that soon the time would come to lay down its responsibilities.

It had done its best to guide the younger races along the proper paths. In its time it had awarded both great riches and terrible punishments. It had created a system by which the Praxis could be maintained after its death, that would hold the empire stable.

Its greatest hope was that, after its death, nothing would change.

Nothing at all. Or ever.

One

'Of course, following the Great Master's death, I will kill myself.'

Lieutenant Gareth Martinez, keeping pace alongside the longer-legged Fleet Commander Enderby, felt himself stumble as he heard the words.

'My lord?' He drove his legs through the stumble to stride, once more, off Enderby's left shoulder. Their heels rang again in unison on the shaved, glittering asteroid material that floored the Commandery.

'I've volunteered,' Enderby said, in his prosaic, literal tone. 'My family needs a representative on the pyre, and I'm the most suitable candidate. I'm at the apex of my career, my children are well established, and my wife has given me a divorce.' He looked at Martinez from beneath his level white brows. 'My death will assure that my name, and my family's name, will be honoured for ever.'

And help everyone to forget that little financial scandal involving your wife, Martinez thought. It was a pity that Enderby's spouse couldn't be the family sacrifice instead of the fleet commander.

A pity for Martinez in particular.

'I'll miss you, my lord,' he said.

'I've spoken to Captain Tarafah about you,' Enderby went on. 'He's agreed to take you aboard as communications officer on the *Corona*.'

'Thank you, my lord,' Martinez said, and tried not to

let his voice reflect the dismay that echoed coldly down his bones.

The Martinez family was among the Peers, the clans that the Great Masters, the Shaa, had placed over all creation. Though all Peers were equal in the sight of the Shaa, the Peers' own views were less Olympian. It wasn't enough just to be a Peer. You had to be the *right kind* of Peer.

And Martinez was definitely the wrong kind. While near omnipotent on its distant home world of Laredo, the Martinez clan were provincial nobodies to the high-caste Peers whose palaces ornamented the High City of Zanshaa. The fine gradations of rank perceived by the Peers had no status in law, but their weight was felt everywhere in Peer society. Martinez' birth entitled him to a place in the Peers' military academy followed by a commission, but that was all.

In six years' service he had risen to lieutenant. That was as far as his father had come in a dozen years, before Marcus Martinez had resigned in frustration and returned to Laredo to devote himself to making money on a grand scale.

What Martinez needed was a powerful patron who would advance him in the service hierarchy. He thought he had found that patron in Fleet Commander Enderby, who seemed impressed with his abilities and was willing to overlook his obscure home and the wretched provincial accent that, try as he might, he had been unable to lose.

What do you do when your senior officer announces his intention to commit suicide? Martinez wondered. Try to talk him out of it?

'Tarafah is a good officer,' Enderby assured. 'He'll look after you.'

Tarafah is only a lieutenant-captain, Martinez thought. So even if Tarafah decided that Martinez was the most brilliant officer he'd ever met — and the chances of *that* were not high — he wouldn't be in a position to give Martinez a promotion to the next rank. He could only recommend

Martinez to a superior, and that superior would be patron to another set of clients whose needs would rank greater than Martinez' own.

I am hip-deep in the shit, Martinez concluded. Unless he could talk the fleet commander into changing his mind about annihilating himself.

'My lord,' he began, and then was interrupted as another officer, Senior Squadron Commander Elkizer, approached with his entourage. Elkizer and his staff were Naxids, members of the first species to be conquered by the Shaa, and Martinez suppressed annoyance as they scuttled across the polished floor towards Enderby. Not only were they interrupting an important moment, the Naxids always made him uncomfortable.

Perhaps it was the way they moved. The Naxids had six limbs, four legs and another, upper pair that could be used as either arms or legs. They seemed to have only two speeds: *stop,* and *very, very fast.* When they moved, the four feet were in continual motion, scrabbling at the ground heedless of terrain or even of success, flinging the body forward as fast as they could; and when Naxids wanted to go particularly fast they lowered their centauroid bodies to the ground and used the front two limbs as well, their bodies snaking from side to side in a liquid whiplike motion that frankly gave Martinez the creeps.

The Naxids' bodies were covered with black, beaded scales ornamented with a shifting pattern of red. The swift-moving scarlet patterns were used for communication among the Naxids, communications that other species found difficult or impossible to decipher. In order not to hamper this communication, the Naxid officers wore uniforms of chameleon weave, that faithfully duplicated the patterns flashing underneath.

On their home world, in their primitive state, the Naxids had travelled in packs led by one dominant personality –

and they still did. Even without rank badges, you could tell by body language and demeanour which Naxids were dominant and which subservient. The high-ranking Naxids were impossibly arrogant, and the lower castes cringingly submissive.

Squadron Leader Elkizer scuttled towards Fleet Commander Enderby and slammed to a halt, his upper body thrown back to bare his throat for the killing stroke.

Kill me if you so desire, my lord: that was the service's ideal of subordination.

Elkizer's entourage – Martinez wanted to use the word *pack* – imitated their superior. Standing at attention, they came up to Enderby's chin, with bodies the size of a very large dog.

'As you were, lords,' Enderby said amiably, and then engaged Elkizer in a discussion of whether one of Elkizer's cruisers would be out of dock in time for the Great Master's death – and Enderby's own suicide, of course. This was complicated by the fact that no one knew when the Great Master's death would come, though everyone was reasonably certain it would be soon.

'Leave nothing undone,' Enderby said to Martinez after the warm-blooded reptiles went on their way. 'You won't mind some extra work helping me with my preparations?'

'Of course not, my lord.' Which meant, damn it, that his meeting with Warrant Officer Amanda Taen was going to have to be postponed.

'We don't know the day,' Enderby said, 'but we must be ready when it comes.'

Martinez felt a sodden, drizzling cloud of gloom press on his skull. 'Yes, my lord,' he said.

Enderby's office had a soft, aromatic scent, something like vanilla. It occupied the southeast corner of the Commandery, with a curving window that made up two walls. From his office Enderby was privileged with a magnificent view which both looked down to the limitless, brooding expanse of the

Lower Town, and upwards to Zanshaa's accelerator ring, the thin arc of brilliant sunlit silver that cut across its viridian sky and circled the entire planet.

But Enderby had always been indifferent to the sight. His desk faced away from the huge window, towards the interior of the Commandery, and beyond it to the nearly-empty Great Refuge of the Masters, where his duty lay.

Martinez had to suppress his admiration for the view while he was with the fleet commander. Enderby had a knack of making himself indifferent to all but the business at hand, but Martinez was more easily distracted. He could have dreamed out the window all day.

Martinez was the fleet commander's communications officer, supervising messages between Enderby and his extensive command, which included the dozens of ships that belonged to the Home Fleet; the installations on the ground on Zanshaa and elsewhere in the system; the paramilitary Antimatter Service that serviced the accelerator ring; the installations, training facilities, docks, and stores on the ring itself; the elevators that ran personnel and cargo from the planet's surface to the ring and back; communication with Enderby's superiors the Fleet Control Board; and of course the intricate communications net that webbed it all together.

Despite the size and complexity of his duties, Martinez usually had plenty of time on his hands. The Home Fleet ran on well-worn routine, established over the thousands of years of the Shaa dominion. Most of the messages reaching Martinez dealt with matters that scarcely required Enderby's attention: routine situation reports, information on stores and requisitions, on maintenance, on personnel entering and graduating from the training academies. These Martinez filed without ever sending them across the fleet commander's screens. Flagged for Enderby's attention were communications from friends or clients, reports on casualties from accidents – which always resulted in a personal note of condolence from the fleet commander – and, more importantly, appeals from the sentences imposed in the event of breaches of discipline or criminal activity. Enderby always paid close attention to these cases, and sometimes sent a series of painfully blunt questions to the accusing officer that resulted in charges being dropped.

Martinez felt relief whenever this happened. He had seen enough of service justice to know how rough it was, and often how lazy the investigating officer. If he should ever be subject to the draconian penalties of the law, he very much wanted someone like Enderby reviewing the case.

During Martinez' time as the fleet commander's aide, nothing like a real emergency had ever occurred to disturb the orderly flow of routine. Procedures were that well honed.

But the leisurely pace of Martinez' regular work was as nothing compared to the private business on which Enderby concentrated that day. Even though Martinez had worked with Enderby almost daily for months, he had no idea how complex Enderby's life was.

Enderby had a thousand details to dispose of, bequests to friends, children, relatives, dependants, and subordinates. He was colossally wealthy, a fact Martinez hadn't quite realized. Though the fleet commander stayed in modest lodgings in the Commandery, he owned a palace in the High City, which he'd closed, apparently, after his divorce. This was left as a bequest to his eldest daughter, who held a high post in the Ministry of Fisheries, though suites were left to other children for their lifetimes. Other pieces of property on Zanshaa and elsewhere had to be dealt with, along with the contents of bank and stock accounts, bonds, and a bewildering array of complex financial instruments.

Martinez sat at his desk in Enderby's office and processed these bequests along with his normal signals traffic. Into the traffic he managed to insert a personal item, a request to Warrant Officer Taen begging a postponement of their date.

Enderby's secretary, an elderly sub-lieutenant named Gupta who had been with him for years, was likewise kept busy, dealing with other aspects of a long, rich, complex life now being brought to a conclusion.

Commanders of fleet rank were allowed to recommend a certain number of promotions on retirement. If a list existed, it did not cross Martinez' desk, and Martinez knew better than to ask Gupta if it had crossed his.

But he very much wished he knew whether his name was on it.

One personal message came to Martinez during the course of his day. Not from Warrant Officer Taen, unfortunately, but from his own sister Vipsania. She looked at him lazily out of the desk display, and tossed her dark hair with a studied gesture. 'We're having a party early next month.' Her tones were even more plummy, if possible, than when he'd last heard them. 'We'd love for you to come, Gareth darling, but I imagine you'll be too busy.'

Martinez didn't send a reply. He knew his sister well enough to know that he had just heard an order to be too busy to attend their party – the 'Gareth, darling' was a clue he couldn't miss.

Vipsania and the two other Martinez sisters, Walpurga and Sempronia, had turned up on Zanshaa just a few months after Martinez had begun his tour of duty. They rented half of the old Shelley Palace and plunged into Zanshaa society. Sempronia was supposedly attending university, and the other two looking after her, but if there was any education going on, it did not seem to be from textbooks.

Martinez' previous memories of his three sisters had been of children – annoying, intelligent, conniving, pestiferous children, admittedly, but still children. The formidable young women who held court in the Shelley Palace seemed not only grown up, but ageless – like nymphs gracing a fountain, they seemed eternal, strangely out of time.

They might have been expected to need Martinez' help in establishing themselves in the capital. But they had come with letters of introduction, and hadn't needed his help – hadn't needed him at all. If anything, they wanted him to stay away. They had lost their Laredo accents somewhere in the course of growing up, and his own speech was a reminder of their provincial origin that might embarrass them in front of their new glit friends.

Sometimes Martinez wondered if he disliked his sisters. But what did fountain nymphs care if they were liked or not? They simply *were*.

By the time Enderby finished his work the sun had set, and Zanshaa's silver accelerator ring had been half-eclipsed by the planet's shadow and was visible now only as a constellation of lights arcing across the night sky. Night birds hunted insects outside the curved window. Sour sweat gathered under Martinez' arms and under the collar of his dark green uniform tunic. His tailbone ached. He wanted to shower and have Warrant Officer Taen massage his shoulders with long, purposeful fingers.

Fleet Commander Enderby signed hard copy of the remaining documents and thumbprinted them. Martinez and Gupta witnessed the documents where necessary. Then Enderby turned off his screens and rose from his seat, rolling his shoulders in a subdued stretch consonant with the dignity of his office.

'Thank you, my lords,' he said, and then looked at Martinez. 'Lieutenant Martinez, will you see the invitations to the ship commanders are delivered?'

Martinez' heart sank. The 'invitations' – not the sort any commander would dare to decline – were to a discussion of fleet dispositions on the day of the Great Master's death, and by service custom such requests had to be delivered by hand.

'Yes, my lord,' he said. 'I'll bring them up to the ring as soon as I can print hard copy.'

The fleet commander's mild brown eyes turned to Martinez. 'No need to go yourself,' he said. 'Send one of the duty cadets.'

A small mercy, at least. 'Thank you, lord commander.'

Sub-Lieutenant Gupta received Enderby's thanks, braced in salute, and made his way out. Martinez put special thick bond paper into the printer – actual trees went into making this stuff – and printed Enderby's invitations. When he finished putting the invitations into envelopes, he looked up to see Enderby turn to gaze out the great curved window. The myriad lights of the Lower Town illuminated and softened Enderby's profile. There was an uncertainty in his glance, a strange, lost vacancy.

For once Enderby could stand in his office and contemplate the view. He had no duty awaiting him.

Nothing was left undone.

Martinez wondered if, at the end of his life, a man as successful as Enderby had any real regrets. Even granted that he was from a clan of the highest caste, he had done well. Though his position had carried him through several promotions, no one was *guaranteed* the rank of fleet commander. He was wealthy, he had added to the honour of his house, his children were all established in life and doing well. The wife was a problem, yes – but the wife's peculations were no stain on the fleet commander, the investigators had gone out of their way to make that clear.

Perhaps he loved her, Martinez thought. Marriages among the Peers were usually arranged by the family, but sometimes love happened. Perhaps, in a situation such as the commander's, it was the love one regretted, not the marriage.

But this wasn't the time to speculate on the fleet commander's private life. This was the time for Martinez to use his cunning, to use all the charm he'd intended to use on Warrant Officer Taen.

Now or never, Martinez thought, and steeled himself.

'My lord?' he said.

Enderby gave a start of surprise, then turned to him. 'Yes, Martinez?'

'You just said something. But I didn't catch what it was.'

Martinez didn't know how to begin this conversation, so he hoped to somehow come to a kind of mutual understanding that Enderby himself had begun it.

'Did I speak?' Enderby was surprised. He shook his head. 'It probably wasn't important.'

Martinez' mind flailed as he tried to keep the conversation going. 'The service is about to go through a difficult period,' he said.

Enderby nodded. 'Possibly. But we've had sufficient time to prepare.'

'In the time that's going to come, we'll need leaders such as you.'

Enderby gave a dismissive twitch of his lips. 'I'm not unique.'

'I beg to differ, lord,' Martinez said. He took a step closer to the commander. 'I've had the honour to work intimately with you these last months, and I hope you'll not take it amiss if I say that in my opinion your gifts are of a rare order.'

Enderby's lips gave that twitch again, and he raised an eyebrow. 'You haven't worked with any other fleet commanders, have you?'

'But I've worked with a lot of *men*, my lord. And a great many Peers. And—' Martinez was deep in the morass now. He could feel the slime rising to his armpits. He took a gulp of air, not daring to stop. '—and I've seen how limited most of them are. And how your own horizons are so much broader, my lord, so much more valuable to the service and to—'

Martinez froze as Enderby fixed him with a glare. 'Lord lieutenant,' he said. 'Will you please bring yourself to the point?'

'The point, lord commander,' Martinez said. 'The point

is—' He reached into his shoes for his courage and dragged it quailing into the light. 'The point is that I was hoping to convince you to reconsider the matter of your retirement.'

He hoped for a softening of Enderby's glance, a sudden shock of concern. Perhaps a fatherly hand placed on Martinez' shoulder, a hesitant question: 'Does it really mean so much to you?'

But instead Enderby's face stiffened, and the older man seemed to inflate, his iron spine growing somehow more rigid, his chest rising. His lower jaw pushed out as he spoke, revealing an even white row of lower teeth.

'How *dare* you presume to question my judgment?' he demanded.

Martinez felt nails bite into his palms. 'Lord commander,' he said, 'I question the necessity of removing a superb leader at such a critical time—'

'Don't you realize that I mean *nothing*!' Enderby cried. '*Nothing!* Don't you understand that elementary fact of our service? We— all this—' He made a savage gesture towards the window with his hand, encompassing all beyond the transparency, the millions in the Lower Town, the great arc of the antimatter ring, the ships and wormhole stations beyond . . .

'It's all *trash*!' Enderby said. His voice was an urgent whisper, as if overwhelming emotion had partially paralysed his vocal cords. '*Trash,* compared to the true, the eternal, the one thing that gives our miserable lives meaning . . .' Enderby raised a fist and for one horrified second Martinez feared that the fleet commander would strike him down.

'*For the Praxis!*' Enderby said. 'The Praxis is all that matters – it is all that is true – all that is beautiful!' Enderby brandished his fist again. 'And *that* is the knowledge for which our ancestors suffered. For which we were *scourged*! *Millions* had to *die in agony* before the Great Masters burned the truth of the Praxis into our minds. And if millions more – billions! –

had to die to uphold the righteousness of the Praxis, it would be our duty to *inflict those deaths!*'

Martinez wanted to take a step backwards to evade the scorching fire in the fleet commander's eyes. With an effort of pure will he kept his shoes planted on the office carpet, and he tipped up his chin, exposing his throat.

He felt the commander's spittle on his neck as Enderby raged on. 'We must all die!' he said. 'But the only death that gives meaning is one in service to the Praxis. Because I am who I am, *at this perfect moment in time,* I am privileged to have *an honourable death,* one that gives both myself and the Praxis meaning – do you know how rare that is?' He gestured again out the window, at the invisible millions below. 'How many of *those* will die in a meaningful way, do you suppose? Practically none!'

Fleet Commander Enderby stepped close to Martinez. 'And you wish to deprive me of a meaningful death? The death proper to a Peer? Who are you to do that, Lieutenant Martinez?'

Instinct managed to find words amid the clouds of fear that shadowed Martinez' mind. He had learned early that when he was caught out, he should always admit it and then beg forgiveness in as endearing a manner as possible. Honesty, he'd found, has its own brand of charm.

'I regret the suggestion extremely, lord commander,' he said. 'I was being selfish and thinking only of my own preferences.'

Enderby glared at Martinez for a few long moments, then took a step back.

'Over the next few hours I shall do my best to forget your very existence, Lieutenant,' he said. 'See that those letters are delivered.'

'Yes, lord commander.'

Martinez turned and marched for the door, ignoring the strong impulse to run.

See if I ever try to save your miserable life again, he thought.
And then, *Damn the Praxis anyway.*

It was the alien Shaa, the Great Masters, who had imposed
their absolutist ethic, the Praxis, on humanity after the surrender of Earth following the destruction of Delhi, Los Angeles,
Buenos Aires, and a dozen other cities by antimatter bombs.
Humanity was the second intelligent species to feel the lash of
the Shaa, the first being the black-scaled, centauroid Naxids,
who by the time of Earth's surrender were sufficiently tamed
to have crewed most of the Shaa ships.

No one knew where the Shaa originated, and the Shaa
were not forthcoming on this or any other aspect of their
history. Their capital, the city of Zanshaa on the planet of
Zanshaa, was clearly not their planet of origin, and had been
chosen in historical times for its convenient location amid
eight wormhole gates through which the Shaa could access
their dominion. The Shaa 'year', .84 Earth years, had no
reference to the period of Zanshaa's orbit about its primary,
or indeed to the orbit of any other planet in their empire. Any
reference to their origins had been erased from the records by
the time their subject species were given access to them.

Another curiosity was the Shaa dating system, which began
in 'the Peace of the Praxis One', some 437 years before their
appearance in the skies above the Naxids' home world. This
suggested a time before the Praxis claimed the Shaa's devotion, but no Shaa could be persuaded to confirm this surmise.
Nor did the Shaa revere whatever Shaa – if it *was* a Shaa –
who first formulated the Praxis, or remember its name.

For the Shaa were adamant that every species – that the
physical universe itself – should submit to terms dictated by
the Praxis. Whole categories of technology were absolutely
forbidden – machine intelligence and autonomy, the translation of organic intelligence into machine or electromagnetic
form, machines constructed so as to manipulate matter at

the molecular or atomic level. Genetic manipulation was also forbidden – the Shaa preferred the slower process of natural selection, the more unsentimental the better.

The iron will behind these prohibitions was demonstrated again and again. Those who offended against the Praxis were punished by death, often horribly and publicly, for the Praxis itself commanded that 'those who offend against the fundamental law shall receive punishment in greater proportion than their crime, so that public virtue may be maintained by this example'. Nor were the Shaa or their followers shy of using the most poisonous and destructive weapons to support their ethic: antimatter bombs sometimes destroyed whole cities for the crimes of a few citizens, and on one occasion, when a small group of Terrans was discovered using genetic technology in hopes of breeding a plague that would kill off the Shaa, their entire planet was bombed to death, the great explosions raising vast clouds of smoke and dust that drew a curtain across the sun, condemning the survivors to lingering, freezing death in a frigid atmosphere poisoned by radiation.

Surviving Terrans, awed by the comprehensive way in which the Shaa destroyed their own subjects, felt supremely lucky that the planet involved was not Earth.

Such examples had their effect. After the lingering death of the planet Dandaphis, the prohibitions against technology embodied within the Praxis were never again subjected to such a radical challenge.

Other elements of the Praxis were devoted to social organization, with every sentient being in the empire given a place in a well-defined hierarchy, one clan ranked below the next, with the Peers over all. Those at the top were given responsibility for the well-being of those at the bottom, while the lower orders were expected to honour the Peers and the Shaa with their meek obedience.

Another clause of the Praxis forbade sentients to 'curse

themselves with immortality'- a curious prohibition, because
the Shaa themselves were immortal. But those among the
Shaa, in a rare display of the reasoning behind one of their
prohibitions, freely admitted that their immortality had been
a mistake, an error sufficient to drive them to eradicate by
gun, flaying knife, or antimatter bomb any others who dared
to seek physical immortality for themselves.

Of the Shaa themselves the Shaa said nothing. Why these
immortal beings, blessed with absolute power, began one by
one to kill themselves remained a riddle. The Shaa refused
to consider their own deaths a tragedy. 'No being should be
immortal,' was their uniform response to any questions.

Whatever the cause, the Great Masters chose to die one by
one, each followed in death by dozens of loyal subordinates.
And now, in the Year 12,481 of the Peace of the Praxis, only
one remained.

And this last was not expected to live long.

Across the foyer of the Commandery was a map of the empire,
showing the wormhole routes connecting Zanshaa to its dominions. The map bore no resemblance to the actual star systems that
surrounded Zanshaa: the wormholes overleaped all the nearby
stars, and could in fact connect any two points in the universe.
Many of the star-systems shown on the map were so remote
from Zanshaa that it was not known where they stood in relation
to any other part of the empire. And the wormholes spanned
time as well as distance – a wormhole that leaped 800 light-years
could also leap up to 800 years into the past, or alternatively into
the future, or any length of time in between.

But there was no paradox when it did so. Because of the
limitations imposed by the speed of light, it was impossible
to get to another star quickly enough to alter its history –
except by using the wormhole, in which case you found that
the Shaa had been there before you.

The overwhelming fact of history was that there was

no escaping the Shaa. There was no escaping the history that made Gareth Martinez a provincial lord, an object of condescension to his betters. There was no going back in time to rectify the error that had caused Fleet Commander Enderby to savage him.

There was no saving him from his mistakes, or the mistakes of civilization, or of history itself. He had to live with them all.

The heavy envelopes containing Enderby's invitations bulked largely under his left arm. He transferred them to his right hand and continued his walk to the cadets' duty room. On the way he checked his sleeve display for any messages.

Some other time maybe.

Warrant Officer Taen's words were printed across the chameleon-weave left sleeve of Martinez' uniform jacket. There was no audio or video, which might have given a clue whether Amanda Taen was angry or not, but from the evidence she hadn't shut him out altogether.

Perhaps this was one mistake from which he could recover.

Martinez triggered the silver sleeve button that acted as a camera, and sent both video and audio in response. 'I'm free now. Is it too late to meet? Or if it's too late, I'll call you tomorrow and we can reschedule.'

Flowers, he thought. If he didn't hear from Amanda Taen soon, he would send flowers along with a written apology.

He turned off the display, and the chameleon weave of the uniform jacket returned to its normal dark green, the precise colour of Zanshaa's viridian sky. He encountered little traffic in the Commandery at this late hour as he walked to the cadets' duty room, and the clicks of his heels on the marble floor echoed in the high, empty corridors. At the door, he straightened his collar with its red triangular staff tabs, stiffened his spine, and marched in.

The four duty cadets didn't see him. As Martinez expected, they were watching sport on the room's video walls – as Martinez remembered from his own cadet years, watching or participating in sport was the default activity, and any cadet who failed to be obsessed by sport was marked as a 'toil', an oddball.

No toils here. The sounds of football blared from one wall, all-in wrestling from another, yacht racing from the third. The cadets lounged on a sofa they'd dragged to face the wall displaying the yacht race, and were draped across the cushions with their jackets unbuttoned and cans of beer in their hands.

There was a problem presented by cadets who had graduated from one or another of the military academies but who hadn't yet gained service experience. Jobs had to be found for them where they could gain seasoning without having the opportunity to damage themselves or others. Cadets were supposed to use the three years between their graduation and their lieutenants' exams to gain experience and study the many technical aspects of their profession, but many preferred the more tempting curriculum of inebriation, dissipation, and gambling away their available funds. 'Glits', such people were called.

Martinez remembered his own temptations very well, and remembered the times he'd given in to them even better. He'd managed to carry off a degree of glithood – in fact, he'd found he was good at it, and only an inner compulsion to somehow be useful prevented him from turning into a complete parasite.

The cadets in the duty room were being used as messengers until useful work could be found for them. Normally someone needing a messenger would have called here and summoned a messenger to pick up despatches, which could give one of these layabouts a chance to finish his drink, spruce up his uniform, and transform himself into something resembling a smart, eager officer before presenting himself to authority.

Martinez parked himself directly behind their couch without anyone noticing. Pleasurable self-righteousness filled his mind. He had tracked the slothful cadet to its lair, where it wasted and loitered and thought not of duty.

'*Scuuuum!*' Martinez bellowed. Cadets were not as yet commissioned, and he didn't have to 'lord' them even though these were almost certainly Peers.

The four cadets – one woman and three men – leaped from the couch, braced their shoulders back, and bared their throats. '*My lord!*' they responded.

Martinez gave them a cold look. He had just had his dignity and fortunes shredded by a superior, and he felt a very powerful, very human urge to pass the pain on to someone else. He said nothing for a few seconds, daring them to relax once they realized they were facing a mere lieutenant – and a provincial at that.

The cadets stayed braced. Rich boy Foote, with his disordered blond cowlick and a clamp on his usual supercilious expression. Chatterji, with her freckles and her red hair clubbed behind her neck. Martinez didn't know the other two.

Eventually he condescended to speak. 'Which of you is at the head of the queue?'

'I am, lord.' It was one of the unknowns who spoke, a small, slim, brown-skinned youth who reeked of the beer he'd splashed on his chest as he leaped from the sofa.

Martinez took a step closer and loomed over him. Martinez was tall, and looming was something he found useful, and he had practised till he could do it well. 'Your name, insect?' he inquired.

'Silva, lord.'

Martinez held out the letters. 'These letters are to be hand-delivered to every ship on the ring station. To the captains personally, or to their aides. Signature-receipts will be collected and returned to Lord Commander Enderby's office.' He looked pointedly at the beery splotch that decorated the cadet's open jacket and the blouse beneath it.

'Are you sober enough for this task, Cadet Silva?'

'Yes, lord!' Barley and hops outgassed from Silva's lungs, but he didn't sway, not even with his heels together and Martinez looming over him. Therefore he probably wasn't so drunk as to bring complete disgrace on himself, Martinez, and Enderby's command.

'The next shuttle for the skyhook leaves in half an hour, insect,' Martinez said. 'That will give you just enough time to shower and change into suitable dress before going topside.' A thought occurred to him, and he added, 'You aren't so drunk you'll upchuck on the elevator, will you, insect?'

'No, my lord!'

Martinez offered him the letters. 'See that you don't. Better put these in a waterproof bag, just in case.'

'Begging my lord's pardon?' said someone else.

The speaker was Jeremy Foote, the big blond with the cowlick that disordered his hair on the right side, and though the cadet was braced, he still managed to speak with something approaching his usual drawling, languid voice. It was a voice he had probably spoken in the cradle, a voice that oozed breeding and social confidence, that conjured images of exclusive smoking rooms, fancy-dress balls, and silent servants. A world to which Martinez, despite his own status as a Peer, had no admittance, not unless he was begging favours from some high-caste patron.

Martinez wheeled on him. 'Yes, Cadet Foote?'

'I may as well take the letters myself, my lord,' Foote said.

Martinez knew Foote well enough to know that this seeming generosity masked an underlying motive.

'And why are you being so good to Silva tonight?' he asked.

Foote permitted a hint of insolence to touch a corner of his mouth. 'My uncle's the captain of the *Bombardment of Delhi,* my lord,' he said. 'After I've delivered the messages, the two of us could have a bit of breakfast together.'

Just like him to ring in his connections, Martinez thought. Well, damn him, and damn his connections, too.

Until Foote had spoken up, Martinez had planned on letting the cadets off with a brief lecture on correct dress and deportment in the duty room. Now Foote had given Martinez every excuse to inflict dread and misery on all of them.

'I fear you'll have to save the cosy family breakfasts for another time, Cadet Foote,' Martinez said. He jerked his chin towards Silva and once more held out the invitations.

'Get up to the station, Silva,' he said. 'And if you don't make the next elevator, believe me I'll know.'

'Lord!' Silva took the invitations and scuttled away, buttoning his jacket as he went. Martinez eyed the other three, one by one.

'I have other plans for the rest of you,' he said. 'I'll oblige you to turn and look at the yacht race, if you will.'

The cadets made precise military turns to face the display on the video wall – except for Chatterji, who swayed drunkenly during her spin. The wall display gave the illusion of three dimensions, with the six competing yachts, along with a planet and its moons, displayed against a convincing simulation of the starry void.

'Display,' Martinez told the wall. 'Sound, off.' The chatter of the commentators cut off abruptly. 'Football, off,' he went on. 'Wrestling, off.'

The yachts now manoeuvred in silence, weaving about the twelve moons of the ochre-striped gas giant Vandrith, the fifth planet in Zanshaa's system. The moons weren't precisely the object of the race: instead each vessel was required to pass within a certain distance of a series of satellites placed in orbit about the moons. In order to avoid the race turning into a mere mathematical exercise best suited to solution by a navigational computer, the satellites were programmed to alter their own orbits randomly, forcing the pilots into off-the-cuff solutions that would test their mettle rather than the speed of their computers.

Martinez maintained an interest in yacht racing, in part because he'd considered taking it up, not only because it might raise his profile in a socially accepted way, but because he thought he might enjoy it. He'd scored his highest marks in simulations of combat manoeuvres, and as a cadet had qualified for the silver flashes of a pinnace pilot. He'd been a consistent winner in the pinnace races staged during his hitch aboard the *Bombardment of Dandaphis*, and pinnaces were not unlike racing yachts – both were purposeful, stripped-down designs that consisted largely of storage for antimatter fuel, engines, and life-support systems for a single pilot.

Martinez *might* be able to afford a personal yacht – he had a generous allowance from his father, which might be increased if Martinez were tactful about it. The little boats were expensive beasts, requiring a ground crew and frequent maintenance, and Martinez would also be obliged to join a yacht club, which involved expensive initiation fees and dues. There would be docking fees and the expense of fuel and upkeep. Not least was the humiliating likelihood that Martinez would probably not be considered for the very best yacht clubs, such as those – for instance – sponsoring the race now being broadcast.

So Martinez had postponed his decision about whether to become a yachtsman, hoping that his association with Fleet Commander Enderby would serve his purposes equally well. Now that his gesture in aid of Enderby's life seemed to have triggered nothing but Enderby's loathing, perhaps it was time to reconsider the yachting strategy again.

Martinez looked at the display, drank it in. The race, though broadcast 'live', was actually delayed by twenty-four minutes, the length of time the telemetry signals took to travel from Vandrith to Zanshaa.

'Cadet Chatterji,' Martinez said, 'can you elucidate the strategy displayed by racer Number Two?'

Chatterji licked her lips. 'Elucidate, my lord?'

Martinez sighed. 'Just tell us what the pilot is doing.'

Racer Two's craft – the display did not offer the name of the pilot, and Martinez didn't recognize the flashy scarlet paint job on the craft – had just rotated to a new attitude and fired the main engine.

'She's decelerating, my lord,' Chatterji said.

'And why is she doing that, Chatterji?'

'She's d-dumping delta-vee in order to— to—' She licked her lips. 'To manoeuvre better,' she finished lamely.

'And what manoeuvre is this deceleration in aid of?'

Chatterji's eyes searched the display in desperation. 'Delta-vee increases options, my lord,' she said, a truism she had learned in tactics class and clearly the first thing to leap to her mind.

'Very true, Chatterji,' Martinez said. 'I'm sure your tactics instructor would be proud to know you have retained a modicum of the knowledge he tried to cram between your ears. But,' he said cheerfully, 'our pilot is *decreasing* delta-vee, and therefore decreasing his options. So tell me *why,* Cadet Chatterji. Why?'

Chatterji focused very hard on the display but was unable to answer.

'I suggest you review your basic tactics, Cadet Chatterji,' Martinez said. 'Persistence may eventually pay off, though in your case I doubt it. *You* – worm there—' Addressing the cadet whose name he didn't know.

'Parker, lord.'

'Parker. Perhaps *you* can enlighten Chatterji concerning our pilot's tactics.'

'She's dumping delta-vee in order to be captured by V9's gravity.' This being the name of Vandrith's ninth moon, counting the innermost as number one. The Shaa didn't much go in for naming astronomical objects in interesting or poetic ways.

'And why is she entering V9's gravity well, Parker?'

'She's planning to slingshot towards the satellite near V11, lord.'

'And Number Four – that would be Captain Chee—' Recognizing the blue-and-silver paint job. 'Why is she *not* dumping delta-vee? Why is she accelerating instead?'

'I—' Parker swallowed. 'I suppose she's trying another tactic.'

Martinez sighed deliberately. 'But *why*, worm, why? The display should tell you. It's *obvious*.'

Parker searched the display in vain, and then Cadet Foote's languid tones interrupted the desperate silence.

'Captain Chee is accelerating, lord, because she's intending to bypass V9 entirely, and to pass between V11 and the satellite to score her point. Since V11 possesses an atmosphere, she'll probably try to use atmospheric braking in order to dump velocity and make her manoeuvre to tag the satellite at the last minute.'

Martinez rounded on Foote and snapped, 'I don't recall asking your opinion, Cadet Foote!'

'I beg the lord's pardon,' Foote drawled.

Martinez realized to his dismay that Foote had just succeeded in making himself the star of this encounter. Martinez had intended to throw a little justified terror into some wastrels caught drunk on duty, but somehow Foote had changed the rules. How had he *done* that?

In children's school fiction, there was always the evil bully, tormenting the youngsters, and then there was the hero, who tried to stand between the bully and his victims. Foote had made a gesture to help Silva, and now had just rescued Parker.

And I'm the bully, Martinez thought. *I'm the wicked superior officer who torments his helpless underlings just to assuage his own pathetic feelings of inadequacy.*

Foote, Martinez realized, had him pegged just about right.

Still, he thought, if he were going to be the villain in this little drama, he might as well do it well.

'Parker should learn that you won't always be there to rescue him from his own stupidity,' he said to Foote. 'But since you've chosen to express an opinion, suppose you tell me whether Chee's manoeuvre will succeed?'

'She shan't succeed, lord,' Foote said promptly.

'*Shan't* she?' Martinez said, mocking. 'And *whyever shan she not?*'

Foote's tone didn't change. 'V11's satellite has altered course, but Chee didn't see it because it was on the far side of the moon at the time. She'll be too late to correct when she finally sees her error.' Foote's tone had grown almost intimate. 'Of course, Captain Blitsharts seems to have allowed for that possibility. His acceleration isn't as great, but he's allowing himself more options.'

Martinez looked at the Number One boat and saw the famous Blitsharts' glossy black paintwork with its ochre-yellow stripes. Blitsharts was a celebrated and successful racer, a glit of the first order, famous not only for his victories but for the fact that he always raced with his dog, a black retriever named Orange, who had his own acceleration bed in *Midnight Runner's* cockpit next to his master's. Blitsharts claimed the dog enjoyed pulling hard gees, and certainly Orange seemed none the worse for his adventures.

Blitsharts also had a reputation for drollery. He was once asked by a yachting enthusiast why he called the dog Orange.

Blitsharts looked at the man and lifted surprised eyebrows above his mild brown eyes. 'Because it's his *name,* of course,' he said.

Oh yes, Martinez thought, there was rare wit in the yacht clubs all right.

'You think Blitsharts will win?' Martinez asked.

'At this stage, it's very likely.'

'I don't suppose Blitsharts is a relative of yours, is he?' Martinez asked.

For the first time Foote hesitated. 'No, my lord,' he said.

'How generous of you,' Martinez said, 'to mention his name in conversation,' and was rewarded by seeing the cadet's neck and ears turn red.

Chee crashed into V11's atmosphere, her craft trailing a stream of ions as it cut through the moon's hydrocarbon murk. She saw her target's change of course too late, altered her heading and burned antimatter to try to make her mark. Her bones must have groaned with the ferocious gees she laid on, but she was a few seconds too late.

Blitsharts, on the other hand, hit the atmosphere with his usual impeccable timing, burned for the satellite, and passed it without breaking a sweat. And then kept accelerating, his torch pushing him onwards past his mark.

'Perhaps, Cadet Foote, you will favour us with an analysis of Blitsharts' tactics *now,*' Martinez said.

'Of course, lord. He's . . .' Foote's voice trailed away.

Blitsharts' boat stood on a colossal tail of matter–antimatter fire and burned straight out of the plane of the ecliptic. Foote stared at the screen in confusion. Blitsharts seemed to be heading away from his next target, away from *all* his targets.

'Blitsharts is . . . he's . . .' Foote was still struggling for words. 'He's . . .'

'Shit,' Martinez said, and bolted for the door.

Two

Operations Command wasn't in the Terran wing of the Commandery, but Terrans were on duty at this hour, none aware of any emergency until Martinez came bursting through the door. The duty officer, Lieutenant Ari Abacha, lounged with his feet on his console, a perfect corkscrew apple peel falling from his paring knife onto the napkin spread over his lap, while the three duty techs dozed over the screens that helped them supervise the automated systems that routed routine traffic.

Martinez batted Abacha's legs out of the way as he rushed for an unoccupied console. The screw of apple peel spilled to the floor, and Abacha bent to pick it up. Footballers careened over a brightly-lit field in one of his displays – he was a big Andiron supporter, Martinez recalled.

'What's the problem, Gare?' Abacha said from somewhere near the floor.

'Vandrith Challenge race. Yacht's out of control.' Martinez dropped onto a seat that had been designed for a Lai-own and called up displays.

'Yeah?' Abacha said. 'Whose?'

'Blitsharts'.'

Abacha's eyes widened. 'Shit,' he said, and leaped from his seat to look over Martinez' shoulder.

Telemetry from *Midnight Runner* had been lost, so Martinez had to locate the yacht by using the passive detectors on Zanshaa's accelerator ring. Blitsharts' yacht had cut its main engine and started tumbling. From the erratic way the boat lurched, it appeared that manoeuvring thrusters were still being fired. It was possible that Blitsharts was trying to regain control, but if so he was failing. Any input from the thrusters just seemed to add to the chaos.

And all this, Martinez reminded himself, had happened over twenty-four minutes ago, with the time-lag increasing as *Midnight Runner* raced towards galactic south.

Martinez asked the computer to calculate how many gees the acceleration had inflicted on Blitsharts' body. A maximum of 7.4, he found, deeply uncomfortable but survivable, especially for a yacht racer in peak condition. Blitsharts might still be alive.

A communicator buzzed on Abacha's console. Abacha stepped towards it and linked it to the display on his uniform sleeve.

'Operations. Lieutenant Abacha.'

The voice came out of Abacha's sleeve. 'My lord, this is Panjit Sesse of Zanshaa All-Sports Networks. Are you aware that Captain Blitsharts' yacht *Midnight Runner* is tumbling out of control?'

'We're working on that, yes.'

Martinez was only vaguely aware of this dialogue. He told the computers to guess where *Midnight Runner* would be in half an hour or so and to paint the area with low-energy ranging lasers aimed from the ring. That might make it easier for rescuers to track the boat.

The reporter's voice went on. '*Who* is working on it, my lord?'

Abacha looked over Martinez' shoulder at the displays again. 'Right now we've got Lieutenant Martinez.'

'Only a lieutenant, lord?'

'He's aide to Senior Fleet Commander Enderby.' Abacha's tone showed impatience. A pair of Peers were dealing with the situation. That should be enough for anybody.

Martinez called up a list of every ship within three light-hours of Vandrith. The closest to Blitsharts were the yacht racers, but they were still engaged in their race, and none of them were suitable as a rescue vehicle. While they'd almost certainly noted Blitsharts' exit, they probably were too busy to analyse the meaning of his trajectory, beyond being pleased to have one less competitor. The large tender that had brought the yachts to Vandrith would need to recover the other yachts before it did anything, and it was built more for comfort than for manoeuvre and heavy accelerations. And it would take twenty-four minutes for Martinez' request to reach them, during which time Blitsharts would continue south.

Martinez scanned the display and found what he was looking for: Senior Captain Kandinski in the *Bombardment of Los Angeles,* one of the big bombardment-class heavy cruisers, which had just finished a refit on the ring dockyards and was now accelerating at a steady one point three gravities toward the Zanshaa Five wormhole gate, heading for the Third Fleet base at Felarus. Currently travelling at approximately .08c and moving slightly southwards of the plane of the ecliptic on direct course for the wormhole. For the next 4.2 standard hours, a rescue boat launched from the *Los Angeles* could take advantage of at least some of the cruiser's speed in its acceleration towards *Midnight Runner.* Not an ideal position for a rescue launch, but it would have to do.

Kandinski was something of a yachtsman himself – *Los Angeles* was a well-polished ship, shiny inside and out, with a white-and-powder-blue paint job Kandinski had paid for out of his own deep pockets. Even the cruiser's pinnaces and missiles had the same glossy light blue finish. Maybe he would feel an affinity for Blitsharts and his shiny yacht.

Martinez reached for the communications console, linked it to his sleeve display.

'Transmission to *Los Angeles*,' he instructed. 'Code status: clear. Priority: extremely urgent, personal to the captain.'

'Identify?' the automated comm system wanted to know.

'Gareth Martinez, Lieutenant, aide to lord commander Enderby.'

A brief moment's pause. Then, 'Approved.'

'Can you tell me what steps are being taken?' Sesse's voice nattered in Martinez' ear from Achaba's sleeve display. Martinez ignored it.

Another chime from the communicator, someone else needing to talk. 'We're very busy right now,' Abacha said. 'Goodbye.'

'Can you just let us *listen*?' Sesse said frantically.

Martinez took a moment to run fingers through his dark hair, then twitched his collar to make certain it was in place. 'Transmit, video and audio,' he said.

He waited for the flashing orange cue in his sleeve display to let him know that transmission had started, then looked at the sleeve button camera and spoke.

'Captain Kandinski, this is Lieutenant Gareth Martinez on lord commander Enderby's staff. The yacht *Midnight Runner* with its captain, Ehrler Blitsharts, is tumbling out of control, heading southwards from Vandrith. There is no telemetry, and there has been no communication from Captain Blitsharts since before the situation started. He may still be alive, but unable to recover command of his boat. If your situation permits, I should like to request that you launch one or more pinnaces on a rescue mission. I will send you the latest course data. Please advise Command on your course of action as soon as possible. This is Lieutenant Martinez at Operations Command. Data follows.'

The message, Martinez knew, was already being pulsed towards *Los Angeles* by powerful military communications lasers, but it would still be over twenty-four minutes before the red-shifted signal reached the cruiser, and at least that much time again before Martinez would know Kandinski's decision.

He added Blitsharts' real and projected course to the end
of the message and ended the transmission. He tried to lean
back, then swayed as he almost toppled from the Lai-own
chair. Abacha was talking to yet another questioner whom he
cut off in mid-sentence. 'Receive military communications
only,' Abacha told his console. 'Log others for reply later.'

'Very good, my lord.'

Abacha turned to Martinez. 'What now?'

Martinez rose from the chair and kicked it away. 'We
wait an hour or more for a reply, while you field calls
from every Blitsharts fan on the planet.' And then a thought
struck him.

'Oh,' Martinez added. 'I suppose we should inform lord
commander Enderby.'

Martinez didn't notice when Enderby arrived in Operations
Command: instead he was busy trying to analyse the way
that Blitsharts' boat was tumbling so that any rescue mission
might better know how to dock with it. The ring's optical
trackers were not ideal for this task, catching only reflections
of Zanshaa's sun flashing on the glossy black surface of the
yacht, hardly ideal data for an analysis. Because even the 3D
displays at Operations would be too small for the kind of
detail he needed of this small vessel very far away, Martinez
got a headset out of storage – one of those designed for
humans – and projected a virtual environment onto the
visual centres of his brain. His mind flooded with an infinite,
empty darkness that seemed to extend light-years beyond the
limits of his skull, and he built a simulation with a picture
and specifications of the craft he'd snagged, using Enderby's
priority code, from the files of Vehicle Registration. Once
he had the model of *Midnight Runner*, he created a virtual sun
at the appropriate angle and of the appropriate intensity, then
sent the model tumbling over and over again in a lengthy
series of simulations until it began to resemble the flashing

visual he was getting from the ring's optical detectors. It could be refined later, after he began getting reflections back from the ranging lasers he'd pulsed out along Enderby's presumed track.

Under normal circumstances, a Fleet pinnace should be able to rendezvous with a yacht like *Midnight Runner* with little trouble. The boats were approximately the same size, and were built for nearly the same purpose: carrying a single passenger very fast, through abrupt accelerations and decelerations and changes of course. In Blitsharts' case this was to enable his boat to make the changes in vector necessary to win a yacht race; in the case of the Fleet boat, it was to avoid destruction long enough to accomplish its mission.

But Martinez was reasonably willing to believe that no one had ever performed a rendezvous like this. The yacht's rolling was wildly complex, as if designed on purpose to baffle anyone attempting to dock with it. Martinez couldn't imagine that Blitsharts could remain in that tumbling craft for very long and remain conscious. There was only one hatch on *Midnight Runner,* and it was rolling over and over in a chaotic series of gyrations. The hatch was forward of the centre of gravity about which the yacht was tumbling, and there was no possible way a rescue craft could dock to it. It would be like docking with the end of a stick being waved in the air by an erratic child.

Martinez worried at the problem, his mind spinning as frantically as the tumbling yacht. He built a model of a standard Fleet pinnace and tried to manoeuvre it near the yacht, only to see it batted away again and again, one potentially crippling collision after another.

It seemed that if he worked really hard, he could help kill *two* pilots, Blitsharts and his rescuer both.

It was the scent of a bruised apple that brought him out of the depths of his study. Abacha's apple, or perhaps just the peel, lying somewhere nearby and reminding him that he hadn't eaten since his noon meal, over half a day ago.

He saved his simulation and pulled off the headset. 'Ari,' he said, turning toward Abacha's console, 'got any of that apple left? Or any food at all?'

It was at this point that he realized that the person he'd sensed standing behind him had far too much braid on his uniform to be a mere lieutenant.

'My lord!'

Martinez leaped to his feet, his chin snapping back. Agonizing pain clamped on his crotch, which had been perched on an alien chair for over an hour.

Fleet Commander Enderby gazed at Martinez with mild eyes. 'Carry on, Lieutenant,' he said.

'Yes, my lord.'

Enderby looked at the displays, which had been showing Martinez' solution.

'A difficult problem, is it not?'

'I'm afraid so, my lord.' Martinez clenched his teeth against the pain. Whatever passion had seized Enderby during their last interview had passed: the fleet commander was his usual self again, keeping himself informed of what was occurring in his command, but content to let lesser beings work out the details. Martinez had never quite made up his mind whether this was a result of Enderby's being profoundly stupid, or profoundly wise.

'I fear Blitsharts has run his last race,' Enderby said. 'I'm certainly not permitting a Fleet vessel to batter itself to pieces attempting a hopeless rescue.' Distant regret tracked across Enderby's features, then he looked at Martinez again. 'Call the commissary and order something, if you want. Use my authority.'

'Yes, my lord.' He reached for his sleeve display, then hesitated. 'Will you have anything, my lord?'

'No. I have dined. Thank you.'

Martinez realized he was ragingly hungry. He ordered soup, a salad, some sandwiches, and a pot of coffee. Trying not to hobble, he removed the Lai-own chair and replaced it with one designed for humans. Gingerly, he sat down, and looked again at the simulation frozen in the displays.

His nostrils twitched to the scent of apple. He turned toward where Abacha sat at his own console. Abacha was looking at his own displays, the stiffness of his spine and neck, and the ostentatious way he went about his business, all showing his awareness of the commander of the Home Fleet standing behind him.

Abacha's handkerchief sat on the long console between them, the screw of apple peel lying discarded on it. Without thinking Martinez reached for it – it was a reflex action for him to keep the fleet commander's vicinity tidy – and he looked for someplace to throw it.

He looked down at the handkerchief, the perfect corkscrew peel lying coiled on the white surface, and froze as a thought occurred to him.

'Lord commander,' he said slowly, 'I think I know how this can work.'

The woman called Caroline Sula fought her way back from nightmare, from a sensation of being smothered with a pillow, the soft pressure filling her nose, her mouth, the screaming pressure in her chest building as she tried to bring in air . . .

She came awake with a cry, hands flailing at an invisible attacker. Then she realized where she was, strapped into the command seat of her pinnace, and then she fought the darkness more rationally, clenching her jaw and neck muscles to force oxygenated blood to her brain. The darkness that swathed her vision retreated just enough so that she could see the cockpit displays directly in front of her. A total stranger looked at her and said, 'You're going to have to *screw* it in,' and then the main engine fired again, the boat groaned in response, and panic flared in her as darkness once more flooded her mind.

An unknown amount of time later she woke gasping for breath, fighting the ton of lead that pressed on her rib cage. There were sensors in her pressure suit that monitored her condition: the computers on her pinnace were instructed to keep her *alive,* but the instructions said nothing about *comfortable.*

In the blackness of her vision there was a circular hole through which a little light came. Sula focused the hole over the engine display, and found that the pinnace was accelerating at a steady 6.5 gravities, which the computer had apparently decided was the optimum both for keeping Sula alive and getting her to where she was going.

The darkness retreated a little from her vision. She panted for breath. She badly wanted to pee.

Sula wrenched her gaze to the speed indicator. She felt as if she had to crowbar her eyeballs around their sockets. She discovered she was travelling $.076c$.

Too bad. It meant that this wouldn't end anytime soon.

The brutal acceleration finally came to an end. The pressure exerted by Sula's suit, soft as foam but firm as steel, withdrew from her arms and legs, bringing them tingling back to life as the blood surged to the muscles. The tingling on her back, caused by the miniwaves pulsed through the acceleration couch to prevent blood pooling and bedsores, faded as she floated free in her harness. The soft darkness retreated from her perceptions, and she could fill her lungs with air.

She checked her own vital signs. Elevated heart rate and blood pressure, but not in the critical ranges. She hadn't stroked out during the acceleration – which sometimes happened even to the fittest young cadets – nor had she given herself some kind of weird heart murmur or arrhythmia.

The composite organics of the ship's hull cracked and

snapped as they reacted to the end of the relentless acceleration. Sula scanned the displays, then raised a hand to send a message both to the *Los Angeles* and to Operations on Zanshaa.

'Cadet Sula reporting. Diagnostics report optimal conditions following acceleration.' *Thanks for not killing me,* she added mentally.

She stretched in her acceleration couch, forcing sluggish blood to her reluctant muscles. The cockpit of the pinnace was tiny, with Sula in her pressure suit taking up most of the available volume. There was even less room than normal, because she was flying a two-seated trainer unit in case she had to take Blitsharts aboard.

Funny. She'd volunteered for pinnace duty in part because it meant getting time to herself, away from ship quarters where the cadets were crammed together, each living in the other's armpit. What she had discovered was that even here, alone in the infinity of space, there wasn't room enough to so much as stretch her arms above her head.

A light glowed on her communications board, the signal that messages had been recorded for her. She'd noted the light since acceleration ceased, but hadn't really felt up to interacting with the command structure till this moment.

She triggered the display and discovered a continuous stream of tracking data from Zanshaa's ring sensors showing Blitsharts' tumbling craft. Another was a communication from Operations Command, a message the pinnace had received directly, followed by a copy of the same message forwarded by the communications officer aboard *Los Angeles*.

Sula played the recorded message. A dark-browed, lantern-jawed young man looked out of the display. There were staff tabs on his collar, the sign of a lord commander's pet, and Sula loathed him on sight.

The lieutenant spoke. 'Lieutenant Martinez at Operations to any rescue pilot. I have analysed the way in which the target

boat is tumbling, and the results don't look very promising.'
A simulation of the *Midnight Runner* filled the display, and
Sula leaned forward, studying the fix Captain Blitsharts had
got himself into.

The voice went on. 'I can't see any way to dock with
the boat's hatch, which is too far forward. At best you'd get
knocked around badly; at worst you'd kill yourself, Blitsharts,
and his dog Orange.'

Har har, Sula thought. Lord commander's pet had a sense
of humour. Wonderful.

'I've worked out a way you can dock with the yacht, if not
with the hatch,' Martinez went on. 'What you'll have to do
is exactly duplicate with your own boat the precise fashion in
which Blitsharts is tumbling, then slip inside his rolling motion
to dock.' A pinnace appeared in the simulation, rolling and
pitching just as Blitsharts' boat was doing, and then the two
moved together to mate, the pinnace fitting very carefully
into a kind of whirlwind corkscrew cone formed by *Midnight
Runner*'s off-centre spinning nose.

'You're going to have to *screw* it in,' Martinez said, and
Sula felt a surge of recognition. She'd heard the message, live,
as she'd received it – only she'd been unconscious through
most of it.

'You can't access the hatch from this position,' Martinez
continued, 'but once you're clamped onto him, you can
use your own manoeuvring thrusters to damp down the
movements of Blitsharts' boat. Once you've got his boat
under control, you can shift your own boat forward to mate
with Blitsharts' hatch.'

Sula frowned at the simulation, which showed exactly that.
It looked possible, but experience had shown her that what
a simulation showed was possible was not necessarily cognate
with the realm of reality.

The picture cut to Martinez.

'There are two problems,' he said. 'The first is that *Midnight*

Runner's thrusters still occasionally fire, which may make the tumbling more chaotic by the time you arrive.'

Oh great, Sula thought. She could do everything perfectly and then Blitsharts' thrusters could cut in and cause a collision.

'The second problem,' Martinez took a breath, 'will be staying conscious. If you attempt to match the movements of Blitsharts' boat, you'll be subjecting yourself to an unforgiving pattern of accelerations, followed by a chaotic combination of roll, pitch, and yaw. You will be in severe danger of blacking out.'

'Oh. Great.' Sula closed her eyes and leaned the back of her head against her helmet pads.

Martinez' closing words echoed in her helmet earphones. 'You are the pilot on the scene. It will be entirely up to you as to whether you attempt this manoeuvre. I am to tell you from the lord commander of the Home Fleet that no blame will attach to you if you decide that the rescue is too risky.'

Sula opened her eyes. *Lord commander of the Home Fleet . . .*

It's not like there was any pressure or anything. She'd only be performing – or demonstrating cowardice or killing herself or fucking up beyond all possible redemption – in front of the individual who commanded the largest division of the Fleet, the defences of the capital, and of course her own personal future.

Thanks a lot.

Martinez' image gazed steadily at her from the displays. 'I'll keep sending updates from our sensors here, though of course anything you'll receive from *me* will be an hour out of date. I'm afraid there is very little assistance I can offer. You're truly on your own. Good luck.'

The image faded, replaced by the orange *end transmission* symbol.

Sula's fist hovered over the transmit button. 'Thank you for sending me on a mission that gives me the choice of suicide or disgrace. Why don't you come and do it yourself if you're so smart?'

She held the fist there for a long moment, hit the transmit button and said, 'Cadet Caroline Sula to Lieutenant Martinez, Operations Command. Your message received. Thank you.'

She hadn't got as far as she had by being stupid.

Sula managed to stay conscious through the next long acceleration burn, as her pinnace swooped over Vandrith's north pole, and slingshot manoeuvre that ended with firing her south, directly on Blitsharts' trail. Her jaws ached from keeping her teeth clamped.

Sula started getting data from the ranging lasers tracking *Midnight Runner,* and she was able to update Martinez' simulation of the tumbling craft. There was an extra wobble in its roll – sure enough, the yacht's manoeuvring thrusters must have fired and added an additional complexity to the acrobatics.

She wondered what could be causing them to fire at random that way. It didn't make any sense. If an automated pitch-and-yaw program had been initiated to stabilize the craft, the thrusters would be firing more regularly and deliberately, and the effect would be to dampen the oscillations, not increase them.

Could Blitsharts be making brief attempts to solve his problem? Coming out of unconsciousness briefly to fire a thruster, but so disoriented he only made his situation worse?

That didn't precisely make sense, either, but it was her best guess.

She studied the simulation. She ate some ration bars. She took a brief nap. And, because she finally couldn't stand the pressure in her bladder any longer, she urinated into her suit.

Elimination was the thing she hated most of living in a vac

suit. She knew perfectly that the crotch of her suit was packed full of absorbent material chock-full of hydrostatic screens and mindlessly happy bacteria that would process the urine into demineralized water and harmless salts, clean her up, and leave her 'fresher than before', which were the words actually used in the suit manual.

Before *what*? she wanted to snarl. Before she was crammed into this giant, unwieldy, vacuum-resistant *diaper*? If the service could only provide her with an honest-to-god *toilet,* she could handle the freshening business herself, thank you very much.

Just before the pinnace inverted to begin deceleration, Sula triggered the boat's radars to give her a better view of her tumbling target. Then the pinnace swung around, aligned its engines very precisely, and began the deceleration burn.

Again she felt the suit gently closing around her arms and legs, forcing the blood to her brain. Again the weight of many gravities compressed her chest. Again she felt the darkness gathering around her vision, the light narrowing to a tiny tunnel bearing only straight forward.

Again she felt the pillow pressing down on her face, throttling her half-formed scream.

Blitsharts, she thought, *you'd better fucking well be alive.*

Enderby had gone to bed hours ago. With dawn, a new shift arrived – not humans but Lai-owns, members of a flightless avian species, taller than humans, covered with grey featherlike hair mottled with black, and with vicious carnivore fangs in an elongated muzzle.

The Lai-owns had provided the Fleet with the only space battles in its long history. Every other species in the dominion of Shaa had been bombarded into submission by overwhelming forces operating from the safety of space. Even those who managed to develop sufficient technology to get into space, like the primitive human tribe-nations on Earth, did not possess an armed presence sufficient to halt the Shaa for even a few seconds. But to the Lai-owns, flightless themselves, space was just an extension of their natural environment, the airy realms where their ancestors had flown. They had spread throughout their home star system, and possessed the fleets to protect their settlements. Had they known to discover and develop the wormholes that orbited their star, they might have been the first to contact the Shaa, not the other way around.

As it was, the Lai-owns gave the Shaa squadrons a bloody nose when the conquerors poured in through the system's wormhole. The Lai-owns were natural tacticians, their avian brains adapted to operating in a three-dimensional environment. And they had fought wars among themselves, which gave them a tactical doctrine based on experience. Their only disadvantage was the light, hollow bones that permitted their ancestors to fly, but which wouldn't stand the ferocious accelerations of space combat.

The Shaa calculated on destroying resistance in a matter of hours. Instead it had taken six days for the Shaa to obliterate the last Lai-own warship and issue a demand for surrender. One of the Lai-own innovations that had so surprised the Fleet had been the use of the pinnace, a small vessel that would shepherd attacking missiles towards the target and update their instructions faster than could the larger ships, which might be lurking light-minutes out of contact.

The pinnaces were valuable tactically, but few had survived actual combat. But in the years since the Lai-own war, cadets had begun to compete for the right to wear the silver flashes of the pinnace pilot, and it had become both a status symbol and an entrée to the fashionable and glamorous world of yachting.

It was a matter for debate concerning how many cadets would have competed so eagerly to be pinnace pilots if there had actually been a war going on. Martinez suspected there would be relatively few.

As he sat with the avians in Operations, Martinez found himself wishing that it had been the Lai-owns who crewed the *Los Angeles,* and not humans. A Lai-own would be able to use Martinez' complex plan for rescuing *Midnight Runner* with little problem, and with no chance of rendering himself unconscious.

Instead an unknown human would do the job, almost certainly an inexperienced cadet. Martinez almost regretted having worked out a plan – if he hadn't, the rescue pilot wouldn't be in jeopardy.

During his long wait, Martinez received two messages. The first was from *Los Angeles,* announcing that, per the lord commander's request, a pinnace had been launched on a rescue mission. The second was from the pinnace itself, a brief announcement, audio only, that his message had been received.

Cadet Caroline Sula. Sula was a name Martinez had heard, but he couldn't recall where. He had seen a Sula Palace in the High City, which meant the Sulas were an old family, Peers of the highest rank. But Martinez couldn't remember hearing of any *other* members of the family, either in government, civil service, or the military, unusual for a family ranked that high. He wondered if this cadet was the last of them.

He hesitated a moment, then used Fleet Commander Enderby's code key to call for her file. Enderby might want a report on the pilot.

Oh my. Martinez, slumped with weariness in his chair, straightened to get a better view of Caroline Sula's face as it materialized on the display. It was extraordinary – pale, nearly translucent skin, emerald-green eyes, white-gold hair worn collar-length. The picture had caught her with a quirk of humour at the corners of her lips, as if she were about to make an ironic remark to the cameraman. And the camera clearly adored her – Martinez threw the picture into 3D and rotated the picture, and Sula didn't have a single bad angle.

Hope she's not married, was Martinez' first thought. His second was that he didn't much care if she were.

And then he noted the title that graced her official records. Caroline, *Lady* Sula. Why hadn't he heard of her?

He paged through her service records. Unmarried – well, good. Her birth as a Peer had guaranteed her a slot in a military academy, and her record there was mixed – low grades the first year, better the second, top marks the third. After graduation she'd received good reports from her superiors – the words 'intelligent' and 'efficient' showed up a lot – though there were two comments regarding her 'inappropriate sense of humour'. She had volunteered for pinnace training after her first year, and again won top marks as a pilot – her marks for high-gee and disorienting environments were good, and made Martinez a little more easy about sending her on this mission.

It seemed as if she was trying very hard to be a good, even outstanding, officer. But Martinez had to wonder why. The higher ranks of Peers considered it bad form to work this hard at anything. Someone with a palace in the High City should rise through the ranks without effort.

He thought to check Sula's family, and there found his answer.

Both Caroline Sula's parents, high officials in the Ministry of Works, had been found guilty of conspiring to steal millions from government contractors. Nine years ago, they and their associates had been publicly flayed and dismembered at the public execution ground in the Lower City. Their property was confiscated, and the remaining family banished from Zanshaa.

Martinez gave a slow, silent whistle. Sula Palace didn't belong to the Sula family any more.

Maybe nothing did.

Cadet Caroline Sula watched Captain Blitsharts' yacht roll and tumble against the cold velvet darkness. She illuminated it with floodlights, and watched it carefully as it yawed and spun. There didn't seem to be anything wrong with *Midnight Runner*, no obvious damage, no clue as to why it had run out of control. Not even a nick on its shiny paint.

Whatever was wrong was on the inside. Damn it.

She nudged her pinnace to a position on the axis of the *Runner*'s spin, the line along which she would have to creep in order to mate with the runaway craft. Proximity alarms blared, and Sula cut them off.

Maybe the alarms were right. The view didn't look encouraging from here, with the yacht's spinning bow lunging towards her with every beat of her heart.

Sula decided not to be stupid and to take some meds to inhibit motion sickness. She'd be sleepy after the adrenalin wore off, but that was better than being sick.

Or dead.

She charged a med injector with the Fleet's standard anti-nausea drug and placed the injector to her neck, over the carotid artery. And hesitated.

Seconds passed. When Sula took the injector away, her hand was trembling.

Not that way.

She put the injector back in the med kit and took out a pair of med patches. She took off her helmet, peeled away the clear polymer backing of the patches, and placed one behind each ear.

It would take longer for the patches to work, but at least there wouldn't be nightmares afterwards.

Her mouth had gone dry. She took a drink of water from the tube built into her seat back, donned and closed her helmet, and reached out towards the comm board so that she could transmit her decisions to Operations Command.

Then she thought better of it. She was alone. They had *sent* her out here alone. It would take half an hour for her signal to reach Operations at the speed of light, hours for a reply to return. They couldn't help her do her job any more than they already had.

You've got to screw *it in.* The words floated into Sula's mind, and she laughed.

Right, Lieutenant Martinez, whoever you are. This is for you.

She touched *Transmit,* sending audio and video both. 'Cadet Sula to Lieutenant Martinez, Operations Command. I am about to attempt rendezvous with *Midnight Runner.* I will send telemetry throughout the manoeuvre.' She hesitated, then twitched her eyebrows towards the camera. 'Please bear in mind that I haven't ever screwed in quite this way before.'

She ended the transmission and arranged to send a continuous broadcast of vehicle telemetry and radar data to Zanshaa's ring, and pointedly avoided sending any data from inside the pinnace, visuals or vital signs from the monitors in her suit. If she passed out, said or did something stupid, shit her pants, or abandoned herself to a fit of screaming terror, at least Lord Commander Enderby wouldn't be watching.

Sula took a deep breath of the canned air in her vacuum suit. Her mouth was dry again.

She decided to go virtual for a better view of the outside environment. The close confines of the cabin vanished from her visual receptors, replaced by the crisp visuals of the outside monitors, with heads-up displays of critical ship systems and controls superimposed on the outside view. At once she thought she'd made a mistake – the view of *Midnight Runner,* made even more alarming by the slight hyperreality of the virtual world, the sense that all this was happening *inside her skull,* was even more frightening than if she'd been peering out a window at the same sight. She could *sense* the mass of that prow coming round like a bludgeon every heartbeat, feel pure malevolence in the way it seemed to *reach* for her . . .

Get a grip, Sula told herself. She fought the fear that pulsed through her veins, took deliberate breaths to lower the trip-hammer beating of her heart. Reached for the manoeuvring controls on the arms of her chair. Tried to time the swing of *Midnight Runner*'s bow. And triggered her thrusters.

One plane at a time. Manoeuvres were calibrated in roll, pitch, and yaw. She started with roll, nudged the control in her left fist. Vertigo shimmered through her inner ear as it sensed her craft starting to tumble, but she mastered it. *Midnight Runner*'s motion shifted relative to her own, began to seem less eccentric. She kept her attention focused not on the runaway yacht, but on the heads-up display and the roll indicator. She kept nudging the boat's roll higher till she saw it match the number that the simulation had predicted for Blitsharts' yacht.

Good. But that was the easy part. Her inner ear could adapt well enough to spinning on one axis, but when she began to alter pitch and yaw, the cockpit – which was well forward in the boat, like Blitsharts' – would swoop and spin through a series of freakish arcs, as if stuck on the end of an erratic pendulum.

Sula began to nudge the pitch control in her right hand. At first the sensation was barely distinguishable, but as pitch increased and the bow of the pinnace began to swoop in larger and larger circles, the vertigo began to build. Fear shivered through her mind. She might not be able to do this for long, possibly not for the length of time it would take to gradually increase her pitch and yaw.

Do it all at once, she thought. She added yaw to her move-ments, both hands working now. She kept her gaze focused fiercely on the *Runner,* trying to ignore the wildly spinning stars in the background. The yacht's complex motions began to moderate relative to Sula's pinnace, until *Midnight Runner* finally stood still in Sula's vision, the bow no longer lunging at her but simply hanging there against the pirouetting star field.

Vertigo swam through Sula's mind in a series of surges, like an inexorable flood tide. Her suit clamped gently on her arms and legs, forcing blood out of her extremities. Her vision was beginning to narrow. It was time to get this over with.

She nudged the controls and began to back her boat, stern-first, towards the yacht. She felt as if her bowels were trying to climb up through her throat – Sula swallowed hard and shook sudden tears from her eyes. She was only a few seconds from grappling, and then she could wrestle both boats to a standstill.

And then Sula saw whiteness blossom in the spotlights that illuminated the scene, and sudden horror surged through her veins. Manoeuvring thrusters had just fired – *Blitsharts'* thrusters. The yacht's bow began to swing. In terror Sula shoved both controls forward, trying to get clear – and then there was a sudden massive jar as tons of yacht shouldered into her pinnace, followed by a horrid rumble and a hideous scraping sound that shivered along the hull. A sudden howling alarm jolted her nerves. For several terrible seconds she felt the prolonged contact in her bones, and then she was free, away from *Runner's* embrace.

Her vision had contracted almost to nothing. She fought the ship's pendulum motion by feel alone, battling the vertigo that swam her mind. She was only certain she had stabilized the ship's motion when the blackness began to retreat from her vision and she saw the virtual world again with its displays.

Bile stung her sinus. She shut off the collision alarm, turned off the virtual displays to bring her cockpit back in her vision again, then lay in her acceleration couch and drew one shuddering breath after another while she tried very hard not to throw up. Probably the only thing that stopped her was the thought of vomit in her suit, which was much less efficient at coping with vomit than with urine.

Eventually the urge to vomit faded, as did the thunderous crash of her heart. She opened her helmet and wiped sweat from her face, and only then remembered that she should have checked hull integrity before opening her suit to the environment.

She went over the displays, then triggered her pinnace's diagnostics and found no sign of damage. Then she checked the exterior displays and found the long scratch on the pinnace's hull where Blitsharts' boat had contacted her own, the light blue paint that had been Kandinski's pride scraped down to the pale resinous hull.

Sula mopped her face again. She shifted the exterior displays to *Midnight Runner,* which was slowly drifting away while still tumbling. It was clear that the yacht's motion was different: the collision, plus Blitsharts' thrusters, had added more complexity to *Runner's* movement.

Damn. She mopped her face again and hoped she was presentable for video, that her next message wouldn't show Enderby a wild-eyed, panicked junior.

She triggered the comm board and tucked in her chin to keep her jaw, and her voice, from trembling. 'Cadet Sula to Operations Command. The rendezvous failed, due to Blitsharts' firing thrusters during the manoeuvre. There was a collision, but hull integrity is uncompromised and ship systems undamaged. I will evaluate *Midnight Runner's* current motion and try to decide whether it is possible to attempt another rendezvous.'

Sula ceased transmission, watched *Runner* spin away through the void, and slowly came to the realization that she was off the hook. The vehicle telemetry she'd sent to Operations would show Blitsharts' thrusters firing and ruining the rendezvous. She could hardly be blamed for not attempting rendezvous again, not with a target that was tumbling in a more dangerous pattern.

The mission had failed, and it wasn't her fault. All she

had to do was take a close look at *Midnight Runner*'s new, more complex tumbling pattern, then decide that it was too dangerous to attempt.

And the failure would be *Blitsharts'* fault. *No blame will attach . . .* For once, perhaps for the only time in her service career, that statement would actually be true.

She was free to abandon the mission.

For a long moment Sula listened to the air circulate through the cockpit and wondered why she didn't feel like celebrating.

She nudged the controls and sent her pinnace after *Midnight Runner*. She parked again along the axis of the *Runner*'s spin, and slowly eyeballed the yacht as it tumbled. Yes, the movement was more complex. More dangerous.

If she went in for the rendezvous again, she'd have to do it faster, give her brain more time to work before it became completely disoriented.

What do you mean if? she demanded of herself. Surely she wasn't going through with this.

'Display: go virtual,' she commanded.

Space expanded in her skull as her view of the cockpit faded. The yacht rolled in the void of stars.

'Display: show only images within one light-second.'

The stars, and the brighter star that was Vandrith, winked out. When the pinnace was tumbling the frenzied dance of the stars was both a distraction and a temptation to motion sickness.

'Display: freeze motion. Display: link pointer to hand controls. Display: pointer is now at target. Display: attach artificial horizon to target at pointer. Display: resume motion. Display: link hand controls to manoeuvring thrusters.'

With these commands, Sula used her attitude controls to manipulate a virtual 'pointer' in the display, attaching an artificial horizon – a flat open gridiron coloured a highly artificial fluorescent orange – to the skin of Blitsharts' boat. This now rolled and pirouetted along with the yacht's motion, a flat plane that danced in a frenzied circle around her.

With further commands, she narrowed the artificial horizon until it was only a strip, an orange carpet that led right to the point on *Midnight Runner* where she could successfully grapple.

'Display,' she commanded, 'reverse angle.'

Instantly her perspective faced directly away from the yacht, and she saw only the artificial horizon in its frenetic dance around her. There were no distractions in the display, no massive prow coming around to threaten her. All she would have to do was match her own boat's motion to the artificial horizon, then back up along the orange carpet till she met the *Runner*.

And of course do it without getting killed. That being the sticky part.

And then Sula realized she had decided to make the attempt, and wondered when that decision had come. She had every justification in the world to back off – she had no reason to think that Captain Blitsharts was alive – and she had every cause to fear the outcome.

But still, she thought. *But still.*

Maybe she was just stubborn.

She closed her helmet and triggered the comm unit.

'Cadet Sula to Operations Control. I'm going to try again.'

As soon as she ended the transmission her hands went to the manoeuvring controls, and – before she could change her mind – she began triggering jets. She wasn't going slowly this time, no cautious addition of yaw to roll to pitch, but moving in all three planes at once. *Don't think about it,* she told herself, *just do it.*

Vertigo surfed through Sula's skull. She felt gravity tug at her lips and cheek, felt her suit clamp down on her arms and legs. She kept her eyes focused on the strip of dancing bright orange, on making the dancing orange carpet stand still.

The orange horizon moved only in two planes now. Stinging acid rose to her throat, and she fought it back down, clamping her jaw and neck muscles to send blood to the brain. Now the horizon moved only in one plane, bobbing up and down like the bow of a rowboat, until she stilled that movement as well. Her stomach made a sudden lunge into her throat, and she battled it back down.

'Display: reverse angle.' The words fell from Sula's lips like a faint prayer. Suddenly the angle was reversed, and she saw *Midnight Runner* standing still in the blackness, the bright orange carpet fixed to its back. She nudged both controls and the yacht began to creep closer. She could feel tears whipping across her face as the boat's frenzied gravities tore them from her eyes, and was thankful that tears could not blur the virtual display burning in her mind.

But gravities would. The orange carpet was not as bright as once it had been. Her vision was going black. She could barely see the *Runner*'s shiny black prow as it slid under her. She braked, hoping she had slowed her boat's movement to a crawl, and as her vision darkened she cried out 'Grapples: engage!'

Both the yacht and the Fleet pinnace were made out of layers of resinous polymer stiffened by longitudinal polycarbon beams – nothing a magnetic grapple would adhere to. But ferrous degaussing strips ran the length of the hull, charged to repel radiation, and these provided a home for the grapples.

There was a shuddering boom as the two hulls came together, followed by a tone in Sula's headset that told her the grapples had successfully adhered. And then she was working the thruster controls again, fighting the two boats' mad tumble through emptiness.

'Display: kill the artificial horizon! Display: show the plane of the ecliptic!' The words came from Sula in a choked scream. Two boats were heavier than the pinnace alone, and sluggish to respond to the controls. She could barely see the plane of the ecliptic even as it was projected onto her visual centres, a green gridiron that flashed over and around and across . . .

She battled the swinging weight of the locked boats, and then a new jolt of terror shrieked through her nerves as she felt something *else* resisting her − Runner*'s thrusters were firing again. Blitsharts was fighting her.* Fury at this treachery raged in her heart. She battled on, struggling against the chaotic movement, battling to remain conscious as her vision darkened . . . A wail rose to her throat, a bubbling cry of frustration and anger . . .

The boat juddered and moaned as gravities warred within its frame. And then Sula gave a shout of triumph as she realized her vision was returning, as she saw the plane of the ecliptic rolling around her in a simple pattern . . . she applied thrust, damping the ship's oscillations, and then she felt a surge of weary triumph as the gridiron plane stilled, stretched like a carpet beneath her feet from one horizon to the other.

Blitsharts' boat gave one last blast from its thrusters, and Sula corrected easily, feeling little but irritation at this final rebellion.

Sula discontinued the virtual display, and then had to shake tears and sweat from her eyes before she could see her cockpit. Wearily, gasping for breath and fighting the rebellious stomach that still pitched and rolled inside her, she called up ship diagnostics. No damage, no hull punctures, antimatter safely contained.

She opened her faceplate and wiped her face. Acid burned in her throat, on her tongue, and she took a long drink of water. Maybe it would settle her stomach.

She wiped her face again, reached for the comm board, and began to transmit.

'Cadet Sula to Operations Control. Rendezvous completed. Both craft now stabilized. In a moment I will grapple to *Midnight Runner*'s hatch and then try to enter.'

Once the transmission was over she took her time before moving, waited for the vertigo to stop swooping through her head and her stomach to stop trying to climb out her throat. Then Sula ungrappled, rolled her boat over onto its back, and slipped it forward along *Midnight Runner*'s hull until the two dorsal hatches could mate.

Sula closed her faceplate again and touched the transmit button.

'Cadet Sula again. I have successfully grappled hatch-to-hatch with *Midnight Runner*. I am going on board.'

She switched on her helmet camera to give everyone at Operations the same view she had herself, unstrapped from her acceleration couch and floated out into the weightless cockpit. Careful not to let her useless legs hit any controls, she rolled over, rolled away the plug of radiation shielding that blocked the exit at the back of the cockpit, and then ghosted down the tunnel that connected the cockpit to the pinnace's small airlock. Once there, she sealed the tunnel behind her, then triggered her helmet lamp and ordered the outside hatch to open.

The hatch obediently rolled back, presenting her with a view of Blitsharts' own glossy black dorsal hatch. She floated to the hatch, looked at the controls, and told the hatch to open.

It did so in silence. Sula pulled herself head-first into *Runner*'s airlock, then braced feet against the sides of the tiny airlock and wrenched the lever that should open the airlock to the interior. It refused. The controls began an annoying meeping sound. Sula looked at the airlock control display. Surprise rang along her nerves.

'This may take a while, Control,' she said. 'There's hard vacuum in there.'

Three

A cold weight lay on Sula's heart. She knew what was inside.

She turned off the airlock alarm. 'I'll have to close and depressurize the lock,' Sula told her distant audience. 'With the hatch shut you won't be receiving my transmissions, so I will record and transmit later.'

She closed the yacht's hatch behind her and then listened to the hiss of air flooding out into the vacuum, the hiss that grew fainter and fainter until there was nothing left in the airlock to carry any sound. Sula braced her feet outwards against the lock walls again and pulled the lever. The inner hatch opened inwards in perfect silence, then caught half open.

Unlike the pinnace, *Midnight Runner*'s lock opened directly into the cockpit. With her helmet jammed against the hatch coaming Sula could see the back of Blitsharts' acceleration couch, with his helmet nestled in webbing. Blitsharts' left hand floated above the thruster control, as if ready to pounce and initiate another chaotic manoeuvre.

Sula tilted her body to scan the cockpit with her helmet lamps, and her heart surged in shock.

The cabin interior was beautifully laid-out, custom-designed and proportioned for Blitsharts himself, made for the reach of his arm, the comfort of his eye. The colours were cream accented with stripes of red, green, and yellow. But something had smashed the cockpit – it looked as if someone had gone over it with a sledgehammer. There were dents and scratches on the instrument panels and cabin walls, and even some of the readouts, built to resist heavy accelerations, had been smashed.

Worse, there was hair, and what looked like blood, smeared over the displays. Sula wondered in shock if someone had murdered Blitsharts. Chopped him up with − with *what*? What could create such a horror?

She tried to shove open the hatch, felt increasing resistance. Something had broken loose and was caught behind the hatch, preventing it from deploying.

Sula groped blindly behind the hatch door with a gloved hand. The obstacle was not within range of her hand at first, and she had to float in the airlock while sweeping her hand along the rim of the hatch. The movement was difficult and awkward in the vac suit, and her bruised muscles strained. Her breath rasped in her helmet, and she felt sweat prickling her forehead. Finally she found the trouble, something wet and bloody and hairy and very, very dead.

The dog Orange. Not that he was recognizable as a dog; he was a battered mass of bloody meat, and had apparently been hurled like a missile around the cockpit as the boat tumbled, the erratic spin subjecting the poor animal to one ferocious acceleration after another.

It was the dog that had bludgeoned the interior of the cockpit, battering the instruments and smearing the compartment with his own blood. It was the dog that had hit the thruster controls and triggered the boat's erratic tumble.

After seeing Orange, Sula had no hope for Blitsharts. She found the captain strapped into his acceleration couch with his faceplate up, open to the vacuum. It had been Orange who fired the manoeuvring thrusters, not the captain. Blitsharts' face, though smeared with dog's blood, had been protected by the frame of the helmet and was undamaged. His expression was pinched and accusing. He had been dead for some time.

It was said that hypoxia was a good way to go, that as the brain slowly starved of oxygen it gave way to euphoria, that the victim's last moments were moments of bliss.

Sula's memories were different. She remembered the body twitching, the heels drumming, the diaphragm going into spasm as the lungs laboured to breathe . . .

She remembered weeping onto the pillow as her friend fought for life. The soft feel of the pillow in her hand, soft as flesh. The pillow that Sula had put over her face to finish her off.

Enderby called Martinez out of Operations Command at the beginning of the shift, but gave him permission to monitor the rescue mission when he wasn't busy forwarding or filing the Fleet's communications.

And so he watched the displays as Sula braked her craft to match velocities with *Midnight Runner,* as she manoeuvred closer for a better view of the tumbling yacht.

He halfway hoped she wouldn't attempt it. He didn't want his plan to kill anyone.

And then came the message, addressed specifically to him. Sula, her astonishing good looks unimpaired by the faceplate that closed her helmet, saying 'I haven't ever screwed in quite this way before.' With an eyebrow tilted, and wicked amusement in her green eyes.

Martinez thought he'd smothered his burst of laughter, but he caught Enderby giving him a sharp look from his desk, and Martinez consciously drew a solemn mask over his amusement.

Sula's face faded from the display, and Martinez watched the telemetry signals as she began using her thrusters, matching her boat's roll to that of the yacht. His hands twitched as they manoeuvred imaginary thrusters. Martinez' heart leaped into his throat when *Runner*'s thrusters began to fire, when *Midnight Runner* began to roll into Sula's pinnace like a great whale breaching over a fishing boat . . . *Get out, get out,* he thought furiously, and fear shivered along his nerves as he saw the collision. He didn't draw breath until Sula had escaped and stabilized her craft.

'I'm going to try again.' Sula looked composed enough in her vacuum suit, but this time there was no mischievous twinkle in her eye – she'd learned well enough that this was no laughing matter. Admiration for her courage warred in Martinez with despair over her foolishness.

But he had to admit she did it beautifully – faster this time, she'd learned her lesson, her boat dancing in all three planes at once. And then the docking, the battle against the great tumbling inertia of the yacht, finally the great triumph in which the two boats flew, linked, through the silent glory of space.

Martinez wanted to shriek and dance. He even found himself looking at Enderby, as if for permission – but the lord commander sat silent at his desk, a slight frown on his face, absorbed in whatever he saw on his own displays. Dancing was not going to be a part of the programme.

Sula's next transmission showed a woman exhausted, limp in her couch, with locks of her golden hair pasted by sweat to her forehead. Martinez could imagine the battle she'd been through. But the gleam in her eye was back, and this time it was a gleam of conquest.

'I am going on board.'

The battle was over, now there was only the inspection of the prize.

When news came that there was no air in Blitsharts' cockpit, Martinez' heart sank only a little. Having had hours in which to think about it, he'd concluded that it was unlikely that the yachtsman was alive.

The next report came after the silence in which the airlock door cut off Sula's transmissions.

'Blitsharts and the dog are dead.' Sula was back in the cockpit of her pinnace, floating within close range of the cockpit camera. 'There was a leak somewhere in the cockpit, and his faceplate was up and he'd turned off most of the cabin alarms. I suppose you shut off a lot of alarms when racing – proximity alarms, acceleration alerts – and when the depressurization alarm went off he probably shut it off without noticing what it was. At some point he released the dog from its acceleration couch, but I doubt he was in his right mind by then – he'd probably lost it from just before that long acceleration burn.' She seemed to shrug inside her vacuum suit. 'I will follow this transmission with the recording I made aboard *Midnight Runner*. This is Cadet Caroline Sula, concluding her report.'

Martinez watched this in fascination. The Cadet Sula who uttered these words was a different person from the woman he had previously seen. She seemed neither the mischievous pilot-cadet nor the weary, triumphant warrior, but, he decided, someone somehow *lost* . . . almost misplaced in time, both older and younger than her actual age. Older, because she seemed timeworn, almost frail. Younger, because there was a helplessness in her glance, like that of a wounded child.

Had she counted so much on Blitsharts being alive? Martinez wondered. Or perhaps she *knew* him, perhaps even loved him . . .

Martinez was tempted to replay the transmission, so he could better understand why her reaction seemed so exaggerated.

'Lieutenant Martinez,' Enderby said.

Martinez gave a start. 'Lord commander?'

'Please convey to Cadet Sula my congratulations on her successful manoeuvre. It required both skill and courage.'

Surprise swam through Martinez' brain. 'Yes, my lord.'

'I have decided to award her the Medal of Merit—'

Enderby hesitated. 'Second class. Please have the necessary documents on my desk by the end of shift.'

'Very good, my lord.'

Enderby had been watching all along, Martinez realized. Watching the transmissions while he sat at his desk, expressionless as always.

'Compose a document for release to the Fleet News Service,' Enderby continued, 'then send it to me for review.'

'Very good, my lord.'

'Oh – another thing.'

'Yes, my lord?'

'In your message, please admonish Cadet Sula for the inappropriate nature of one of her remarks. Official communications are not to be used for levity.'

'Very good, my lord.'

Martinez realized he would miss the old man, when he was gone.

Enderby sent Martinez and Gupta home early so that he could attend the football match between the crews of *The Glory of the Praxis* and *The Sublime Truth of the Praxis,* two of the goliath Praxis-class battleships that formed the core of the Home Fleet.

Fleet commanders were often as fanatic about sport as any cadet. Sport was the closest anyone in the Fleet was ever likely to come to real combat.

Martinez himself attended the games as often as not, but today he wanted nothing so much as a shower, a bed, and – come to think of it – a drink to help relax the kinks in his muscles. He stopped by the junior officers' club on his way out of the Commandery, and there he encountered Ari Abacha, fortifying himself before his shift at Operations Control. Abacha waved him over to the bar as he entered, and Martinez took a chair, wincing at the pain caused by that inhuman seat in Operations.

'Buy you a drink?'

'Thanks, Ari. I'll have some of that Sellaree.'

A glass of ruby wine was placed in front of Martinez. It was one of the Commandery's special tulip glasses, rimmed with the same glossy white ceramic out of which the bar had been shaped, and with a stripe of the same pale green as the carpet, a colour scheme intended to set off to advantage the darker green of the officers' tunics.

'I say. Gare.' Abacha's words were unusually tentative.

Martinez looked at him. 'Yes, Ari?'

Abacha gave a laugh. 'I don't know whether you'll be annoyed by this or not – I think it's amusing actually – but it seems you're famous.'

Martinez raised his heavy brows. 'I? Famous?'

'I'm afraid so. Do you remember yesterday, when that fellow from All-Sports Network called Operations Control?'

Martinez scratched his two days' beard. 'Panjit something, wasn't it?'

Abacha gave a nervous laugh. 'Panjit Sesse, yes. Well – things were getting busy, you'll recall – and I was going to cut the fellow off. But I *didn't* – he *suggested* that I keep transmitting to him, and it appears that I *did*. Without thinking about it. He heard *everything*.'

'Everything,' Martinez repeated, trying to remember if he'd said anything particularly embarrassing.

'Everything up till the time my shift ended and I left. Everything we did was broadcast on All-Sports Network.'

'And the censors didn't—?'

'The censors seem to have taken the night off. Maybe they were watching the football match – it was Lodestone versus Andiron, you know.'

Martinez probed carefully, like a tongue exploring a painful tooth. 'I – *we* – didn't say anything that . . .'

'Oh no.' Abacha laughed. 'Nothing that will haunt us. You were quite decisive, in fact – sent your message to Kandinski requesting a rescue mission before informing lord commander Enderby that a situation even existed.'

Martinez' brittle laugh was a poor imitation of Abacha's, and his head buzzed with calculation as he laughed.

Did Enderby know? If he didn't, someone was sure to tell him. But of course Enderby *already* knew, he knew that *someone* must have requested a rescue mission from Kandinski.

If only Enderby's informant didn't rub his nose in it. If only someone didn't jog him with an elbow at the football match and say, 'By all the virtues, Enderby, you allow your aides a deal of latitude.'

But someone was bound to. The Fleet sailed not so much in the starry void as on a sea of rumour, an incoherent mass of information, speculation, gossip, intrigue, interest, and collusion. Martinez, without seeking them out, was nevertheless privy to an outrageous number of secrets, some of which – if true – were blood-chilling. But it hardly mattered whether they were true or not, they were things that the Fleet *knew*. It was *known* that the Naxid Fleet Commander Toshueen, finding his son disappointing, had cut off the youngster's head and eaten it; it was *known* that Squadron Commander Rafi had ordered cadets to tie and beat him, and as for Enderby's wife . . . well, a lot was *known* about Enderby's wife.

That Martinez had good, authoritative reasons to disbelieve all these stories scarcely mattered: the Fleet always told stories about itself, and the sorts of stories it told about itself were eternal. There was a *need* in the Fleet for stories, and now there was a new story, how lord commander Enderby had been made a fool of by his aide.

Martinez had always hoped he would be the subject of one of these stories, but this wasn't the sort he had in mind.

Martinez had the sense that his promotion, already slipping from his fingers, had just floated beyond his reach.

His sense of grievance, however, was only momentary. He was too tired to feel anything for very long.

He said goodbye to Abacha and took a cab to the apartment he kept in the High City, let his clothes fall on the floor for his orderly to pick up, and fell into bed.

His orderly woke him at the usual hour, and Martinez dragged himself to breakfast. Lieutenants were entitled to two servants, paid for by the Fleet – the service was nothing if not generous to its officers – but Martinez had never found duties enough for more than one. This was Khalid Alikhan, a master weaponer of more than thirty years' service, a man Martinez saved from retirement when the old *Crisis* was decommissioned. He was tall and grave, with iron-grey hair and the curling mustachios and goatee favoured by senior warrant and petty officers.

As a servant Alikhan was adequate: though he kept the place tidy and looked after Martinez' uniforms, he was an indifferent cook, and both his manners and accent were rough. But that didn't matter – Martinez could always hire more polished servants if he wished to entertain. It was Alikhan's thirty years spent in the Fleet weapons bays that Martinez found invaluable, the fund of Fleet wisdom and experience to which Alikhan gave Martinez access.

Alikhan knew more of the Fleet's *stories* than anyone Martinez had ever met.

'There are quite a few messages, my lord,' Alikhan said as he poured the first coffee of the day. 'They started coming in yesterday morning.'

Alikhan's words brought the day's first cloud of despair overhead: Martinez felt his head sinking between his shoulders. 'Reporters, I suppose?' he said.

'Yes, my lord.'

Alikhan offered Martinez his breakfast of porridge and pickled mayfish. The jellylike mayfish, splayed across the plate's Martinez crest, trembled greenly in the morning light.

'I saw the broadcasts, my lord,' Alikhan said. 'When you didn't turn up the other night, I checked the video to see if some crisis might be detaining you.'

'Was it exciting?' Martinez shoved porridge into his mouth. He was rarely awake enough in the mornings to care what his breakfasts tasted like, and this one, so far as he could tell, tasted more or less like the others.

'Well,' Alikhan said, 'the broadcasters really didn't know what to make of it, but to anyone with real experience,' by which he meant the Fleet, 'to anyone who knew what was happening, it was . . .' He made an affirmative movement with one shovel-fingered hand. 'It was suspenseful, my lord. Very interesting.'

'Let's hope the lord commander isn't too *interested*,' Martinez said savagely.

'He might decide that you're a credit to the service, my lord,' Alikhan offered. He sounded as dubious about this idea as Martinez.

'He might,' Martinez agreed, then added, 'He's decorating that cadet, Sula . . . nothing was said about decorating *me*.'

The pickled mayfish oozed over Martinez' palate. He washed it down with coffee, and Alikhan topped up his cup.

'*People* are interested in you,' he said. 'There's that.'

'That's nice, I suppose. But that's not going to matter in the service.'

'But those people could be, I don't know . . . useful.'

Something in Alikhan's manner made Martinez straighten. 'How do you mean?' he said.

'Well,' Alikhan began, 'I recall a lieutenant on the old *Renown,* name of Salazar. There was a problem with one of the missile launchers during an exercise – the missile ran hot in the tube, was spraying gamma rays all through the bay, could have blown up . . . Salazar was the officer in command, took charge and got the missile out of the tube – those were the old Mark Seventeen launchers, my lord, very unreliable unless they were maintained properly, and these weren't. That's what the Board of Inquiry determined – there were two officers cashiered over that one, and a master weaponer and two weaponers first class were broken in the ranks.'

'They took it seriously, then,' Martinez said. Weaponers were broken in rank often enough, he supposed, but if they cashiered a couple of Peers instead of shifting them to meaningless duty, then their dereliction must have been serious.

'It spoiled a very large Fleet exercise,' Alikhan said. 'Lord commander Fanaghee – that's the clan-elder of the Fanaghee that's got the Naxid squadron at Magaria – he was humiliated in front of Senior Fleet Commander El-kay. And of course we could have lost the *Renown*. The destruction of the *Quest* had already been blamed on the Mark Seventeen, and cautions sent around the Fleet.'

'I see,' Martinez said. 'So how did Salazar make out?'

'Well, he was decorated, of course – the hero of the hour. Very popular. But it was what he did *with* his celebrity that caught my attention.'

Martinez had forgotten the existence of his breakfast. 'And what was that?' he asked.

'He was interviewed. And in the interviews he stressed the discipline of the Fleet under lord commander Fanaghee, the inspiring example of his seniors, the capability of the instructors who had taught him how to manage the missile launchers.'

'He flattered everybody,' Martinez said.

'He turned what had been a black eye for the Fleet into something that reflected well on the service. Fanaghee ordered him promoted to lieutenant-captain even though he'd only passed for lieutenant nine months before.'

Martinez decided that Salazar's example was certainly worth pondering. He cocked an eye up at Alikhan.

'What became of Salazar? I never heard of him.'

'He died, my lord, a few months later. Too many gamma rays flooding that missile bay.'

At least there were no gamma rays in Martinez' case.

'I can't talk to reporters without clearing it with the lord commander,' he said.

'I would advise obtaining permission, my lord,' Alikhan agreed.

'Damn Abacha, anyway!' Martinez said. 'This is all his fault.'

Alikhan refrained from comment.

Martinez concentrated on his breakfast. The taste, he reflected, wasn't bad at all.

Enderby granted Martinez permission to talk to reporters, comforted perhaps by the fact that Fleet censors would have the final say in what finally reached the public. Martinez found his opportunity when Enderby was called to a meeting, leaving Martinez with nothing to do but monitor signals traffic.

Martinez spoke to several reporters from his comm station in Enderby's office. He told them that it was the example of Fleet Commander Enderby and his other seniors that had inspired him during the rescue mission. Enderby saw that the Home Fleet was trained and disciplined and brought up to the mark. It was thanks to Enderby that the Home Fleet was ready for anything.

'It is one of the glories of the Praxis that lines of responsibility are clearly defined,' he said. 'I have my job and am responsible to my lord commander, just as others are responsible to me. When I undertake a task, I know that it is because my lord commander has entrusted me with it, and I do my best to ensure that it will be performed up to his expectations.'

The reporters listened to this and took dutiful notes, if
for no other reason than it was the sort of thing the censors
would like to see in their reports. They asked questions about
Martinez' history, his family. They seemed equally interested
in Cadet Caroline Sula, however, and the fate of the dog
Orange. They wanted to know if it were possible to interview
Cadet Sula.

'I'll ask,' Martinez said. 'But I have to remind you that
she's still some distance out. It's not going to be a sparkling
dialogue, with her answers taking half an hour to get back
to you.'

He sent the reporters as much information about Sula as he
felt appropriate for them to know, with no mention of the
miserable fate of her parents. He sent them her picture, which
he was sure would pique their interest, if not their lust.

And then, looking at the picture, that glorious face, he
began to think about Cadet Sula. She was out there alone,
hours beyond reach of even the simplest message, and in
a tiny vessel with no comforts. Her nearest neighbour was
a corpse.

What was she thinking about? he wondered. Her last message, the shocking picture of the fragile, strangely aged Sula,
had suggested that her thoughts were not comfortable ones.

If she were to think about anything, he considered, perhaps
she ought to be thinking about Gareth Martinez.

He reached for his comm set to send her a message.

Sula lay in the darkness of the cockpit, afraid to sleep. She
had managed to function throughout her evaluation of the
situation on *Midnight Runner,* through the return to her
own pinnace through the airlock, and her brief report to
Operations Control. She had done well as she ungrappled,
shifted the pinnace to provide a better purchase on the yacht,
engaged the grapples again, and fired the main engine.

Midnight Runner, out of control and with its crew dead,

had been boarded by a Fleet vessel. That made it salvage, Fleet property. Her duty was to bring it to Zanshaa where it would be sold, or – very possibly – turned into personal transportation for some high-ranking Fleet commander.

Sula began with a very gentle acceleration while she monitored the magnetic grapples carefully. She was pleased to discover that two vessels could maintain an acceleration of half a gravity before any strain on the grapples became apparent.

Half a gravity was something she could maintain very well, easy on the bruised bones and kinked muscles that still ached from her earlier, more brutal, accelerations. She plotted her course with half a gravity in mind and began the long, long burn.

Thirteen and a half days to the halfway point, where she'd turn and begin a half-gravity deceleration burn for another thirteen and a half days.

Twenty-seven days altogether, alone, in this little room.

Once everything was plotted on the computer and the torch began to fire, she had nothing to do. And it was then that her mind began to be enfolded by the cold, slow, nightmare tentacles of memory . . .

The worst part was that she knew what was happening. She knew that the asphyxiated body of Blitsharts had brought forward the memories she most dreaded, the past she'd tried her best to bury, bury deep in the innermost frozen ground of her self . . . bury there, like a corpse.

It would be twenty-seven days to Zanshaa. Days spent in the night of space, alone with a dead man and live memories. Of the two, the dead man was preferable company.

Sula considered giving herself something to help her sleep, but she dreaded the moment before the drug would take her, the darkness enfolding her consciousness in its dark wings, followed by the surrender to the tide of night . . .

It was too much like smothering.

She ran ship diagnostics over and over, finding nothing wrong but hoping the repetition would lull her to dreamless sleep. It didn't help, of course. She was condemned to the memories.

Memories of the girl called Gredel.

Gredel's earliest memories were of cowering in the darkness while violence raged on the other side of the flimsy door. Antony screaming at Nelda, the sound of his slaps on Nelda's flesh, the crash of furniture as it was broken against other furniture or against the walls.

Antony was very hard on furniture.

Gredel, unlike many of the children she knew, had actually met her father, and her father was not Antony. She had met her father twice, when he'd passed through the Fabs on his way to somewhere else. On both occasions he'd given Nelda money, and Nelda had taken a little of the money and bought Gredel a frozen treat at Bonifacio's in Maranic Town.

Nelda looked after Gredel because her mother, Ava, was usually away. When Ava came she usually brought Nelda money, but Nelda didn't seem to mind when Ava didn't.

Ava and Nelda had been to school together. 'Your ma was the beautiful one,' Nelda said. 'Everyone loved her.' She looked at Gredel and sighed, her hand thoughtfully stroking Gredel's smooth cheek. 'And you're going to have that trouble, too. Too many people are going to love you, and none for the right reasons.'

Nelda lived in the Fabs, the many streets of prefabricated apartment buildings, all alike, down the Iola River from Maranic Town. Poor people lived in the Fabs, though everyone in the Fabs had some money at least for rent. People with no money at all slept in the street until the Patrol picked them up and shipped them off to the agrarian communes that covered most of the land surface of Spannan.

Though the Patrol didn't sweep through the Fabs very often, and sometimes people lived on the streets for years.

Gredel's mother Ava had spent time in an agrarian commune, not because she had no money, but because she was involved in some business of Gredel's father. Gredel's father hadn't been arrested, though he had to leave the Fabs for a long time. Nelda explained that Gredel's father had 'linkages' that kept the Patrol from arresting him, though the linkages hadn't worked where Ava was concerned. 'Someone had to pay,' Nelda said, 'and people decided that person was your ma.'

Gredel wondered who it was who decided such things. Nelda said it was all very complicated and she didn't know the whole story anyway.

Nelda worked as an electrician, which paid well when she was working. Usually there was no work, however, and she earned money by hooking people illegally to the electric mains.

Antony, the man who bellowed and roared and hit Nelda, was Nelda's husband. He wasn't around much, however, because he wandered from town to town and job to job. When he returned to the Fabs it was because he didn't have work, and he needed Nelda's money to pay for liquor. When he was drinking, it was wise to stay out of his sight.

When Gredel's mother Ava returned to the Fabs from her sentence in the country, it didn't look as if she had suffered very much – Ava was beautiful, with the golden hair and creamy skin that she shared with Gredel, and with large blue-grey eyes. She was dressed wonderfully – a blue blouse, with the upswept collar that turned into a glittering, gem-encrusted net for her hair, and a skirt that wrapped around her twice and showed her figure. Her hands had long, curved nails painted a glossy shade of blue-grey, to match her eyes. The scent she wore made Gredel want to stop and just inhale. Gredel's mother had already found someone to take care of her.

Ava took Gredel on her lap and smothered her with kisses. Ava told Gredel what she did in the country. 'I processed food,' she said. 'I roasted grain for Naxids, and I processed soy curd for Terrans. It wasn't hard work. It was just boring.'

Most of the work on the farms was automated, Ava said. Not many people were needed in the country, and that's why most of the countryside was empty and all the people were packed into the cities, most of them in places like the Fabs.

Gredel adored her mother, but never had the chance to live with her. The men who took care of Ava – and there were several over the years, all 'linked' in some way – didn't want children around, and when Ava was without a man, she didn't want Gredel with her because it would make a man harder to get.

Gredel thought that she didn't miss living with Ava that much. She had a place with Nelda, and Antony wasn't around often. Nelda had two children of her own, a boy and a girl, and a boy named Jacob she was looking after for another friend. She just liked having children around. She made sure that the children in her charge were fed and clothed and attended school.

School was something Gredel liked, because she could learn about places that weren't the Fabs. She spent hours on the display terminal, both at home and at school, working with the instructional programs connected with her classwork, and often simply looking up things on her own.

There were advantages to working with the terminal. If she was quiet, Antony wouldn't notice her.

Once she stumbled across a picture of the Arch of Macedoin, with its triple towers. She was struck by the sight: the Arch's ornate, eerie architecture was so unlike the Fabs. It was even different from Maranic Town. She shifted the display into three-dimensional projection and looked at it more intently, seeing towers crowned by pinnacles that looked as if they were made of white icing, the niches below in which stood the Colossi of Macedoin.

The Colossi, she was surprised to discover, were all Terrans. Louis XIV, she read, Henry VIII, M. Portius Cato, Shih Huangdi, V.I. Lenin, Alexander son of Philip, Mao Zedong, Marcus Aurelius, Kongfuzi . . . All heroes of Earth, she learned, those who had, before the arrival of the Shaa, striven to bring into being something like the Praxis, which of course was the most perfect form of government possible.

Earth, she learned, was also called Terra, a word that meant the same thing in another dead language – Earth had apparently once had *lots* of languages, which must have been difficult for people when they wanted to talk to one another. Earth, she learned, was where her ancestors had come from.

She became fascinated by Earth. It wasn't a very important planet in the Shaa dominion, because most of its wormhole gates didn't lead anywhere useful, but there were still billions of Terrans living there or in its star system. Most of them, Gredel was disappointed to discover, lived in places more like the Fabs than the Arch of Macedoin, but still there were ancient cities on Earth of great beauty and majesty, Byzantium, Nanjing, SaSuu, Lima . . .

Gredel devoured everything she could find about Earth. She knew the succession of dynasties in China, learned the names of the kings of France, and could tell the difference between a saker and a demiculverin. She even learned to speak with an Earth accent from watching videos of Earth people. Her mother Ava, on one of her visits, was astonished that her little girl spoke of the members of the Capetian court on the same familiar terms with which she referred to her neighbours.

Her friends started calling her 'Earthgirl'. It wasn't intended as a compliment particularly, but Gredel didn't care. Earth history seemed at least as interesting as anything anyone in the Fabs got up to.

But eventually her interest in Earth history waned, because Nelda's prediction came true.

Gredel had grown older, and – they said – beautiful. And, as Nelda had predicted, she was loved, and for all the wrong reasons.

'Hey Earthgirl! I got someone for you to meet!'

Stoney was excited. He was almost *always* excited. He was one of Lamey's lieutenants, a boy who hijacked cargo that came over the sea to Maranic Port and sold it through Lamey's outlets in the Fabs. Stoney wore soft felt boots and a puffy padded jacket with rows of tiny little metal chimes that rang when he moved, and a hard round plastic hat without a brim, the clothes that all Lamey's linkboys wore when they wanted to be noticed.

Gredel came into the room on Lamey's arm. He had dressed her in a gown of short-haired kantaran leather set off with collar and cuffs of white satin, big clunky white ceramic jewellery inlaid with gold, shiny little plastic boots with nubbly surfaces and tall heels. The height of fashion, at least as far as the Fabs were concerned.

Lamey liked shopping for Gredel. He took her to the stores and bought her a new outfit two or three times each week.

Lamey had earned his name because he once had a defect that made him walk with a limp. It was something he'd got fixed as soon as he had the money, and when Gredel first met him he glided along like a prince, putting each foot down with deliberate, exaggerated care, as if he were walking on rice paper and didn't want to tear it. Lamey was only twenty-five years old in Shaa measure, but already he ran a set of linkboys, and had linkages of his own that eventually ran up to some of the Peers responsible for running places like the Fabs. He had millions, all in cash stashed in various places, and three apartments, and half a dozen small stores through which he moved the material acquired by his crews.

He also had a seventeen-year-old girlfriend called Earthgirl.

Lamey had offered to set her up in an apartment, but Gredel still lived with Nelda. She wasn't sure why. Maybe it was because Gredel hoped she could protect Nelda against Antony. Or maybe because once she moved into a place that Lamey bought her, she'd have to spend all her time there waiting for him to come see her. She wouldn't be able to leave for fear that he'd come by and find her gone and get angry; and she couldn't have her friends visit because they might be there when Lamey turned up and that would probably make him mad, too.

That was the kind of life Ava had always led, waiting in some apartment somewhere for some man to turn up. That's why Ava had never been able to see her daughter when she wanted to. Gredel wanted a different life for herself. She had no idea how to get it, but she was paying attention, and maybe some day she'd learn.

Gredel still attended school. Every afternoon, when Gredel left her school, she'd find Lamey in his car waiting for her, Lamey or one of his boys who would take Gredel to wherever Lamey waited.

Gredel's attending school was something Lamey found amusing. 'I'm going around with a schoolgirl,' he'd laugh, and sometimes he'd remind her to do her schoolwork when he had to leave with his boys on some errand or other. Not that he left her much time for schoolwork. Her grades had plunged to the point where she would probably get kicked out of school before she graduated.

Tonight, the eve of the Festival of Spring, Lamey had taken Gredel to a party at Panda's place. Panda was another of Lamey's linkboys, and he worked on the distribution end. He'd pointed Stoney and his crew at a warehouse full of wine imported from Cavado and pharmaceuticals awaiting shipment to a Fleet hospital on Spannan's ring. The imported wine was proving difficult to sell, there not being much of a market in the Fabs for something so select; but the pharmaceuticals were moving fast through Panda's outlets and everyone was in the mood to celebrate.

'Come on, Earthgirl!' Stoney urged. 'You've got to meet her!'

A warning hummed through Gredel's nerves as she saw everyone at the party looking at her with eyes that glittered from more than whatever they'd been consuming earlier in the evening. There was an anticipation there in those eyes Gredel didn't like. So she dropped Lamey's arm and straightened – because she didn't want these people to see her afraid – and she walked to where Stoney waited.

'Earthgirl!' Stoney said. 'This is Caro!' He was practically jumping up and down with excitement, and instead of looking where Stoney was pointing, Gredel just gave Stoney a long, cool glance, because he was just so outrageous this way.

When she turned her head, her first thought was, *She's beautiful.* And then the full impact of the other girl's face struck her.

'Ah. Ha,' she said.

Caro looked at her with a ragged grin. She had long golden hair and green eyes and skin smooth as butter-cream, flawless . . .

'It's your twin!' Stoney almost shouted. 'Your secret twin sister!'

Gredel gaped while everyone laughed, but Caro just looked at her and said, 'Are you really from Earth?'

'No,' Gredel said. 'I'm from here.'

'Help me build this pyramid.'

Gredel shrugged. 'Why not?' she said.

Caro wore a short dress and a battered jacket with black metal buckles and boots that came up past her knees –

expensive stuff. She stood by the dining table carefully building a pyramid of crystal wine glasses. 'I saw this done once,' she said. 'You pour the wine into the one glass on the top, and when it overflows it fills all the others. If you do it right you fill all the glasses and you don't spill a drop.'

Caro spoke with a kind of drawl, like Peers or rich people did on video.

'We're going to make a mess,' Gredel predicted.

'That's all right, too,' Caro shrugged.

When the pyramid was completed Caro got Stoney to start opening bottles. It was the wine his crew had stolen from the warehouse in Maranic Port, and it was a kind of bright silver in colour, and filled the glasses like liquid mercury.

Caro tried to pour carefully but, as Gredel predicted she made a terrible mess, the precious wine bubbling across the tabletop and over onto the carpet. Caro seemed to find this funny. At length all the glasses were brimming full, and she put down the bottle and called everyone over to drink. They took glasses and cheered and sipped. Laughter and clinking glasses rang in the air. The glasses were so full that the carpet got another bath.

Caro took one glass for herself and pushed another into Gredel's hand, then took a second glass for herself and led Gredel to the sofa. Gredel sipped cautiously at the wine – there was something subtle and indefinable about the taste, something that made her think of the park in spring, the way the trees and flowers had a delicate freshness to them. She'd never tasted any wine like it before.

The taste was more seductive than she wanted anything with alcohol to be. She didn't take a second sip.

'So,' Caro said, 'are we related?'

'I don't think so,' Gredel said.

Caro swallowed half the contents of a glass in one go. 'Your dad was never on Zanshaa? I can almost guarantee my dad was never here.'

'I get my looks from my Ma, and she's never been any-where,' Gredel said. Then, surprised, 'You're from Zanshaa?'

Caro gave a little twitch of her lips, followed by a shrug. Interpreting this as a yes, Gredel asked, 'What do your parents do?'

'They got executed,' Caro said.

Gredel hesitated. 'I'm sorry,' she said. Caro's parents were linked, obviously. No wonder she was hanging with this crowd.

'Me, too.' Caro said it with a brave little laugh, but she gulped down the remains of the wine in her first glass, then took a sip from the second. She looked up at Gredel.

'You heard of them maybe? The Sula family?'

Gredel tried to think of any of the linkages with that name, but couldn't. 'Sorry, no,' she said.

'That's all right,' Caro said. 'The Sulas were big on Zanshaa, but out here in the provinces they wouldn't mean much.'

Caro Sula finished her second glass of wine, then got two more from the pyramid and drank them, then reached for Gredel's. 'You going to drink that?'

'I don't drink much.'

'Why not?'

Gredel hesitated. 'I don't like being drunk.'

Caro shrugged. 'That's fair.' She drank Gredel's glass, then put it with the others on the side table. 'It's not being drunk that I like,' she said, as if she were making up her mind right then. 'But I don't dislike it either. What I don't like,' she said carefully, 'is standing still. Not moving. Not changing. I get bored fast, and I don't like *quiet*.'

'In that case you've come to the right place,' Gredel said.

Her nose is more pointed, Gredel thought. And her chin is different. She doesn't look like me, not really.

I bet I'd look good in that jacket, though.

'So do you live around here someplace?' Gredel asked.

Caro shook her head. 'Maranic Town.'

'I wish I lived in Maranic.'

Caro looked at her in surprise. 'Why?'

'Because it's . . . not here.'

'Maranic is a hole. It's not something to wish for. If you're going to wish, wish for Zanshaa. Or Sandamar. Or Esley.'

'Have you been to those places?' Gredel asked. She almost hoped the answer was no, because she knew she'd never get anywhere like that, that she'd get to Maranic Town if she was lucky.

'I was there when I was little,' Caro said.

'I wish I lived in Byzantium,' Gredel said.

Caro gave her a look again. 'Where's that?'

'Earth. Terra.'

'Terra's a hole,' Caro said.

'I'd still like to go there.'

'It's probably better than Maranic Town,' Caro decided.

Someone programmed some dance music, and Lamey came to dance with Gredel. A few years ago he hadn't been able to walk right, but now he was a good dancer, and Gredel enjoyed dancing with him, responding to his changing moods in the fast dances, moulding her body to his when the beat slowed down.

Caro also danced with one boy or another, but Gredel saw that she couldn't dance at all, just bounced up and down while her partner manoeuvred her around.

After a while Lamey went to talk business with Ibrahim, one of his boys who thought he knew someone in Maranic who could distribute the stolen wine, and Gredel found herself on the couch with Caro again.

'Your nose is different,' Caro said.

'I know.'

'But you're prettier than I am.'

This was the opposite of what Gredel had been thinking. People were always telling her she was beautiful, and she had to believe they saw her that way, but when she looked in the mirror she saw nothing but a vast collection of flaws.

A girl shrieked in another room, and there was a crash of glass. Suddenly Caro's mood changed completely: she glared towards the other room as if she hated everyone there.

'Time to change the music,' she said. She dug in her pocket and pulled out a med injector. She looked at the display, programmed a number, and put the injector to her throat, over the carotid. Little flashes of alarm pulsed through Gredel.

'What's in there?' she asked.

'What do you care?' Caro snarled. Her eyes snapped green sparks.

She pressed the trigger, and an instant later the fury faded, and a drowsy smile came to Caro's lips. 'Now that's better,' she said. 'Panda's got the real goods, all right.'

'Tell me about Zanshaa,' Gredel said.

Caro lazily shook her head. 'No. Nothing but bad memories there.'

'Then tell me about Esley.'

'Sure. What I can remember.'

Caro talked about Esley's black granite peaks, with a white spindrift of snow continually blowing off them in the high perpetual wind, and the shaggy Yormak who lived there, tending their equally shaggy cattle. She described glaciers pouring in ageless slow motion down mountain valleys, high meadows covered with fragrant star flowers, chill lakes so clear that you could see all the way to the bottom.

'Of course I was only at that mountain resort for a few weeks,' Caro added. 'The rest of the planet might be burning desert for all I know.'

Lamey came back for more dancing, and when Gredel returned to the sofa Caro was unconscious, the med injector in her hand. She seemed to be breathing all right, though, lying asleep with a smile on her face. After a while Panda came over and tried to grope her, but Gredel slapped his hands away.

'What's your problem?' he asked.

'Don't mess with my sister when she's passed out,' Gredel told him. He laughed, not exactly in a nice way, but he withdrew.

Caro was still asleep when the party ended. Gredel made Lamey help her carry Caro to his car, and then got him to drive to Maranic Town to her apartment. 'What if she doesn't wake up long enough to tell us where it is?' Lamey complained.

'Whatever she took will wear off sooner or later.'

'What if it's next week?' But he drove off anyway, heading for Maranic, while Gredel sat with Caro in the back seat and tried to wake Caro up. Caro woke long enough to murmur the fact that she lived in the Volta Apartments. Lamey got lost on the way there, and wandered into a Torminel neighbourhood. The nocturnal Torminel were in the middle of their active cycle, and Lamey got angry at the way they stared at him with their huge eyes as he wandered their streets.

Lamey was furious by the time he found the apartment building. He opened the passenger door and practically dragged Caro out of the car onto the sidewalk. Gredel scrambled out of the car and tried to get one of Caro's arms over her shoulders so she could help Caro get to her feet.

A doorman came scrambling out of the building. 'Has something happened to Lady Sula?' he demanded.

Lamey looked at him in surprise. The doorman stared at Gredel, then at Caro, astonished by the resemblance. But Gredel looked at Caro.

Lady Sula? Gredel thought.

Her twin was a Peer.

Ah, she thought. *Ha.*

*   *   *

The cold touch of the med injector.

Pressed to the throat.

Followed by the hiss . . .

Cadet Sula thrashed awake from the nightmare memory, only gradually prying its frozen talons from her mind. A light flashed on her instrument panel, accompanied by a soft tone.

Incoming transmission. Right.

'Display,' she said.

It was the lantern-jawed staff lieutenant, Martinez. 'Cadet Sula,' he said, 'I was wondering if you're lonely.'

Surprise brought a savage laugh to Sula's throat. *Lonely? How could you think that?*

'I'm sending you some entertainment,' Martinez said. 'It's all from my personal collection. I don't know what sort of thing you like, so I'm sending a wide spectrum of stuff. If you'll tell me the sort of thing you'd prefer, I'll try to get it to you.'

He smiled 'Enjoy.' Then he hesitated, and added. 'I'm receiving requests from reporters who want to interview you in regard to the Blitsharts rescue. The lord commander's given his permission, so all that's up to you. You've become sort of famous, here.' And then he brightened again.

'Let me know if you need anything. Aside from a hot bath, that is.'

The transmission ended. Sula looked at the comm display and saw the light steadily winking that indicated her communications buffer was being filled with compressed audiovisual files.

Entertainment?

Anything was better than lying here alone, with nothing but memories for company.

She watched Spate in the knockabout comedy *Extrovert,* enjoying his excellent timing, the sheer physicality of his movements. She absorbed Loralee Pang and the Lai-own

Far-fraq in the melodramas *Dr An-ku Investigates* and *Dr An-ku and the Mystery Skull*. She watched Aimee Marchant in the sophisticated comedy *Fleet Exercises,* with its totally unreal life aboard a battleship, and Cannonball Li in the frantic, classic *Crazy Vacation,* which she decided was overrated. She avoided the dramas *Righteousness* and *Life of Evil* — grim explorations of despair and violence were not what she wanted to watch right now, despite the happy endings mandated by the censors.

'Send more Spate,' she sent in a private message to Martinez. 'And tell the reporters to go eat rocks.'

Martinez proved to be quite a connoisseur of low comedy. In addition to more Spate vehicles, he sent The Deuces in *High-Low Boys* and Mary Cheung in *Who's on the Slab?*

It was while watching Spate do his famous Mushroom Dance in *Spitballs!* that Sula felt the tide of sorrow begin to flow out of her, propelled by a wind of laughter. She laughed till cramp lay like a fist in her belly, till tears spilled from her eyes. She felt the sadness retreat, flow away until she could dam it up again, until it was safe behind its iron wall.

Thank you, Martinez, she thought. *Thank you for saving me . . . from me.*

Four

There had been a party at the Ngeni Palace the night before, and the decorations were still coming down. Golden shay blossoms taller than a man were being lowered from the upper regions of the barrel-vaulted hall, ribbons of gold and white were being unwound from the columns that supported the long balconies, and the dark red marble floor was being thoroughly scrubbed by a gang of servants under the direction of a Daimong in livery. Mingled scents of perfume and decay wafted from the hundreds of faded flowers dumped into a hopper near the front door.

Judging by its remnants, the party had been quite large, thronging the halls and corridors. Were Martinez the sort to pay attention to the society reports, he could probably have read rapturous descriptions that morning of the decorations, costumes, and guests that had filled the palace the previous night.

Perhaps Martinez *would* examine the society reports, at least as far as studying the guest list. It would be interesting to speculate who had rated an invitation and who hadn't, and why.

Martinez, for example, hadn't rated an invitation, despite being one of Lord Ngeni's clients. It was Ngeni and his clan who represented the Martinez clan's interests here in the capital.

But Lord Ngeni was absent – the Ngeni clan head had taken up the governorship of Paycah, leaving clan affairs in the hands of his son, Lord Pierre Ngeni. It had been Pierre's party that had filled the palace the previous day.

Martinez followed the palace majordomo through the courtyard – filled with orderly rows of greenery and larger-than-life statues of Ngeni ancestors – to Lord Pierre's office. There were several individuals in the waiting room, not all of them human, not all of them respectable-looking. Martinez was not made to wait.

At least he rated *some* consideration.

Pierre Ngeni was a broad-shouldered, round-headed young man with a resonant baritone voice and the jaws of a mastiff. He, like his father, wore the dark red uniform that marked him as a convocate – a member of the Convocation, the body that provided the empire's top administrators, and which was permitted to 'petition' the Shaa. (When a petition was accepted by the Shaa, it changed its status to a 'law'.) The Convocation would have charge of the empire when the last of the great masters finally ended its life.

Lord Pierre's uniform was well-tailored, but not the extreme epitome of style – at least Pierre was not a glit. Quite the contrary, he was a serious man, dry, who always gave the impression of being busy. His desk was covered with orderly stacks of papers and two secretaries sat in the room to take notes or dictation, as he required.

'My lord,' Pierre said, rising from behind his desk.

'Lord convocate.' Martinez briefly braced himself military-style, tilting his chin high, a salute to the other man's senior status.

'Please sit down.'

Martinez sat in a straight-backed chair clearly designed to discourage people from taking up too much of the lord convocate's time. Lord Pierre's chair was a more comfortable one, and its cushions sighed as it took his weight. Pierre leaned his chair back at a generous angle and evaluated Martinez with his mild brown eyes.

'I've seen you in the news,' he said. 'That rescue you helped engineer – that's been well spoken of.'

'Thank you, Lord Pierre.'

'A pity you couldn't bring back Blitsharts alive, or at least the dog.' Zanshaa, or at least the Terran parts of it, were displaying extravagant mourning for the dog Orange, more than they seemed to show for his owner.

Martinez gave a shrug. 'I'm afraid that wasn't up to us,' he said.

'I suppose it wasn't.' There was a moment's pause, then Pierre, businesslike, inclined himself and his chair forward. 'How may I help you this morning?'

'I was hoping you might be able to arrange another appointment for me.'

Lord Pierre seemed taken aback. 'As I recall,' he said slowly, 'my father went to some effort to recommend you to lord commander Enderby.'

'And I'm very grateful to him, my lord.'

Pierre's look turned accusatory. 'But it hasn't worked out? Enderby has taken some dislike to you?'

'Not that I know of,' Martinez hedged. 'The problem is that lord commander Enderby has decided to follow the last Shaa into eternity.'

Lord Pierre's eyes flickered in surprise. 'Ah. I see.' He stroked his heavy jaw. '*Most* inconvenient, after all we've done. And you have no indication whether his deathbed petition will recommend you for promotion or not?'

'I can't *count* on any such recommendation,' Martinez said carefully. His hands twitched at the creases of his trousers. 'He's arranged for me to take a post as communications officer on the *Corona*. It's more or less the same job I'm doing now, but it's a small ship under a junior commander, and . . . .'

'A far less prestigious post than aide to the commander of the Home Fleet,' Pierre said.

'Yes.'

'It's almost as if he were going out of his way to demote you,' Pierre said. The accusing look re-entered his eyes.

'He probably thinks it's time I had ship duty,' Martinez said weakly.

'I will see what I can find,' Pierre said. 'The problem is, I have very little influence in the Fleet at the moment – my great-aunt's retired, and no one in the service owes us any favours right now.' He frowned and lowered his voice, almost speaking to himself. 'If you wanted a post in the civil service I'd stand a greater chance of finding you something.'

'I'd appreciate anything you can do, my lord,' Martinez said. 'And perhaps my . . . recent celebrity . . . may be of some assistance.'

Lord Pierre tilted an eyebrow at this thought, and then his hands reached for the arms of his chair, as if he were about to rise and dismiss Martinez from both his office and his thoughts, but then he seemed to think better of it and settled back into his seat.

'How are your lady sisters?' he asked. 'I've seen them here and there, since you made their introductions here, but I haven't had a chance to speak to them.'

'They're well,' Martinez said. 'Very active in the social life of the capital.'

'Have you made marriage plans for them?'

The question took Martinez aback. 'Ah – no,' he said. 'No plans.' *I wouldn't dare,* he added silently.

'I have a cousin,' Lord Pierre said, 'who I believe would be improved by marriage. His name is Pierre also, though we call him PJ.'

Martinez blinked. 'Which of my sisters did you have in mind?'

Lord Pierre shrugged. 'It doesn't matter, I suppose, so long as she brings a competence with her. And I assume your lord father can find employment for PJ on Laredo . . . ?'

Warning bells clanged loud and long in Martinez' mind. 'Perhaps you can tell me a little more about PJ,' he said.

Lord Pierre's answer made much of Lord PJ's sunny personality and winning ways. He was a popular fellow, apparently, beloved by all who knew him. Under Martinez' careful questions, it was revealed that PJ had not – quite – finished university, and had never entered either of the two career courses traditional for Peers, the civil service or the military. He had never, in fact, had a career at all.

By the time this was revealed, anger had begun to simmer dangerously in Martinez' veins. Lord Pierre had a useless glit cousin who had dissipated his inheritance and/or embarrassed everyone with his behaviour, and the Martinez family was to take him off the Ngenis' hands – and be *grateful*, presumably, for the chance to marry upwards. The reference to a 'competence', and to finding PJ employment off in the provinces, made it clear that the Martinez clan would be expected to support this character once he connected himself with them.

Martinez badly wanted to shove this offer back between Lord Pierre's perfect white teeth, but instead he said, 'Well, I'll talk to my sisters, but I don't think they're contemplating matrimony at present.'

Lord Pierre offered a little frown. 'Surely you don't leave it up to them?'

The answer that came to Martinez was, *If you were their brother, you would, too.* But what he said was, 'It's my father's choice in any case. I'll write to him with the particulars, if you like.'

'Oh – perhaps we should just contrive to introduce PJ into their circle. They entertain frequently, I suppose?'

'Among their set,' Martinez said.

If Lord Pierre thought Martinez was going to drag this PJ person to one of his sisters' parties, he was very much mistaken. *No,* he thought, *you're going to have to invite us here, which so far you have conspicuously failed to do.*

Lord Pierre's little frown deepened, but whatever answer he intended, it was interrupted by one of his secretaries.

'Lord convocate,' the man said, 'beg pardon for interrupting, but I just received a signal that the Convocation is commanded to meet this afternoon, in three hours' time.'

Both Martinez and Lord Pierre unconsciously straightened in their chairs at the announcement. There was only one entity that could *command* the Convocation to meet, and that was Anticipation of Victory, the last of the Great Masters.

'Cancel the rest of my appointments,' Lord Pierre said. He turned to Martinez as he rose from his chair. 'I beg your pardon, my lord . . .'

Martinez rose also. 'I understand.'

There was only one reason to summon the Convocation at this time, and that was to announce the hour at which the last great master would kill itself.

Once outside the palace, Martinez turned uphill, towards the Commandery. He knew he would be needed there.

'Forty-one days,' Martinez told Cadet Sula. 'Enough time for the news to reach the farthest corners of the empire, with twenty or so days left over to make preparations.' And forty-one, a prime number, was a significant number for the Shaa, who loved primes and multiples of primes. Martinez' look darkened. 'Forty-one days for me to find a better appointment than the one Enderby's stuck me with.'

Amusement trickled through Sula. The woes of her superior officers rarely stirred her sympathy.

At least Martinez *had* an appointment, even if it wasn't one he particularly wanted. She, on the other hand, had no prospects at all once she delivered Blitsharts' yacht to the yards on Zanshaa's ring station. Her few acquaintances in the Fleet had been left behind on *Los Angeles,* and she knew no one on Zanshaa other than Martinez, who she'd never met in person.

She could be assigned anywhere, or nowhere, on the whim of the service.

Sula didn't reply to Martinez. She was still over fifteen light-minutes from Zanshaa, and it was impossible to have anything resembling a regular conversation. Instead Martinez' transmissions were more in the nature of video letters, skipping from topic to topic at Martinez' whim. The replies she sent tended to be much shorter, as her days generated very little in the way of news or interest.

Martinez' expression changed, turned a little sly. 'If you have any idea of the nature of the air leak on *Midnight Runner*, you might want to send me a follow-up report to the one you've already filed. Or if you're feeling a little ambitious, you might suit up and try to track it down. There has already been some litigation filed in regard to Blitsharts' estate.'

Oh really? Sula thought. She found herself leaning forward in her couch, her mind already working on the possibilities.

'It seems that Blitsharts was bankrupt and heavily in debt,' Martinez said. 'He was betting on races, apparently, and not just his own, and not very lucky either way. His creditors were getting ready to file for the seizure of *Midnight Runner,* and this might have been his last race. His creditors have now filed a petition for the Fleet to turn *Midnight Runner* over to them—' *Fat chance,* Martinez' expression seemed to say, the Fleet wasn't about to hand over a choice piece of salvage to private interests. '—and his insurance company has filed a petition to examine the boat, a petition lord commander Enderby has been pleased to consider. If it can be shown that Blitsharts sabotaged his own boat in order to commit suicide, the insurance company won't have to pay off. But the creditors *want* the company to pay off so the settlement will go to them, so unless there's clear physical evidence one way or another the question of how Blitsharts died will be decided in court.'

Interesting, Sula thought. Blitsharts' last long acceleration burn *might* have been calculated to take him out of range of any rescue, and the erratic tumble that followed *might* have been intended to make any docking impossible – all could certainly be interpreted as an attempt to hide a suicide attempt.

But even if Blitsharts *had* killed himself, the case would be difficult to prove. The sabotage itself could have been done very subtly, a matter of a loose connector here or an overlooked fastening there ... unless Blitsharts had done something so direct as to drill a hole in his hull with a hand laser, there would be no evidence of intent.

'Blitsharts' friends are up in arms about it, of course,' Martinez went on. 'The centrepiece of their argument is the claim that Blitsharts would never have deliberately done anything so cruel as to murder his dog.'

Sula's answer to that was a wolfish smile. If Blitsharts was a sufficient egotist – and there was nothing to indicate that he wasn't – he might have thought of Orange as merely an extension of himself, an aspect of his own personality. In which case he would have sacrificed Orange without a second thought.

Martinez paused for a moment, then shrugged. 'Well,' he said, 'maybe you can find something that will solve the mystery.'

Sula knew there was no way she was ever again going on board that ship of the dead, no way short of a direct order, and she would resist even that. She had climbed out of one dark nightmare pit, she wasn't about to descend into another. The mystery, if there was one, could be solved without her.

Martinez shifted to another topic. 'I'm running out of Spate to send you,' he said. 'I found an old interview, however, and I'll send it along on this transmission. I'm also enclosing two comedies with The Deuces, one of them a minor masterpiece, plus the latest instalment of *Oberon* and the most recent plans for the Great Master's funeral.' His face assumed a bland pleasantness. 'I hope the weather's fine where you are. I'll transmit again when duties permit.'

The view screen went dark. Sula considered replaying it, then decided to save it for later, if she got lonely enough.

Aside from monitoring her engine and life-support boards, twice-a-day isometric exercise and the consumption of bland rations, Sula literally had nothing to do, and of course nowhere to go. Her pinnace had been designed for voyages of hours, not many days. Martinez' broadcasts, which averaged two a day, were the only human contact she could expect to receive until she requested docking instructions for the Zanshaa ring.

She wondered why Martinez bothered. Of course men constantly reminded her of the fact they considered her attractive, but surely there were other women on Zanshaa, and besides, conducting a courtship at a distance of light-hours seemed excessive.

Maybe he just felt sorry for her, stuck out here in the middle of nowhere with only a vacuum-mummified corpse for company.

But though Sula wondered about his reasons, she found she didn't care what they were. He appeared on her viewscreen twice a day, offered news, commentary, and human warmth; he demanded nothing; and he beamed her entertainment that kept her amused in the darkness. She was deeply grateful. She was even nearing the point where she hardly noticed his accent.

'I'd appreciate it if you could send me some texts,' Sula said. 'I can't be watching passive entertainment all the time, enjoyable though it is. I'd like something to chew on.'

Martinez sipped at his cocktail as he glanced at the list she'd appended to the message: *Kwa-Zo's Fifth Book of Mathematical Puzzles, Proceedings of the Seventeenth Quee-ling Conference on the Textural Mapping of Wormhole Space, Pre-Conquest Earth Porcelains: Asia.* Not the lightest of reading.

He was beginning to believe that Cadet Sula was a toil.

'If there are any charges for the texts, I'll reimburse you,' Sula said.

The download fees, if any, would be insignificant, but it was nice to know that Sula was conscientious that way.

Martinez looked at the display. Sula lay on her acceleration couch with the helmet and upper half of her vacuum suit removed – the lower half was presumably retained for sanitary purposes. Her hair was stringy, her shirt was rumpled and sweat-stained, and she looked in need of a shower, but her gaze was lively and interested, and she seemed much better than the pale, stricken ghost he'd seen after she'd found Blitsharts dead in his cockpit.

'Thank you for taking such an interest in me,' Sula went on. 'I enjoy your messages and everything you've sent me, and I only wish I could send you messages at least as interesting and amusing as yours. But—' She gave a little sigh. 'I'm afraid the news from here has been pretty dull. The most exciting events of the day involve bowel movements, and I'll spare you the data unless you have an unusually morbid turn of mind.'

She could still joke, then, Martinez noted. For some reason this cheered him. He took another sip of his cocktail in celebration.

Sula shifted on her couch, moving easily in the half-gravity of her ship. 'Thanks for the information about Blitsharts' insurer and creditors. I'm not going to go poking around about *Midnight Runner,* though – I don't want the official investigators complaining that an overeager cadet messed up their evidence. Sorry—' She gave a wan smile. 'I hope you'll forgive me for declining the opportunity to pass on something interesting for a change.'

Martinez shrugged. He knew that in the same situation he personally would have been over *Midnight Runner* with a magnifying glass and a toothbrush to find out what had happened to Blitsharts. At the very least he'd have downloaded everything he could from the onboard computer.

Oh well. Maybe Sula didn't have that kind of curiosity.

'Thanks again for keeping in touch,' Sula said. 'I'll work on making up something exciting for the next transmission.' Her eyes flicked off-camera. 'Computer,' she commanded, 'end transmission.'

The end-stamp appeared on the screen.

Pneumatics sighed as Martinez leaned his long body back in his desk chair. He was in his apartment, whiling away the moments between the end of his shift and the time when he'd have to leave for a scheduled supper with his sisters.

He considered sending a reply to Sula, then decided there wasn't enough time. He finished his cocktail and was on the verge of blanking the screen when it chimed to indicate an incoming call. He answered and found himself staring at Warrant Officer Amanda Taen.

'Hello?' she queried, 'I'm back on station.' A broad smile spread across her face as she saw that Martinez had answered in person.

Martinez was momentarily derailed as he tried to switch tracks from Sula to the woman he had, until recently, been pursuing. Warrant Officer Taen was a contrast to Cadet Sula in almost every particular: where Sula was a pale-skinned blonde, Taen had abundant, glossy chestnut hair, dark eyes, and a rosy complexion. Sula's figure – so far as Martinez could tell from the video, anyway – was certainly feminine, but it was also slim; whereas Taen's was so lush as to be almost tropical in its abundance.

Taen exuded a sense of mischief and readiness for fun that haloed her like a cloud of pheromones. Martinez suspected that she had no acquaintance whatsoever with *Kwa-Zo's Fifth Book of Mathematical Puzzles*.

'Where have you been?' he asked.

'Satellite maintenance. The usual.'

Warrant Officer Taen was second-in-command of a small vessel that maintained, replaced, and repaired the hundreds of communication and sensing satellites in the Zanshaa system. She was frequently absent for days at a time, but her furloughs were equally long, and more than compensated for the length of her missions.

'I'm engaged for this evening,' Martinez said. 'What are you doing tomorrow night?'

Taen's smile broadened. Her look was so direct that Martinez felt it more in his groin than in his mind.

'I have no plans,' she said. 'I hope you can make some for me.'

Martinez did so, feeling regret as he did so that it wasn't Sula who had just landed, with a furlough and time on her hands.

Oh well, he thought. The Fleet did not consider junior officers' preferences when it made its schedules. Taen was available and Sula was not, and he would be a fool to deny himself one pleasure just because another was half a light-hour away.

After speaking to Amanda Taen, Martinez changed into semi-formal evening clothes – nothing was *ever* casual with his stylish sisters – and took a cab to the old Shelley Palace, where the Martinez salon had been established.

Along the way Martinez passed the famous statue of The Great Master Delivering the Praxis to Other Peoples, with its life-size Shaa – twice the size of a Terran – standing on its thick legs with its prow-shaped head lifted towards the horizon. Grey folds of skin draped artfully from the arm that thrust out a display on which the Praxis itself had been carved, beginning with the proud, rather ominous declaration, *All that is important is known*. Before the Great Master knelt representatives of the subject races, all frozen in postures of astonishment and delight.

Martinez glanced at the statue with a morose eye and went on his way.

The Shelley Palace was a huge old thing, several buildings connected by galleries and passages, built over centuries in a succession of architectural styles, horned stone demons capering on the rooftop next to sleek, metallic abstracts of the Devis mode. Lord and Lady Shelley now lived in a smaller, more modern building on a more fashionable street, rented the front part of their old palace to the Martinez sisters, and used the buildings at the back as storage for old retainers and penniless relations, who were often seen drifting about the courtyard garden like ancient, homeless ghosts.

Martinez was let into the building by a young maidservant who possessed the virtue of being homely – no woman in the household was allowed to outshine the Martinez sisters. Martinez was taken to the south drawing room, the one with the view of the Lower City, where he found his sisters Vipsania and Walpurga. They rose so that he could buss their cheeks.

'Cocktail?' Vipsania asked.

'Why not?'

'We've just made a pitcher of blue melon.'

'That would suit.'

Martinez took his drink – which was neither blue nor contained melon – and took a chair facing his sisters.

Vipsania wore a mauve gown, and Walpurga a turquoise one. Otherwise the sisters looked very much alike, sharing Martinez' olive skin and dark hair and eyes. Vipsania's face was perhaps a little sharper, and Walpurga's jaw a little fuller. Like Martinez, they were tall, and like Martinez their height was in the length of their spine, not their legs. Both were imposing more than beautiful, and intelligent much more than not.

Martinez couldn't imagine how he came to be related to either one of them.

'We heard from Roland,' Walpurga said. 'He's coming to Zanshaa.'

Roland was Martinez' older brother, the presumed heir to the feudal privilege enjoyed by the Martinez clan on Laredo.

'Why?' Martinez asked.

'He's coming for the Great Master's end.'

Mental calculations flickered through Martinez' mind. 'Word hasn't reached Laredo by now, surely.'

'No. He anticipated.'

'He wants to be in at the death?' Martinez wondered.

'He wants to be in at the *beginning*,' Vipsania said. 'He wants to petition the Convocation to open Chee and Parkhurst to settlement.'

Under Martinez patronage, of course. That was clear but unstated.

Chee and Parkhurst were two habitable worlds that had been discovered by the Exploration Service in the heyday of planetary discovery, ages ago. So far as was known, each could be reached only by way of wormholes in Laredo's system. Both had been scheduled for settlement, but as the number of Great Masters had grown smaller, so had their ambitions. The expansion of the empire had halted, and the Exploration Service reduced to a fragment of its former self.

It had long been the ambition of the Martinez clan to sponsor habitation of the two nearly-forgotten worlds. To be patrons of *three* worlds – now *that* would elevate them to the highest, most rarified ranks of the Peerage.

'I wouldn't expect the lords convocate to alter the Great Masters' policy with any speed,' Martinez asked.

Vipsania shook her head. 'There are *plenty* of little projects left unfinished. Not all planets to be settled, of course, but appointments to be made, contracts awarded, grants offered, awards rendered, revenues to be collected or disbursed . . . If Roland, with Lord Pierre's help, can find enough allies in the Convocation, I think the project can move along very well.'

Martinez grimaced. 'I hope Roland can get more action out of Lord Pierre than I can,' he said. 'And speaking of Lord Pierre, he's got a cousin named PJ who—'

'Gareth!'

Martinez rose as his youngest sister Sempronia rushed into the room. She flung her arms around him and hugged him fiercely. He returned the embrace with pleasure.

Martinez genetics had reached back many generations to find whatever had built Sempronia. Her wavy light-brown hair had lightened to gold in the sun, and her hazel eyes were likewise flecked with gold, both hair and eyes contrasting dramatically with the Martinez olive complexion. Her nose was tip-tilted, her lips full, her legs long. She was the only one of his sisters in whom Martinez could at all see the lively girl he had left behind, years ago, on Laredo.

'What have I missed?' Sempronia asked.

'I was about to broach the subject of your marriage,' Martinez said.

Sempronia's eyes widened. '*My* marriage?'

'One of you, anyway. It doesn't seem to matter which.'

He explained about Lord Pierre's cousin PJ. 'I don't see why we should marry into a family that won't even invite us to their palace,' he concluded, 'particularly as the fellow's going to be a complete burden on his in-laws.'

'We don't absolutely *know* that,' Vipsania said. A little frown perched between her eyebrows. She turned to Walpurga. 'What do we know of PJ?'

'He's a social creature,' Walpurga said. 'Quite popular, I understand – well dressed, well connected of course, good-looking. I could ask Felicia about him – she's in a better position to know.'

'You're not taking this seriously,' Martinez protested.

Vipsania turned her frown towards him. 'Not yet,' she said.

'But the Ngenis are a family who could be useful to us in the matter of Chee and Parkhurst.'

'They're our patrons. They're supposed be useful to us anyway.'

'And in that case we'd have to cut them in on any profits,' Walpurga said. 'It might be cheaper to take PJ off their hands.'

'Which of you,' Martinez asked, 'plans to marry this wart on the body politic?'

'Not me!' Sempronia declared. 'I'm still in school!'

Martinez grinned at her. 'Good for you!'

Vipsania's frown deepened. 'There are worse things than marriage to a highly popular, well-connected man, even if he *has* run through his funds.'

'Then *you* do it,' Sempronia said. Martinez hid a smile: this was a sentiment that Martinez hadn't quite dared to express himself.

Vipsania shrugged. 'Perhaps I will.'

'We're getting ahead of ourselves,' Walpurga said. 'We've not yet seen any advantages to the match at all.'

'True,' Vipsania said. 'And I'm not about to marry into any family that won't see us socially.' She turned to Martinez. 'Which means, Gareth dear, that you'll contact Lord Pierre and inform him that we are willing to be introduced to his cousin, but since Lord Pierre is the only member of the Ngeni family we know, he'll have to be the one doing the introductions.'

'Very well,' Martinez said. Perhaps it was the blue melon on top of the cocktail he'd already had at home, but he was unable to entirely suppress the thought that came next. He turned to Sempronia.

'You'll have to be the one who gets engaged,' he said. 'That's the way that makes sense.'

Sempronia blinked at him, startled eyes wide. 'I won't marry him! I already said I wouldn't!'

Martinez grinned at Sempronia over the rim of his cocktail glass. 'I didn't say *marry*,' he said. 'I said you'll have to be the one who *gets engaged*.'

Vipsania narrowed her eyes. 'Explain yourself, Gareth,' she said.

'The whole point of getting engaged to PJ is access,' Martinez said. 'Access to the Ngenis' circle. And the best means of prolonging access is an engagement – a *long* engagement.'

Vipsania gave a slow, thoughtful nod. 'Go on.'

'There's no reason why you or Walpurga can't marry after a short engagement, especially if Roland's here,' Martinez said. 'So it'll have to be Sempronia who gets engaged to PJ, because we'll be able to insist that she can't marry till she's finished with school.' He looked at Sempronia. 'How many years do you have left, Proney?'

'Two,' Sempronia said suspiciously.

'Surely you can fail a few courses and make it three,' Martinez said. 'And after that, some post-graduate work might be necessary to fully round your education. And of course our lawyers can drag out the negotiations for the marriage contract for, well, ages I suppose.'

Light glimmered in Vipsania's eyes. 'And in the meantime—' she said.

'In the meantime,' Martinez echoed, 'we have access to the most exclusive circles in the High City. Roland will be able to pitch his planetary development scheme to the leaders of the Convocation, and surely *one* of you—' Addressing Vipsania and Walpurga. '—*one* of you will find someone in that circle for a husband. Probably both of you, if I know you at all. And pick someone, if you please, who can assure me a promotion or a staff job, or both. And then—' He smiled at Sempronia. 'Surely with such a man as PJ is likely to turn out to be, you can find some reason to break the engagement. Drunken behaviour in public, a dread secret from the past, a mistress stowed away in a closet, an unacceptable number of natural children, *something*. Unless of course,' he added as an afterthought, 'you actually fall in love with the poor brute, in which case I'm personally packing you into a crate and shipping you back to Laredo.'

There was a moment of silence in which all three sisters looked at Martinez. Vipsania gave a little nod, then turned to Sempronia. 'We'll have to discuss this again, Proney dear.'

'No we won't!' Sempronia said.

Walpurga echoed Vipsania's nod. 'Oh yes we shall,' she said.

Sempronia turned to Martinez. 'I can't believe you're making me do this!' she said.

'I'm not,' Martinez said. 'If it were up to me, I'd give PJ a swift kick off the planet for daring even to think of marrying any of my precious sisters. But since Vipsania and Walpurga are insisting on taking this seriously, I thought I'd better work to minimize any possible damage.'

'Thanks a lot.'

'You're welcome!' Martinez said brightly, and sipped his blue melon.

Poor PJ, he thought. The man didn't know what he was getting into.

At that point the door chime rang, and the other guests began arriving. There was a lawyer named Gellimer who was very attentive towards Vipsania, two young women Sempronia knew from school, a pair of elderly Shelley relatives who lived in the rear of the palace and who acted as chaperones, their presence permitting the young ladies to entertain gentlemen. Arriving a bit late was someone named Castro from the Treasury who followed yachting and was very interested in Martinez' description of his solution to the problem of Blitsharts' runaway yacht. Martinez demonstrated the gyrations of *Midnight Runner* by hanging a table knife from his thumb and forefinger and rotating it in a complicated way, and he looked across the table to find Vipsania's eyes on him.

'Do you know Lady Sula well?' she asked.

Martinez was surprised. 'We speak now and again,' he said. 'Of course she's half a light-hour out.'

'Do you think she would be interested in coming to our party?'

Martinez was even more surprised. 'I'll ask her,' he said, and then smiled.

His sisters rarely made such a useful suggestion.

'Introducing me to your family already?' Sula said. 'I suppose I should be flattered.' Her face showed weary but genuine pleasure. 'Well,' she said, 'why not? The needs of the Fleet permitting, I'd be honoured to accept.'

Martinez smiled. He felt a warm buoyancy enter his soul, and was willing to accept the possibility that sisters had their uses after all.

He listened to the rest of Sula's brief message, then checked the time display to see when lord commander Enderby could be expected to return. Not yet – he and Gupta were at yet another one of the interminable planning sessions relating to the Great Master's end, leaving Martinez in charge of communications while they were gone. Since he had time available, he called Lord Pierre. At the moment he felt as if he could handle a dozen Lord Pierres.

'My sisters have agreed to be introduced to your cousin,' he said.

For a moment Lord Pierre seemed puzzled, as if he didn't recall quite what Martinez was talking about, and then comprehension entered his eyes.

'Shall I bring him to the—' He hesitated. 'Where is it that your sisters are staying?'

Martinez affected surprise. Lord Pierre wasn't about to get away with that. 'You can hardly bring PJ to the Shelley Palace

for a cold-blooded inspection,' he said. 'He's not a stud horse.'
Though of course that's exactly what he is, Martinez thought
quietly to himself. 'It's you that will have to play host, I'm
afraid. And since I doubt it would be very comfortable for
PJ to have my sisters descend on him like the Three Fates,
there should be more than the six of us in the party.'

'Six?' Lord Pierre raised an eyebrow. 'You're planning on
attending yourself?'

'A chaperon should be present, don't you think?'

A frown knit between Lord Pierre's brows. 'You're going
to be formal as all that?'

'These are my *sisters,*' Martinez said virtuously.

The whole business of chaperonage was something Martinez
didn't quite understand: things were handled otherwise in
a Fleet where recreational tubes were installed on every
ship. But some of the old families insisted on keeping their
bloodlines unblemished, and would only marry those with a
certificate of purity.

Lord Pierre conceded with an annoyed flap of one hand.
'Very well,' he said. 'I'll check my schedule and get back
to you.'

'Thank you, lord convocate.' And smiled as sweetly as
he could.

After that he recorded another rambling message to Sula,
and sent it along with downloads of *Kwa-Zo's Fifth Book of
Mathematical Puzzles* and *Pre-Conquest Earth Porcelains: Asia.*

When he returned to his apartment he found his evening
clothes laid out for him, along with a fragrant corsage of
eskartori blossoms, and remembered his date with Amanda
Taen. The memory came as a mild surprise. He had been so
occupied with making plans for meeting Caroline Sula and
arranging a sham engagement for Sempronia that he'd pushed
Amanda to the back of his mind. An injustice, he thought,
and he'd spend the rest of the evening setting it right.

He told Alikhan to lay out a small cold buffet for later and to chill a bottle of sparkling wine. Alikhan, not unaccustomed to these sorts of commands, nodded without speaking. Martinez shaved again, then changed into the civilian suit, with the braided collar and cuffs and the elastic stirrup than ran under his glossy shoes at the instep – all the accessories that said *fashionable* without quite saying *glit* – then summoned a cab to pick up Amanda at her warrant officers' quarters. She wore a gown of russet material quietly stuffed with all the byproducts of modern materials science: it supported her lush figure in all the right places, while tucking her in elsewhere. In front the gown modestly covered her to the throat, but there was no back at all. Her chestnut hair had been pinned up by long golden needles topped by walnut-sized chunks of artificial ruby – cheap stuff, but deployed massively and to great effect – while rubies and gold also glittered on her fingers and at her throat.

Her smile was as brilliant as her jewellery. 'It's not too formal, is it?' she asked.

'Not at all.' He put a hand on her naked back and helped her to the cab.

He took her to the Penumbra Theatre for a comedy, a sex farce of the sort that humans loved and that other races found incomprehensible. Amanda laughed in all the places where Martinez could have hoped she might have laughed.

After the show Martinez took her to a restaurant in the High City for supper – not one of the absolutely first-class places, which tended to be too starched and formal, but a large, noisy restaurant with overhead galleries, smiling, busy waitrons, and with what Martinez had been assured was excellent food. Ari Abacha was drinking in the bar as Martinez entered, and silently raised his glass at the sight of Amanda. Martinez ate modestly, watched Amanda tuck into her bison steak, and thought how pleasing it was to meet a girl with such unconcealed appetites.

Afterwards he took her to a club for dancing, then to his apartment, and then to bed. When he drew off her gown, her abundant flesh seemed to leap into his hands. She was as much fun as he expected, a gloriously healthy young female animal who took what she wanted with both generosity and laughter.

The evening would have been perfect, if it hadn't been for the fact that in his mind he kept seeing Sula, her image and eyes, her voice, and her imagined scent, some fanciful combination of clean skin and lilac and arousal.

While Sula, alone in her sour-smelling cockpit, wondered why Martinez hadn't sent his usual evening message. She had got used to hearing Martinez' voice two or three times every day, and now that the voice hadn't come, she realized how much she missed it.

Sula decided that his commander had him working late, and she opened the file on Earth porcelains. She spent the hours gazing at one image after another of vases and bowls and jugs, all ancient and unbelievably rare and precious. In her mind she touched the lovely objects, stroking surfaces glossy or crackled or smooth, her fingertips caressing the unreachable creations of those immeasurably skilled, unknown, long-dead hands.

Five

'He's old. I hate him.'

Sempronia's fierce whisper hissed in Martinez' ear. He looked at his youngest sister with sympathy.

'Sorry, Proney.'

'He keeps following me around the room. What if he wants to *touch* me?'

'You'll have to endure it. Think of the family.'

Sempronia narrowed her eyes and glared at him. 'I *am* thinking of the family. I'm thinking of *you* – because this whole scheme is all *your fault*.'

'Ah – here you are.' PJ Ngeni materialized at Sempronia's elbow, a drink in either hand. 'I thought I'd bring you another cocktail.'

Sempronia turned to PJ with a brilliant smile. 'Why, thank you! How very thoughtful!' She put down her untouched drink and replaced it with another.

Martinez had to admire her skill under pressure. Sempronia was so good at *playing* a vivacious young thing that he sometimes had to remind himself that she *was* a vivacious young thing, at least most of the time. He could only tell the difference between a performance and the genuine article by the slight tensing of the muscles around the eyes.

PJ didn't seem the type to much care about whether Sempronia's conduct was genuine or not. His own behaviour was clearly a performance of some sort, in his case that of an attentive and considerate cavalier. He was a tall, thin, elegant man, and with arched, amused eyebrows and a little moustache. He lacked the cannonball head and large jaws of most of the Ngenis, and the hair was beginning to recede atop his long skull. Though suspicious, thus far Martinez had found nothing in the man he could object to save the bracelets and lapel braid made of bleached and woven human hair, a typical glit affectation.

PJ looked at Martinez. 'Such a shame about Blitsharts,' he said. 'Too bad you couldn't rescue him.'

'I rescued him all right,' Martinez said. 'The pity is that he was dead by then.'

PJ's tented brows arched even higher, and he gave a laugh. 'Blitsharts was a good fellow,' he said. 'Witty. Like you. I won quite a lot, betting on him in the old days.' He shook his head. 'Not so much lately, though. He wasn't lucky.'

'Are you a gambler, then?' Sempronia asked. Her eyes clearly asking, *Is this why you need my dowry?*

PJ shrugged. 'I have a flutter now and again. A fellow has to, you know. It's expected.'

'What else is a fellow expected to do?' The brilliant smile across Sempronia's face, Martinez knew, was intended to mask the vengeful glimmer in her eyes.

The question took PJ aback. 'Well,' he said. 'Dress well, you know. Mix with people. Have nice things.'

Sempronia took his arm. 'There must be more to it than that. Please tell me simply *everything*.'

Martinez watched as Sempronia drew him away with the clear intention of ferreting out his every vicious secret. PJ, he decided, was going to pay dearly for his family's marital ambitions.

Martinez, for his part, was enjoying himself. Lord Pierre had added the Martinez clan to a dinner party already on his schedule, which meant that Martinez would soon be sitting to supper with the sort of people normally out of his reach, in this case three convocates, a judge of the High Court, the commander of the Legion of Diligence for the Metropolis of Zanshaa, a fleet commander on the retired list, and a captain and a squadron commander who weren't.

Martinez wore his uniform, something he normally didn't do on a social engagement, and it contributed to his being recognized. The captain and the squadron commander asked for details on the Blitsharts rescue, and Martinez was pleased to oblige. He was just getting to his description of how he had used the virtual simulation to work out how *Midnight Runner* was tumbling when the dinner gong rang. 'I'll go into the rest later,' Martinez promised.

Particularly the part where he expressed admiration for lord commander Enderby's decision to terminate his life, and happened to mention that as a result he was lacking a posting.

Martinez gave his arm to a lady convocate and led her from the tapestry-lined parlour to the dining room done in parquetry, tens of thousands of slivers of various kinds of wood jigsawed together in the form of portraits of prominent Ngenis of the past. Lord Pierre had only been doing his duty when he placed Martinez between the lady convocate and the retired fleet commander, a short, leathery-skinned woman.

Servants in livery began putting down plates of soup, and the scent of onions and tomatoes rose in the room. The retired fleetcom – she was Lord Pierre's great-aunt – turned to Martinez and looked him up and down. Long white hairs clustered on her chin, Martinez noticed. 'You're the Martinez who got Blitsharts back, aren't you?'

'Yes.' Martinez reached for his soup spoon and readied the story of the rescue.

'Bad business,' the fleetcom said. 'Wish you hadn't.'

'My lady?'

The fleetcom glowered. 'Now all sorts of things that should have been private will come out. Things that will discredit the poor man. You should have let the fellow die in peace.'

'No doubt, my lady,' Martinez murmured. One never disagreed with a fleet commander.

The fleetcom's gaze shifted searchingly to her plate. 'Hope the soup's good,' she muttered. 'Last time they burnt the onions.'

Which ended *that* conversation. The lady convocate on the other side of Martinez was engaged in a complicated discussion over a piece of legislation involving the protection of the gold-bearing seaweeds of Hy-Oso. Martinez glanced across the table, where PJ seemed relieved to find himself sitting next to Vipsania. Lord Pierre had doubtless seated them together on the theory that since Vipsania was the eldest, she'd be most desperate to marry.

Martinez applied himself to his soup and thoughts of Sula and Amanda Taen. He'd seen Amanda twice since he'd first taken her out, with results as filled with delight as the first time. None of the delight, however, had quite got Cadet Lady Sula out of his mind.

Well. He'd see her soon. That would probably settle his thoughts one way or another.

At the end of the long deceleration burn Sula turned *Midnight Runner* over to the tugs that would take it to fleet quarantine. Sula guided her pinnace into her assigned berth, and as the docking clamps locked she began to feel the ring's gravity pushing her onto her back, pressing her into her acceleration couch at a full gravity, twice what she'd experienced during the journey to Zanshaa. She waited till the docking tube had extended and formed a seal around the hatch, and then pulled off her helmet and took a deep, relieved breath. People were supposed to wear vac suits when docking in small craft, and it had been a mental struggle to get the faceplate closed.

Once her helmet was off, Sula shut down the pinnace and took two small data foils out of the computer and put them into envelopes.

One foil was the log of the journey, and went into an official envelope which would be turned over to the Fleet Records Office for examination and filing. The other contained her personal information, the communications from Martinez and all the books and entertainment he'd sent her.

She put the private data into the small bag of personal gear she'd carried onto the pinnace with her, then sealed the bag into the thigh pocket of her vac suit. She popped the door into the airlock trunk, grabbed the hand bar over her head and hauled herself out of the couch. The airlock was now 'down', and she lowered herself into it, clumsy in the suit, shut off the lights in the pilot's compartment, and sealed the door behind her.

She didn't spare the interior of the pinnace another glance. She was glad to see the last of it.

The hatch hissed open, and Sula crawled down the docking tube until she emerged in the ready room, blank white walls and floor, the better to show any dirt or contamination. Hands reached down to help her stand, and it wasn't until Sula got to her feet that she realized that the hands belonged to Martinez. He wore his undress uniform and a broad smile.

Vertigo eddied through Sula's inner ear. 'My lord,' she said.

'Welcome back to the world, cadet.' His hands guided her a step or two forward, and three expressionless, disinterested riggers in sterile disposable smocks and caps descended on her and began to strip off her vac suit. Martinez relieved her of the official envelope containing the pinnace log. 'Is this the log? I'll take it, then.'

'I'm supposed to deliver it myself.'

'I'll sign a chit for it,' Martinez said. 'It has to be delivered to the Investigative Service, not to Fleet Records.'

'Oh.'

'Lawyers armed with writs have already descended on

Midnight Runner. Not that it will do them any good –
the Fleet has lawyers as good as anyone's, and I'm sure it's
already been decided which senior officer is going to get the
new toy.'

Efficient hands opened all the vac suit's pockets, retrieved
her personal belongings, some tools, and a pony bottle of air.
The air supply and recycler was detached from the seat, the
valves sealed, and the upper suit section detached from the
lower. The riggers shoved her arms above her head, then
pulled the top of the suit off.

Sula, arms high, was suddenly aware that she didn't smell
very good. She lowered her arms as the riggers began to
prepare to drop the lower half of the vac suit. Sula looked
up at Martinez.

'Would you mind turning your back?'

Martinez turned and the riggers stripped the suit and its
sanitary gear down Sula's legs. Martinez looked down as
he took a datapad from his belt and wrote on it. One
of the riggers held out a pair of sterile drawers, and Sula
stepped into them. Martinez pressed a button and the datapad
spat out a foil, which Martinez took and held over his
shoulder.

'Your chit.'

'Thanks.' Collecting it. 'You can turn around.'

Martinez did so. The expression of polite interest on his
face betrayed no consciousness of the fact that he was looking
at an unwashed, slack-muscled woman with greasy hair, pasty
skin, and a shirt stained with prominent sweat patches that
hadn't been changed in many long days. Sula had to admire
his self-control.

'I've got you a room in the cadets' quarters at the
Commandery,' he said.

'I don't have to live on the ring?' Sula was impressed.
'Thanks.'

'I'm using my staff privileges while they last. You can

shower in your quarters, and get a bite if you want, and
then we've got an appointment with my tailor.'

'Tailor?'

'Lord commander Enderby is going to decorate you in
a ceremony tomorrow. You can't show up in what you're
wearing.'

'Oh. Right.' *Decorate?* she thought.

'I got your height and weight and so on out of your records.
The tailor's put a uniform together from that, but you'll still
need the final fitting.'

Elastic snapped around Sula's ankles as the riggers knelt
and put slippers on her feet. The vac suit was carried off for
checkout, refurbishment, sterilizing, and storage. A thought
struck her. 'I don't have to wear parade dress, do I?'

'Full dress, not parade dress.'

'Oh, good. My feet and ankles are swollen from sitting all
this time on that couch, and I'd hate to get fitted for a pair
of boots right now.' And then Sula remembered.

'Decorate?' she asked.

'Medal of Merit, Second Class. You'll be decorated with
nine others, after which there will be a reception and questions from reporters.' He gave her a significant look. 'The
yachting press. Answer their questions fully and freely, and if
you want to give credit to my brilliant plan for your success,
I think it would only be just.'

Sula looked at him. This last was said with a jocular tone,
but perhaps with more emphasis than was necessary.

'I think I'd like to take a shower now,' Sula said. She knew
that showers were always adjacent to the sterile ready rooms,
and her whole body shrieked for soap and hot water.

'Certainly. This way.'

He directed her to the changing room, and politely held
the door for her.

'I'm likely be here a while,' she said.

'Take all the time you like.' He smiled. 'By the way, I

arranged a furlough for you, starting in two days. It'll last until the death of Anticipation of Victory, and then all furloughs are off anyway.'

He smiled again and let the door sigh closed behind her. Sula turned and propped the door open with one hand. He looked at her, his heavy brows raised.

'Are you always this efficient?' she asked.

Martinez tilted his head as he considered the question. 'Yes,' he said. 'Yes, I believe I am.'

Sula, wearing her new uniform and medal, sat in the Commandery's cadet lounge, where three separate football games blared from the video walls. She was perched on a chair of carbon-fibre rods with a lemon-flavoured beverage in her hand, while Cadet Jeremy Foote lounged before her in another, deeper, overstuffed chair.

'Martinez?' Foote said. 'He's got you in his sights, has he?'

'Sights!' snorted Cadet Silva from the sofa. 'Bang! Another virgin gone!'

Silva, Sula thought, was very drunk.

'Virgin?' Foote said. He turned to Sula and raised an eyebrow. 'You're not a virgin, are you? That would be original.'

'I'm pure as the void itself,' Sula said, and enjoyed the expression that crossed Foote's face as he tried to work out exactly what she meant.

She had sought out the cadet lounge because it was one of the few places in the Commandery where an off-duty cadet was permitted. Senior officers and politicians apparently preferred to work, drink, and dine without having to rest their eyes on the gauche, ill-mannered, pimpled, and inebriated apprentice officers.

After a brief exposure to Cadet Silva, Sula was beginning to think they had a point.

'So is there anything *wrong* with Martinez?' she asked.

'Nothing, if you're attractive, female, and a shop girl,' Foote said. 'He's got money and a degree of charm and a limited sense of style, and I'm sure he gives his usual sort of companion no reason to complain. But those from a higher station in life can't be so very impressed.' He gave Sula a significant look. '*You* could do much better, I'm sure.'

'Troglodyte!' Silva called. 'That's what *we* call him!' His voice grew excited. '*Goal!* Did you see that? Point for *Corona!* A header off the goalie's hand!'

'Troglodyte?' Sula asked.

Foote smiled thinly and swiped at the cowlick on his blond head. 'It's those short legs of his. And the long arms. Have you noticed? He must be a throwback to some primitive form of human.'

'But he's tall,' Sula protested.

'It's all in his back. The legs are short.' He nodded. 'Mind you, he's got a good tailor. The cut of the jacket hides it, except it can't hide the hands that hang almost to his knees.'

The comm unit on the wall chimed. Foote told the video walls to be quiet, rose from his chair, and answered. He turned to Silva.

'Package at the Fleet Office, Silva,' he said. 'Needs hand delivery. Take it, will you?'

'You're first in the queue,' Silva said.

Irritation crossed Foote's face. 'Just go, will you, Silva?'

'The score's tied two-all,' Silva complained, but he rose, buttoned his tunic, and headed for the door.

'Breath, Silva,' reminded Foote. He tossed Silva a small silver aerosol flask, and Silva gave his palate a shot of mint. Silva tossed the flask back to Foote, who pocketed it, and Silva departed.

'Do you make a point of easing life for your drunken friends?' Sula asked as Foote resumed his seat.

Foote was surprised. 'Friends help each other out,' he said. 'And as for drinking, you have to do something here to keep away the boredom. For myself, I'm thinking of taking up yachting.' A thought struck him. 'Why don't we *both* take it up?' he asked. 'You showed real skill capturing the *Midnight Runner*. I'm sure you'd do well.'

Sula shook her head. 'I'm not interested.'

'But why not?' Foote urged. 'You've won the silver flashes – surely you must have considered yachting. And the Fleet will encourage you, because it'll improve your piloting.'

Sula felt a certain comfort in the fact that Foote hadn't checked her family history. Her membership in the Peerage was genuine enough, for all that the Sula clan had no members other than herself. Her trust fund might support a modest apartment in the High City, but would hardly extend to a yacht.

She could simply tell Foote that she hadn't got her inheritance yet, but for some reason she didn't want to. The less Jeremy Foote knew about her the better.

'I spend too much time in small boats as it is,' Sula said. 'Why ask for more?'

At that moment a red-haired cadet entered and looked at Sula in surprise. 'I saw you on vid this morning,' she said. 'You salvaged the *Runner*.'

Foote introduced Ruth Chatterji, who wanted to know if Lord Commander Enderby was as ferocious as rumour made out. Sula said he *looked* ferocious enough, but hadn't behaved with any noticeable brutality when hanging the medal around her neck.

'So tell me what it was like on *Midnight Runner*,' Chatterji said. 'Is it true that Blitsharts got an embolism and vomited up his lungs?'

Sula rose to her feet. 'I'd better go. Thanks for the chat.'

'Time for your date with the trog?' Foote said. He slouched in his chair and tossed his head back, looking at Sula under half-lowered lids as she passed him. 'Tell you what,' he said. 'Why don't I show you a proper evening? I'm having dinner with my uncle tomorrow night – he's captain of the *Bombardment of Delhi*. He's always keen to meet a promising officer – maybe he could do you some good.'

Sula looked down at Foote and smiled sweetly. 'Captain Foote of the *Delhi*?' Sula asked. She wrinkled her brow as if trying on a memory for size. 'He's the yachtsman?'

'Yes. That's the fellow.'

Sula let her smile twist into an expression of distaste. 'I don't know,' she said doubtfully. 'I've always thought yachtsmen were the most boring people in the whole fucking world.'

Mean pleasure sang in Sula's heart as she left Foote blinking in slow surprise, and Chatterji staring.

Though the afternoon in the cadet lounge wasn't without its effect. When Martinez arrived for her, she found herself looking at his legs as she walked beside him through the Commandery.

They *were* perhaps a little short, she decided.

Vipsania raised her glass. 'Before we go in to supper,' she said, 'I would like to salute our special guest. To Lady Sula, who so bravely and skilfully retrieved the *Midnight Runner* and the bodies of Captain Blitsharts and Orange.'

Martinez repressed a stab of jealousy as he raised his glass and murmured Sula's name along with everyone else. Really, he thought, it *was* his plan.

He imagined it was too much to suppose that Vipsania would ever bother to offer a toast to Martinez. He was just her brother, after all.

But envy faded into admiration as he contemplated Sula, who stood slim and straight as a lance in the parlour of the Shelley Palace, her porcelain complexion lightly flushed at being the centre of attention. Her dark green dress tunic served to heighten the intrigue of her emerald eyes. Martinez' tailor had done a superb job with fitting the uniform, and a bath, a haircut and modest use of cosmetic had done wonders to repair the pallor and poor skin tone that were consequences of her long, cramped journey.

Martinez touched his glass to his lips and drank to Sula with complete sincerity.

Sula raised the glass of sparkling water she'd been nursing since the start of the evening. 'I would like to thank Lady Vipsania, Lord Gareth—' With a look at Martinez. '—and the entire Martinez clan for their gracious hospitality.'

Martinez modestly refrained from lifting his glass as the guests saluted him. He cast a glance about the room and saw PJ Ngeni, a few paces away, looking at Sula with glowing eyes. 'Superb!' Martinez heard beneath the crowd's murmur. 'Wonderful girl!'

Martinez smiled privately. *You'll have no luck with this one, my man,* he thought, *unless you know the works of Kwa-Zo.*

The Martinez sisters' party seemed to be a success. Martinez saw several faces he'd first seen at Lord Pierre's dinner party, and PJ had arrived with a couple of his male friends who were less successful than he at concealing their fundamentally decorative nature. Walpurga, Martinez saw, was in a corner of the room, laughing and smiling with an advocate she had first met at the Ngeni Palace, a man who represented the interests of the Qian clan. Sempronia was speaking near the garden door to a young brown-haired man in the viridian uniform of a Fleet lieutenant.

And Sula, Martinez saw, had since her public introduction become the centre of a number of young men, including PJ's two glit friends. Martinez was thinking about rescuing her when the dinner gong boomed and saved him the trouble.

He wasn't seated near Sula, who was placed between two of the guests his sisters had poached from the Ngeni Palace, but he had a clear view of her. She was framed perfectly by the chair back, which was made of carved, ancient, darkened

Esker ivory that admirably set off Sula's pale complexion. Despite the other guests and the elaborate floral arrangements that had perfumed the air with their scent, Caroline Sula was clearly the object in the room most worth looking at.

Martinez was shifting from the dining room to the drawing room when Sempronia briefly touched him on the left arm. 'This is *your* fault!' she hissed. 'He's at me to join him for a walk in the garden!'

'It's a pleasant garden,' Martinez said.

'Not with PJ in it.'

'Besides,' Martinez said, 'it's your sisters' fault and you know it.'

She glared at him. 'You should stand up to them for me!' she said. 'What are brothers for?' She strode off.

Martinez mingled for a while, and was on the verge of seeking out Sula when PJ Ngeni touched him on the right arm. Symmetry, he thought.

'May we speak?' PJ said, and touched his narrow little moustache.

'Certainly.'

'I have asked, um, your sister Sempronia if she would join me for a walk in the garden,' he said.

Martinez drew a smile onto his face. 'That will be pleasant,' he said.

'Well.' PJ hesitated. 'The fact is, I've become quite fond of Sempronia in a very short time.'

Martinez nodded. 'That's not unusual. She's a popular girl.'

'I thought – if I could get her in the garden – I might ask for her hand.' His voice trailed off. 'In marriage,' he clarified.

'I never thought otherwise.'

'So I thought I'd ask your advice,' PJ finished, and looked brightly up at Martinez.

Martinez gazed down at the man. For someone who was

supposed to have led some kind of debauched life, PJ seemed remarkably short of social confidence.

'What's the problem?' Martinez asked. 'Haven't you propositioned a woman before?'

PJ flushed. 'Well, yes,' he said, 'purely in a sporting way, of course. But I have never proposed marriage, with all its,' he gave a little cough, 'responsibilities and duties, and . . .' He looked bleak. '. . . so forth.' His voice trailed away, and he looked up at Martinez again. 'Do you have any objection to my asking for your sister's hand?'

'No.' *Not for asking,* Martinez thought. *Actually marrying, I'd have to shoot you.*

This answer didn't relieve PJ's anxiety. 'Do you think she . . . do you think darling Sempronia will accept me?' He licked his lips. 'She seems to be rather avoiding me, actually.' He cast a glance to a corner of the room, where Sempronia was still talking to the brown-haired young officer.

'She's one of the hostesses, she's got a lot to do,' Martinez said. 'I think if you ask her, the answer would please you.' It was time to get PJ on his errand. He clapped the man on his shoulder. 'Go to it,' he said. 'Courage!'

PJ eyes seemed to be looking not at Sempronia, but at the abyss. 'Very good of you,' he murmured. 'Thanks.'

He marched towards Sempronia as if to his execution. Martinez smiled at the thought of the two people, neither of whom wanted a life with the other, stumbling their way towards the engagement that would satisfy their families. He decided he would prefer not to witness the painful outcome, whatever it was, but instead looked for Sula and found her sipping a cup of coffee and miraculously free of admirers.

'We don't have to stay all night,' he said. 'I know a place in the Lower Town that's fun.'

Sula tasted her coffee and returned the cup to its matching saucer of hard-paste porcelain. 'Is this the new Spenceware Flora pattern?' she asked.

Martinez looked at the cup as if seeing it for the first time. There was a pattern of violets and a faint, matching purple stripe.

'I don't know,' he said. 'To me it looks like, well, a cup.'

Sula looked up from the saucer. 'I can ask your sisters when we say goodnight.'

They bade farewell to Vipsania and Walpurga, who told Sula that the cup was in fact the new Flora and thanked her effusively for coming. The presence of the recently-decorated Sula, Martinez knew, was enough to assure a mention of the party in tomorrow's society reports, and that had been his sisters' object in inviting Sula in the first place. They wanted to get certified as fashionable hostesses before the official period of mourning for the last Shaa brought large society functions to a close for a full year.

Martinez took Sula down the funicular railway to the Lower Town, and they gazed through the rail car's transparent roof at the great expanse of the huge metropolis rising to embrace them like a wide, golden sea. Gusts of wind made little excited screams against the car's hard edges. Martinez turned to one side and saw the old Sula Palace towering on the edge of the high city, its distinctive stained-glass dome glowing blue, and with a start he turned to Sula, remembering the way her parents had died and lost their property. Sula was looking towards the palace as well, but her face was relaxed. Maybe, after all these years, she didn't recognize the place.

Martinez took Sula to a cabaret off the city's main canal, sat her in a quiet corner, and ordered a bottle of wine. He was surprised when Sula put a hand over the mouth of her glass and asked for sparkling water instead.

'Don't you drink at all?' he asked.

'No. I—' She hesitated. 'I used to have a problem with alcohol.'

'Oh.' There was a moment of surprised silence. Then he

looked at the wine bottle in his hand. 'Does it bother you if I drink? Because if it does, I'll—'

'I don't mind. Have all you like.' She smiled thinly. 'Just don't expect me to carry you home.'

'I haven't had to be carried yet,' Martinez said, an attempt to carry off the awkward moment with a little bravado.

He sipped his wine but decided to strictly limit his intake. The idea of being inebriated in Sula's presence was suddenly very distasteful.

'So,' he said, 'you're an expert on porcelain? I remember sending you that book.'

'I'm hardly an expert,' Sula said. 'I'm just very interested.' Her eyes brightened, and she seemed as relieved as he to leave the awkward subject of alcohol behind. 'Did you know that fine porcelains were invented on Earth? That porcelain was one of the few things, along with tempered tuning, the Shaa thought a worthy contribution to interstellar civilization?'

'No. I didn't know that. You mean no one had pots until Earth was conquered?'

Sula's eyes narrowed. 'Of course they had pots. They had all sorts of ceramics. Stoneware, even. But translucent, vitrified ceramics, white clay mixed with feldspar – real porcelain, the kind that rings when you tap your finger against it – that was invented on Earth.' Her lecturing tone suggested that Martinez' question had disappointed her.

Martinez disliked disappointing beautiful women, and decided not to risk her disapproval by asking about tempered tuning, whatever that was. He took a careful sip of his glass and decided to try the compliment direct.

'I'm reminded of porcelain when I look at you,' he said. 'Your complexion is extraordinary, now that I can appreciate it in person. I'm having a hard time not staring.'

She turned away from him, an ambiguous smile twisting her lips. And then she gave a brief laugh, tossed her head, and looked him in the eye.

'And my eyes are like emeralds, right?' she said.

Martinez answered with care. 'I was going to say green jade.'

She nodded. 'Good. That's better.' She turned away again. 'Perhaps we can save the descriptions of any remaining parts for another time,' she murmured.

At least the thought of her other parts – this time or next – was cheering.

'Do you collect porcelain?'

Sula shook her head. 'No. I— Not with the way I'm living now. Not if I'm sharing cadet quarters with five other pinnace pilots. Nothing would survive.'

It was also possible, Martinez realized, that Sula couldn't afford the kind of ceramics she'd like to own, not if she were actually living on her cadets' pay. He didn't know what financial resources the execution of her parents had left her.

'There's a whole wing of porcelain in the Museum of Plastic Arts,' Martinez said. 'We could go there some day, if you like.'

'I've seen it,' Sula said. 'It was the first place I went, when the *Los Angeles* came here to refit.'

He could scratch the museum tours off his agenda, Martinez thought. Though it might have been fun, seeing porcelain with an expert as lovely as any of the ceramics on display.

'Any luck in finding a good posting?' Sula asked.

'No. Not yet.'

'Does it have to be a staff job?'

Martinez shook his head. 'I don't mind ship duty. But I'd like it to be a step up, not a step back or sideways.' He put his arms on the table and sighed. 'And it would be nice to be in a position to occasionally accomplish something. I have this ridiculous compulsion not to be totally useless. But that's difficult in the service, isn't it? Some days it's a struggle to find a point in it all. Do you know what I mean?'

Sula looked at him and nodded. 'We're in a military that

hasn't fought a real war in thirty-four hundred years, and most of its engagements before and since consisted of raining bombs on helpless populations. Yes, I know what you mean.' She cocked her head, silver-gilt hair brushing her shoulders. 'Occasionally we pull off a nice rescue,' Sula said. 'Though we hardly need cruisers or battleships for that, do we? But all those big ships make terrific platforms for enhancing the grandeur and self-importance of senior captains and fleet commanders, and grandeur and self-importance are what holds the empire together.'

Martinez blinked. 'That's blunt,' he said.

'I'm allowed to be blunt. I understand my position very well.' She looked at him. 'You know about my family?'

Martinez gave a cautious nod. 'I've seen your file.'

'Then you know that the military is the only career I'm allowed. But even though I'm a clan head, there's no clan for me to be head of, so there will be no powerful relatives to help me get promotions. I can get a lieutenancy on my own, but once I pass the exam that's about all I can expect. If I astonish everyone with my genius, I might be promoted to elcap, and if I make full captain it will probably happen only on retirement.' She gave a cold smile. 'The consolation of my position is that I can say what I damn well please,' she said. 'None of it will change anything.' She looked thoughtful. 'Except . . .' she began.

'Yes?'

'If I do an absolutely brilliant exam. Sometimes senior officers take an interest in the cadet who scores first. Or even second.'

Martinez nodded. It had been known to happen. Even commoners could do well if they had the right patron. 'I wish you the best of luck,' he said.

'I hope luck has nothing to do with it,' Sula said. 'I've never got anywhere by counting on luck.'

'Fine,' Martinez said amiably. 'No luck to you, then.'

She smiled. 'Thanks.'

'You're welcome.'

There was a brief silence, and then Sula spoke. 'In the last couple days, since I've arrived on Zanshaa, I've started getting messages from people. People who say they were friends of my parents.' She shook her head. 'I don't remember any of them. I don't remember things very well from that period.'

'You should meet them.'

'Why?'

'Maybe they could help you. They may feel that they owe your parents that.'

Sula considered this for a moment, and then her eyes hardened. She shook her head. 'It's the job of the dead to stay dead,' she said. 'Isn't it?'

Sula raged inwardly against her certainty that everything she said was wrong. She was making a botch of the whole evening, and all because she didn't know how to talk to someone who liked her.

She had been another person once, and then decided not to be that person again, and to avoid anything, like alcohol, that might bring that person back. But she didn't know how to be a new person very well, and she kept getting it wrong.

It's the job of the dead to stay dead. Nice light cocktail-bar conversation, that.

She reminded herself that Martinez was only trying to help.

Of course he was also trying very hard to get her into bed. This was a prospect that wasn't entirely without its attractions, though she'd been chaste for so long that she wondered if she'd have any idea how to behave. It would be on a par with everything else this evening to somehow make a total botch of it.

Martinez could probably handle any problem that might arise, she decided. She could trust to his efficiency that way.

She might as well surrender. It's not as if chastity had benefited her in any way that she could see, and Martinez could hardly make her life worse than it was.

Fortunately entertainment began before she could completely poison the conversation. A pair of singers and a band mounted the stage and began a series of dance tunes, and Martinez seemed pleased that it was she who asked him to dance and not the other way around.

Sula had once enjoyed dancing, but her only practice in recent years had been at the academy, with everyone standing nervous and perspiring in dress uniforms, and hampered by a rigid etiquette. She was out of practice at dancing for pleasure, but fortunately Martinez was an able partner – those stumpy legs knew their business, she decided – and his expertise neutralized her initial awkwardness. She discovered in herself a tendency to bounce on the balls of her feet with each step, but reminded herself that the whole point was to keep a low centre of gravity, and told herself sternly to glide, not bound like an eager puppy.

As the evening progressed her awkwardness faded, and she relaxed into the movements, the steps, and Martinez' arms. Their bodies moved into a close synchrony, and she found herself responding easily to the merest suggestion of his touch, the lightest impulse on her palm or hip or back. Her body moulded to his during the slow dances, and warm blood flushed her skin at his nearness. There seemed progressively less point to the whole chastity business.

They danced for an hour and then stepped outside to cool off. Clouds scudded low overhead, obscuring Zanshaa's ring, and gusts of wind blustered around the corners of the buildings. A pleasure boat floated past on the canal, darkened but with its contours outlined in cool blue neon – it looked like a skeleton boat, a visitation from another plane. Martinez dabbed sweat from his brow with a handkerchief and opened his high uniform collar. 'Next time,' he said, 'I'll wear civvies.'

'Thank you for reminding me how much fun this is,' Sula said. 'I've only been to formal balls for – oh, years.'

'Service dances?' He looked at her. 'They *can* be deadly, can't they?' He turned to the canal, saw the neon-lit pleasure boat floating past, and his eyes lit with an idea. 'I have a notion. Would you like to go for a ride on the canal?'

'I—'

'Come on!' He took her by the hand and set off at a trot. She followed, the wind tearing a laugh from her lips.

A short distance ahead was an stand for excursion boats. Martinez showed the elderly Torminel attendant his credentials and was shown to a small, two-person canal boat, with strands of coloured lights hanging from its stumpy mast and its canopy folded halfway back over a sofa seat. Martinez wiped water from the seat with his handkerchief, then helped Sula down from the stone quay – the light, resinous hull swayed as she stepped in, and water made a viscous sucking sound against the moss-draped stone – and then he seated himself next to her and instructed the autopilot.

Iodine, weed and moss, bird droppings, things that were dead and floating in the chill dark water – the scent of the canal struck like a bludgeon at Sula's memory. She hadn't tasted air like this in a long time. Suddenly she wanted to protest the whole excursion, but Martinez was near and smiling, happy in his adventure; and she didn't want to ruin the evening, not after it had finally begun to go well.

The silent electric motor accelerated smoothly. Sula tried to relax against Martinez' arm. 'There's a lovely view of the High City coming up,' he said in her ear.

Put him in the river, Gredel had said, years of pent-up hatred burning in her words.

The High City was obscured by low cloud. Martinez

murmured his disappointment. 'I'll have to show it to you another time,' he said.

A chill wind shivered along Sula's bones. She thought of the body slipping in silence beneath the surface of the Iola, streetlight shimmering gold on the spreading, dying ripples, the water rising over the mouth and nose, rising in Sula's mind like the obdurate flood of memory, the scent of river and time and death.

Lady Sula?

She wasn't even Lady Caro, she was Lady *Sula*. She wasn't just any Peer, she was head of the whole Sula clan.

Lamey's fury faded away quickly – it did that, came and went with lightning speed – and he picked Caro up in his arms and carried her to the elevator while the doorman fussed around him. When they arrived on the top floor, the doorman opened Caro's apartment, and Lamey walked in as if he paid the rent himself and carried Caro to her bedroom. There he put Caro down on her bed, and had Gredel draw off the tall boots while Lamey covered her with a comforter.

Gredel had never admired Lamey so much as at that moment. He behaved with a strange delicacy, as if he were a Peer himself, some lord commander of the Fleet cleaning up after a confidential mission.

The doorman wouldn't let them stay. On the way out Gredel saw that Caro's apartment was a terrible mess, with clothes in piles and the tables covered with glasses, bottles, and dirty dishes.

'I want you to come back here tomorrow,' Lamey said as he started the car. 'I want you to become Caro Sula's best friend.'

Gredel fully intended this, but she wondered how Lamey's mind and her own were running on the same track. 'Why?'

'Peers are rich,' Lamey said simply. 'Maybe we can get some of that and maybe we can't. But even more than the money, Peers are also the keys to things, and maybe Caro can open some doors for us. Even if it's just the door to her bank account, it's worth a try.'

It was very, very late, almost dawn, but Lamey wanted to take Gredel to one of his apartments. There they had a brisk five minutes' sex, hardly worth taking off her clothes as far as Gredel was concerned, and then Lamey took Gredel home.

As soon as she walked in the door she knew Antony was back. The apartment smelled different, a blend of beer and tobacco and human male and fear. Gredel took off her boots at the door so she wouldn't wake him, and crept in silence to her bed. Despite the hour she lay awake for some time, thinking of keys and doors opening.

Lamey didn't know what he wanted from Caro, not quite, he was operating on an instinct that told him Caro could be useful, give him connections, links that would move him upwards. Gredel had much the same intuition where Caro was concerned, but she wanted Caro for other things. Gredel didn't want to stay in the Fabs. Caro might show her how to get out, how to behave, perhaps, or how to dress, how to move up, and maybe not just out of the Fabs but off Spannan altogether, loft out of the ring station on a tail of fire to Esley or Zanshaa or Earth, to a glittering life that she felt hovering around her, a kind of potential waiting to be born, but that she couldn't quite imagine.

She woke just before noon and put on her robe to shower and use the toilet. The sounds of the Spring Festival zephyrball game blared from the front room, where Antony was watching the video. Gredel finished her business in the bathroom and went back into her room to dress. When she finished putting on her clothes and her makeup she brushed her hair for a long time, delaying the moment when she would leave her sanctum to face Antony, but when she realized what she was doing she got angry at herself and put the brush down, then put her money in the pocket of her jacket and walked through the door.

Antony sat on the sagging old sofa watching the game on the video wall. The remains of a sandwich sat on a plate next to him. He was a man of average height but built powerfully, with broad shoulders and a barrel chest and long arms with big hands. He looked like a slab on legs. Iron-grey hair fringed his bald head, and his eyes were tiny and set in a permanent suspicious glare.

He wasn't drinking, Gredel saw, and felt some of her tension ease.

'Hi, Antony,' she said as she walked for the apartment door.

He looked at her with his glaring black eyes. 'Where you going dressed like that?'

'To see a friend.'

'The friend who bought you those clothes?'

'No. Someone else.' She made herself stop walking and face him.

His lips twitched in a sneer. 'Nelda says you're whoring now for some linkboy. Just like your mother.'

Anger flamed along Gredel's veins, but she clamped it down and said, 'I've never whored. Never. Not once.'

'Not for money, maybe,' Antony said. 'But look at those clothes on you. And that jewellery.' Gredel felt herself flush. Antony returned his attention to the game. 'Better you sell that tail of yours for money,' he muttered. 'Then you could contribute to your upkeep around here.'

So you could steal it, Gredel thought, but didn't say it. She headed for the door, and just before it swung shut behind her she heard Antony's parting shot. 'You better not take out that implant! You get pregnant, you're out of this place! I'm not looking after another kid that isn't my own!'

Like he'd ever looked after any kid.

Gredel left the building with her fists clenched and a blaze of fury kindled in her eyes. Children playing in the front hall took one look at her and got out of her way.

It wasn't until the train was halfway to Maranic Town that the anger finally ebbed to a normal background buzz, and Gredel began to wonder if Caro would be at home, if she would even remember meeting her the previous night.

Gredel found the Volta Apartments quickly now that she knew where it was. The doorman – it was a different doorman this time – opened the door for her and showed her right to the elevator. Clearly he thought she was Caro. 'Thank you,' Gredel smiled, trying to drawl out the words the way a Peer would.

She had to knock loudly, several times, before Caro came to the door. Caro was still in her short dress from the previous night, and tights, and bare feet. Her hair was disordered, and there was a smear of mascara on one cheek. Her slitted eyes opened wide as she saw Gredel at the door.

'Earthgirl,' she said. 'Hi.'

'The doorman thought I was you. I came over to see if you were all right.'

Caro opened the door and flapped her arms, as if to say, *I am as you see me.* 'Come in,' she said, and turned to walk towards the kitchen.

The apartment was still a mess, and the air smelled stale. Caro went to the sink in the little kitchen and poured herself a glass of water.

'My mouth tastes like cheese,' she said. 'The kind with the veins in it. I hate that kind of cheese.'

She drank her water while Gredel walked around the disorderly apartment. She felt strangely reluctant to touch anything, as if it was a fantasy that might dissolve if she put a finger on it.

'So,' she said finally, 'you want to go and do something?'

Caro finished her water and put down her glass on a counter already covered with dirty glasses. 'I need some coffee first,' she said. 'Would you mind going to the café on the corner and getting some for me while I change?'

'What about the coffee maker?' Gredel asked.

Caro blinked at the machine as if she were seeing it for the first time. 'I don't know how to work it,' she said.

'I'll show you.'

'I never learned how to do kitchen stuff,' Caro said, as she made way for Gredel in the kitchen. 'Till I came here we always had servants. I had servants *here,* but I called the last one a cow and threw her out.'

'What's a cow?' Gredel asked.

'They're ugly and fat and stupid. Like Berthe when I fired her.'

Gredel found coffee in a cupboard and began preparing the coffee maker. 'Do you *eat* cows, or what?' she asked.

'Yeah, they give meat. And milk, too.'

'We have vashes for that. And zieges. And swine and bison, but they only give meat.'

Gredel made coffee for them both. Caro's coffee cups were paper thin and delicate, with a platinum ring around the inside and a design of three red crescents. Caro took her cup into the bathroom with her, and after a while Gredel heard the shower start to run. She sipped her coffee as she wandered around the apartment – the rooms were nice, but not *that* nice. Lamey had places just as good, though not in such an exclusive building as this. There was a view of the Iola River two streets away, but it wasn't that nice a view, there were buildings in the way, and the window glass was dirty.

Then, because she couldn't stand the mess any longer, Gredel began to pick up the scattered clothes and fold them. She finished that and was putting the dirty dishes in the washer when Caro appeared, dressed casually in soft wool pantaloons, a high-necked blouse, and a little vest with gold buttons and lots of pockets slashed one on top of the other. Caro looked around in surprise.

'You cleaned up!'

'A little.'

'You didn't have to do that.'

'I didn't have anything else to do.' Gredel came into the front room. She looked down at one of the piles of clothing, put her hand down on the soft pile of a sweater she had just folded and placed neatly on the back of a sofa. 'You have some nice things,' she said.

'That's from Yormak cattle. They have wonderful wool.' She eyed Gredel's clothing. 'What you're wearing, that's – that's all right.'

'Lamey bought it for me.'

Caro laughed. 'Might have known a man picked that.'

What's wrong with it? Gredel wanted to ask. It was what everyone was wearing, only top quality. These weren't clothes hijacked at Maranic Port, they were bought in a *store*.

Caro took Gredel's arm. 'Let's get some breakfast,' she said, 'and then I'll take you shopping.'

The doorman stared comically as Caro and Gredel stepped out of the elevator. Caro introduced Gredel as her twin sister Margaux from Earth, and Gredel greeted the doorman in her Earth accent. The doorman bowed deeply as they swept out.

An hour later in the restaurant, Gredel was surprised when Caro asked her to pay for their meal. 'My allowance comes first of the month,' she said. 'And this month's money supply is *gone*. This café won't run a tab for me.'

'Weren't we going shopping?'

Caro grinned. 'Clothes I can buy on credit.'

They went to one of the arcades where exclusive shops sheltered under a long series of graceful arches of polymerous resin, the arches translucent but grown in different colours, so that the vaulted ceiling of each glowed with subtle tones that merged and flowed and blended. Caro introduced Gredel as her sister, and laughed when Gredel used her Earth accent. Gredel was called Lady Margaux and surrounded by swarms of clerks and floorwalkers, and she was both surprised and flattered by the attention. This is what it was like to be a Peer.

If she'd been merely Gredel, the staff would have been there all right, but following her around to make sure she didn't steal.

The arcades didn't serve just Terrans, so there were Torminel there, and Naxids, and some pleasure-loving Cree who wandered through the shops burbling in their musical voices. It was unusual for Gredel to see so many non-humans in one place, since she rarely had any reason to leave the Terran parts of the Fabs. But the Peers, Gredel concluded, were almost a species of their own. They had more in common with each other than they had with other folk.

Caro bought an outfit for herself and two for Gredel, first a luxurious gown with a cape so long it dragged on the floor, and next a pyjama-like lounging outfit. Gredel had no idea where she would ever wear such things. Caro nodded at the lounging suit. 'Made of worm spit,' she said.

'Sorry?' Gredel said, startled.

'Worm spit. They call it "silk".'

Gredel had heard of silk – she'd read about it in her researches on Earth history – and she touched the fabric with a new respect. 'Do you think it came from Earth?' she asked.

'I doubt it.' Dismissively. 'Earth's a hole. My mother was there on government service, and she told me.'

Caro bought everything on credit. Gredel noticed that she signed only *Sula,* leaving out her first name and the honourific *Lady*. She seemed to carry a tab in every store in the arcade. When Gredel thanked her for the presents, Caro said, 'You can pay me back by buying dinner.'

'I don't think I can afford that,' Gredel said doubtfully.

Caro laughed. 'Guess we better learn to eat worm spit,' she said.

Gredel was intrigued by the way everyone lined up to give Caro credit. 'They know I'm good for it,' Caro explained. 'They know I'll have the money eventually.'

'When?'

'When I'm twenty-three. That's when the funds mature.' She laughed again. 'But those people still won't get paid. I'll be off the planet by then, in the Fleet, and they can chase me through space if they like.'

Gredel was intrigued by this, too. There tended to be serious consequences in the Fabs for people who didn't pay their debts. Maybe this, too, was different for Peers.

'So is this money your parents left you?' Gredel asked.

Caro looked dubious. 'I'm not sure. My parents were caught in some kind of scheme to swindle government suppliers out of a lot of money, and they lost everything – estates, money—' She tapped her neck significantly. 'Everything. I got sent to live with Jacob Biswas in Blue Lakes.' This was an exclusive area outside of Maranic Town. 'The Biswas clan were clients of the Sulas, and Dad got Biswas the job of Assistant Port Administrator here. I'm not sure if the money is something Dad got to him, or whether it came from my dad's clients or friends, but it's in a bank on Spannan's ring, and the interest comes to me here every month.'

'You don't live with Biswas anymore, though. Did he leave Spannan?'

'No, he's still here. But he got divorced and remarried, and the new wife and I didn't get along – we were fighting every day, and poor old Jacob couldn't take it any more, so he got me the place in the Volta until it was time for me to join the Fleet.'

Caro went on to explain that her family was forbidden to be in the civil service for three generations, both as punishment for what her parents had done and to minimize the chance to steal. But as a Peer she had an automatic ticket to one of the Fleet academies, and so it had been planned for her to go there.

'I don't know,' Caro said, shaking her head. 'I can't see myself in the Fleet. Taking orders, wearing uniforms ... under all that discipline. I think I'd go crazy in ten days.'

The Fleet, Gredel thought. The Fleet could carry you away from Spannan, through the wormhole gates to the brilliant worlds beyond. Zanshaa, Esley, Earth ... The vision was dazzling. For that she could put up with uniforms.

'I'd do it in a second,' Gredel said.

Caro gave her a look. 'Why?'

Gredel thought she may as well emphasize the practical advantages. 'You get food and a place to sleep. Medical and dental care. And they *pay* you for it.'

Caro gave a disdainful snort. '*You* do it, then.'

'I would if I could.'

Caro made a disgusted noise. 'So why don't you? You could enlist.'

'They wouldn't let me. My mother has a criminal record.'

The Fleet had their pick of recruits: there were plenty of people who wanted those three free meals per day. They checked the background of everyone who applied.

Unless, Gredel thought, someone she knew could pull strings. A Peer, say.

They took a taxi back to Caro's apartment, but when the driver started to pull up to the kerb, Caro ducked into the back seat, pulled a bewildered Gredel down atop her, and shouted at the driver to keep going.

'What's the matter?' Gredel asked.

'A collector. Someone come to get money from me. The doorman usually chases them off, but this one's really persistent.'

Apparently living on credit wasn't as convenient as Caro let on.

The driver let them off in the alley behind the apartment building. There was a loading dock there, and Caro's codes opened the door. There were little motorized carts in the entryway, for use when people moved in furniture or other heavy belongings.

They took the freight elevator to Caro's floor and looked for something to eat. There wasn't much, just biscuits and an old piece of cheese. 'Have you got food at your place?' Caro asked.

Gredel hesitated. Her reluctance was profound. 'Food,' she said, 'but we've got Antony, too.'

'And who's that?'

Gredel told her. Caro's disgusted look returned. 'He comes near me,' she said, 'I'll kick him in the balls.'

'That's wouldn't stop him for long,' Gredel said, and shivered. 'He'd still slap your face off.'

'We'll see.' Caro's lip curled again.

'I'm serious. You don't want to get Antony mad. I bet even Lamey's boys would have a hard time with him.'

Caro shook her head. 'This is crazy,' she laughed. 'You know anyone who could buy us some food?'

'Well. There's Lamey.'

'He's your boyfriend, right? The tall one?'

'He carried you up here last night.'

'So I *already* owe him,' Caro laughed. 'Will he mind if I mooch dinner off him? I'll pay him back, first of the month.'

Gredel called Lamey on her phone, and he was amused by their dilemma and said he'd be there soon.

Gredel made coffee while they waited, and served it in the paper-thin cups. 'So tell me about Lamey,' Caro said.

So Gredel told Caro about Lamey's business. 'He's linked, you know? He knows people, and he moves stuff around. From the Port, from other places. Makes it available to people at good prices. When people can't get loans, he loans them money.'

'Aren't the clans' patrons supposed to do that?'

'Sometimes they will. But, you know, those mid-level clans, they're in a lot of businesses themselves, or their friends and allies are. So they're not going to loan money for someone to go into competition with them. And once the new businesses start, they have to be protected, you know, against the people who are already in that business, so Lamey and his people do that, too.'

'It's the Peers who are supposed to protect people,' Caro said.

'Caro,' Gredel said, 'you're the first Peer I've ever seen outside of a video. Peers don't come to places like the Fabs.'

Caro gave a cynical grin. 'So Lamey just does *good* things, right? He's never hurt anybody, he just helps people.'

Gredel hesitated. They were entering the area of things she tried not to think about. She thought about the boy Moseley, the dreadful dull squelching thud as Lamey's boot went into him. The way her own head rang after Lamey slapped her that time.

'Sure,' she said finally, 'he's hurt people. People who stole from him, mostly. But he's really not bad,' she added quickly, 'he's not one of the violent ones, he's *smart*. He uses his intelligence.'

'Uh-huh,' Caro said. 'So has he used his . . . *intelligence* . . . on you?'

Gredel felt herself flush. 'A few times,' she said quickly. 'He's got a temper. But he's always sweet when he cools down, and buys me things.'

'Uh-huh,' Caro said.

Gredel tried not to bristle at Caro's attitude. Hitting was what boyfriends *did*, it was normal, the point was whether they felt sorry afterwards.

'Do you love him?' Caro asked.

Gredel hesitated again. 'Maybe,' she said.

'I hope at least he's good in bed.'

Gredel shrugged. 'He's all right.' Sex seemed to be expected of her, because she was thought to be beautiful and because she went with older boys who had money. For all that it had never been as pleasurable as she'd been led to expect, it was nevertheless pleasurable enough so that she never really wanted to quit.

'Lamey's too young to be good in bed,' Caro declared. 'You need an older man to show you what sex is really about.' Her eyes sparkled, and she gave a diabolical giggle. 'Like my Sergei. He was really the best! He showed me *everything* about sex.'

Gredel blinked. 'Who was Sergei?'

'Remember I told you that Jake Biswas remarried? Well, his wife's sister was married to Sergei. He and I met at the wedding and fell for each other – we were always sneaking away to be together. That's what all the fighting in the family was about. That's why I had to move to Maranic Town.'

'How much older was he?'

'In his forties somewhere.'

Black, instant hatred descended on Gredel. She could have torn Sergei to ribbons with her nails, with her teeth.

'That's sick,' she said. 'That man is disgusting.'

Caro gave a cynical laugh. 'I wouldn't talk if I were you,' she said. 'How old is Lamey? What kind of scenes does *he* get you into?'

Gredel felt as if Caro's words had slapped her across the face. Caro gave her a smirk.

'Right,' she said. 'We're models of stability and mental health, we are.'

Gredel decided to change the subject. 'This is lovely,' she said, and held up the cup.

Caro look at it without expression. 'I inherited that set. That's the Sula family badge, those three crescents.'

'What do they mean?'

'They mean three crescents. If they mean any more than that, nobody told me.'

Caro's mood had sweetened by the time Lamey turned up. She thanked him for taking her home the previous night, and took them both to a restaurant so exclusive that Caro had to give a thumbprint in order to enter. There were no real dinners on the menu, just a variety of small plates that everyone at the table shared. Gredel had never heard of some of the ingredients. Some of the dishes were wonderful, some weren't. Some were simply incomprehensible.

Caro and Lamey got along well, to Gredel's relief. Caro filled the air with vivacious talk, and Lamey joked and deferred to her. Towards the end of the meal he remembered something, and reached into his pocket. Gredel's nerves tingled as she recognized a med injector.

'Panda asked me if you wanted any more of the endorphin,' Lamey said.

'I don't have any money, remember?' Caro said.

Lamey gave an elaborate shrug. 'I'll put it on your tab.'

Don't, Gredel wanted to shout.

But Caro gave a pleased, catlike smile, and reached for the injector in Lamey's hand.

Gredel and Caro spent a lot of time together after that. Partly because Lamey wanted it, but also because Gredel found that she liked Caro, and she liked learning from her. She studied how Caro dressed, how she talked, how she moved. And Caro enjoyed dressing Gredel up like one of her dolls, and teaching her to walk and talk as if she were Lady Margaux, the sister of a Peer. Gredel worked on her accent till her speech was a letter-perfect imitation of Caro's. Caro couldn't do voices the way Gredel could, and Gredel's Earthgirl voice always made her laugh.

Gredel was learning the things that might get her out of the Fabs.

Caro enjoyed teaching her. Maybe, Gredel thought, this was because Caro really didn't have much to do. She'd left school, because she was a Peer and would get into the academy whether she had good marks or not, and she didn't seem to have any friends in Maranic Town. Sometimes friends from Blue Lakes came to visit her – usually a pack of girls all at once – but all their talk was about people and events in their school, and Gredel could tell that Caro got bored with that fast.

'I wish Sergei would call,' Caro said. But Sergei never did. And Caro refused to call Sergei. 'It's his move, not mine,' she said, her eyes turning hard.

Caro got bored easily. And that was dangerous, because when Caro got bored she wanted to change the music. Sometimes that meant shopping or going to a club, but it could also mean drinking a couple of bottles of wine or a bottle of brandy, or firing things into her carotid from the med injector, or sometimes all of the above. It was the endorphins she liked best, though.

The drugs weren't illegal, but the supply was controlled in various ways, and they were expensive. The black market provided pharmaceuticals at more reasonable prices, and without a paper or money trail. The drugs the linkboys sold weren't just for fun, either: Nelda got Gredel black market antivirals when she was sick, and fast-healers once when she broke her leg, and saved herself the expense of supporting a doctor and a pharmacy.

When Caro changed the music she became a spiky, half-feral creature, a tangled ligature of taut-strung nerves and overpowering impulse. She would careen from one scene to the next, from party to club to bar, having a frenzied good time one minute, spitting out vicious insults at perfect strangers the next.

At the first of the month Gredel urged Caro to pay Lamey what she owed him. Caro just shrugged, but Gredel insisted. 'This isn't like the debts you run up at the boutique.'

Caro gave Gredel a narrow-eyed look that made her nervous, because she recognized it as the prelude to fury. 'What do you mean?'

'When you don't pay Lamey, things happen.'

'Like what.' Contemptuously.

'Like—' Gredel hesitated. 'Like what happened to Moseley.'

Her stomach turned over at the memory. 'Moseley ran a couple of Lamey's stores, you know, where he sells the stuff he gets. And Lamey found out that Moseley was skimming the profits. So—' She remembered the way Lamey screamed at Moseley, the way his boys held Moseley while Lamey smashed him in the face and body. The way that Lamey kept kicking him even after Moseley fell unconscious to the floor. Her nerves leaped at the memory the thuds of the boots going home.

'So what happened to Moseley?' Caro asked.

'I think he died.' Gredel spoke the words past the knot in her throat. 'The boys won't talk to me about it. No one ever saw him again. Panda runs those stores now.'

'And Lamey would do that to *me*?' Caro asked. It clearly took effort to wrap her mind around the idea of being vulnerable to someone like Lamey.

Gredel hesitated again. 'Maybe you just shouldn't give him the chance. He's unpredictable.'

'Fine,' Caro said. 'Give him the money then.'

Caro went to her computer and gave Gredel a credit foil for the money, which Gredel then carried to Lamey. He gave the tab a bemused look – he was in a cash-only business – and then asked Gredel to take it back to Caro and have it cashed. When Gredel returned to Caro's apartment the next day, Caro was hung over and didn't want to be bothered, so she gave Gredel the codes to her cash account.

It was as easy as that.

Gredel looked at the deposit made the previous day and took a breath. Eight hundred and forty zeniths, enough to keep Nelda and her assortment of children for a year, with enough left over for Antony to get drunk every night. And Caro got this every *month*.

Gredel started looking after Caro's money, seeing that at least some of the creditors were appeased, that there was food in the kitchen. She cleaned the place, too, tidied the clothes Caro scattered everywhere, saw that the laundry was sent out and, when it returned, was put away. Caro was amused by it all. 'When I'm in the Fleet, you can join, too,' she said. 'I'll make you a servant or something.'

Hope burned in Gredel's heart. 'I hope so,' she said. 'But you'll have to pull some strings to get me in – I mean, with my mother's record and everything.'

'I'll get you in,' Caro assured.

Lamey was disappointed when Gredel told him about Caro's finances. 'Eight hundred and forty,' he muttered, 'it's hardly worth stealing.' He rolled onto his back in the bed – they were in one of his apartments – and frowned at the ceiling.

'People have been killed for a lot less than that,' Gredel said. 'For the price of a bottle of cheap wine.'

Lamey's blue eyes gave her a sharp look. 'I'm not talking about killing anybody,' he said. 'I'm just saying it's not worth *getting killed over,* because that's what's likely to happen if you steal from a Peer. It won't be worth trying until she's twenty-two, when she gets the whole inheritance, and by then she'll be in the Fleet.' He sighed. 'I wish she were in the Fleet now, assigned to the Port. We might be able to make use of her, get some Fleet supplies.'

'I don't want to steal from her,' Gredel said.

Lamey fingered his chin thoughtfully and went on as if he hadn't heard. 'What you do, see, is get a bank account in *her* name, but with *your* thumbprint. Then you transfer Caro's money over to your account, and from there you turn it into cash and walk off into the night.' He smiled. 'Should be easy.'

'I thought you said it wasn't worth it,' Gredel said.

'Not for eight hundred it isn't,' Lamey said. He gave a laugh. 'I'm just trying to work out a way of getting my investment back.'

Gredel felt relief that Lamey wasn't really intending to steal Caro's money. She didn't want to be a thief, and she especially didn't want to steal from a friend like Caro.

'She doesn't seem to have any useful contacts here.' Lamey continued thinking aloud. 'Find out about these Biswas people. They might be good for *something*.'

Gredel agreed. The request seemed harmless enough.

Gredel spent most of her nights away from Nelda's now, either with Lamey or sleeping at Caro's place. That was good, because things at Nelda's were grim. Antony looked as if he was settling in for a long stay. He was sick, something about his liver, and he couldn't get work. Sometimes Nelda had fresh bruises or cuts on her face. Sometimes the other kids did. And sometimes when Gredel came home at night Antony was there, passed out on the sofa, a bottle of gin in his hand. She took off her shoes and walked past him quietly, glaring her hatred as she passed him, and she would think how easy it would be to hurt Antony then, to pick up the bottle and smash Antony in the face with it, smash him until he couldn't hurt anyone ever again.

Once Gredel came home and found Nelda in tears. Antony had slapped her around and taken the rent money, for the second time in a row. 'We're going to be evicted,' Nelda whispered hoarsely. 'They're going to throw us all out.'

'No they're not,' Gredel said firmly. She went to Lamey and explained the situation and begged him for the money. 'I'll never ask you for anything ever again,' she promised.

Lamey listened thoughtfully, then reached into his wallet and handed her a hundred-zenith note. 'This take care of it?' he asked.

Gredel reached for the note, hesitated. 'More than enough,' she said. 'I don't want to take that much.'

Lamey took her hand and put the note into it. His blue eyes looked into hers. 'Take it and welcome,' he said. 'Buy yourself something nice with the rest.'

Gratitude flooded Gredel's eyes. Tears fell down her cheeks. 'Thank you,' she said. 'I know I don't deserve it.'

'Of course you do,' Lamey said. 'You deserve the best, Earthgirl.' He kissed her, his lips coming away salty. 'Now you take this to the building agent, right? You don't give it to Nelda, because she might give it away again.'

'I'll do that right away,' Gredel said.

'And—' His eyes turned solemn. 'Does Antony need taking care of? Or need encouragement to leave? You know what I mean.'

Gredel shrank from the idea. 'No,' she said. 'No – he won't stay long.'

'You remember it's an option, right?' She made herself nod in answer.

Gredel took the money to the agent, a scowling little woman who had an office in the building and who smelled of cabbage and onions. She insisted on a receipt for the two months' rent, which the woman gave grudgingly, and as Gredel walked away she thought about Lamey and how this meant Lamey loved her.

Too bad he's going to die. The thought formed in her mind unbidden.

The worst part was that she knew it was true.

People like Lamey didn't survive for long. There weren't many *old* linkboys – that's why they weren't called link*men*. Sooner or later they were caught and killed. And the people they loved – their wives, their lovers, their children – paid

as well, with a term on the labour farms like Ava, or with
their own execution.

The point was reinforced a few days later, when Stoney was
caught hijacking a cargo of fuel cells in Maranic Port. His trial
was over two weeks later, and then he was executed the next
week. Because stealing private property was a crime against
common law, not against the Praxis, he wasn't subjected to
the tortures reserved for those who transgressed against the
ultimate law, but simply strapped into a chair and garotted.

The execution was broadcast on the video channel reserved
for punishments, and Lamey made his boys watch it. 'To
make them more careful,' he said simply.

Gredel didn't watch. She went to Caro's instead and
surprised herself by helping Caro drink a bottle of wine.
Caro was delighted at this lapse on Gredel's part, and was
her most charming all night, thanking Gredel effusively for
everything Gredel had done for her. Gredel left with the
wine singing in her veins. She had rarely felt so good.

The euphoria lasted until she entered Nelda's apartment.
Antony was in full cry. A chair lay in pieces on the floor and
Nelda had a cut above her eye that wept red tears across her
face. Gredel froze in the door as she came in, and then tried to
slip towards her room without attracting Antony's attention.

No such luck. Antony lunged towards her, grabbed her
blouse by its shoulder. She felt the fabric tear. 'Where's the
money?' Antony shouted. 'Where's the money you get by
selling your tail?'

Gredel held out her pocketbook in trembling hands.
'Here!' she said. 'Take it!'

It was clear enough what was going on, it was Antony
Scenario Number One. He needed cash for a drink, and he'd
already taken everything Nelda had.

Antony grabbed the pocketbook, poured coins into his
hand. Gredel could smell the juniper scent of the gin reeking
off his pores. He looked at the coins dumbly, then threw

the pocketbook to the floor and put the money in his pocket.

'I'm going to put you on the street myself, right now,' he said, and seized her wrist in one huge hand. 'I can get more money for you than this.'

'No!' Gredel filled with terror, tried to pull away.

Anger blazed in Antony's eyes. He drew back his other hand.

Gredel felt the impact not on her flesh but in her bones. Her teeth snapped together and her heels went out from under her and she sat on the floor.

Then Nelda was there, screaming, her hands clutching Antony's forearm as she tried to keep him from hitting Gredel again. 'Don't hit the child!' she wailed.

'Stupid bitch!' Antony growled, and turned to punch Nelda in the face. 'Don't ever step between me and her again!'

Turning his back was Antony's big mistake. Anger blazed in Gredel, an all-consuming blowtorch annihilating fury that sent her lunging for the nearest weapon, a chair leg that had been broken off when Antony had smashed the chair in order to underscore one of his rhetorical points. Gredel kicked off her heels and rose to her feet and swung the chair leg two-handed for Antony's head.

Nelda gaped at her, her mouth an O, and wailed again. Antony took this as a warning and started to turn, but it was too late. The wooden chair leg caught him in the temple, and he fell to one knee. The chair leg, which was made of compressed dedger fibre, had broken raggedly, and the splintery end gouged his flesh.

Gredel gave a shriek powered by fifteen years of pure, suppressed hatred and swung again. There was a solid crack as the chair leg connected with Antony's bald skull, and the big man dropped to the floor like a bag of rocks. Gredel dropped her knees onto his barrel chest and swung again and again. She remembered the sound that Lamey's boots made going into Moseley and wanted badly to make those sounds come from Antony. The ragged end of the chair leg tore long ribbons out of Antony's flesh. Blood splashed the floor and walls.

She only stopped when Nelda wrapped Gredel's arms with her own and hauled her off the unconscious man. Gredel turned to swing at Nelda, and only stopped when she saw the older woman's tears.

Antony was making a bubbling sound as he breathed. A slow river of blood poured out of his mouth onto the floor. 'What do we do?' Nelda wailed as she turned little helpless circles on the floor. 'What do we do?'

Gredel knew the answer to the question perfectly well. She got her phone out of her pocketbook and went to her room and called Lamey. He was there in twenty minutes with Panda and three other boys. He looked at the wrecked room, at Antony lying on the floor, at Gredel standing over the man with the bloody chair leg in her hand.

'What do you want done?' he asked Gredel. 'We could put him on a train, I suppose. Or in the river.'

'No!' Nelda jumped between Antony and Lamey. Tears brimmed from her eyes as she turned to Gredel. 'Put him on the train. Please, honey, please.'

'On the train,' Gredel repeated to Lamey.

'We'll wake him up long enough to tell him not to come back,' Lamey said. He and his boys picked up Antony's heavy body and dragged it towards the door.

'Where's the freight elevator?' Lamey asked.

'I'll show you.' Gredel went with them to the elevator. The tenants were working people who went to bed at a reasonable hour, and the building was silent at night and the halls empty. Lamey's boys panted for breath as they hauled the heavy, inert carcass with its heavy bones and solid muscle. They reached the freight elevator doors and the boys dumped Antony on the floor while they caught their breath.

'Lamey,' Gredel said.

Lamey looked at her. 'Yes?'

She looked up at him, into his accepting blue eyes.

'Put him in the river,' she said.

Something floated by on the surface of the water, and Sula tried not to look at it. Martinez gathered Sula in his arms and began to kiss her. She kissed him back, briefly, distractedly. She jerked and gave a shiver as a fat raindrop spattered on the back of her hand.

'Are you cold? Let me close the canopy.'

Martinez pushed a lever and the boat's plastic canopy flapped forward, cutting off the breeze. Suddenly there was no air. Sula lunged forward and heaved the canopy back with a cry.

'What's wrong?' Martinez asked, startled.

'Boat!' Sula commanded. 'Go to the quay! Now!'

Panic flapped in her chest like torn canvas flogging in the wind. Raindrops spattered on her face. Martinez took her by the hand.

'What's wrong? Are you all right?'

'No!' she managed to shout, and she wrenched her hand free. The boat slid against the quay and Sula launched herself for dry land. Pain jolted her shins as they barked against the stone quay, but after a brief scramble she was on her feet and walking briskly away. Martinez remained behind, his arms thrown out for balance, ridiculous in the swaying little boat.

'What did I do wrong?' he called, his voice bewildered. Rain hit her face in cold little slaps.

'Nothing!' she answered over her shoulder, and increased her pace.

Six

The catafalque of the last Great Master rolled past, moving at a silent, glacial glide along the length of the Boulevard of the Praxis, all the way from the Great Refuge at the peak of the city's acropolis to the Couch of Eternity on the other end of the High City's great rock. Atop the monstrous catafalque was an image of the last Shaa itself, twice life size. The massive body reclined amid sculpted folds of slack grey skin, its flat-topped, prow-shaped head erect, like some lonely butte in a distant desert country, and gazing ahead into a future that only those as wise as the Shaa could expect ever to see.

Martinez had been standing under grey skies for what seemed hours. He wore parade mourning dress, with cape and brocade and epaulettes and jackboots, and a tall black leather shako atop his head. Service colours were reversed in mourning garb, so instead of green tunic and trousers with silver buttons and braid, the tunic and trousers were the white of mourning, with green collar, cuffs, braid, buttons, and brocade. The cape was white and lined with green, and weighted at the corners to preserve its line.

The uniform was stiff with starch and unfamiliarity, and the tall collar chafed the underside of Martinez' chin. The jackboots were hot and heavy, and the shako with its silver plate sat like a millstone on his skull. The scabbard of the sickle-shaped dress knife, with which he was supposed to slice the throats of subordinates who displeased him, banged against his thigh when he walked.

The catafalque crept past, followed by a band – all Cree, with motorized booming kettledrums and double-reed flutes that wailed a weird, wild chant like the keening of some half-savage species from the dawn of time. These were followed by a float that held the various machines that – rumour maintained – had been connected to Anticipation of Victory during the latter portion of its life. These were covered with white shrouds, and would be burned along with the last Shaa, taking their secrets with them.

Martinez couldn't help but think this was a pity. The Shaa had been very private where their anatomy and physiology were concerned, let alone their mentation. On their decease, each Shaa had been cremated along with their personal servants and gear, and the surviving Shaa had made certain that all proper procedures were followed. Whatever was going on beneath those folds of skin, or in those prow-shaped heads, remained a secret of the Shaa alone.

But now there *were* no surviving Shaa to ensure that the evidence was destroyed. This was a perfect opportunity for a post-mortem if not an actual dissection. If Martinez had been in charge of arrangements, the funeral and its solemn procession would have been postponed for days if not months, while expert pathologists sought out every last secret of Shaa physiology, and the best cyberneticians examined the machines to determine if they were, in fact, repositories of Shaa memory.

But Martinez was not in charge, and the secrets of the Shaa would die with the last of their kind.

Following Anticipation of Victory and its machines came the senior mourners, all in their reversed mourning uniforms. The white and deep red of the lords convocate, the white and brown of the civil service, the white and green of the Fleet, each service organized by species, in order of the seniority of conquest. The Naxids were first, their long bodies curving right and left in order to maintain the slow pace, followed by the Terrans, the Torminel, and so on. The only species missing were the Yormaks, who centuries ago had received special dispensation never to leave their home world.

Lord Pierre Ngeni was somewhere amid the lords convocate, but Martinez didn't see him. Amid the white uniforms of the Fleet, Martinez saw Senior Fleet Commander Jarlath, the new commander of the Home Fleet. He was a Torminel, his large nocturnal eyes covered by shaded spectacles even on such a grey day as this, and with his plump, furry body swathed to the chin in mourning white. The combination of fur and an elaborate uniform could result in deadly overheating in his species – in less formal circumstances, Torminel officers usually wore only vests and short pants – and there were probably refrigeration units in his uniform to keep his body cooled to a reasonable temperature. Martinez knew that many Torminel in official posts would bleach to white their grey-and-black fur for the duration of the mourning period rather than having to risk heat stroke every day.

Martinez knew nothing of Fleet Commander Jarlath, and wished to know less. For Jarlath had replaced Fleet Commander Enderby, and after today Martinez would have to remove from his collar the red staff tabs that marked him as an officer of distinction.

Following the mourners of the Fleet came the white-and-blue of the Exploration Service, then the black-and-gold of the Legion of Diligence. The Legion alone had no mourning dress, which symbolized the fact that even mourning could not interrupt their incessant search for the foes of the Praxis.

After these came the bodies of those who had decided to follow the Great Master in death, first among them the lady senior of the Convocation, the highest-ranking individual in the empire not to have been born a Shaa. She moved past slowly on her catafalque, the wind whipping the scant feathery hair atop her hollow-boned body. Following the lady

senior and other convocates came the biers of high-ranking
civil servants. Each had taken massive doses of poison, and had
presumably died with their loyal family members worshipfully
clustered about them – possibly to make certain they went
through with it, or to pour the poison down their throats if
they balked.

For the first time in his life Martinez felt grateful that the
Martinez clan wasn't of the first rank. He couldn't help but
wonder that, if his family were expected to offer up one of
their own, they wouldn't have handed the cup to him. His
brother Roland was the presumed heir to Laredo and too
important to die, and his sisters were – for the most part,
anyway – a united front against all adversity. Perhaps a family
council would have decided that the unfortunate Gareth,
employed uselessly with the Fleet and with few prospects
for aiding the others in their projects, would have been the
most expendable.

Martinez was saved from further morbid thoughts by the
sight of someone he knew – PJ Ngeni, dressed all in white,
walking slowly in the procession with an unusually solemn
look on his insipid face. He marched with other Ngenis
behind the bier of one of their clan members, an elderly
man with a distinguished white moustache who wore the
uniform of a retired senior civil servant. Strange to think
that the Ngenis would spare this one sooner than PJ.

PJ's sojourn in the Shelley Palace garden with Sempronia
proved successful – certainly more successful than Martinez' boat
ride with Sula – and Martinez was now obliged to treat PJ
as a future brother-in-law. If Martinez didn't know that the
whole thing was a sham, he would have been deeply offended,
but as it was he found himself almost genial around PJ.

Which was more than could be said for Sempronia, who
was clearly keeping her fiancé at arm's length. What PJ
thought of being engaged to a girl who was doing her best to
avoid his presence had not, so far, come to Martinez' ears.

After the civil servants came the biers of the Fleet. Fleet Commander Enderby, without the fierce rigidity that animated him in life, looked shrunken and mournful in death. Martinez felt a surge of sadness at the sight.

He should have followed my advice, Martinez thought.

Enderby's daughter, looking trim in the white-and-brown of the civil service, stepped from her place near Martinez and walked to the tail of her father's bier. She held her own daughter, a child of nine or ten, by the hand.

The famous wife was nowhere in evidence.

'Party — forward!' called the senior captain on Martinez' right, and Martinez stepped out with the others of Enderby's family and staff. The small formation, Enderby's official family, performed a left wheel and placed themselves into the procession behind Enderby's daughter and granddaughter, his chief mourners.

Other formations placed themselves in the procession. Among them, Martinez saw, was Cadet Foote. Apparently the Footes had sacrificed one of their own to the glory of their clan, though the solemnity of the occasion had done nothing to tame Foote's cowlick.

Martinez was pleased to be moving, even if it was at this glacial pace. He was not allowed to step naturally, as the glacial solemnity of the death march meant each foot had to hang in the air for a beat or two before it could be placed on the ground. The polished jackboots looked dashing and romantic, but they were very heavy for suspending in the air that way. The rest of the uniform had its disadvantages as well: when the procession moved into gaps between the palaces that lined the road, the wind caught at his tall hat and whipped the cape of the next in line into his face.

He blinked and adjusted his hat, which earned a frown from the captain on his right.

The procession crept on. The scabbard of the curved knife banged against his right thigh with every step. Formations of cadets lined the road to keep order, and Martinez found himself searching for the bright hair and brilliant eyes of Cadet Sula. He failed to find her, and then he reprimanded himself for looking for Sula in the first place.

He had been angry enough when she'd bolted and left him standing foolishly in the excursion boat. His temper hadn't improved when he'd returned to his apartment and found the cold supper that Alikhan had left for two, and which Martinez unceremoniously shoved into the fridge on his way to bed.

His anger had faded to annoyance by morning, and faded yet again when he received a message from Sula. The message had been written on her datapad in a precise, uniform hand, and sent from the datapad without being recorded on video. Perhaps she was embarrassed to be seen by him, even on a screen.

'It's entirely my fault,' she'd written. 'Since I'm not fit company for man nor beast, I'm going to spend the rest of my furlough away from the capital, studying for my exams.'

It had been a few hours before his ire faded to the point where he returned her message, scrawling her a note – this handwriting was contagious – to the effect that he'd be happy to speak with her whenever she felt like talking.

Apparently she didn't feel much like conversation, because he'd never heard from her again. He had managed to console himself somewhat with Amanda Taen, who by this point he was finding refreshingly uncomplicated.

He didn't see Sula during the long, slow march, but that wasn't surprising. Every cadet, every officer, every warrant and petty officer, and every recruit was on duty at this hour, and only a minority of them in the High City. Also on alert was every member of the Legion, every member of every police force, and even the few remaining members of the Exploration Service. All public areas were guarded, and a platoon of armed troops guarded each end of the skyhooks tethered to the ring. They were all as ready as they could be for . . . well, for *something*.

The truth, as Martinez was beginning to see it, was that no one knew what to expect after the death of the last member of the order that had ruled with such terror and absolute unquestioning certainty for the last ten thousand years. Despair and panic were widely predicted. Projections ran from mass suicides to riots and insurrections. Lord commander Enderby and the other senior officers had redeployed half the Fleet to make sure that warships were available to intervene anywhere in the empire at short notice.

Martinez himself suspected that little or nothing would happen. Yes, there would be hysterics who would try to kill themselves, though most of them wouldn't succeed; and perhaps there would be a few individuals who ran out of control while under the impression that, with the last Shaa dead, life would turn into some kind of fair. But while these people doubtless existed, those Martinez encountered fitted neither of these types.

Most were *waiting*. They hadn't worked out what the death of Anticipation of Victory meant, and neither had anyone else.

And then he remembered standing in the foyer of the Commandery, looking at the map of the empire's wormhole systems and thinking that there was no escaping the Shaa.

Perhaps, he thought, he *had* just escaped. Perhaps everyone had. Perhaps some of the weight of history had been taken off everyone's shoulders.

This idea sufficiently intrigued him that he barely noticed the long, slow parade until it finally came to an end at the Couch of Eternity, the long, rectangular mausoleum, sheathed in marble of a brilliant cake-icing white, where the Great Masters were cremated and shelved for infinity. The mausoleum was built at the base of a series of long white steps, an artificial amphitheatre, with a ramp descending to the building's entrance with its peculiar two-tier arch. The catafalque rolled slowly down the ramp and beneath the arch, and the mourners following wheeled off and took their places ranked on the tall wide steps on either side.

As Enderby's body crept beneath the arch, Martinez' formation wheeled again to follow Enderby's daughter past the more senior mourners to their place. To Martinez' right the lower town sprawled out beneath the uncertain autumn skies, marked by the patterns of cloud that scudded overhead. He was beginning to feel very cold. The march hadn't been swift enough to warm him.

The slow procession went on until finally the elaborate doors of blackened steel closed behind the last of the dead.

There was a long, long pause. The mourners stood in disciplined rows, coats and cloaks flapping in the cold wind. And then there was a rushing noise, as if the wind had been channelled into a tiny tunnel, and then fire burst from the mausoleum roof, a column of white-hot flame that broke its confines and licked towards the viridian sky.

Martinez felt a collective sigh from the assembled multitude. The era of the Shaa had come to an end.

The column of flame died away, scattering atoms of Anticipation of Victory onto the cold wind. In a series of shouted commands the mourners were dismissed. Martinez stood with the others to speak briefly to Enderby's daughter – the proper form was to offer congratulations rather than condolences on someone permitted to die with a Great Master, but Martinez knew his congratulations probably sounded more mournful than not – and then he made his way back along the parade route through the High City.

He passed the Shelley Palace on the way, where he knew his sisters, along with PJ Ngeni, were hosting a small reception for his brother Roland, who had arrived three days ahead of the funeral. It wasn't a party, since parties on the day of the last Shaa's death would have been bad form. It would be a mourning function, a kind of wake, and was restricted by custom to twenty-two guests.

Martinez wasn't one of them. The Fleet was still on alert, and he would be spending the next shift in the Commandery, handling the signals traffic that might result from an emergency, should there actually be one.

Then he would turn in the Commandery ID that entitled him to enter the building, after which he would go to his apartment and give Alikhan his jacket, so that his orderly could pick away the tiny stitches that fixed the red staff tabs to his collar.

Sula spent the day commanding a guard detail on a skyhook terminus on the first level of Zanshaa's accelerator ring. The ring was built in two sections: the lower part rotated at the same speed as the planet below, which gave it a very light gravity, and was used for antimatter generation, storage, and utility conduits. The second, outer section glided atop the inner ring like the second hand of a clock spinning faster than the hour hand; it moved at nine times geosynchronous speed in order to maintain one standard gravity. It was the second level that contained docks, repair bays, and housing for the population of the ring.

Sula's dozen recruits carried stun batons, and she herself wore a sidearm on one hip and a viridian-green helmet on her head. She couldn't help but wonder what this pathetic force was supposed to do in the event of a raving mob of anarchists charging down from the outer ring to seize the skyhook, other of course than to die pointlessly with all the bravery they could muster.

Nothing happened. Civilian traffic was nil, and military traffic nearly so until her relief arrived, a detail of Naxids armed with gatling guns and grenade launchers.

Naxids didn't fool around, Sula concluded.

She took her detail to the outer ring, where she turned in her sidearm and her detail's stun batons, and then wondered what to do next. Mourning had closed down all entertainment, on the planet or off it, and filled all hotels so she couldn't get a room.

In the end she requested a billet in the travelling cadets' hostel and found half a dozen cadets passing a bottle around while shooting dice. She let them get drunk, won their money, and then retired to her rack filled with a rare, pleasing sense of accomplishment.

'Reporting aboard *Corona*, my lord.'

Martinez, head thrown back before his new captain, gazed with level eyes above the captain's head at the massive gleaming structure on the shelf behind him, the Home Fleet Trophy that *Corona*'s football team had just won in a short season truncated by the death of the last Shaa.

One other Home Fleet Trophy stood on a special shelf in the corner, locked into place and braced against high accelerations. A second-place trophy sat on a somewhat less special shelf. Other, lesser trophies, all topped by gleaming crystal footballers, crowded Tarafah's desk on all sides.

'At ease, Lieutenant Martinez,' said Lieutenant-Captain the Lord Fahd Tarafah, which allowed Martinez to drop his chin and contemplate his new commander. Still under thirty, Tarafah was a compact, well-formed man with a shaven head and neatly-trimmed goatee. On his left sleeve, just above the cuff, was the stylized football insignia that all the Coronas were entitled to wear for the next year.

'You've reported to Garcia?' Tarafah asked, referring to the officer on watch.

'Yes, my lord. She's shown me my quarters and given me the code to my safe. She was going to give me a more thorough orientation after her watch.'

'It'll be useful to have another watch-keeping officer

aboard. Your orders and records have been logged on the computer?'

'Yes, my lord.'

Tarafah opened his collar, took his captain's key from around his neck, and called Martinez' records onto his displays. His eyes scanned back and forth, then halted, no doubt focused on the candid evaluations of Martinez' abilities and character provided by Martinez' former commanders, evaluations which Martinez carried around with him as part of his permanent record but did not possess the codes to read.

'What sports did you do at the academy?' Tarafah asked. Which, Martinez knew, was the question that might well doom him.

'An absolute fanatic about football,' Ari Abacha had said approvingly, when Martinez had asked him about Tarafah at the junior officers' club. 'Pulls every string he can to get the top players on his ship, and when strings won't work, he lays out the cash. Rumour has it that he bought Captain Lord Winfield a new yacht in order to guarantee the transfer of a new outside forward.'

Abacha approved of the Fleet's fanatic football officers, and if his own devotion to languor hadn't been so all-encompassing, he would probably have been one himself, either a player or coach or manager. As it was, Abacha contented himself with absorbing everything known about the subject, the players, the statistics, the tactics, the managers and coaches, and had a profitable sideline running a sports book for other officers.

Corona's appearance only confirmed Abacha's assessment. Tarafah had painted his ship green, not the viridian green of Zanshaa's sky but the bright lawn green of a football pitch, with the white midfield stripe bisecting the frigate lengthwise and a motif of white soccer balls bouncing down the ship's sides.

Corona was a small ship to field such an important team.

With a crew of only sixty-one, to get a first-rate team of eleven players, plus alternates and coaches and support – enough to make a serious bid for the Home Fleet Trophy, against ships with ten times the crew strength – required single-minded dedication and deep pockets.

'I did fencing and swimming, my lord,' Martinez said. Sports where his long arms and comparatively short legs worked to his advantage.

He suspected it wouldn't help to mention that he was school champion at hyper-tourney, an abstract positional game with a computer-generated playing field. Hyper-tourney was probably a little too intellectual for Tarafah and the *Corona*.

'We do football on the *Corona*,' Tarafah said. Which Martinez couldn't help but think was like saying, *In the Legion of Diligence, we do fanaticism.*

'Yes, my lord,' Martinez said. 'Everyone in the Fleet knows the quality of *Corona*'s team.'

The compliment indirect, Martinez thought. One should start small, then work slowly upwards towards finding the appropriate level of flattery for one's commander.

The praise at least persuaded Tarafah to ask Martinez to sit. Martinez drew up a chair and watched the lieutenant-captain with all due attention.

Tarafah folded his hands atop his desk and leaned slightly forward. 'I don't believe that any officer can succeed on his own, Lieutenant,' he said. 'I believe that a ship's company is a team, each dependent on the others for success.'

'Very true, my lord.' Martinez tried to suggest that this was an idea he had never encountered before.

'That's why I expect the entire ship's company to pull together for the common good. In making *Corona* look its absolute best – during fleet manoeuvres, during inspections, and on the football field. Each must do his part.'

'Very good, my lord,' Martinez repeated.

'That's why I expect everyone to support the team. The

team makes us *all* look good, just as polished panelling and spotless floors give us the look of a ship where everything is completely up to the mark. Do you understand?'

'Yes, my lord. In fact,' Martinez added, 'that's why I hope to contribute directly to the success of the team. I know that I'm probably unsuitable as a player, but I thought I might serve as a coach, or some kind of manager . . .'

Martinez fell silent as he saw the thin, disapproving look on Tarafah's face. 'I coach the team myself, as well as manage,' he said. 'And Weaponer Mancini assists.'

'Yes, my lord,' Martinez said, his hopes for the tour sinking fast. He played his last card. 'By the way,' he added, 'I'm bringing only one servant on board.'

Tarafah was taken aback. 'Yes? Do you want the first officer to appoint another?'

'No. I merely thought that, if for any reason you needed another reserve player aboard, you could make the player my second servant.'

'Oh.' Calculation flickered across Tarafah's face. 'That might be useful,' he judged. 'I intend to win the Second Fleet Championship next year, at Magaria.'

Surprise filled Martinez. 'Magaria?' he said. 'We're shipping out?'

'Yes. We're replacing *Staunch*, which is going into refit. You've got six days to wind up your personal affairs and get your division up to the mark.'

'Yes, my lord.'

Tarafah fingered the touch pads on his desk. 'I've configured your third lieutenant's key. Here you are.'

Martinez accepted the key on its elastic strap and thought, *This is going to be a long, long tour.*

'Brilliant. Quite brilliant. I'm sure your parents would be proud.'

'I'm glad you think so,' Sula said.

'May I get you another drink?'

'I'm having water, thanks.'

Lord Durward Li decanted some water into Sula's glass and refreshed his own mig brandy. 'It's a pity we're in a period of mourning,' he said. 'Usually we have *swarms* of guests at these affairs, but now it's only twenty-two, alas.'

'Twenty-two,' Sula mused. 'I wonder why. The Shaa usually preferred to play with primes.'

'Oh – you don't know the story behind that? You see, ages ago, just after the Torminel conquest . . .'

Sula sipped her water and listened to Lord Durward rattle on.

After the debacle with Martinez she had fled the capital to a resort town in the highlands. While other visitors hiked trails or lounged in the communal bath or enjoyed the mountain scenery, Sula rarely left her room and spent her days studying for her lieutenants' exams.

When she'd grown so weary of cramming that she couldn't make her eyes focus on the screen, she closed her eyes and lay on the bed and tried to rest. On the backs of her closed lids she saw Martinez standing in the boat, his hands thrown out in exasperation.

Stupid, stupid. She had to learn how to behave around people.

She remembered the invitations she'd received and thought that perhaps Martinez had been right about them. Her parents' friends might help, and in any case it was probably a good idea to meet some people other than those the service threw in her way. The alternative, after all, was the cadet lounge, with Foote and his clique.

She'd sent her regrets to all invitations taking place before the Great Master's funeral, which disposed of all the people who only wanted her to ornament their parties because she had become a kind of celebrity. And then she'd done a modest amount of research through public databases concerning those who remained, and discovered that the Li clan had definitely been clients of the Sulas, and after the fall of Clan Sula had been assured of the patronage of the Chen clan instead. Lord Durward's was the first invitation she had accepted.

Apparently the Lis had done well for themselves in the years since the death of Lord Sula. The new Li Palace, built on the site of an older place that had been torn down, occupied a large frontage on the Boulevard of the Praxis. The facade was of some pale, semi-translucent stone veined with pink, which, when lights were turned on at night, seemed to glow, as if the building itself were a living thing.

Inside, the reception hall was draped in what Sula at first thought were tapestries and lace, but which on closer inspection turned out to be marble, cream and green and pale red, that had been carved into the shape of draped fabric, all the little lace-points and filigree cunningly shaped into the stone. Sula was stunned by the tens of thousands of man-hours that must have gone into the work.

The parlour was less intimidating, with plush furniture and portraits of horses and country scenes on the walls. Fortunately the furniture was set with wide lanes between the pieces, so that the three Naxid guests – Lady Kushdai, a convocate come into the city for the Great Master's funeral, and her kin – could manoeuvre without knocking things over. Sula admired greatly the crackled surface on the porcelain jars, each taller than a man, that stood in the room's corners.

'So you see,' Lord Durward finished, 'it all has to do with the Twenty-Two Martyrs for the Perfection of the Praxis. One wants to invite them to one's mourning feasts, to show them that they didn't die in vain.'

'I see,' Sula said.

'Ah.' Lord Durward's ginger brows rose as he turned to the parlour door, where a Fleet captain had just entered with an elegant young woman on his arm. 'Have you met my son Richard?' And then he smiled. 'Well, of course you have. I forgot.'

Sula's mind whirled as she tried to remembered where she might have met Captain Lord Richard Li. He didn't seem the sort of man one would forget: he was taller than his father, dark-haired, with a smooth, handsome face of the sort that would look youthful well into middle age.

'Caro,' Lord Richard said, taking Sula's hand. 'It's good to see you after all this time.'

Sula felt herself bristling, and told herself to behave.

'Caroline,' she corrected. 'I'm not Caro any more.'

Amusement crinkled the corners of Lord Richard's eyes. 'You don't remember me at all, do you?'

'I'm afraid not.' *Behave,* she told herself. *These people are trying to be your friends.*

Lord Richard's smile was very white, his eyes very blue. 'I put you on your first pony, in our garden at Meeria.'

'Oh,' Sula said. Her eyes widened. 'That was *you?*'

'I haven't changed *that* much, have I?' he said. 'Do you still ride at all?'

'Not in ages.'

Lord Richard looked at his father, then back at Sula. 'We still keep stables at Meeria. If you'd like to go down and spend some time riding, I'm sure we'd love having you. We also have excellent fishing.'

Lord Durward nodded agreement.

'Thank you,' Sula said. 'I'll think about it. But it's been so long . . .'

Lord Richard turned to the young woman by his side. She was tall and willowy, with dark almond eyes and a beautiful, shining fall of black hair.

'This is my fiancée, Lady Terza Chen. Terza, this is Caroline, Lady Sula.'

'A pleasure. I saw you on video.' Lady Terza's voice was

low and soothing, and the graceful hand she extended was unhurried but warm and welcoming in its gentle clasp.

Sula knew it was far too early to hate her, to resent the ease and privilege and serenity that oozed from Terza's every pore, but somehow she managed it. *Shove off, sister,* she thought. *You think you can get between me and the man who put me on my first pony?*

'What a beautiful necklace,' Sula said, the first civil thing that popped into her head.

Lord Richard turned adoring eyes to his bride-to-be. 'I wish I could say I'd given it to her,' he said. 'But she chose it herself – her taste is so much better than mine.'

Sula looked at him. 'You're a lucky man,' she said.

It's not as if she wouldn't have bollixed the relationship anyway.

A trim, broad-shouldered man in the uniform of a convocate arrived, along with Lady Amita, Lord Durward's wife. The newcomer was introduced as Maurice, Lord Chen, Terza's father. Sula's knowledge of the status of Peer clans in relationship to each other was hazy, but she understood enough to know that the Chens were on top of the pile. Lord Chen and Lord Richard and Lord Durward then engaged in a brief contest concerning who could offer Terza the most compliments, with Sula adding plaudits of her own now and again out of politeness. Then Lord Chen turned to Sula and said equally polite things about her parents, and about her rescue of *Midnight Runner*.

It was a polite group altogether, Sula thought.

'The problem is,' Sula said, 'I'm not likely to see the end of *Midnight Runner* for some time. I've had to give a deposition for the court of inquiry, but I've been contacted by advocates representing Lord Blitsharts' insurance company. *They* want to prove it was suicide.'

'It wasn't, was it?' Lady Amita asked.

'I found no evidence one way or another.' Sula tried not to shiver at the memory.

'However complicated it gets,' Lady Amita said, 'I'm so glad it was you who got the medal, and not that dreadful man.'

'Dreadful man, my lady?' Sula asked, puzzled.

'The one who talked all the time during the rescue. The man with the horrible voice.'

'Oh.' Sula blinked. 'That would be Lord Gareth Martinez.'

'That's what the news kept insisting, that he was a Peer.' Lady Amita made a sour face. 'But I don't see how a Peer could talk like that, not with such a horrid accent. Certainly *we* don't know any such people. He sounded like some kind of criminal from *The Incorruptible Seven*.'

Lord Durward patted his wife's arm. 'Some of these decayed provincial Peers are worse than criminals, take my word on it.'

Sula felt a compulsion to defend Martinez. 'Lord Gareth isn't like that,' she said quickly. 'I think he's a kind of a genius, really.'

Lady Amita's eyes widened. 'Indeed? I hope we never meet any such geniuses.'

Lord Durward gave her an indulgent smile. 'I'll keep you safe, my dear.'

The point of the evening, it turned out, was to demonstrate Lady Terza's accomplishments before a select group of Lis and their friends. After supper, which was served on modern Gemmelware with a design of fruits and nuts, they all gathered in a small, intimate theatre built at the back of the Li Palace – it was built in the form of an underwater grotto, with the walls and proscenium covered with thousands of sea shells arranged in attractive patterns, and blue-green lighting to enhance the effect. All listened as Lady Terza sat before a small chamber ensemble and played her harp – and played it extremely well, so far as Sula could tell. Terza's concentration on the music was complete, her face taking on an intent look, almost a ferocity, that belied the serene exterior she had shown with her family and friends.

Sula knew next to nothing about chamber music, and had always dismissed it as the kind of music where you have to make up your own words. But Terza's concentration led Sula into the piece. From the other woman's expressions – the way Terza held her breath before a pause, then nodded her satisfaction at the chord that ended the suspense; the way her eyes grew unfocused as she made a complicated attack; the way she seemed to relax into the slow passages, her movements growing dreamy, evocative – Sula felt the music enter her, caressing or stimulating or firing her nerves, dancing in her blood.

After the music ended there was a pause, and then Sula helped to fill it with applause.

'I'm glad to have a chance to hire an orchestra,' confided Lady Amita, her hostess, during the interval. 'Musicians aren't going to be in very great demand during the mourning period.'

This aspect of mourning hadn't struck Sula till now. 'It's good of you to give them work,' she said.

'Terza suggested it. She has so many friends among the musicians, and she's concerned for them.' Her face assumed a touch of anxiety. 'Of course, once she's married, we don't imagine she'll be spending so much time with—' Tact rescued her in time. 'With those sorts of people.'

The interval ended, and the orchestra began to play again. Sula watched Terza's intent face hovering near the strings, and then Sula glanced across the aisle at Maurice Chen and Lord Richard, both gazing with shining eyes at the graceful woman on stage. Sula suspected her own accomplishments would never gather quite that level of admiration – she was a good pilot and a whiz with maths, but she'd already destroyed any hope of a relationship with the one person who had ever shown appreciation for that particular blend of skills.

Not that she would have had a chance with Martinez anyway, not in the longer term, and certainly not with someone like Lord Richard. She had long ago discovered that her looks attracted eligible men right up to the point where their parents found out she had no money or prospects, after which the young men were dragged off to look elsewhere. Strangely enough, however, this made her attractive to their fathers, men who had married once for the sake of procreation and family advantage, and who now, widowed or divorced, were looking for fun in their declining years, and someone beautiful on their arm for other men to admire.

If Sula had been interested in older men, she supposed she could have done very well for herself. But she would have been lost in the complex, intricate world that those men lived in – she hadn't grown up in it the way they had, or had a fraction of their experience – and she didn't fancy being in the position of a pampered, addled, half-imbecile doll, trotted out for show or a romp in bed, then sent off to the boutique or the hairdresser whenever anything important went on.

The Fleet, for all its frustrations and disadvantages, was at least something that she understood. Given a chance, perhaps only the merest breath of a chance, the Fleet was a place where she could do well.

After the concert, Sula complimented Terza on her playing. 'What instrument do you play?' Terza asked.

'None, I'm afraid.'

Terza seemed surprised. 'You didn't learn an instrument at school?'

'My schooling was . . . a bit spotty.'

Terza's surprise deepened. 'You were taught at home, Lady Sula?'

Clearly no one had told Terza about Sula's past.

'I was in school on Spannan,' Sula said. 'The school wasn't very good and I left early.'

Something in Sula's tone perhaps suggested to Terza that the matter was best left unpursued, and so it was. Sula raised her coffee cup.

'This is the Vigo hard-paste, isn't it?'

Which led to a discussion of porcelain in general, and a tour of some of the family's collection led by Lord Richard.

It never hurts to know a genial senior officer, Sula told herself, and exerted herself not to tell him he was an idiot when he got something wrong.

The vote appointing Akzad as lord senior of the Convocation was unanimous. There was no opposition, as in fact Akzad's choice was obvious. Lord Convocate Akzad was a member of an exemplary and dignified Naxid clan that had provided scores of distinguished civil servants and high-ranking officers of the Fleet, he had served in the Convocation most of his life, and he was a prominent member of the previous lady senior's administration.

There was a certain amount of speculation concerning why Akzad hadn't retired or committed suicide along with contemporaries. Privately the convocates admitted to one another that Akzad wanted the highest office in the empire more than he wanted his ashes to rest with the Great Masters. But it was also admitted that he deserved the office and that his administration would be smoothly run and free of innovation. The Convocation was not in favour of innovation, especially now, when citizens were uneasy after the death of the Shaa and continuity was most to be desired.

Maurice, Lord Chen rose from his seat when the vote was called, and then remained on his feet and applauded as Akzad took his seat at the dais, and with great ceremony was cloaked in the stiff, brocaded robe of the lord senior, and presented with the overlong wand, burnished copper with silver bands, that he would use to call the Convocation to order, to recognize speakers, and to command the audio pickups that would broadcast the speaker's words to the six hundred and thirty-one members of the Convocation.

Behind Akzad's dais was a transparent wall with a spectacular view of the Lower Town, the Apszipar Tower prominent on the far horizon. The Convocation's meeting room was a large fan-shaped building tucked beneath a wing of the Great Refuge, a stone amphitheatre with the seat of the lord senior at its focal point. The grey-white granite of the acropolis was carved in abstract, geometric patterns and inset with other stones, marble and porphyry and lapis. Each convocate had a seat appropriate to his species, along with a desk and display.

The applause ending, Lord Chen took his seat and paged through his correspondence while Lord Akzad gave his speech of acceptance. When his turn came, he rose to congratulate the lord senior on his appointment and express confidence in Akzad's forthcoming administration. With any luck he'd get an appointment himself, command a department or chair a more important committee than that of Oceanographic and Forestry on which he now sat.

After the long round of congratulations, the Convocation was adjourned. Akzad would need several days in which to form his government and make his appointments.

As Lord Chen made his way out of the hall, he found himself walking alongside Lord Pierre Ngeni. The young convocate walked with his head bent, frowning at the floor, his heavy jaw grinding some particle of a thought to powder.

'Lord Pierre,' Maurice Chen said, 'I hope your father is well.'

Pierre gave a start and looked at up. 'I beg your pardon, Lord Chen. I was thinking of— Well, never mind. My father is well, and I wish he was here. He'd be certain to be a part of this new government, but I'm too young, alas.'

'I encountered one of your clients the other day. Lord Roland Martinez.'

'Ah.' His heavy jaw ground once. 'Lord Roland, yes. He's arrived from Laredo.'

'A three-month journey, he told me.'

'Yes.'

'He's the brother of the fellow that helped Caro Sula try to save Blitsharts, isn't he?'

Lord Pierre looked as if he had just been struck by indigestion. 'His brother, yes. Lord Gareth.'

Maurice Chen waved at a friend across the lobby. 'Dreadful accent the man's got,' he said.

'Both brothers. The sisters' voices are sweeter, but more insistent.'

'You're marrying PJ to one of them, aren't you?'

Lord Pierre shrugged. 'PJ's got to marry someone. A Martinez is probably as high as he can hope.'

Lord Chen guided Pierre into the lobby lounge, where legislators, meeting clients or family, were thick on the deep pile carpet before the bar. He caught the eye of one of the waiters, and signalled for two of the usual.

'The Martinez family's very wealthy, I understand,' he said.

'And they're doing their best to display it while they're here.' Sourly.

'They don't seem vulgar, though, from what I've seen of them. I haven't seen them making the mistakes the newly arrived usually make.'

Lord Pierre hesitated, then agreed. 'Nothing gauche,' he said. 'Except their accents.'

'Lord Roland spoke to me of his plan for the opening of Chee and Parkhurst.'

Lord Pierre looked at Chen in surprise. 'He only spoke to me of it a few days ago. I've barely had time to consider the scheme.'

'The scheme seemed fairly complete to me.'

'He should have let me present it to people, once I'd had a chance to review it. The Martinez clan are always in a hurry.' Lord Pierre shook his head. 'They have no patience, no sense of occasion – everything's a rush with them. My father tells me it was the same with their father, the current Lord Martinez.'

'Lord Roland has only a limited time on Zanshaa. I'm sure he'd like to get things in train before he leaves. And he's certainly done his homework.'

Drinks arrived. Lord Pierre raised his glass to his lips, began to drink, then hesitated. 'I say, Lord Chen,' he said, 'what's your interest in Roland Martinez?'

Lord Chen spread his hands. 'Just that he seems a very . . . *thorough* young man. He's looked into a number of schemes that have got jammed up one way or another, what with uncertainty and inertia and the death of the Great Masters. Including the station at Choy-on, which should have been expanded to a full-scale antimatter ring ages ago.'

Lord Pierre's pebble eyes gazed unblinking at Maurice Chen. 'You have shipping interests at Choy-on,' he said.

'And I also have ships that could also be leased long-term to help settle Chee and Parkhurst.'

'Ah.' Lord Pierre took a long, deliberate swallow of his drink, and seemed to chew it on the way down. 'Since you've taken such an interest in Clan Martinez,' Lord Pierre said, 'I wonder if you might consider helping Lord Gareth.'

'Lord Gareth needs help?'

'Lord Gareth needs promotion. I really don't have any family remaining in a position to help him, not since my great-aunt retired.' His lips tightened in what might have been a smile. 'But *you*, I seem to remember, have a squadron commander in the family.'

'My sister, Michi.'

'And your daughter is marrying a captain, I seem to remember.'

'But Lord Richard can't promote anyone to command. He has no command himself, at present.'

'Your sister can, and does.'

'*Possibly* my sister can,' Lord Chen qualified. 'I'll inquire and see what she can do.'

'You'll have my gratitude.'

'And you already have mine. For letting me bore you with this subject.'

'Not at all.'

Later, as he left the lounge, Maurice, Lord Chen reflected on the conversation and decided that things had, for a change, gone very well.

Now if only he could get out of Oceanographic and Forestry and into something more useful.

Sula raised her glass to the newly-commissioned Sub-Lieutenant Lord Jeremy Foote, and toasted his good fortune. Foote had insisted on filling the glass with champagne despite her protests. She moistened her lips with the wine and put the glass down.

'Thank you,' Foote said. 'I appreciate you all turning up for my farewell dinner.' He unleashed a bright white smile. 'I wonder how many of you would have shown if I hadn't been paying for it.'

Sula allowed herself to smile as the predictable laughter rolled from the guests.

It would have been impolite to refuse Foote's invitation. The Fleet hadn't found her employment other than to run messages in the Commandery, which put her in the cadets' lounge every day. After a few straightforward attempts to get her into bed, and some equally unsuccessful tries at bullying her into doing his work, Foote had seemed to accept that she wasn't interested in playing his games, and then treated her with a brotherly familiarity calculated to annoy her. But they had survived the time in the cadets' lounge without actually plunging daggers into one another, and Sula supposed that this was worth a toast or two, especially as she'd never have to toast him again.

She had to admit that Foote looked fine in his new white uniform with its dark green collar and cuffs, his sub-lieutenant's narrow stripe bright on his shoulder boards. Foote hadn't actually done anything so unfashionable as to pass his lieutenants' exams: his uncle, as a senior captain commanding the *Bombardment of Delhi*, was allowed to raise two cadets to a lieutenancy every year provided he had vacancies in his own ship, and Foote had long been marked for one of these. Tomorrow Foote would take up his post as *Delhi*'s navigation officer, where well-trained subordinates and a computer would doubtless assist him in not diving the heavy cruiser straight into the nearest star.

Foote had thrown a splendid party. He had rented a private dining room in the eight-hundred-year-old New Bridge restaurant in the High City, and provided entertainment as well, a raucous six-piece band that had the floorboards throbbing beneath Sula's feet. The food arrived in fourteen courses – Sula counted – and the drinks were unending. Cadet Parker seemed to have ordered up a woman to go along with the food and drink – at least Sula hadn't yet met any woman who dressed that way for free – and Sula wondered if Foote was paying for that as well.

After Foote started grabbing his guests and shoving them under the long table so that they could sing the 'Congratu-lations' round from *Lord Fizz Takes a Holiday,* Sula slipped from her place, opened one of the tall doors, and stepped out onto the balcony. Drunken chanting echoed behind her as she braced her arms on the wrought-iron and polished-brass rail and gazed down at the night traffic. Peers walked or drove on their usual evening round of parties and dinners and meetings; servants slumped along to the funicular that would take them to their homes in the Lower Town; groups of young people walked, half-dancing, on their way to a night of adventure.

It had been a while since Sula had been part of such a group, on her way to such an adventure. She wondered if she missed it.

Sometimes, she decided. Sometimes she missed it very much.

She had seen Martinez once, at the Imperial, a performance of *Kho-So's Elegy*, about the most exciting sort of entertainment permitted in the month following the Great Master's death. Sula had been in the Li family box with Lady Amita and some of her friends, and saw Martinez in the stalls below in the company of a woman with an astounding hourglass figure and glossy dark hair. *So that's the kind he likes,* Sula thought, and then immediately regretted the injustice – Martinez had seemed to like her well enough until she'd ruined everything.

She didn't think Martinez had seen her. She'd stayed in the box through the intermission, chatting to Lady Amita, and delayed their leaving as much as she could.

A pair of arms went around Sula from behind. She found herself relaxing into them, and then Foote spoiled the illusion by talking.

'You looked lonely,' he said. 'This party isn't your sort of thing, is it?'

'It was, once,' Sula said. 'Then I turned seventeen.'

'There's been talk about you.' Foote nuzzled her hair to one side and spoke at close range into her ear. 'We've been wondering if you're really a virgin. I bet the others that you aren't.'

'You lose,' Sula said. She detached his arms from her and turned to face him, and felt a fierce inward satisfaction as she thought, *Good. Open season on you, then.*

Foote brushed invisible lint off his new tunic, then glanced out at the city.

'That's your old home by the funicular, isn't it? The one with the blue dome.'

Sula didn't look. 'I guess it must be,' she said.

He looked at her. 'I know about your family. I looked it up.'

Sula affected surprise. 'Don't be silly. *You* – actually looking something up? You paid someone to do it.'

Foote looked nettled, but he let that one go by.

'You really should be friends with me. I could help you.'

'You mean your uncle the yachtsman could.'

'He would if I asked him. And *I* could, eventually. I'll get promoted as fast as it's legally allowed, the next few steps are already worked out. Then I'll be able to help people. And you don't have any patronage in the Fleet. You've got to have friends or you'll be stuck as a lieutenant for ever.' His look softened. 'You're at the head of one of the most senior human clans. Eminent as my own. It's unjust that someone with your ancestors shouldn't be promoted to the highest ranks.'

Sula smiled. 'So how many times do I have to join you in the fuck tubes for this injustice to be corrected?'

Foote opened his mouth, closed it.

'Would six times a month be enough?' Sula went on. 'We could put it in a contract. But you'd have to do your part – if I don't make lieutenant at the earliest legal opportunity, you could pay a fine of, say – ten thousand zeniths? And twenty thousand if I don't make elcap, and so on. What do you say? Shall I take it to my lawyer?'

Foote turned to face the party on the other side of the tall glass doors, and leaned back against the iron rail with his arms crossed. His handsome profile was undisturbed. 'I don't know why you talk this way.'

'I just think everything should be clear and understood right from the beginning. It only makes sense to put a business arrangement in a contract.'

'I was just offering to help out.'

Sula laughed. 'I get offers of that sort every week. And most of them are better than yours.'

A massive exaggeration, but one Sula decided was justified under the circumstances.

Sula decided she should exit before Foote regrouped. She gave his sleeve a pat of mock consolation and strolled through the open door into the dining room.

Save for Parker and his companion, the guests had climbed from beneath the table. The band was making a lot of noise. Sula sat at her place, reached for her sparkling water, and discovered that someone had spiked it with what seemed to be grain alcohol.

These youngsters and their hijinks, she thought wearily.

For a moment she thought about downing the drink and chasing it with her untouched champagne. The idea had a certain attractive gaiety to it. She remembered the person she'd been the last time she was drunk, and smiled . . . these people wouldn't like that person at all.

The problem was, she wouldn't either.

She put the glass back on the table, and then, a moment later, knocked it and its contents into the lap of the person next to her.

'Oh, so sorry,' she said. 'Would you like a match?'

'Signal from flag, my lord,' Martinez said. '*Second division, alter course in echelon to two-two-seven by one-two-zero relative, and accelerate at two point eight gravities. Commence movement at 27:10:000 ship time.*'

'Comm, acknowledge,' said Tarafah. He sat in his rotating acceleration couch in the middle of the command centre. The padded rectangular room was unusually quiet, with the lighting subdued in order not to compete with the glowing pastel lights of the various station displays, green and orange and yellow and blue. Through the open faceplate of his helmet, Martinez could smell the machine oil that had recently relubricated the acceleration cages, all mixing with the polymer plastic scent of the seals of his vac suit.

Martinez, whose couch was behind the captain's, observed that Tarafah's body was so rigid with tension that the rods and struts of the acceleration cage vibrated in sympathy with his taut, quivering limbs.

'Yes, lord elcap,' Martinez said. 'Elcap', the accepted shorthand for Tarafah's grade, came more easily than 'lieutenant-captain' to a Fleet officer in a hurry.

Tarafah stared at his displays, one muscle working in his cheek, a fact observable because Tarafah hadn't put on his helmet, a breach of the procedure permitted in a captain but scarcely anyone else. Tarafah gazing at his displays had the attitude of a footballer deep in concentration on an unfamiliar playbook. Martinez figured that Tarafah was desperate not to wreck the assigned manoeuvre, a greater possibility than usual since so many of his top petty officers, the noncommissioned officers who were the backbone of his ship, were useless dunces.

Fortunately Martinez had only one such dunce in his own division, Signaller First Class Sorensen, otherwise known as *Corona*'s star centre forward. It wasn't so much that Sorensen wasn't willing to learn his official duties – he seemed cheerful and cooperative, unlike some of the other players – but that he seemed incapable of understanding anything the least bit technical.

No, Martinez thought, that wasn't exactly true. Sorensen was perfectly capable of understanding the complex series of lateral passes that Tarafah had built into the Coronas' hard-charging offensive, and all that was technical enough – and besides, Martinez took his hat off to *anyone* who could understand the intricacies of custom, interpretation, and precedent that made up the Fleet League's understanding of the offside rule. It was just that Sorensen couldn't understand any complexities beyond football, to which he seemed dedicated by some unusually singleminded force of predestination.

All that wouldn't have mattered so much if Sorensen hadn't been promoted past recruit first class. But Tarafah had wanted to boost his players' pay beyond the hefty under-the-table sums he was doubtless handing them, and so he'd promoted eight of his first-string players to specialist first class. No doubt he would have promoted them to Master Specialist if that rank hadn't required an examination that would have exposed a complete ignorance of their duties.

Leaving aside the senior lieutenant, Koslowski, who despite playing goalkeeper seemed a competent enough officer, there were ten additional first-string players, plus an alternate (the second alternate being an officer cadet fresh from a glorious playing season at the Cheng Ho Academy). To these were added a coach in the guise of a weaponer second class, all of which made up a lot of dead weight in a crew of sixty-one.

Thus it was that Martinez found what Captain Tarafah had meant when he said he wanted the entire ship's company to pull together. It meant that everyone else had to do the footballers' jobs.

Martinez could have coped easily enough if it had meant covering for the genial but inept Sorensen. But because Tarafah was consumed with football, and the premiere was a player, it meant that Martinez did much of Koslowski's work as well, and even some of the captain's. And sometimes stood their watches as well as his own.

And this was during a period in which football wasn't even in season. Martinez dreaded the time when the games actually started.

He also envied *Corona*'s second officer, Garcia. A small, brown-skinned woman, she wasn't a suitable footballer, and she spoke with a provincial accent almost as broad as Martinez' own, but she'd got herself in with the captain as, in effect, First Fan. She had organized the non-footballer crew to attend and cheer for the Coronas at the games, and made up signs and banners and threw parties in the players' honour. Thus she had worked her way into the captain's circle, though she was also obliged to keep her own watch and do her own work, and probably a little of the premiere's as well.

'Pilot, rotate ship,' Tarafah said. A little ahead of time, Martinez thought. The other ships in the division hadn't rotated yet, but no harm done.

'Rotating ship,' called Pilot/2nd Anna Begay, who was doing the job of Pilot/1st Kostanza, a long-legged hairy-wristed halfback who sat behind her in the auxiliary pilot's position, and whose displays had been set to an archived edition of *Sporting Classics*.

The acceleration couches swung lightly in their cages as *Corona* rotated around them. Martinez kept his eyes focused on his signals display board in front of him.

'Two-two-seven by one-two-zero by relative, lord elcap,' Begay reported.

'Engines, prepare for acceleration,' said Tarafah.

'Engines signalled,' said Warrant Officer Second Class Mabumba, who was doing a class on propulsion to prepare for his exams for warrant officer/1st.

The little muscle ticked in Tarafah's cheek as he watched the digital readout on his displays. 'Engines, accelerate on my mark,' he said, and then, as the counters ticked to 27:10:000, 'Engines, fire engines.'

Gravity's punch in the chest, and the gee suits tightening around arms and legs, told everyone in the ship that the engines had fired, but Mabumba reported the fact anyway, as protocol dictated. Acceleration couches swung to new attitudes as gee forces piled on, and began to generate the pulsing miniwaves that kept blood from pooling. The second division of Cruiser Squadron Eighteen, echeloned so that each ship wouldn't fry the one behind with its torch, blazed out towards the target.

Martinez saw that Tarafah seemed to relax once the engines were fired. There hadn't been the slightest chance that they *wouldn't* fire, of course: the dour, impatient Master Engineer Maheshwari had the engines well in hand, even considering the two footballers stuck in his department, one rated engineer/1st and supposedly in charge of his own watch.

The problems, if any, would come when weapons began to fire. Since *Corona* had never fired a weapon in anger the weapons bays had seemed a useful sort of place to stuff excess footballers, and the weapons department carried more than its share.

But now missiles were actually going to be launched, from launchers maintained and loaded by crews supervised by bogus weaponers, and Martinez figured that if anything was going to go amiss, it would be there.

Martinez had tried to head off trouble by sending Alikhan, his orderly, to the weapons bays instead of to the damage control or medical sections, as was normal. Alikhan had retired a master weaponer, and Martinez reckoned *Corona*'s weapons division could use him.

Still, if anything went wrong, Martinez hoped it wouldn't involve antimatter.

Quietly, he configured his screen so as to show the view of the security camera in the weapons bay. He tucked the image into a corner of his display, then jumped back to his real job as a new message flickered onto his screens.

'Message from flag,' he reported. *'Second division, alter course in echelon to one-zero-zero by zero-eight-zero relative, execution immediate.'*

Martinez touched the pad that would send the new course to the captain, pilot, navigator, and engine control, which would assure that they would all receive the same information and that it wouldn't be garbled in transmission.

'Signals, acknowledge,' Tarafah said. 'Engines, cut engines.'

'Engines cut, lord elcap.' Suddenly everyone was weightless in their straps.

'Pilot, rotate ship.'

'Rotating ship, lord elcap. New heading one-zero-zero by one-nine-zero by zero-eight-zero relative.'

'Engines, fire engines.'

Again that punch in the solar plexus, the swinging of the couches in their cages. Somewhere a couch wheel gave a little metallic scream.

'Engines fired, my lord.' Redundantly.

Over Tarafah's shoulder, Martinez caught a glimpse of the navigation displays. The ships of the second division had all made the course change in their own time, leaving their line slightly ragged. *Corona,* at one end of the line, was headed just for the enemy, exactly according to plan.

'Weapons,' Tarafah commanded, 'prepare to fire missiles.'

Martinez reflected that if it hadn't been for Tarafah's worry over whether one of his nominal petty officers was going to make him look bad, the current operation would scarcely have had any suspense at all.

Martinez had yet to see Magaria, *Corona*'s new base. Not that it was worth viewing: Magaria had been chosen as a major Fleet installation not because the world was a desirable one, but because the system had seven useful wormhole gates, only one fewer than Zanshaa itself, and the Second Fleet squatting at the wormhole nexus could therefore hold much of the empire in its power.

Magaria had been a hellishly hot planet when it was discovered, shrouded in clouds of acid and swept by typhoon winds, and thousands of years of tinkering with its climate had barely succeeded in making the place habitable. The population of Magaria's accelerator ring was higher than that of the planet proper, several million who lived off the money the military brought in, or who existed as middlemen for cargoes passing through the port, but a few towns crouched at artificial oases near the skyhook termini, hiding from the scouring sandstorms, their economies largely based on supporting and supplying the Fleet and entertaining its crews. Most of the inhabitants were Naxids, who were more suited for hot, dry weather than other species.

The local Fleet commander was a Naxid as well, Senior Fleet Commander Fanaghee, known as a ferocious disciplinarian, who ruled her domain from a luxurious suite aboard the *Majesty of the Praxis,* one of the huge Praxis-class battleships that provided vast planet-slagging firepower as well as the splendour and magnificence which the customs of the service demanded for senior officers.

Because no one had known quite what to expect following the death of the last Shaa, Fleet elements had been dispersed around the empire in order to preserve order. Now that order seemed to have been preserved without the intervention of the Fleet, the squadrons were reassembling – but they were also reshuffling. Two of Fleetcom Fanaghee's squadrons were new to the Magaria station, and so she had declared a series of manoeuvres, the two Naxid squadrons versus the other three. It was a reasonably even match, as the Naxid ships were more heavily armed, and included the only battleship.

Corona had arrived on station just as the manoeuvres were beginning, and to Tarafah's alarm had been added to the second division as its smallest ship, the rest being medium and light cruisers.

Manoeuvres weren't common in the Fleet. Squadrons had to spend a month or more at high accelerations beforehand, and the same amount of time decelerating afterwards. Martinez had participated in manoeuvres only once before, years ago, when he was a young cadet on the *Dandaphis*.

Live-fire exercises, particularly on short notice, had not exactly been Tarafah's speciality. So Martinez wasn't surprised to hear renewed tension in his captain's voice as he spoke to the weapons officer.

'Weapons, this is a drill,' Tarafah said, following form. 'Target salvo one at trailing enemy cruiser. This is a drill.'

'This is a drill, my lord. Salvo one targeted at trailing enemy cruiser.'

'Weapons, this is a drill. Fire salvo one.'

There was a brief, suspenseful pause as gauss rails flung missiles into space – there was of course no recoil detectible in Command centre – after which solid-fuel boosters carried the missiles to a safe distance before their antimatter engines ignited. An instant later, Cadet Kelly was hurled after them in her pinnace.

'Salvo one away, lord elcap. Pinnace one away.' She paused and only then remembered her disclaimer. 'This is a drill.'

Martinez glanced at the corner of his screen that showed the weapons bays. Nothing was happening, a good sign, and the weaponers all were in the safety of their hardened shelters.

The missiles raced off on their pre-programmed tracks, followed by the pinnace that was supposed to shepherd them. Naturally they wouldn't actually explode – not unless someone in the weapons department had *really* bollixed something up – but their effects would be simulated, or at least their assumed effects would.

Not that what the missiles actually did would matter: the fate of all the ships, not to mention their missiles, had already been decided. Fleetcom Fanaghee and her staff had laboured many hours to script the manoeuvres to the last detail. The two Naxid squadrons, designated the 'defenders of the Praxis', were holding one of Magaria's wormholes against 'mutineers', and the Praxis, along with Fanaghee's squadrons, would inevitably triumph.

As for *Corona*, it would attack with the second division against the enemy's light squadron. The first salvos fired by each side were scheduled to annihilate each other in a simulated spray of antimatter radiation, thus confusing sensors and masking manoeuvres from the other side – the missiles wouldn't actually detonate, and the sensors' confusion was programmed. The second salvo from the enemy would mostly fall to point-defence weapons, but one would detonate near enough to *Corona* to damage one of the weapons bays and require the venting of one of the antimatter storage tanks, thus providing some useful drill for the frigate's damage-control teams.

Corona would fight on, launching several more waves of missiles, until annihilated by an oncoming barrage from the flagship at 29:00:021 precisely. The entire battle could have been loaded into the ships' computers and fought without a single officer having to give an order, except that this was specifically forbidden. The officers were to have practice at giving orders, even if the orders were scripted well in advance.

'Weapons, this is a drill. Fire salvo two. This is a drill.'

The officers were very scrupulous indeed to give the right orders. They and their ships would be judged by how well they followed the plan. The point of the manoeuvre wasn't who won, but who best did what they were told.

'This is a drill. Salvo two away, lord elcap. This is a drill.'

The tension in Command seemed to fade with news of the two successful launches.

'Enemy light squadron firing missiles,' reported Navigation. 'Missile tracks heading our way. Estimated time of impact, eight point four minutes.'

The missiles in question had actually been fired some minutes ago, but the limitations of the radars' speed of light had prevented the information from reaching *Corona* till this moment.

'Starburst, lord elcap!' Navigation managed to simulate surprise. 'Enemy starburst!'

Which meant that the target squadron, perceiving incoming missiles, were now trying to separate from one another as swiftly as they could. To keep their ships firmly under their control, squadron commanders usually wanted to keep them clustered about them as long as possible – one or two light-seconds was normal – but ships that were clumped together also made overlarge targets, with a possibility of one strike destroying more than one ship. The question of when and when not to order a starburst was one of the questions that junior officers debated ceaselessly in their wardrooms. If the senior officers debated this subject, or indeed anything at all, they gave no sign.

Tarafah frowned down at his displays. 'Weapons, this is a drill. Power up the point-defence lasers.'

'This is a drill, lord elcap. Point-defence lasers powered.'

As the enemy's second salvo came in, the point-defence lasers fired away at low power, perhaps even scoring hits. Whether hit or not, most of the salvo had been declared destroyed days before they were fired, and were deactivated. Whether hit or not, one missile was assigned to penetrate the defensive shield and detonate, its (simulated) radiation burning away the control systems on the number two engine, setting off a potential runaway antimatter leak that required a fuel tank to be vented into space. Other damage would include the disabling of an entire bank of missile launchers and sensors burned away along one whole flank of the frigate.

A message flashed onto Martinez' displays. Relief danced in his heart as he reported it to Tarafah. 'General message from flagship *Majesty*.' The qualifier was to distinguish it from the heavy cruiser that was the flagship of the mutineers' squadron. '*Bombardment of Kashma* has failed to launch pinnace number three. All ships are to proceed as if the pinnace was launched.'

'Comm, acknowledge,' Tarafah said. He could barely contain his delight. Some *other* ship had screwed up, and furthermore one in Fanaghee's own squadron.

Corona could look on the rest of the manoeuvres with a rising optimism. Even if they made some hideous mistake, they wouldn't be alone.

The hideous mistake came some twelve minutes thereafter, when the simulated damage occurred to a bank of eight missile launchers. The damage was not to be repaired by actual members of the crew, because the powerful and unpredictable accelerations of a warship might fling them against the nearest bulkhead. Instead weaponers, from the safety of their thick-walled shelters, cleared the missiles from the tubes with remote-controlled robots, massive machines built on the lines of spiders, with multiple arms that would clamp on stanchions fixed to the ship's polycarbon frame, move from one stanchion to the next while the powerful arms secured themselves against accelerations, and smaller manipulator arms did the work.

The movements of the two robots seemed at first to go well. One of the robots moved very slowly, but it moved precisely. 'Damaged' control systems were replaced, and the robots began to yank missiles from their tubes. Then somehow one of the multilegged machines fouled the other, and in an effort to break free tore away the other robot's central hydraulic reserve. Hydraulic fluid jetted out into the weightless missile compartment, forming a spray of perfect azure globes, and the second robot died.

Now both robots were useless, since the dead robot was blocking the one that still functioned.

Martinez watched the silent little video picture with the same fascination with which he would watch any disaster that he was helpless to prevent. The footballers with whom Tarafah had stuffed the weapons division might have just finished off their patron's career.

Martinez glanced up from his screens to tell Tarafah what was happening, but then hesitated. The captain couldn't affect whatever was going in the weapons bays, not now, not from Command. Perhaps he would be happier not knowing.

And besides, Martinez recalled he wasn't supposed to be spying on other divisions.

And then he looked back at the video at the sight of motion in the weapons bay. Little suited figures were shooting weightless into the bay.

The figure in the lead seized a stanchion with one hand and, gesturing, directed the others to the work. From the leader's erect posture, and something of his air of command, Martinez recognized him as his own orderly, Alikhan. The retired master weaponer was trying to set things right.

How long till the next acceleration? The terrifying question shot through Martinez' mind. And suddenly his fingers were tapping his screens in an attempt to call up the script for the manoeuvre.

Unsuccessful, damn it. Tarafah had the whole thing under his captain's key. Martinez glanced in claw-handed frustration at his displays.

Two of the suited figures had wrestled a missile out of its tube and were now guiding it through tangle of robotic limbs between it and the disposal bay. At least the missile hadn't received its antimatter, and was therefore relatively light.

How long? Martinez clenched his teeth. He thought about shouting out, 'Crew in the weapons bay!', which would presumably halt any future accelerations.

No. No acceleration would occur without Tarafah's command, and if Tarafah gave the order, Martinez could announce the danger in time.

Or so he hoped.

Another missile was being wrenched out of its tube, by a single straddle-legged figure braced against the weapons bank. At least the footballers could be counted on for brawn.

A message flashed across screens. 'Message from flag,' he found himself repeating. '*Second division, alter course in echelon to two-two-seven by three-one-zero relative. Accelerate at four point five gravities. Execute at 28:01:000 ship time.'*

He glanced at the time display. That was six minutes from now.

He was never more thankful for the regulation that made certain his helmet was sealed. He touched his controls and said into his helmet mic, 'Page crewman Alikhan.'

'My lord?' The answer came within seconds.

'You've got five minutes before the next acceleration.'

There was a moment of silence as Alikhan calculated the odds. 'Three missiles remaining. We're not going to make it.'

'No. Get the people to the acceleration couches, and I'll tell the captain what's happening.' Martinez looked at the hopeless situation, the awkward crew in their vac suits guiding a missile past the tangled arms of the robots, and then he said, 'Halt that. Wait a minute.' He paused a brief second to think his idea through. 'No, what you do is this. Get someone on the robot controls. Have the others yank the missiles from the tubes and then just hand them to the robot manipulator arms. The robot can hang onto them till the manoeuvre is over. There's no antimatter and no danger, and after the manoeuvre's completed you can finish the job manually.'

'Very good, my lord.' Alikhan cut his comm very fast, and from then on Martinez had to watch in silence. Alikhan himself bounded out of frame, presumably to Weapons Control and the robot controls. The other crew popped the hatches, pulled the missiles, and boosted them very gently in the direction of the functioning robot. In another few seconds, the robot's manipulator arms snatched the missiles from midair and then froze.

The suited figures bounded from the weapons bay in the direction of their armoured shelter. Martinez looked at the time display.

26:51:101
Two minutes to spare.

'Oh, it was a shambles in the weapons bays, my lord,' said Alikhan as he buffed Martinez' number two pair of shoes. 'No one was in charge. The master weaponer was so drunk he couldn't manage a single order that made sense or had anything to do the situation. One of our two weaponer/1sts was a footballer, and so was one of the weaponer/2nds. And the two cadets who usually help out — nice young people, really, they're learning fast — were stuffed into pinnaces and fired out of the ship.'

'I'm glad I thought to put you on the scene,' Martinez said. 'But still, I could have got you killed.'

Alikhan put the shoe down and tapped the inactive communications display on his left sleeve. 'I had Maheshwari on the comm. He would have aborted any accelerations if we'd still had anyone in the weapons bay.'

Martinez nodded slowly. The senior petty officers had their own networks, their own intelligence, their own way of surviving the officers that the Fleet had placed over them.

If you can find a master specialist who isn't a drunk, isn't crazy, and who retains most of his brain cells, Martinez' father had told him, *then grab him.*

Martinez blessed his father for the advice.

Martinez helped himself to some whisky from his private stash, the dark-panelled cabinet under his narrow bed. On taking command Captain Tarafah had repanelled the officers' quarters, and his own, with rich, dark mahogany, complemented by brass fixtures and dark tiles with a white and red geometric pattern. Officers' country was now scented faintly with lemon oil, at least when it didn't whiff of brass polish.

Martinez needed the whisky, having just finished a double shift, standing watch in Command while *Corona* picked up its pinnaces and spent missiles, and Tarafah and the senior lieutenant shuttled to the flagship for a debriefing with the other captains and the fleetcom. The neat whisky scorched Martinez' throat, and he could feel his bruised muscles begin to relax.

'I'm glad we're not in a real war,' Martinez said. 'You would have all been shot through with gamma rays.'

'In a real war,' Alikhan said, 'we would have stayed safe in our bunker and used a different bank of missiles.'

Martinez fingered his chin. 'Do you think the captain will find out what happened?'

'No. The jammed robots were repaired as soon as we secured from quarters. The damaged missile will be written off the inventory somehow – there are all sorts of ways to make a missile disappear.'

'I take no comfort in this knowledge,' Martinez said. He took another sip of whisky. 'Do you think the captain *should* find out?'

By which Martinez meant, Do you think the captain should find out that *we* saved him during the manoeuvres?

Alikhan looked sober. 'I'd hate to end the career of a thirty-year man just short of retirement. And it's the master weaponer who'd be blamed, not the footballers.'

'True,' Martinez said. He hated the idea of doing something clever, and of no one ever finding out. But getting the master weaponer cashiered would not endear him to Alikhan, and he found Alikhan too valuable to offend.

'Well,' he shrugged, 'let it go. Let's hope *Corona* doesn't get into a war before the master weaponer retires.'

'Hardly likely, my lord.' Alikhan brushed his moustache with the back of a knuckle. '*Corona* has survived worse commanders than Tarafah,' he said. 'We'll get her through it, never fear.'

'But will *I* get through it?' Martinez asked. He sighed, then reached into the mahogany-panelled hutch beneath his bed

and withdrew another bottle of whisky. 'This might help
your cogitations,' he said. 'Don't share it with anyone in the
Weapons Division.'

Alikhan accepted the bottle with gravity. 'Thank you,
my lord.'

Martinez finished his drink and decided not to pour himself
another, at least not yet. The example of the master weaponer
was a little too strong. 'Too bad it's the only reward you're
going to get for saving the captain from disgrace.'

'It's more than I usually get,' Alikhan remarked and, with
an ambiguous smile, braced in salute and left.

Two days later, after the last of the meetings in which
the commanding officers refought the manoeuvre, Fleet
Commander Fanaghee announced a Festival of Sport that
would take place at Fleet facilities. Teams from every ship
in Fanaghee's command would participate, and *Corona's*
football team would face Magaria's own champions from the
Bombardment of Beijing in a special match. Tarafah announced
an intensified programme of training for his team, beginning
immediately, before the ship even docked.

When Martinez crawled off his watch that night, he didn't
stop at one drink. Or at two.

The bank was built of granite, a miniature Great Refuge
complete with dome, probably built to suggest permanence
but now, in the absence of the Great Masters, perhaps
suggesting something else. Mr Wesley Weckman, the trust
manager, was a young man with a prematurely grave manner,
though the style of his glossy boots and his fashionable bracelet
of human hair suggested that his life outside the bank was not
as sedate as his working hours.

'Interest has stayed at three percent in the years since you
entered the academy,' he said. 'And since you've returned
most of your allowance to the bank since that time, I'm
pleased to report that the total sum now exceeds twenty-nine

thousand zeniths, all of which I can put in your hands when your trust fund matures on your twenty-third birthday.'

Which was in eleven days. Which made her, in Terran years – she had once known someone who calculated 'Earthdays' – just past twenty.

Sula briefly calculated what twenty-nine thousand zeniths might buy her. A modest apartment in the High City, or an entire apartment building in a decent section of the Lower Town. A modest villa, with extensive grounds, in the country.

At least a dozen complete outfits from the most fashionable designers of Zanshaa.

Or one perfectly authentic rose Pompadour vase from Vincennes dating from four centuries before the conquest of Terra, conveniently up for auction at the end of the month.

Sula figured that given prices like that, those antimatter bombs had broken a lot of porcelain.

It was a ridiculous fantasy to spend her entire inheritance on a vase, but Sula felt she'd been working hard for a long time now, and deserved a moment of complete irrationality.

'What do I have to do to get the principal?' she asked.

'A small amount of paperwork. I can do it now, if you like, and it will take effect on your birthday.'

Sula grinned. 'Why not?'

Weckman printed out the papers in question, then handed them to Sula along with a fat gold-nibbed pen. Then he activated the thumbprint reader and pushed it across his desk.

'You've got my thumbprint?' Sula asked in surprise. 'From all those years ago?'

Weckman looked his screens to make certain. 'Yes. Of course.'

'I don't remember giving it.' Sula crossed her legs, laid the papers on her thigh, and read them carefully. Then she put the papers on the desk, raised the pen above the signature line, and hesitated.

'You see,' she said, 'I don't know what I'm going to do with the money.'

'The bank employs several investment counsellors,' Weckman said. 'I can introduce you to Miss Mandolin – I see that she's at her desk.'

Sula capped the pen. 'The problem is, I'm in transit. I don't even know what my next assignment is going to be.' She put the pen on the desk before Weckman. 'Maybe I'll just leave it in the trust fund, at least till I make lieutenant.'

'In that case, you need do nothing at all.'

'Is it all right if I keep the papers?'

'Of course.'

She rose, and Weckman bowed as he showed her out of his office.

What would she do with a vase anyway? she thought. She didn't even own any flowers to put in it.

She decided to visit the auction house again, and say goodbye.

She should have known better than to permit herself certain dreams.

'Put him in the river,' Gredel said. 'Just make sure he doesn't come up.'

Lamey looked at her, a strange silent sympathy in his eyes, and he put his arm around her and kissed her cheek. 'I'll make it all right for you,' he said.

No you won't, she thought, *but you'll make it better.*

The next morning Nelda threw her out. She looked at Gredel from beneath the slab of grey healing plaster she'd pasted over the cut in her forehead, and she said, 'I just can't have you here anymore. I just can't.'

For a moment of blank terror Gredel wondered if Antony's body had come bobbing up under Old Iola Bridge, but then Gredel realized that no, that wasn't it. The previous evening had put Nelda in a position of having to decide who she loved more, Antony or Gredel. She'd chosen Antony, unaware that he was no longer an option.

Gredel went to her mother's, and Ava's objections died the moment she saw the bruise on Gredel's cheek. Gredel told her what happened – not being stupid, she left out what she'd asked Lamey to do – and Ava hugged her and told her she was proud of her. She worked with cosmetics for a long time to hide the damage.

And then she took Gredel to Maranic Town, to Bonifacio's for ice cream.

Ava and Lamey and Panda helped carry Gredel's belongings to Ava's place, arms and boxes full of the clothing Lamey and Caro had bought her, the blouses and pants and frocks and coats and capes and hats and shoes and jewellery, all the stuff that had long ago overflowed the closets in her room at Nelda's, that was for the most part lying in neat piles on the old, worn carpet.

Panda was highly impressed by the tidiness of it. 'You've got a *system* here,' he said.

Ava was in a better situation than usual. Her man was married and visited only at regularly-scheduled intervals, and he didn't mind if she spent her free time with family or friends. But Ava didn't have many friends – her previous men hadn't really let her have any – and so she was delighted to spend time with her daughter.

Lamey was disappointed that Gredel didn't want to move into one of his apartments. 'I need my Ma right now,' Gredel told him, and that seemed to satisfy him.

I don't want to live with someone who's going to die soon. That was what she thought to herself. But she wondered if she was obliged to live with the boy who had killed for her.

Caro was disappointed as well. 'You could have moved in with *me*!' she said.

Shimmering delight sang in Gredel's mind. 'You wouldn't mind?'

'No!' Caro was enthusiastic. 'We could be sisters! We could shop and go out – have fun.'

For days Gredel basked in the warm attentions of Caro and her mother. She spent almost all her time with one or the other, enough so that Lamey began to get jealous, or at least to *pretend* that he was jealous – Lamey was sometimes hard to read that way. 'Caro's kidnapped you,' he half-joked over the phone. 'I'm going to have to send the boys to fetch you back.'

Gredel began to spend nights with Caro, the nights when Ava was with her man. There was a lot of room in the big bed. She found that Caro didn't so much go to sleep as put herself into a coma: she loaded endorphins into the med injector and gave herself one dose after another until unconsciousness claimed her. Gredel was horrified.

'Why do you do it?' she asked one night, as Caro reached for the injector.

Caro gave her a glare. 'Because I *like* it,' she snarled. 'I can't sleep without it.'

Gredel shrank away from Caro's look. She didn't want Caro to tear into her the way she ripped into other people.

One night Lamey took them both to a party. 'I've got to take Caro out, too,' he told Gredel. 'Otherwise I'd never see *you*.'

The reason for the party was that Lamey had put up a loan for a restaurant and club, and the people hadn't made a go of it, so he'd foreclosed and taken the place over. He'd inherited a stockroom of liquor and a walk-in refrigerator full of food, decided it may as well not go to waste, and invited nearly everyone he knew. He paid the staff for one more night and let all his guests know the food and drinks were free.

'We'll have fun tonight,' he said, 'and tomorrow I'll start looking for somebody to manage the place.'

It was the last great party Gredel had with Lamey and his crew. The big room was filled with food and music and people having a good time. Laughter rang from the club's rusted, reinforced iron ceiling, which was not an attempt at decor but a reminder of the fact that the floor above had once been braced to support heavy machinery. Though Gredel didn't have anything to drink she still got high simply from being around so many people who were soaking up the good times along with the free liquor. Gredel's mind whirled as she danced, whirled like her body spinning along the dance floor in response to Lamey's smooth, perfect, elegant motion. He leaned close and spoke into her ear.

'Come and live with me, Earthgirl.'

She shook her head, smiled. 'Not yet.'

'I want to marry you. Have babies with you.'

A shiver of pleasure sang up Gredel's spine. She had no reply, only put her arms around Lamey's neck and rested her head on his shoulder.

Gredel didn't know quite how she deserved to be so loved. Lamey, Caro, her mother, each of them filling a dreadful hollowness inside her, a hollowness she hadn't realized was there until it was filled with warmth and tenderness.

Lamey danced with Caro as well, or rather guided her around the dance floor while she did the jumping-up-and-down thing she did instead of dancing. Caro was having a good time. She drank only a couple bottles of wine over the course of the night, which for her was modest, and the rest of the time danced with Lamey or members of his crew. As they left the club she kissed Lamey extravagantly to thank him for inviting her. Lamey put an arm around both Caro and Gredel.

'I just like to show my beautiful sisters a good time,' he said.

He and Gredel took Caro to the Volta Apartments, after which they intended to drive back to the Fabs to spend the dawn in one of Lamey's apartments. But Caro lingered in the car, leaning forward out of the back seat to prop her head and shoulders between Lamey and Gredel. They all talked and laughed, and the doorman hovered in the Volta vestibule, waiting for the moment to let Lady Sula past the doors. Finally Lamey said it was time to go.

'Save yourself that drive back to the Fabs,' Caro said. 'You two can use my bed. I can sleep on the sofa.'

Lamey gave her a look. 'I hate to put a beautiful woman out of her bed.'

Caro gave a sharp, sudden laugh, then turned to kiss Gredel on the cheek. 'That depends on Gredel.'

Ah. Ha, Gredel thought, surprised and not surprised.

Lamey, it seems, was looking for a return on his investment. Gredel thought a moment, then shrugged.

'I don't mind,' she said.

So Lamey took Gredel and Caro up to the apartment and made love to them both. Gredel watched her boyfriend's pale butt jigging up and down over Caro and wondered why this scene didn't bother her.

Because I don't love him, she decided. *If I loved him, this would matter.*

And then she thought, *Maybe Caro loves him.* Maybe Caro would want to stay with Lamey in the Fabs, and Gredel could take Caro's place in the academy and go to Earth.

Maybe that would be the solution that would leave everyone happy.

Caro apologized the next day, after Lamey left. 'I was awful last night,' she said. 'I don't know what you must think of me.'

'It was all right,' Gredel said. She was folding Caro's clothes and putting them away. *Cleaning up after the orgy,* she thought.

'I'm such a slut sometimes,' Caro said. 'You must think I'm trying to steal Lamey away from you.'

'I'm not thinking that.'

Caro trotted up behind Gredel and put her arms around her. She leaned her head against Gredel's shoulder, and put on the lisping voice of a penitent little girl. 'Do you forgive me?'

'Yes,' Gredel said. 'Of course.'

Suddenly Caro was all energy. She skipped around the room, bounding across the carpet as Gredel folded her clothes. 'I'll make it up to you!' Caro proclaimed. 'I'll take you anywhere you want today! What would you like? Shopping?'

Gredel considered the offer. It wasn't as if she needed new things – she was beginning to feel a little oppressed by all her possessions – but on the other hand she enjoyed Caro's pleasure in purchasing them. But then another idea struck her.

'Godfrey's,' she said.

Caro's eyes glittered. 'Oh yes.'

It was a glorious day – summer was coming on, and warm breezes flowed through the louvred windows on the private rooms at Godfrey's, breezes that wafted floral perfume over Gredel's skin. She and Caro started with a steam bath, then a facial, a lotion wrap, a massage that stretched all the way from the scalp to the toes. Afterwards they lay on couches, talking and giggling, caressed by the breezes and drinking fruit juice as smiling young women gave them manicures and pedicures.

Every square inch of Gredel's skin seemed flushed with summer, with life. Back at the Volta, Caro dressed Gredel in one of her own outfits, the expensive fabrics gliding over nerve-tingling, butter-smooth flesh. When Lamey came to pick them up, Caro put Gredel's hand in Lamey's, and guided them both towards the door.

'Have a lovely night,' she said.

'Aren't you coming with us?' Lamey asked.

Caro only shook her head and laughed. Her green eyes

looked into Gredel's – Gredel saw amusement there, and secrets that Lamey would never share.

Caro steered them into the hall and closed the door behind them. Lamey paused a moment, looking back.

'Is Caro all right?' he asked.

'Oh yes,' Gredel said. 'Now let's go find a place to dance.'

She felt as if she was floating, moving across the floor so lightly that she almost danced on her way to the elevator. It occurred to her that she was happy, that happiness had never been hers before but now she had it.

All it took was getting Antony out of the picture.

The first crack in Gredel's happiness occurred two afternoons later when she arrived at the Volta late due to a blockage on the train tracks from the Fabs. Gredel let herself in, and found Caro snoring on her bed. Caro was dressed to go out, but she must have got bored waiting for Gredel to turn up, because there was an empty wine bottle on the floor and the med injector near her right hand.

Gredel called Caro, then shook her. There was no response at all. Caro was pale, her flesh cool and faintly bluish.

Another long, grating snore shredded the air. Gredel felt her heart turn over at the pure insistence of the sound. She seized the med injector and checked the contents: endorphin analogue, something called Phenyldorphin-Zed.

Caro began another snore, and then the sound simply rattled to a halt. Her breathing had stopped. Terror roared through Gredel's veins.

She had never dealt with an overdose, but there was a certain amount of oral legend on the subject that circulated through the Fabs. One of the fixes involved filling the victim's pants with ice, she remembered. Ice on the genitals was supposed to wake you right up. Or was that just for men?

Gredel straddled Caro and slapped her hard across the face.

Her own nerves leaped at the sound, but Caro gave a start, her eyelids coming partway open, and she gasped in air.

Gredel slapped her again. Caro gasped again and coughed, and her lids opened all the way. Her eyes were eerie, blank screens of green jasper, the pupils so shrunk they could barely be seen.

'What—' Caro said. 'What are you—?'

'You've got to get up.' Gredel slid off the bed and pulled Caro by the arm. 'You've got to get up and walk around with me, right?'

Caro gave a lazy laugh. 'What is— What—'

'Stand up now!'

Gredel managed to haul Caro upright. Caro found her feet with difficulty, and Gredel got Caro's arm around her shoulders and began to drag Caro over the floor. Caro laughed again. 'Music!' she snorted. 'We need music if we're going to dance!'

This struck her as so amusing that she almost doubled over with laughter, but Gredel pulled her upright and began moving her again. She got Caro into the front room and began marching in circles around the sofa.

'You're funny, Earthgirl,' Caro said. 'Funny, funny.' Laughter kept bubbling out of her throat. Gredel's shoulders ached with Caro's weight.

'Help me, Caro,' she ordered.

'Funny funny. Funny Earthgirl.'

When she couldn't hold Caro up any more, Gredel dumped her on the sofa and went to the kitchen to get the coffee maker started. Then she returned to the front room and found Caro asleep again. She slapped Caro twice, and Caro opened her eyes.

'Yes, Sergei,' she said. 'You do that. You do that all you want.'

'You've got to get up, Caro.'

'Why wouldn't you talk to me?' Caro asked. There were

tears in her eyes. Gredel pulled her to her feet and began walking with her again.

'I called him,' Caro said as they walked. 'I couldn't stand it anymore and I called him and he wouldn't talk to me. His secretary said he was out but I knew he was lying from the way he said it.'

It was three or four hours before Gredel's fear began to ebb. Caro was able to walk on her own, and her conversation was almost normal, if a little subdued. Gredel left her sitting on the sofa with a cup of coffee and went into the bedroom. She took the med injector, and two others she found in the bedroom and another in the bathroom, plus the cartridges of Phenyldorphin–Zed and every other drug cartridge she could find, and she hid them under some towels in the bathroom so that she could carry them out later, when Caro wasn't looking. She wanted to get rid of the liquor, too, but that would be too obvious. Maybe she could pour most of it down the sink when she had the chance.

'You stopped *breathing*,' Gredel told Caro later. 'You've got to stop using, Caro.'

Caro nodded over her cup of coffee. Her pupils had expanded a bit, and her eyes were almost normal-looking. 'I've been letting it get out of hand.'

'I was never so frightened in my life. You've just got to stop.'

'I'll be good,' Caro said.

Gredel was sleeping over three nights later, when Caro produced a med injector before bed and held it to her neck. Gredel reached out in sudden terror and yanked the injector away.

'Caro! You said you'd stop!'

Caro smiled, gave an apologetic laugh. 'It's all right,' she said. 'I was depressed the other day, over something that happened. I let it get out of hand. But I'm not depressed any more.' She tugged the injector against Gredel's fingers. 'Let go,' she said. 'I'll be all right.'

'Don't,' Gredel begged.

Caro laughingly detached Gredel's fingers from the injector, then held it to her neck and pressed the trigger. She laughed while Gredel felt a fist tightening on her insides.

'See?' Caro said. 'Nothing wrong here.'

Gredel talked to Lamey about it the next day. 'Just stop selling to her,' she said.

'What good would that do?' Lamey said. 'She had sources before she ever met any of us. And if she wanted, she could just go to a pharmacy and pay full price.' He took her hands and looked at her, concern in his blue eyes. 'You can't help her. Nobody can help a user when they've gone this far. You know that.'

Anxiety sang along Gredel's nerves. She didn't want Lamey's words to be true. She would just have to be very careful, and watch Caro to make sure there weren't any more accidents.

Gredel's happiness ended shortly after, on the first hot afternoon of summer. Gredel and Caro returned from the arcades tired and sweating, and Caro flung her purchases down on the sofa and announced she was going to take a long, cool bath. On her way to the bathroom Caro took a bottle of chilled wine from the kitchen, opened it, offered some to Gredel, who declined, then carried the bottle and a glass into the bathroom with her.

The sound of running water came distantly to the front room. Gredel helped herself to a papaya fizz and for lack of anything else to do turned on the video wall.

There was a drama about the Fleet, except that all the actors striving to put down the mutiny were Naxids. All their acting was in the way their beaded scales shifted colour, and Gredel didn't understand any of it. The Fleet setting reminded her of Caro's academy appointment, though, and Gredel shifted to the data channel and looked up the requirements for the

Cheng Ho academy, where the Sulas bound for the military traditionally attended.

By the time Caro came padding out in her dressing gown, Gredel was full of information. 'You'd better find a tailor, Caro,' she said. 'Look at the uniforms you've got to get made.' The video wall paged through one picture after another. 'Dress, undress,' Gredel itemized. 'Ship coveralls, planetary fatigues, formal dinner dress, parade dress – just look at that hat! And Cheng Ho's in a temperate zone, so you've got greatcoats and jackboots for winter, plus uniforms for any sport you decide to do, and a ton of other gear. Dinner settings! In case you give a formal dinner, your clan crest optional.'

Caro blinked looked at the screen as if she were having trouble focusing on it all. 'What are you talking about?' she said.

'When you go to the Cheng Ho academy. Do you know who Cheng Ho *was,* by the way? I looked it up. He—'

'Stop babbling.' Gredel looked at Caro in surprise. Caro's lips were set in a disdainful twist. 'I'm not going to any stupid academy,' she said. 'So just forget about all that, all right?'

Gredel stared at her. 'But you have to,' she said. 'It's your career, the only one you're allowed to have.'

Caro gave a little hiss of contempt. 'What do I need a career for? I'm doing fine as I am.'

It was a hot day and Gredel was tired and had not had a rest or a bath or a drink, and she blundered right through the warning signals Caro was flying, the signs that she'd not only had her bottle of wine in the bath, but taken something else as well, something that kinked and spiked her nerves and brought her temper sizzling.

'We *planned* it,' Gredel insisted. 'You're going into the Fleet, and I'll be your orderly. And we can both get off the planet and—'

'*I don't want to hear this useless crap!*' Caro screamed. Her

shriek was so loud that it stunned Gredel into silence and
set her heart beating louder than Caro's angry words. Caro
advanced on Gredel, green fury flashing from her eyes. 'You
think I'd go into the Fleet? The Fleet, just for *you*? *Who do
you think you are?*'

Caro stood over Gredel. Her arms windmilled as if they
were throwing rocks at Gredel's face. 'You drag your ass all
over this apartment!' she raged. 'You – you wear my clothes!
You're in my bank accounts all the time – *where's my money,
hey! My money!*'

'I never took your money!' Gredel gasped. 'Not a cent! I
never—'

'*Liar!*' Caro's hand lashed out, and the slap sounded louder
than a gunshot. Gredel stared at her, too overwhelmed
by surprise to raise a hand to her stinging cheek. Caro
screamed on.

'I see you everywhere – everywhere in my life! You tell
me what to do, how much to spend – I don't even have any
friends anymore! They're all *your* friends!' She reached for the
shopping bags that held their purchases and hurled them at
Gredel. Gredel warded them off, but when they bounced to
the floor Caro just picked them up and threw them again, so
finally Gredel just snatched them out of the air and let them
pile in her lap, a crumpled heap of expensive tailored fabrics
and hand-worked leather.

'Take your crap and get out of here!' Caro cried. She
grabbed one of Gredel's arms and hauled her off the sofa.
Gredel clutched the packages to her with her other arm, but
several spilled as Caro shoved her to the door. 'I never want
to see you again! Get out! Get out! *Get out!*'

The door slammed behind her. Gredel stood in the corridor with a package clutched to her breast as if it was a
child. Inside the apartment she could hear Caro throwing things.

She didn't know what to do. Her impulse was to open the

door – she knew the codes – to go into the apartment and try to calm Caro and explain herself.

I didn't take the money, she protested. *I didn't ask for anything.*

Something hit the door hard enough so that it jumped in its frame.

Not the Fleet. The thought seemed to steal the strength from her limbs. Her head spun. *I have to stay here now. On Spannan, in the Fabs. I have to . . .*

What about tomorrow? a part of her whined. She and Caro had made plans to go to a new boutique in the morning. Were they going or not?

The absurdity of the question struck home and sudden rage possessed her, rage at her own imbecility. She should have known better than to press Caro on the question, not when she was in this mood.

She went to her mother's apartment and put the packages away. Ava wasn't home. Anger and despair battled in her mind. She called Lamey and let him send someone to pick her up, then let him divert her for the rest of the evening.

In the morning she went to the Volta at the time she had planned with Caro. There was a traffic jam in the lobby – a family was moving into the building, and their belongings were piled onto several motorized carts, each with the Volta's gilt blazon. Gredel greeted the doorman in her Peer voice, and he called her 'Lady Sula' and put her alone into the next elevator.

She hesitated at the door to Caro's apartment. She knew she was grovelling, and knew as well that she didn't deserve to grovel.

But this was her only hope. What choice did she have?

She knocked, and when there wasn't an answer she knocked again. She heard a shuffling step inside and then Caro opened the door and blinked at her groggily through disordered strands of hair. She was dressed as Gredel had last seen her, bare feet, naked under her dressing gown.

'Why didn't you just come in?' Caro said. She left the door open and withdrew into the apartment. Gredel followed, her heart pulsing sickly in her chest.

There was litter inside the door. Broken bottles, pillows, packages, and the shattered remains of porcelain cups, the cups with the Sula family crescents on them.

There were more bottles lying on tables, and Gredel recognized the juniper reek that oozed from Caro's pores. 'I feel awful,' Caro said. 'I had too much last night.'

Doesn't she remember? Gredel wondered. Or is she just pretending?

Caro reached for the gin bottle and the neck of the bottle clattered against a tumbler as she poured herself two fingers' worth. 'Let me get myself together,' Caro said, and drank.

A thought struck Gredel with the force of revelation. *She's just a drunk,* she thought. *Just another damn drunk.*

Caro put the tumbler down, wiped her mouth, gave a hoarse laugh. 'Now we can have some fun,' she said.

'Yes,' Gredel said. 'Let's go.'

She had begun to think it might never be fun again.

Perhaps it was then that Gredel began to hate Caro, or perhaps the incident only released hatred and resentment that had lain, denied, for some time. But now Gredel could scarcely spend an hour with Caro without finding new fuel for anger. Caro's carelessness made Gredel clench her teeth, and her laughter grated on Gredel's nerves. The empty days that Caro shared with Gredel, the pointless drifting from boutique to restaurant to club, now made Gredel want to shriek. Gredel deeply resented her tidying up after Caro even as she did it. Caro's surging moods, the sudden shifts from laughter to fury to sullen withdrawal, brought Gredel's own temper near breaking point. Even Caro's affection and her impulsive generosity began to seem trying. *Why is she making all this fuss over me?* Gredel thought. *What's she after?*

But Gredel managed to keep her thoughts to herself, and at times she caught herself enjoying Caro's company, caught herself in a moment of pure enjoyment or unfeigned laughter. And then she wondered how this could be genuine as well as the other, the delight and the hatred coexisting in her skull.

It was like her so-called beauty, she thought. Her alleged beauty was what most people reacted to; but it wasn't her *self*. She managed to have an inner existence, thoughts and hopes entirely her own, apart from the shell that was her appearance. But it was the shell that people saw, it was the shell that most people spoke to, hated, envied or desired. The Gredel that interacted with Caro was another kind of shell, a kind of machine she'd built for the purpose, built without intending to. It wasn't any less genuine for being a machine, but it wasn't her *self*.

Her *self* hated Caro. She knew that now.

If Caro detected any of Gredel's inner turmoil, she gave no sign. In any case she was rarely in a condition to be very observant. Her alcohol consumption had increased as she shifted from wine to hard liquor. When she wanted to get drunk, she wanted the drunk *instantly,* the way she wanted everything, and hard liquor got her there quicker. The ups and downs increased as well, and the spikes and valleys that were her behaviour. She was banned from one of her expensive restaurants for talking loudly, and singing, and throwing a plate at the waiter who asked her to be more quiet. She was thrown out of a club for attacking a woman in the ladies' room. Gredel never found out what the fight was about, but for days afterwards Caro proudly sported the black eye she'd got from the bouncer's fist.

For the most part Gredel managed to avoid Caro's anger. She learned the warning signs, and she'd also learned how to manipulate Caro's moods. She could change Caro's music, or at least shift the focus of Caro's growing anger from herself to someone else.

Despite her feelings she was now in Caro's company more than ever. Lamey was in hiding. She had first found out about this when he sent Panda to pick her up at Caro's apartment instead of coming himself. Panda drove her to the Fabs, but not to a human neighbourhood: instead he took her into a building inhabited by Lai-owns. A family of the giant birds stared at her as she waited in the lobby for the elevator. There was an acrid, ammonia smell in the air.

Lamey was in a small apartment on the top floor, with a pair of his guards and a Lai-own. The avian shifted from one foot to the other as Gredel entered. Lamey seemed nervous. He didn't say anything to Gredel, just gave a quick jerk of his chin to indicate that they should go into the back room.

The room was thick with the heat of summer. The ammonia smell was very strong. Lamey steered Gredel to the bed. She sat, but Lamey was unable to be still: he paced back and forth in the narrow range permitted by the small room. His smooth, elegant walk had developed hitches and stutters, uncertainties that marred his usual grace.

'I'm sorry about this,' he said. 'But something's happened.'

'Is the Patrol looking for you?'

'I don't know.' His mouth gave a little twitch. 'Bourdelle was arrested yesterday. It was the Legion of Diligence who arrested him, not the Patrol, so that means they've got him for something serious, something he could be executed for. We've got word that he's bargaining with the prefect's office.' His mouth twitched again. Linkboys did not bargain with the prefect, they were expected to go to their punishment with their mouths shut.

'We don't know what he's going to offer them,' Lamey went on. 'But he's just a link up from me, and he could be selling me or any of the boys.' He paused in his pacing, rubbed his chin. Sweat shone on his forehead. 'I'm going to make sure it's not me,' he said.

'I understand,' Gredel said.

Lamey looked at her. His blue eyes were feverish. 'From now on, you can't call me. I can't call you. We can't be seen in public together. If I want you, I'll send someone for you at Caro's.'

Gredel looked up at him. 'But—' she began, then, 'When?'

'When . . . I . . . want . . . you,' he said insistently. 'I don't know when. You'll just have to be there when I need you.'

'Yes,' Gredel said. Her mind whirled. 'I'll be there.'

He sat next to her on the bed and took her by the shoulders. 'I missed you, Earthgirl,' he said. 'I really need you now.'

She kissed him. His skin felt feverish. She could taste the fear on him. Lamey's unsteady fingers began to fumble with the buttons of her blouse. *You're going to die soon,* she thought.

Unless of course it was Gredel who paid the penalty instead, the way Ava had paid for the sins of her man.

Gredel had to start looking out for herself, before it was too late.

When Gredel left Lamey, he gave her two hundred zeniths in cash. 'I can't buy you things right now, Earthgirl,' he explained. 'But buy yourself something nice for me, all right?

Gredel remembered Antony's claim that she whored for money. It was no longer an accusation she could deny.

One of Lamey's boys drove Gredel from the rendezvous to her mother's building. Gredel took the stairs instead of the elevator because it gave her time to think. By the time she got to her mother's door, she had the beginnings of an idea.

But first she had to tell her mother about Lamey, and why she had to move in with Caro. 'Of course, honey,' Ava said.

She took Gredel's hands and pressed them. 'Of course you've got to go.'

Loyalty to her man was what Ava knew, Gredel thought. She had been arrested and sentenced to years in the country for a man she'd hardly ever seen again. She'd spent her life sitting alone and waiting for one man or another to show up. She was beautiful, but in the bright summer light Gredel could see the first cracks in her mother's facade, the faint lines at the corners of her eyes and mouth that the years would only broaden. When the beauty faded, the men would fade, too.

Ava had cast her lot with beauty and with men, neither of which were reliable in the long term. If Gredel remained with Lamey, or with some other linkboy, she would be following Ava's path.

The next morning Gredel took a pair of bags to Caro's place and let herself in. Caro was asleep, so far gone in torpor that she didn't wake when Gredel padded into the bedroom and took her wallet with its identification. Gredel slipped out again and went to a bank, where she opened an account in the name of Caroline, Lady Sula, and deposited three-quarters of what Lamey had given her.

When asked for a thumbprint, she gave her own.

Seven

'My lord?' said Cadet Seisho. 'I'm looking at a transmission and Recruit Levoisier says something about the captain that I'm not sure about . . .'

Martinez glanced at his sleeve display, which showed the cadet's smooth-cheeked face.

'Does she say that she's going to kill the captain, maim him, assault him, or disobey the captain's orders?' Martinez asked.

Seisho blinked. 'No, my lord. It's . . . more personal than that.'

More personal? Martinez wondered. Then decided it was better not to know . . .

'If it's not assault, death, disobedience, or sabotage, it's not treason,' he said. 'Pass it.'

Seisho nodded. 'Very good, my lord.'

'Anything else?'

'No, my lord.'

'Then goodbye.'

The sleeve returned to its normal mourning pallor. Martinez turned back to his own work – or rather Koslowski's. The senior lieutenant was off with the team practising, and Martinez was standing Koslowski's watch as well as his own.

Pulling together with the team involved more than just standing watches. Martinez had been put on a hellish number of boards and other collateral duty assignments. He was the Library and Entertainment Officer, the Military Constable

Officer, and the Cryptography Security Officer – at least cryptography was more in his line. He was on the Wardroom Advisory Board and the Enlisted Mess Advisory Board. He audited the accounts for the officers' and general mess, which called for accounting skills that he didn't possess. He was on the Hull Board and the Weapons Safety Board, as well as the Cadet Examination Board, the Enlisted Examining Board, and the Cryptography Board.

He was on the Relief Board, intended to help people in distress, which meant that enlisted personnel were constantly hounding him with their hard-luck stories in hopes of getting money.

And lastly he was also officer in charge of censoring the ship's mail, a job he was happy to shovel off onto Seisho and a couple of other cadets.

In fact the cadets and some of the more reliable warrant officers were getting as much of his work as he could safely unload, though anything involving equipment or funds was kept in his own hands.

At the moment he was puzzling over wardroom funds. The three lieutenants were required to contribute sums to their mess, intended for the most part to be spent on liquor and delicacies, though some money vanished as under-the-table payoffs to maintain the style of the wardroom steward, in civilian life a professional chef, and large sums seemed to be employed for the purposes of gambling on football games. Since *Corona* had a successful season, and most of the bets were winners, this didn't seem to be a problem.

What disturbed Martinez most was inventory. The wardroom mess had paid for a good many items that were no longer in stock. It was possible that enlisted personnel were somehow pilfering, though it seemed unlikely given that wardroom supplies were kept separately under lock and key. It was likewise possible that the wardroom steward, who had a key, was skimming. But since most of the items seemed to have vanished since *Corona* had been docked at Magaria's ring station, Martinez suspected that it was the officers themselves who were taking the stuff away, perhaps to give as presents to women friends in Magaria's ring station or skyhook towns.

But in that case, why didn't the officers simply sign for the items? They'd paid for them, after all.

Martinez had verified with his own eyes that the items had existed. He had signed for them. And now they were gone.

He drummed his fingers on the edge of the display. This might be another good moment to schedule a talk with Alikhan.

His left cuff button chirped again, and Martinez, assuming another query from Seisho, glared as he told the display to answer the call.

'Martinez. What is it?'

The face that appeared on his sleeve answered his glare with an apologetic look. 'This is Dietrich at the airlock, my lord. The military constables are here with three of our liberty people.'

Dietrich was one of the two guards on duty at the port to the ring station. 'Are they drunk?' Martinez asked.

Dietrich's eyes cut away, outside the frame of the camera, then back to Martinez. 'Not at the moment, my lord.'

Martinez restrained the impulse to sigh. 'I'll be there in a minute and sign for them.'

Such were the joys of the designated Military Constabulary Officer.

He put the wardroom accounts back in their sealed password file and rose from his chair. *Corona* was moored nose-on to the ring station, which meant the forward airlock was 'up' from Command, where Martinez was standing watch. In dock, a continuous belt elevator – essentially a mobile stepladder – was rigged in a central tunnel, and Martinez stepped onto this for the ride to *Corona*'s forward airlock.

Rigger/1st Dietrich was waiting just inside the airlock, his sidearm, stun baton, and handcuffs on his wide scarlet waist belt, and the red elastic military constabulary band on his arm. 'Zhou, Ahmet, and Knadjian drunk and disorderly. Busted up a bar in the course of getting themselves thrashed by a gang from the *Storm Fury*.'

Zhou, Ahmet, and Knadjian. Martinez hadn't been on the ship long, but he already knew better than to feel sympathy for these three.

After Martinez went up the long umbilical to the station he found the three handcuffed recruits with their torn clothing, blackened eyes, and cut lips. Knadjian seemed to have had a fistful of hair torn from his scalp. After *Storm Fury*'s recruits finished with them, the Naxid constables who had broken up the fight had probably got in a few licks as well. The miscreants had spent the night in the local lockup and they smelled about as good as they looked.

The Fleet's enlisted personnel were known with varying degrees of affection as hardshells, holejumpers, or – from the hard gees they pulled – crouchbacks, pulpies, or pancakes. Whatever they were called, they tended to fall into certain well-defined areas on the military spectrum. Zhou, Ahmet, and Knadjian were in the part of the spectrum that involved brawls, floating dice games, drunkenness, the plunder of military supplies, and intrigues with women of low character. If their roles hadn't been so well-defined and traditional, Martinez would probably have been more annoyed at the three. Instead he was aloof and amused.

Martinez read the charges given him by the constable/1st, who stood braced as far back as a Naxid could rear. Martinez signed the charge sheet, presented in electronic form on the constable's overlarge datapad, and then the other document accepting custody of the prisoners, and as he did so he sensed the Naxids twitching at the presence of something behind him. He turned.

Squadron Commander Kulukraf, Fanaghee's flag captain,

was marching along the ring with a pack of twenty or so of his officers. Martinez figured that the Naxid MCs were twitching to restrain the impulse to grovel in the face of someone so senior.

Martinez sent electronic copies of the documents to his station on *Corona,* then handed the datapad back to the constable. 'You can take off their handcuffs, Constable,' he said.

'Very good, my lord.'

The crouchbacks, released from restraint, rubbed their wrists and eyed the MCs sidelong, as if tempted by the idea of clouting them now their fists were free. Martinez decided to cut this dangerous thought off with some ideas of his own.

'You have twenty minutes to shower, clean up, and present yourselves to Rigger Chaves for fatigues. The captain will hear your wretched excuses and award punishment in the morning. Get moving.'

The recruits moved. Martinez smiled and considered which toilets needed cleaning and which brassware the most needed polishing. *All,* he decided.

He turned back to the head constable. 'Thank you, Constable. You may—'

He noticed that the constable was braced at the salute facing into the ring, and the other constables with him. Martinez whipped around and braced.

Squadron Commander Kulukraf had moved closer, and was pointing at *Corona*'s hatch with one dark-scaled hand. The Naxid officers looked from Kulukraf to *Corona,* then to their sleeve displays and back to Kulukraf again. Red patterns on their chests flashed complex patterns at one another, the chameleon-weave jackets transmitting the colour shifts of the beaded scales beneath. None of them spoke.

Kulukraf ignored Martinez and the others braced at the docking tube, then made his way onwards, fast-moving feet beating at the rubberized surface of the ring station's main thoroughfare. Martinez watched him go, then relaxed.

'Thank you, constable,' he repeated. 'You may go.'

'Very good, my lord.' The constables braced briefly, turned, and thrashed deck after Kulukraf.

Curious, Martinez looked after Kulukraf. The Naxid squadcom and his officers had stopped at the next docking tube on the station, that of the light cruiser *Perigee,* and were going through the same routine, pausing and staring and making notes.

'The squadcom was here yesterday with a different bunch,' Dietrich volunteered.

'Was he?' Martinez looked at him. 'Do you know what he's up to?'

'No idea, lord lieutenant. They just flashed at each other, like today.'

Martinez wondered if there was some kind of big surprise inspection scheduled. But only a total swine of a fleetcom would schedule an inspection two days before the Festival of Sport.

Right. And Fanaghee wasn't exactly known for dripping sweet compassion over her subordinates, was she?

Martinez decided he'd better have a quiet word with the warrant officers who ran each of the ship's departments. And, while he was at it, make sure his own communications rigs, both the primary and auxiliary, were immaculate, and his subordinates at their most presentable.

'May I speak with you privately?'

Lord Richard Li was the only person at the reception besides Sula who was wearing dress mourning whites, and Sula only wore her uniform because she didn't have anything elegant or expensive enough for this company. Lord Richard, she presumed, had some other reason.

'Privately?' Sula looked at him in surprise. 'Yes, of course.'

It was Terza Chen, Lord Richard's fiancée, who had invited her to this function at the ornate Chen Palace, but

Terza had glided off in her elegant way, and left Sula with the Lord Richard.

Lord Richard took Sula's arm and led her to a library off the front hall, dark wood carved with a pattern of holly, and ancient leather-bound books sealed behind glass, their delicate contents preserved by a mixture of rare gasses. The very sight made Sula want to lunge for the cabinets, pop the seals, and indulge in an orgy of reading.

On the desk was a small fountain, water trickling over small stones, that gave the air a slight scent of brine. Lord Richard gazed at the fountain for a moment, then turned to face Sula.

'Lord Richard?'

'I heard about the *Midnight Runner* verdict,' he said. A Fleet Court of Inquiry had just proclaimed Blitsharts' death an accident, the result of a faulty water intake coupling.

'Unfortunately it's only the *first Midnight Runner* verdict,' Sula said. 'There's going to be a lawsuit before the insurance company will part with any money. They're going to say that Blitsharts damaged the coupling intentionally. So I'll be stuck here giving depositions for years, unless I can get ship duty.'

A smile crossed Lord Richard's chiselled features. 'Well, as to that,' he said, 'I've just returned from the Commandery. That's why I'm in uniform. The announcement won't be made for a few days, but I've been informed that I'll have command of the *Dauntless* when it comes out of refit. We'll be joining the Second Cruiser Division, Home Fleet.'

'Congratulations, my lord.' *Dauntless* was a new heavy cruiser that was finishing its first refit, with everything that hadn't worked properly on its first tour repaired, replaced, or redesigned. It was a perfect command for this stage of Lord Richard's career, and spoke well of Fleet Commander Jarlath's confidence in him.

'I know you'll do well,' Sula said.

'Thank you.' Lord Richard inclined his head as he looked at Sula. Behind him, the little fountain chimed.

'You know,' he said, 'that I get to promote two lieutenants into *Dauntless* when I get command of her. In view of your family's kindness to mine over many years, I wish to offer you one of those places.'

Sula's heart gave a surprised little skip. A captain's promotions were usually *quid pro quo* arrangements within or between families – 'I'll promote your youngster, and you'll see my cousin gets the supply contract for the satellite relays on Sandama.' But Sula didn't have anything to offer in exchange – this was pure kindness on Lord Richard's part.

Sula found herself flushing with the effort to compose her thanks. Composing thanks wasn't one of the things she did well.

'Thank you, Lord Richard,' she said. 'I— I appreciate your – your confidence.'

He smiled with his perfect white teeth. Sula observed that there were little crinkles around his eyes when he smiled. 'We'll consider it done, then,' Lord Richard said.

'Ah – my lord.' She felt herself flush. 'You know that I've been cramming for my exams.'

'Yes. Well, now that won't be necessary. You can enjoy yourself.' Lord Richard began to step towards the exit across the deep pile of the Tupa carpeting.

'I was going for a first, my lord,' Sula said. Lord Richard hesitated in mid-stride.

'Really?' he said.

'Ah – yes.' Her cheeks must be pouring out nova heat, she thought.

'Do you think you have a chance?'

There, Sula reflected, was the key question. The cadet who achieved a first – the highest score of all lieutenants' exams given throughout the empire during a year – was almost certain to acquire a name in the service, and very possibly some patrons to go with it. She wouldn't be dependent entirely on Lord Richard for promotion: with a first, many more doors would open to her.

'I've been working the practice exams and doing very well,' Sula said. 'Though of course a first is – ah – well, it's unpredictable.'

'Yes.' He knitted his brows. 'Well, the exams are in a mere ten days or so, correct?'

'Yes, my lord.'

He gave a modest shrug. 'My offer will remain open, then. I won't need a lieutenant in the next ten days, and if I get someone who was first in the Year 12,481 then *Dauntless* will only gain by the prestige.'

'I— Thank you, my lord.' Gratitude still had her tripping over her tongue.

Lord Richard took her arm again and steered her for the door. 'Good luck with all that, Caro – Caroline. I was never very good at exams – that's why I was happy to take my uncle Otis' offer of a lieutenancy.'

Sula paused in surprised contemplation at the thought of a Lord Richard who wasn't good at something, then dismissed the thought as modesty on the captain's part.

Sula and Lord Richard rejoined the reception, Lord and Lady Chen and their twenty-two guests. Terza floated towards them, looked at Sula, and said, 'Is it decided?'

'Lord Richard has been very kind,' Sula said.

'I'm so pleased,' Terza said, and clasped Sula's hand.

Suddenly Sula knew that the offer of promotion had been Lady Terza's idea.

'He'll be able to set you on your career,' Lady Terza said.

'Well, turns out it's a little more complicated than that,' Lord Richard said, 'but Lady Sula will be set on her career one way or another, and very soon.'

Terza hesitated, then decided to smile. 'Well,' she said, 'that's very good.'

Sula's nerves gave a warning tingle as Lady Vipsania Martinez walked into sight on the arm of a exquisitely dressed man with a receding hairline. Lady Vipsania's eyes widened slightly as her eyes crossed with Sula's, and then she strode towards Sula with impressive dignity, the man following in her wake.

'Lady Sula,' she said, 'I'm sure you remember Sempronia's fiancé, Lord PJ Ngeni.'

Sula didn't remember Lord PJ at all, but she said, 'Of course. Is Sempronia here?'

Melancholy touched PJ's long face. 'She's over there.' He nodded towards a corner of the room. 'With those officers.'

Sula turned to see Sempronia speaking to a pair of men in civilian suits. 'They're officers?' she asked. She didn't recognize them.

'They're *always* officers,' PJ said, the melancholy only growing.

'Go and fetch her, my dear,' Vipsania advised. 'I'm sure she'd like to speak to Lady Sula.'

'That's a lovely gown,' Sula said. It was, too. Some elderly seamstress had probably grown blind sewing on all those thousands of beads.

'Thank you.' A look of modest concern crossed Vipsania's brows. 'We've been sorry you haven't been able to attend our little get-togethers.'

'I left town,' Sula said. 'I was cramming for my exams.'

'Ah.' She nodded in apparent satisfaction. 'It hadn't anything to do with my brother, then.'

Sula's heart gave a jolt. 'Lord Gareth?'

'He thought he might have offended you in some way. He can be a dreadful idiot some times.'

'Dreadful idiot?' queried Sempronia as she arrived with PJ. 'We're talking about Gareth, I presume?'

Sula decided to set the record straight. Or straighter,

anyway. 'He hasn't offended,' Sula said flatly. 'And he's quite the opposite of an idiot.'

Sempronia narrowed her hazel eyes. 'I hate him,' she said. 'I refuse to hear a word said on his behalf.' She smiled as she said it, but those narrowed eyes weren't smiling.

Lord Richard seemed both amused and a little discomfited to find himself in the midst of this family drama. 'What do you have against my brother officer?' he said finally.

Sempronia gave PJ a flicker of a glance. 'That's between me and Gareth,' she said.

'Sometimes I feel as if I'm marrying into a pack of tigers,' PJ said. 'I'm going to have to watch myself night and day.'

Sempronia patted his arm. 'Retain that thought, my dear,' she said, 'and we'll get along fine.'

PJ adjusted the line of a lapel, then gave his collar a tweak, as if suddenly finding himself a little warm.

'Lady Sula,' Terza said in her soft voice, 'Richard tells me that you're interested in porcelain. Would you like to see some of our collection?'

'I'd love it,' Sula said, happy for Terza's tactful shift of subject. 'And I wonder,' she ventured, 'if I might glance at some of the books as well.'

Terza was mildly surprised. 'Oh. Those. Certainly. Why not?'

'Do you have any books,' Sula asked, 'that come from old Terra?'

'Yes. But they're in languages that no one reads any more.'

Sula gave a contented smile. 'I'll be very happy just to look at the pictures,' she said.

The case of the missing wardroom supplies was solved when Martinez went into the wardroom that evening for a cup of coffee and found Lieutenant-Captain Tarafah rummaging through the steel-lined food locker. Tarafah had just returned with the team after a day's practice, and he was placing a couple of smoked cheeses in the hamper carried by his orderly. Martinez observed that the hamper already contained three bottles of wine and two bottles of excellent brandy.

'My lord?' Martinez asked. 'May I help you?'

Tarafah looked over his shoulder at Martinez, then nodded. 'You may, lord lieutenant Martinez.' He reached into the locker and withdrew two bottles of aged cashment. 'Do you prefer the pickled or the kind soaked in vermouth?'

'The pickled, my lord.' Martinez hated the stuff and would be glad to see the last of it.

The pickled cashment went into the hamper, followed by some canned butter biscuits, purple-black caviar from Cendis, and a wedge of blue cheese. 'That should do it,' Tarafah said with satisfaction, then closed the heavy doors and locked them with his captain's key.

The captain's key opened the wardroom store and spirit locker, Martinez noted. Interesting.

The smoky odour of the cheeses floated up from the hamper, which sat on the narrow cherrywood table built to serve *Corona*'s three lieutenants and one or two of their guests. Martinez called up the inventory, and jotted the captain's acquisitions onto the wardroom screen.

'My lord?' he said. 'Would you sign for the stores?'

'I can't sign. I'm not a member of the wardroom mess.'

Which was perfectly true. Martinez reflected that the captain certainly had the facts at his fingertips.

Time, he thought, for the query discreet

'Are the captain's stores running low, my lord?'

'No.' Offhand, as he tucked his key away into his tunic. 'I'm contributing as well.'

'Contributing, lord elcap?'

Tarafah looked at him with impatience. 'To our series of feasts for the *Steadfast*'s officers. They're providing the officials and referees for the game, and it's necessary to keep on their good side.'

'Ah. I see.'

'The chief referee is being very sensible about the offside rule. We need to keep him sweet.' Tarafah shouldered his way past Martinez and into the corridor that led to his own cabin. 'Koslowski, Garcia, and I won't be back till late. You're on watch tonight, right?'

'Ah – no, my lord.' But Tarafah was gone, followed by his orderly, before Martinez could explain that he'd just got off his double watch, and that the watch tonight would be kept by *Corona*'s master weaponer, who would be drinking himself into unconsciousness in Command while Cadet Vonderheydte performed all necessary watchkeeping tasks from an auxiliary station he'd set up forward, near the umbilical.

But Tarafah wasn't very interested in these arrangements, anyway.

Martinez watched the broad-shouldered back of the captain recede, and then returned to the wardroom and signed out all missing stores as a 'contribution to captain's personal charity'. Then he signed out a can of caviar – the last – a tin of macaroons, another of crackers, a bottle of smoked red peppers, a duck preserved in its own fat, a brace of cheeses, a couple of bottles of wine, and a bottle of brandy, from which he made a splendid cold meal, the remainder of which he stowed in his own cabin.

If he was going to be paying for someone else's feast, the least he could do was have one of his own.

The exam proctor was a Daimong and scented the room with the faint putrescence of her perpetually-dying, perpetually-renewed flesh. Strips of dry, light-grey skin, weightless as the empty husks of insects, hung from the Daimong's cuffs and long, long chin, and her round, deepset black eyes gazed at the assembled cadets with the fixed Daimong combination of melancholy and alarm.

'Electronic devices must now be turned off,' she said in her chiming voice. 'Any electronic devices will be detected and the user marked down as a cheat.'

It would have been hard to smuggle electronic devices into the examination room in any case. The cadets – all in this room were Terran – all wore their black examination robes, silk with viridian stripes for Peers, synthetics without markings for commoners. They had been made to change into these just moments ago, and their clothing was being held for them till the end of the day. The rest of the costume consisted of felt slippers and a soft, floppy round hat, the Peers' version of which had a green pompon.

Sula supposed she might have smuggled some electronics in her underwear, but how she would read them past the densely-woven black silk was beyond her imagination.

The Daimong checked the telltales on her electronic scanners. Apparently the result was satisfactory, because the next command was, 'Activate your desks.'

Sula did so. The exams existed only in electronic form, and had been loaded into the desks only moments before by the proctor herself. Though the computers in the desks could be used to help solve problems, there was no information in their memories that could give the cadets any help beyond doing the numbers.

The first exam was mathematics – a snap, Sula reckoned. Then astrophysics, with an emphasis on wormhole dynamics, followed by theoretical and practical navigation, which was maths and astrophysics combined. All things Sula prided herself as being good at.

The next day's exams included history, military law, and engineering, all subjects in which Sula felt confidence. The third, final day featured tactical problems and the only exam for which Sula felt trepidation, 'The Praxis: Theory, History, and Practice'. It was, as the old joke had it, the only exam where too many wrong answers could earn you the death penalty. Even though the Praxis was supposed to be eternal and unvarying, in practice the ground of interpretation tended to shift uneasily over time, and Sula had saved studying Praxis theory till last in hopes her answers would reflect the current official line.

'You may toggle on the first question,' the Daimong said. 'You have two hours and twenty-six minutes to complete the series.'

Sula toggled, and the first question appeared:

Under what circumstances does the identity
$$f(x) = f(x_1) + (x-x_1) [x_1 \, x_2] + (x-x_1)(x-x_2) [x_1 \, x_2 \, x_3]$$
$$+ (x-x_1)(x-x_2)(x-x_3) [x_1 \, x_2 \, x_3 \, x_4] + R_4(x)$$
give the following:
$$f(x_1) + (x-x_1) [x_1 \, x_2] + (x-x_1)(x-x_2) [x_1 \, x_2 \, x_3] +$$
$$(x-x_1)(x-x_2)(x-x_3) [x_1 \, x_2 \, x_3 \, x_4]$$

The answer was obvious: when $x = x_1, \, x_2, \, x_3$, etc. and $R_4(x)$ vanishes. She gave this as her answer.

Then she read the question over again just to make sure there wasn't something hidden in it.

Are they all going to be this *easy?* she wondered.

During the next afternoon watch in Command, Martinez made certain one of the displays set to reveal images sent from the exterior security camera placed outside the airlock was working properly. If the high command had a surprise inspection scheduled for his watch, Martinez wanted to see it coming.

He had done his best to prepare. He'd told the first lieutenant, Koslowski, of his suspicions, and Alikhan had alerted the senior warrant and petty officers; and as a result *Corona*'s crew – at least those who weren't involved in football – had joined Zhou, Ahmet, and Knadjian in furiously applying scrub brushes, polish, or lemon wax to every surface in sight.

Even the missiles in the tubes had been hand-buffed, and any scrapes from the automatic loaders to their special lawn-green paint had been repaired.

And now, Martinez saw, a party of Naxids was on its way, their scurrying, pounding feet driving them at their usual rocketing pace along the broad rubberized passage along the outside of the ring station. The party came to a lurching stop at the airlock of the *Steadfast,* the cruiser docked off *Corona*'s spinward flank. Through the display, Martinez could see their chameleon-weave jackets flashing as they looked at *Steadfast*'s airlock and at their sleeve displays.

He couldn't imagine what they were doing. They certainly weren't inspecting anything.

Martinez reached for the joystick that controlled the security camera and zoomed toward the Naxid party.

Kulukraf wasn't in charge of this group, he saw: instead there was a senior captain, a half-dozen lieutenants, and – strangely – twice that number of warrant officers. They were going through the same routine Martinez had seen yesterday – pointing, conferring, flashing. Whatever they were up to, Martinez saw, it required senior specialists. He was about to zoom in closer in order to distinguish the speciality patches on the warrant officers' uniforms when the group moved, their scrabbling feet throwing their long bodies out of the camera frame.

Martinez panned the camera after them and found them halted about fifteen paces in front of *Corona*'s airlock. Their chameleon-weave jackets were already flashing red patterns, and frustration gnawed at Martinez at his inability to read what the Naxids were saying.

And then he remembered that a rather imperfect Fleet translation program existed for the Naxid pattern language, and that it was probably installed on *Corona*'s computers. Martinez triggered the *record* button, figuring he'd try to read the conversation later, and then zoomed in closely enough so that he could see the sleeve badges on the group of warrant officers that hovered respectfully behind their seniors.

Weaponer patches, he saw. Engineers. And military constabulary, though without the usual red belts and armbands they wore on duty.

Why those three? Martinez supposed that weaponers and engineers might assist with inspections of weapons bays and engine rooms, but he'd never known them to be a part of any such inspection. And in any case, why were the constabulary in the mix?

The Naxids swept on to the *Perigee* in the downspin berth and went through the same routine. Martinez kept the camera on them, kept recording the red patterned flashes. And then he wondered, *What* else *are the Naxids doing?*

He could access most of the military station's security cameras from his own station, and he began throwing them up on other displays.

Other Naxid patrols were moving along the ring, demonstrating the same sort of behaviour they'd shown along *Corona*'s stretch of dockyard. The Terran light squadron had its own set of visitors, and the heavy division crewed by Daimong.

There was no unusual activity near the berths occupied by the two Naxid divisions. The only dockyards visited by the Naxids were those occupied by the three non-Naxid divisions, those labelled 'Mutineers' during the recent exercises.

Weaponers, he thought. Engineers. And the constabulary.

If you were to take a ship by boarding, he thought, the first thing you'd want to secure would be the missiles with their lethal antimatter warheads, and you'd need weaponers for that. Engineers would be required to secure the engines, which used dangerous antimatter as fuel and whose blazing torch could itself be used as a weapon. Officers would be needed in Command and Auxiliary Command. And armed military cops would make the whole job all that much easier.

A warning bell began to chime in Martinez' thoughts. He zoomed the security cameras in on the Naxid parties and began to record the feed.

And then he started to dig through menus for the program that would translate the Naxid flash patterns.

What he discovered was that the bead patterns didn't translate very well. The patterns had evolved in order to help packs of Naxids chase down prey on the dry veldt of their home continent, and they tended to be idiomatic and strongly dependent on context. There were, for instance, about twenty-five ways to flash 'yes', depending on the situation and who was being addressed, and the patterns could mean anything from a simple affirmative to 'this unworthy one is staggered by the percipience of your excellency's reasoning.'

There was a rigid pattern of symbols, with unambiguous meanings, that were to be used in military situations where absolute clarity was required, but the Naxids weren't using these. They seemed to be having the equivalent of an informal, slangy conversation, which Martinez thought was suspicious considering there were officers and enlisted both. The Naxids were instinctively submissive to pack leaders, who in turn behaved with a highly formalized arrogance to underlings: he couldn't imagine the Naxid superiors using this kind of informal language to their subordinates.

The only reason Martinez could think of for the idiomatic quality of the flash-dialogue was that the Naxids were striving to make their silent conversation as incomprehensible as possible to outsiders.

Nevertheless some of it translated. Repeated more than

once was a pattern that meant either *distant coordinates, dusty ground,* or *target* – Martinez was betting *target.* Other patterns were less ambiguous: *Move swiftly. Make secure. Swarm,* which the program explained was a hunting tactic designed to bring down a large prey animal. There were a number of patterns along the lines of *Your lordship shall be obeyed without question,* and *This unworthy one marvels at the dimensions of your* – of something which was either *hindquarters,* or *gemel tree,* neither of which seemed suitable to the occasion.

There were other references to *cold ocean* and *divan chamber,* phrases which were sufficiently idiomatic that the translation program declined to attempt to assign them meaning. The program declined even to guess at the rest.

Martinez followed the Naxid parties with the security cameras until their mission was completed. The enlisted returned to their individual ships, but the officers went to *The Majesty of the Praxis,* Fleet Commander Fanaghee's flagship, presumably to report.

Martinez thought for a long, sombre moment as he stared at the multiple displays, then saved all the recordings and the translations into his personal file. He wiped the screens, thought for another moment, and then triggered his sleeve display.

'Contact Alikhan,' he said.

Alikhan answered the call within a few seconds. 'My lord.'

'Meet me in Auxiliary Command at once.'

Alikhan betrayed no hint of surprise at this unusual order. 'Very good, my lord.'

Martinez rose from his seat and glanced around Command. Cadet Vonderheydte was at the position that monitored ship's systems, bent over a display and probably censoring mail. Signaler/2nd Blanchard, in Martinez' own division, day-dreamed over the communications board. Otherwise Command was empty.

'Vonderheydte,' Martinez said.

The small, yellow-haired cadet shook himself and straightened at his station. 'Lord lieutenant.'

'The watch is yours till I return.'

'The watch is mine, my lord.'

Martinez pushed his displays up until they clicked into place and stepped out of the locked Command cage. He made his way to the exit and then hesitated – Vonderheydte had kept watches before, but usually Koslowski or Martinez had backed him up with an experienced warrant officer.

'Vonderheydte,' Martinez said.

'My lord?'

'Contact me in Auxiliary Command in the case of anything unusual or important. Particularly if anyone requests permission to come aboard.'

The cadet blinked in surprise. 'Very good, my lord.'

Martinez went down the central belt elevator to Auxiliary Command, the armoured battle station aft intended for use if Command was destroyed by an enemy or was in the hands of mutineers. He paused outside the hatch, then stepped a little to one side to check the six long, low rooms referred to officially as 'biological recreation chambers'. None of the crew were having a romp at present, not surprising considering that such of the crew as remained on *Corona* were employed in polishing everything to a golden gleam, something guaranteed to make Martinez beloved among the pulpies if they ever found it was his idea.

Martinez waited for Alikhan's arrival, then opened Auxiliary Command with his lieutenant's key. The armoured door rolled shut behind them as the lights automatically came on.

Auxiliary Command was smaller than Command, the stations more cramped and the gimballed chairs placed closer together. Nevertheless the metal cages gleamed, and the scent of polish wafted on the breeze: the place had been carefully sleekened and burnished just that morning.

'I'd like your opinion, Alikhan,' Martinez said as he squeezed between two of the cages to sit in one of the couches at the communications station. 'Sit on my right here, watch some video, and tell me what you think.'

Alikhan eased himself into the couch and lowered the displays until they locked in front of him. Martinez opened his private files and showed Alikhan the Naxid parties marching along the rows of ships, the officers, weaponers, engineers, and constables. He showed the translations the program had made, but offered no comment on them.

'What are your conclusions?' Martinez asked.

Alikhan stared at the displays, the deep lines of his face set in a frown. 'I don't like to speculate on such things, my lord,' he said.

'Talk, Alikhan.' Martinez said. 'I really need you to help me.'

Alikhan's mouth worked beneath his spreading moustache. And then he sighed, and gave a slow nod.

'They're going to take the ship, my lord.' His voice was filled with a kind of tremulous, exalted despair, terror and awe all mingled together. 'They're going to take all the Terran and Daimong ships. Probably tomorrow, when most of the crews will be on Magaria with their teams.'

Relief trickled through Martinez's veins. He wasn't alone in this madness, he had an ally.

'But why?' Martinez asked. 'Is it a mutiny? Or is Fanaghee acting to *stop* a mutiny?'

Alikhan shook his head. 'I don't know.'

'The Terran and Daimong divisions were labelled "Mutineers" during the exercises. And the exercises were aimed at holding a wormhole gate against attackers. Are they expecting a counterattack from the Home Fleet after they take the Second Fleet?'

Alikhan turned to Martinez. 'There are Naxid squadrons in the Home Fleet, too, my lord.'

Martinez felt cold fingers caress his spine. This was a factor he hadn't considered.

'Here the Naxids are two-fifths of our strength,' he said, and hoped his tone was optimistic. 'In the Home Fleet they're a smaller percentage.'

Alikhan's expression was careful to avoid utter hopelessness. 'That's true, my lord.'

Martinez turned towards the displays, looked at the images of Naxids marching between docking ports. 'I'll have to tell the captain.'

Alikhan's expression did not change. 'The captain may not be . . . receptive,' he ventured.

'I'll speak to Koslowski first, if I get the chance.'

'And if the lord premiere is also distracted?'

Martinez felt a sudden, angry urge to leap from the acceleration couch and pace around the room. For Martinez, planning and motion were best performed simultaneously. But the room was too crowded with the close-packed acceleration cages, and so he settled for savagely wiping the screen of Naxids.

'I'm trying to think of other officers I know on this station,' he said. 'Salzman on the *Judge Di*. Aragon and Ming on the *Declaration*. Mukerji the Younger on the *Steadfast*.' He banged a fist on his armrest in frustration. 'That's all, damn it,' he said, more to himself than to Alikhan. 'I did a cipher course with Aidepone on the *Bombardment of Utgu* but I don't know him that well. And I don't know any of the captains at all. And worse than that—'

Alikhan's calm voice cut off the flow of words. 'How do you plan to communicate with these officers, my lord? The Naxids may be intercepting communications.'

Despair clawed at Martinez' heart as he stared hopelessly across the small armoured room. He couldn't even use coded communications: all the Second Fleet had the same codes in common, and Fanaghee or her minions would be able to read anything he tried to send.

He sighed, then straightened on the couch, and put his hands on the control panel in front of him as if he were going to take *Corona* out of dock. On his right sleeve glittered the soccer ball worn by the Home Fleet champions. 'Right,' he said. 'So how do we save *our* ship?'

'You'll speak to the officers. And I'll speak to others.'

Martinez looked at him. 'Speak to who?'

'Maheshwari. If we have to run, I wouldn't want to take the ship out of dock without him minding the engines.'

'Good. And—?'

Alikhan looked uncertain. 'I suppose I should choose only from those likely to be on the ship tomorrow, during the sporting exercises?'

Martinez nodded. 'For the moment, let's say yes.'

Alikhan's voice grew firm. 'In that case, no one. Maheshwari's the only one with sufficient, ah, gravity to appreciate the situation.'

Martinez's fingers tapped the control panel. 'I'm sending you a copy of the recordings and translations. Show them to Maheshwari.'

'Yes, my lord.'

Martinez blanked the screen, unlocked the displays, and swung them up and out of the way. A strong sense of relief swept through him: he was accomplishing something, working against the threat he'd knew existed.

He bounded to his feet like a man escaping prison. And then he remembered that his next task was to speak to the captain, and again his heart sank.

Lieutenant-Captain Tarafah looked up from his ocoba-bean salad. 'Ah. Lieutenant Martinez. I'd been wanting to speak with you.'

Irrational hope blazed in Martinez' heart. Tarafah and the rest of the team had just returned from their day's practice, and the elcap, the lieutenants Koslowski and Garcia, and the trainer, Weaponer/1st Mancini, were settling down to a meal at the captain's table. They were all still in their sweats, with *Corona*'s blazing badge on their breasts, and smelled of exercise and the outdoors. The captain's table was scattered with bottles and cold dishes as well as papers and diagrams of plays.

And now Tarafah actually wanted to speak to him. Martinez had worried about being resented for intruding on the captain's time, but it seemed he wasn't entirely out of the captain's thoughts.

'Yes, lord elcap?' he answered.

Tarafah looked at him with cool eyes. 'When you joined at Zanshaa you offered to have a player as one of your servants,' he said. 'I'd like to take advantage of your offer, if I may.'

Martinez was surprised. He had long ago assigned his spare-servant scheme to the realm of unsuccessful ploys.

'Of course, lord elcap,' he said.

'Good. Our only weakness is defence, and Conyngham on the *Judge Jeffreys* has agreed to trade us one of his backs. He'll be your orderly until, umm, we can work him in elsewhere.'

Till he can be promoted to specialist/1st in some poor fool's division, Martinez thought. *Let's hope it isn't mine.*

But he agreed, of course, and as heartily as he could manage. 'When will he come aboard?'

'In the next few days, so we can have him in place when the season starts.'

'Very good, my lord.'

The captain's cook brought in the main dish, a steaming casserole fragrant of allspice and onions, and placed it before the captain. 'Ragout of beef, lord elcap,' he said, and then his eyes turned uncertainly to Martinez. 'Shall I set Lieutenant Martinez a place, my lord?'

Tarafah favoured Martinez with a brilliant white smile. 'Certainly. Why not?'

'Thank you, lord elcap.'

Martinez sat at the end of the polished mahogany table while the captain's steward provided him a place setting and poured him a glass of dark ale from the pitcher in the centre of the table. The others were in a exuberant mood: the day's practice must have gone well. Martinez tried not to fidget with his silverware.

Tarafah's shaved head bent over his plate for a moment as he sampled the ragout, and then he looked up at Martinez, his face glowing with enthusiasm. 'Lord Gareth,' he said, 'I'm pleased to say that I've reviewed every recording of *Beijing*'s games last season – and now I know their weakness! Three times in the last season their left half and their left back were drawn out of position in exactly the same way – a goal each time! No one's noticed it till now.'

'Excellent, my lord,' Martinez encouraged. 'Very perspicacious.'

'So for us, it's Sorensen to Villa to Yamana to Sorensen to Digby – and goal!' Tarafah brandished his fork in triumph. 'We were drilling it all afternoon.'

'Superb, lord elcap! Congratulations!' Martinez raised his glass. 'To our coach!'

Tarafah beamed while the others toasted him. Martinez took a breath. Certainly there would never be a better moment.

'Apropos tactics,' he began. 'I've noticed the Naxid squadrons are up to something odd. May I show you?'

'Show us?' Tarafah bent over his plate again.

'May I use the display here?' Without waiting for permission Martinez reached over the pink head of the plump, bald Mancini and touched the control of the wall screen. He activated his own sleeve display and slaved the wall screen to it.

'For the last three days,' Martinez said, 'Naxid officers have been making an extraordinary tour of the non-Naxid berthing areas. For the first two days, Squadron Commander Kulukraf brought parties of officers along the berthing bays, and today the officers brought noncoms with them. These are recordings I made this afternoon . . .'

He went through the evidence piece by piece, just as he had with Alikhan. The others ate in silence as he spoke, Mancini and Garcia occasionally craning around to view the display behind them. At the end, with the screen frozen on a Naxid officer flashing the symbol for *target,* Martinez turned to the captain.

'I wonder, lord elcap,' he said, 'what you make of it?'

Tarafah raised his napkin to dab gravy off his goatee. '*Should* I make anything of it?'

Garcia spoke hesitantly. 'They're obviously rehearsing something.'

'And it's a manoeuvre that requires weaponers, engineers, and the constabulary,' Martinez said.

Koslowski, the premiere, frowned at him. He was a long-legged, broad-handed man, as befitted his position of goalkeeper. 'This morning,' he said, 'you told me that you thought that all this was the rehearsal for a surprise inspection . . .'

He barely got out the words before Tarafah thumped a hand down on the table and made the plates jump. 'Just before the game? When we're all distracted? That Fanaghee's a vicious monster, isn't she?' He looked at Koslowski. 'I'll have to inspect the ship myself tomorrow morning before breakfast, right when I was hoping to have a last talk with the team.'

'The lord premiere and I have been preparing for the inspection,' Martinez said. 'I've had the people hard at work all day.'

Tarafah seemed little mollified. 'That's good. But I still

can't believe that Fanaghee would take advantage of the Festival of Sport in this way. It just isn't right!'

'My lord,' Martinez said. 'I no longer believe that the Naxids are planning a surprise inspection.'

Tarafah blinked at him. 'What?' he said. 'Why are you bothering us, then?'

Martinez tried to settle his leaping wits. 'You don't need weaponers or engineers or constables to pull an inspection, lord elcap,' he said. 'You need weaponers to control the weapons bays. Engineers to control the engines. And constables to control the crew – *and* the officers.'

Tarafah's brows knitted as he tried to puzzle it out. 'Yes. That's true. But what are you saying?'

Martinez took a deep breath. 'I think the Naxids are going to board the ship and take her. Take *all* the ships they don't have already.'

Tarafah gave a puzzled frown. 'Why would Fanaghee do that? She doesn't need to capture our ships. She's *already* in command of us.'

To prevent his hands from trembling with eagerness and frustration, Martinez clamped them on the butter-smooth edge of the table and squeezed.

'She could be acting to suppress a mutiny she believes is about to break out,' Martinez said. 'Or it could be a rising of some kind.'

The trainer, Mancini, seemed even more puzzled than his captain. 'On the *Festival of Sport*?' he demanded in a high, peevish voice. 'A rising on the *Festival of Sport*?'

'What better time?' Martinez asked. 'Most of the crew, and all the senior officers, will be off the ship watching the games.'

'The Naxids are *participating* in the festival,' Koslowski said. 'They're having a huge tournament of lighumane, and—' He hesitated. 'Some of the other sports they do.'

'On the *Festival of Sport*?' Mancini repeated. 'Spoil the

football and disappoint the fans? That's the most ridiculous thing I've ever heard.'

'It doesn't make any sense,' Tarafah said. 'Why should Fanaghee lead a rising? She's at the top of her profession – she's a *fleet commander*, for all's sake.'

'I don't know,' Martinez said. He hesitated – he knew this might sound dangerously absurd – but it was the only argument he had left. 'Maybe it's not just Fanaghee,' he said. 'Maybe *all* the Naxids are rising.'

The others stared at him. Then Koslowski lowered his eyes and shook his head, his lips quirked in a tight smile. '*All* the Naxids?' he murmured. 'That's too ridiculous.'

'The Naxids are the most orthodox species under the Praxis,' Tarafah said. 'There's never been a single rebellion in Naxid history.'

'They're pack animals,' Koslowski said. 'They always submit to authority.'

'*They'd* never spoil the football,' Mancini proclaimed, and smacked his lips as he drank his ale.

'Then what could they possibly be doing?' Martinez asked. 'I have no other explanation.'

'That doesn't mean there isn't one,' Koslowski said reasonably. 'Maybe Fanaghee's decided to drill her people on boarding. Maybe it's a familiarization tour for new arrivals. Who knows?'

Tarafah seemed happy to agree with his goalkeeper. 'This speculation is useless,' he said. 'I'm not going to get inside Fanaghee's mind, or Kulukraf's, either.' He turned to Martinez. 'Lord Gareth, I appreciate your . . . diligence. But I think you've let your imagination run away with you.'

'Lord elcap.' Desperately. 'I—'

'Perhaps we should return to tomorrow's game,' Tarafah said. 'That's something a little more within our sphere.'

Martinez suppressed the impulse to hurl his glass at his captain's face.

'To our winning play!' Mancini said, and raised his glass. 'Sorensen to Villa to Yamana to Sorensen to Digby – and *goal*!'

Martinez drank with the others, as despairing, unvoiced shrieks echoed one after another in his skull.

Martinez didn't manage to eat much of his dinner. When the elcap proposed another review of the videos of *Beijing*'s game, Martinez excused himself and made his way to his cabin. Once there, he sent messages to the other officers he knew on station, asking if they'd care to meet him in one of the bars on the station. Salzman didn't reply, Ming sent his regrets, Aragon said that he was participating in the wushu tournament in the Festival of Sport and was making an early night of it. Aidepone was likewise preparing for tomorrow's game of fatugui, and only Mukerji accepted. Viewing the transmission, with its sonic interference, Martinez knew that Mukerji was already in a bar.

Martinez joined him in the Murder Hole, a dark, nebulous, and noisy place, with ear-shattering music and dancing. Mukerji bought three rounds of drinks while Martinez showed Mukerji the Naxid manoeuvres on his sleeve display, and then explained his theory.

Mukerji put a friendly arm around Martinez' shoulders. 'I always thought you were mad!' he said cheerfully. 'Totally mad!'

'You can tell your captain!' Martinez shouted over the music. 'I can give you the data! He might be able to save his ship!'

'Totally mad!' Mukerji repeated. He pointed to a couple of Fleet cadets standing by the bar. 'If it's my last night of freedom, I want some recreationals,' he said. 'Who do you want – the redhead or the other?'

Martinez excused himself and made his way out onto the ring station with whisky fumes swirling through his head.

Perhaps he *was* mad, he thought. No other officer credited his theory about the Naxids, and perhaps they'd been right about the absurdity of his premise. It made no sense for the most obedient and orthodox species under the Praxis to suddenly turn rogue.

He admitted to himself that he didn't like Naxids and never had. It was, he likewise admitted, an irrational prejudice. Naxids had always made him uneasy, unlike the other species united beneath the Praxis. Perhaps he had let his bias run in advance of the facts.

He thought again of those parties marching up and down the ring station's broad avenue, and at the thought a chill certainty went through his frame.

No. He *was* right. The Naxids were going to board the ship. It was possible there was some rational explanation for it other than a rising, some reason that hadn't occurred to him, but the boarding *would* happen.

And if the boarding were to be prevented, it would be Martinez who would prevent it.

Martinez returned to his cabin aboard *Corona* and called Alikhan.

'My lord?'

'No good with the captain,' Martinez said. 'Or with anyone else.'

Alikhan didn't seem surprised. 'I have spoken to the master engineer,' he said.

'And?'

'Maheshwari agrees with your lordship.' Spoken carefully, in case of eavesdroppers.

Martinez sighed. Maheshwari was something, at least.

'Very well,' Martinez said. 'Let me know if—' He fell silent, defeated, then finished, 'Let me know if *anything*.'

'Very good, my lord.'

The orange *end transmission* symbol appeared on Martinez' sleeve display, and he blanked it.

Fully aware that this was the last time he might ever do these things, Martinez took off his clothes, hung them neatly in his tiny closet, and prepared for bed.

Plans for saving *Corona* eddied through his head, all fog and futility.

Sorensen to Villa to Yamana to Sorensen to Digby, he thought.

And goal.

Eight

Martinez, with most of *Corona*'s crew, stood on the station rim outside the airlock and cheered and clapped as Tarafah led *Corona*'s team out of the ship. Tarafah, immaculate in white sweats with *Corona*'s blazon on his chest and his lieutenant-captain's shoulder boards pinned on, grinned and waved as if he were jogging into a stadium filled with ten thousand fans. Koslowski followed at the head of the players.

'*Corona! Corona!*' the crew chanted. Martinez pounded his big hands together till they were sore.

The team jogged away to the rim train station that would take them to the skyhook terminal, and were followed by the waddling figure of their trainer, Mancini. Lieutenant Garcia, in undress mourning whites, whooped and waved her cap over her head.

'Let's go!' she shouted. 'Let's give the Coronas our support!'

Shouting, most of the crew poured after the team, leaving behind the cadets condemned to spend the day aboard, and Dietrich and his partner Hong, both looking depressed at having to play military constable while the rest of the crew was off on a lark.

Served them right for being large and handsome, Martinez thought. Since the airlock guards were the members of *Corona*'s crew most often seen by outsiders, Tarafah chose them for their imposing appearance rather than for any skill at policing.

Lieutenant Garcia herself remained behind, cheering and clapping as the crew pounded after their team. Then she turned to Martinez and stepped up to him.

'Take this,' she said in a soft voice, and Martinez felt something warm and metallic pressed into his palm. 'Just in case you're right.'

Martinez glanced at his half-opened hand, saw Garcia's second lieutenant's key, and felt his mouth go dry. He shut his fist on the key.

'Koslowski doesn't wear his key while playing,' Garcia murmured. 'I don't know where he keeps it. Try his safe.'

Martinez managed a nod. 'Thank you,' he said.

Garcia's dark eyes held his. 'If they take the fleet,' she said, 'blow everything. The ships, the ring, everything.'

Martinez stared into the dark eyes. His nerves wailed like violin strings tuned to the breaking point. 'I understand,' he said.

Garcia gave a quick, nervous nod, then turned and ran after her crew.

Martinez let his breath out slowly as he watched Fleet personnel stream past along the rim. They laughed and shouted, carrying banners and signs, their officers striding with them, happy to let them have fun. It was their first holiday since the period of mourning began, and they were ready for a deliriously good time, already drunk on freedom and anticipation.

Martinez watched them go by and wondered what would happen if he just ran out among them and started shouting, 'Back to your ships! There's a rising! If you go down to the planet, all is lost!'

He'd be laughed at if he was lucky. If he was unlucky, he'd be hit on the head by the constables and dragged off to jail.

Blow everything, he thought again. There were thousands of personnel on the ships and the ring station, and millions of civilians, all to be vaporized or blown to bits – but only if he was right about the Naxid rising. If his fears were justified, everything was *already* lost.

Except maybe *Corona*. Maybe he could save his ship.

He put Garcia's key in his pocket, then turned to face the airlock. Dietrich and Hong stood there, stiff-spined in the presence of officers, along with Warrant Officer First Class Saavedra, a middle-aged, mustachio'd man who had double duty as *Corona*'s secretary and supply officer, and Cadet Kelly, a lanky, clumsy pinnace pilot in charge of the weapons department in the absence of the drunken master weaponer.

'Kelly. Saavedra. After you.' Martinez made shooing motions with his arms, and the two turned obediently and headed into the airlock. Martinez began to follow, then paused by the two constables. Dietrich and Hong braced as they detected his inspection.

'I want you to understand,' Martinez said, 'that no one comes aboard *Corona* without my permission.'

'Yes, lord lieutenant,' the two chorused, eyes forward.

'And by that I mean *anyone*,' Martinez continued, speaking with forceful emphasis that he hoped did not sound either fanatic or insane. 'If Anticipation of Victory himself comes back from the dead and demands to be let on board, you are not to him aboard without my express permission.'

The two blinked in surprise. 'Very good, lord lieutenant,' Dietrich said.

Martinez looked from one to the other. His mouth was dry and he hoped his voice wouldn't break. 'And furthermore,' he said, 'you will use all necessary force to *prevent* anyone from coming aboard who does *not* receive my permission. Do you understand?'

'Yes, lord lieutenant,' the two chorused again, though Martinez could see more of their eyewhites than he should, a sure indication they thought the third lieutenant was out of his mind.

'There is a special order I wish to give you,' Martinez said. 'If I think it necessary for you to retreat from this post through the airlock and into the ship, I will transmit the words "Buena Vista."' He looked at them, then repeated with special emphasis. '"Buena." "Vista." Repeat the words, please.'

'Buena. Vista.' In chorus.

'Buena Vista,' Martinez repeated again. The name of the house on Laredo where he had been born, the name given by his romantic mother in an antique Terran language no longer spoken, and read only by scholars.

He could see, drawn through the ether between the two constables in invisible letters, the conviction that Martinez was insane.

'Very good,' Martinez finished. 'I'll send Alikhan out with refreshments every so often. Remember what I said.'

There were four doors between Martinez and the interior of *Corona,* two at the rim airlock, where Dietrich and Hong stood guard, and two on the frigate's bow lock, with the docking tube in between. Martinez moved along this series of barriers and entered his kingdom.

A kingdom with nineteen subjects, most present in obedience to the regulation that required every vessel in commission to carry sufficient crew aboard, even in dock, in case an emergency require that the ship be manoeuvred. A dozen of those aboard were intended to work the ship, and the rest consisted of the two constables and a full kitchen staff preparing a huge celebratory meal in anticipation of *Corona*'s victory.

Martinez let himself into the ship's small armoury with his lieutenant's key, then summoned Alikhan and Maheshwari. While he waited he signed out a sidearm and strapped the weapon on its constable-red belt around his waist. He signed two more out to Alikhan and Maheshwari, then handed Alikhan a pistol as he arrived, along with a red constable's armband and helmet.

'I'm thinking of sending you to the airlock,' he said. 'Those boys might need some stiffening.'

'Very good, my lord.' Alikhan looked at the armoury datapad, then signed for his weapon and pressed his thumb to the weapon's ID scanner..

'And another thing,' Martinez said. 'I want you to go to the riggers' locker and get whatever you'll need to drill the first lieutenant's safe.'

Alikhan nodded. 'Do you wish that done immediately, my lord?'

'No.' Breaking into the premiere's safe in search of his key was, among other things, a capital crime, and if he were discovered it would be a race between the Criminal Investigation Division and the Legion of Diligence to see who would kill him first. Martinez wasn't quite willing to commit himself to the executioner's garotte just yet.

'Just have the equipment ready in the lord lieutenant's cabin. If we have to burn gees out of here, it'll be easier to have what you need on hand rather than have you try to haul it to Koslowski's cabin under three and a half gravities.'

'Very good, my lord.'

Maheshwari arrived and braced to the salute. He was a small, mahogany-skinned man, with crinkly hair gone grey and a pointed beard and mustachios dyed a spectacular shade of red. Martinez handed him a sidearm.

'I hope this won't be necessary,' he said.

'There won't be trouble in *my* division,' Maheshwari said as he signed for the weapon and scanned in his thumbprint. 'But I can't speak for some of the other folk on board.'

'In a short while I'm going to call for an engine startup drill. It takes forty minutes or so to ready the engines for a cold start, yes?'

Maheshwari smiled with brilliant white pebble-sized teeth. 'It can be done much faster, my lord.'

'Let's not. I want the drill to seem as normal as possible.'

As possible was the key here. No drill was going to be normal on the Festival of Sport.

'The electrical and data connections are dropped at three minutes forty, if I remember,' Martinez said. 'We'll start the drill and then hold at four minutes.'

'Beg pardon, my lord,' Maheshwari reminded, 'but water and air connections are dropped at four minutes twenty.'

'Oh. Right. We'll hold at five, then.'

'Very good, my lord.'

Dropping water, air, electrical, and data connections to the ring station would be the station's first warning if *Corona* left its berth unexpectedly. Martinez wanted to delay the warning as far as he could.

At least he was confident that, if necessary, he could leave his berth when he wanted to, whether the engines were ready or not. Six hundred and forty-one years ago, a raging fire had broken out in Ring Command on Zanshaa's ring station, subsequently spreading to seven berthed ships, all destroyed along with their crews. The ships could not unberth, or even close their airlock doors, without permission from Ring Command, which by then had been gutted by fire.

Since then, regulations had insisted that a ship under threat could unberth without permission, and had complete control of its airlock doors. Martinez could get *Corona* out of its berth, the only question being whether the other warships would permit her to survive past that point.

Martinez did his best to pretend that he had his imperturbable, omnipotent officer's face on, and ventured to give the master engineer a confident smile.

'Good luck, Maheshwari.'

Maheshwari's response was courtly. 'The same to you, lord lieutenant.'

The engineer braced in salute and returned to Engine Control.

Martinez locked the armoury and went to the central

belt elevator that would take him to Command, then hesitated, one hand on the wide belt that held his sidearm and stun baton.

If he walked into Command wearing this thing everyone would know him insane. If the Naxids did nothing, or if what they did had a rational explanation, then the entire crew would know by the end of the day. He'd become a laughing stock.

He stood in the hatch and heard the laughter in his mind, laughter ringing down the years as long as he remained in the service. If he were wrong he could expect nothing less. Everything Fanaghee and Kulukraf were doing could have an innocent explanation – well, not *innocent* exactly, but at least *rational*. If he had missed that, if the Naxids were doing anything else but a rising, he would never hear the end of it. The story would become one of those Fleet legends that would follow a person for his entire career, like the story of Squadron Commander Rafi ordering the cadets to bind and beat him.

The endless belt of the central elevator rustled past. Suddenly he wanted very much to return to the weapons locker, check his pistol back in, and go to the wardroom to watch the game on video and cheer on *Corona*'s team.

The hell with it, he thought. He was *already* a laughing stock to most of the crew.

He put a foot on the next descending rung, took a handhold onto the rung above, and stepped into the central trunk corridor. He stepped off two decks below, and immediately saw Zhou, the brawler he'd released from arrest two days before, polishing the silverware in the officer's mess, across the corridor from Command.

Wonderful, Martinez thought. He had Zhou, Ahmet, and Knadjian in his crew, as well as every other miscreant that the captain had condemned to labour instead of the games.

Zhou, polishing away, gave Martinez a dubious look from

his blackened eyes, which widened when he saw the pistol belt. Martinez gave a curt nod and walked into Command.

'I am in Command,' he announced.

'The officer of the watch is in Command.' Cadet Vonderheydte agreed, speaking from his position at the comm board. The scent of coffee, wafting from the cup he'd propped near one hand, whispered invitingly in the room.

Martinez stepped into the locked captain's cage. 'Status?' he asked.

Vonderheydte, whose cage was directly behind the captain's, saw the pistol belt, and his eyes widened. 'Um – ship systems are normal,' he said. 'And – oh yes! The dishwasher in the enlisted galley blew a circuit breaker, and it's being looked into.'

'Thank you, Vonderheydte.' He turned his back on the cadet and sat in the captain's chair. Cushions sighed beneath his weight, and he adjusted the pistol to a more comfortable position, then reached over his head and drew down the captain's displays until they locked in front of him.

He set one display to the security camera. Crewmen were still streaming past the airlock towards the rim rail stop. Nothing untoward was visible, but then Martinez didn't expect anything for a few hours yet, not until the crews had descended to the planet's surface and all the remainder were distracted by the sports.

He settled back in his chair. 'We'll be having an engine drill presently,' he said, and then listened to the profound, astonished silence that followed his words.

Sorensen to Villa to Yamana to Sorensen to Digby – and goal. Martinez heard Vonderheydte give a shout as the ball shot past *Beijing*'s goalkeeper and into the net.

Warrant Officer/2nd Mabumba punched the air with a fist. He sat at the Engineering station, and in his excitement at *Corona*'s second goal had forgotten to be resentful of Martinez for the engine drill that put Mabumba in Command instead of the warrant officers' lounge, where he could have watched the game in comfort, and with a glass of beer by his hand.

Maheshwari in Engine Control was holding the engine countdown at five minutes. Martinez had doubtless won the enduring love of the entire engineering division for calling the drill on a sports holiday, and keeping them at their stations.

Martinez had left Command only once, to help Alikhan bring food, coffee, and comfort to the two guards at the outside airlock, where Martinez had made it clear to Dietrich and Hong that any orders from Alikhan were to be treated as if they were orders from Martinez himself.

Clearly, the silent faces of the sentries suggested, there was more than one madman aboard the ship.

Next Martinez tried to see what he could do about sending alarms to other elements of the Fleet, perhaps to Zanshaa. A check with data on file at the Exploration Service, which crewed and maintained the wormhole stations that stitched the empire together with communications lasers that pulsed messages and data from one system to another, showed that there was no chance of getting word outside the Magaria system. In the previous few months, on a leisurely schedule, the crews of each station had been replaced – with Naxids.

Another possibility existed. There were civilian ships in the system, outbound. He could send a message to each of these, and hope that at least some information escaped the system. He checked the navigation plots and discovered that there were sixteen civilian ships in the Magaria system. He checked their registration, and after discounting the three large inbound transports belonging to a corporation called Premiere Axiom, based on the Naxid homeworld of Naxas, produced a list of ships to which he might appeal.

He'd tell them when the time came. And he still had ground-line communication to other ships berthed in the Fleet dockyard. He might be able to save some of them yet.

Another of Martinez' displays shifted through a succession of other security monitors, particularly those on the Naxid stretch of the ring station. The Fleet enclave was nearly deserted: everyone, even the civilian workers, had been given tickets to the Festival of Sport and a day off. The only living presence in the Fleet areas were the two guards posted by every airlock.

A third display showed the football match between the Coronas and the Beijings. Tarafah's offensive strategy had thus far scored two goals and held the opposition scoreless. Martinez had to admire his captain's ability as a strategist – he was a truly superb and inspiring sports tactician.

A fourth, smaller display scrolled slowly between the other games being played at the same time. His friend Aragon of the *Declaration* had won his wushu match with a joint lock in the second round, but Aidepone's team from the *Utgu* wasn't faring very well in their game of fatugui, a game involving a large ovoid ball being flung across a field by what looked like giant teaspoons held in the matchstick arms of the Daimong players. Two of Aidepone's side had been declared dead, in fatugui a temporary condition, but their opponents now had the advantage of numbers and had scored several points, and their own team kept stumbling over them.

Senior Fleet Commander Fanaghee was enthroned, with Kulukraf and others of her senior staff, in the stadium where two champion Naxid teams were deeply involved in lighumane, a game of position and movement that seemed like an unlikely combination of chess and rugby football – at one moment players carrying large white or black placards were participating in diabolically subtle manoeuvres on a green field, and then all periodically dissolved into riot and violence. The camera frequently returned to Fanaghee, as if to demonstrate to everyone that she was here watching sport instead of, say, conspiring at mutiny aboard the *Majesty*.

All these displays, however, were little more than a distraction to Martinez. A fifth, central display was open to a navigation plot. Martinez had been trying to find an escape route for *Corona* once he got her out of dock, and the possibilities weren't promising. The direct wormhole route to Zanshaa was blocked by the cruiser *Judge Kybiq*, which had departed the station en route to Zanshaa three days earlier.

Other than Zanshaa, the nearest Fleet concentration was the Fourth Fleet headquarters at Felarus, but Fanaghee had cleverly blocked that as well, with the heavy cruiser *Bombardment of Turmag*, shaking down after a period of refit. The refit, Martinez suspected, had been timed very precisely in order to provide Fanaghee with an excuse to order the cruiser out of dock.

Corona would have to return to Zanshaa the long way round, through Magaria Wormhole Four, then through a series of three other wormholes leading through uninhabitable or sparsely-inhabited systems. It would add twenty to forty days to *Corona*'s journey, depending on how hard Martinez wanted to push the acceleration.

And then Martinez had to cope with the possibility that once he arrived at Zanshaa, he would find that the capital itself might have fallen to the rebels. In that case Martinez could launch whatever missiles he had at Zanshaa's ring station, he supposed, try to kill whatever enemy ships were there before he was destroyed himself, and then go down marked in history as Nature's very own fool.

His navigation plot was complicated by the fact that he hadn't any real-world experience as a navigator, only basic training, and that long ago. Martinez double- and triple-checked everything, and leaned heavily on the computer for assistance. He realized he had been staring at his navigation plot for some time without thought, and reached for the communications button to call to the officers' galley for a flask of coffee, when a movement caught his eye, and a cold chill eddied along his flesh. His second display was automatically flicking through a series of security camera shots from the Naxid part of the ring, and quite suddenly there was movement.

A lot of movement, and on *every* camera.

Naxids were pouring off their ships. Whole long columns of them, swarming out of the airlocks four abreast.

He scrambled upright on his seat and only caught the yell of alarm that rose in his throat just in time to keep it from breaking out. *It's really happening,* he thought.

'Damn! Damn-damn-damn!' It was Mabumba cursing, and it took Martinez a staggered second to realize that he was lamenting the fact that the Beijings had just scored a goal.

Martinez stabbed at the alarm switch and missed — his overexcited thumb overshot the target and skiddered along the smooth metal console surface — and then he swiped at the switch with his entire hand and managed to shove it over. Furious, urgent bells blared throughout the ship. Mabumba almost jumped out of his chair, and stared at Martinez with wild, disbelieving eyes.

Martinez reached for the headset with its earphones, built-in microphones, and virtual reality projectors, put it on his head, and snapped the chin strap shut. He took a moment to get ahold of his leaping nerves, then spoke into the microphone.

'Communications,' he prefaced to the computer. 'General announcement to ship's company.' He waited a half-second or so, and then spoke again.

'General quarters,' he said. 'This is the officer of the watch. Everyone to their action stations.'

He thought about adding the words *This is not a drill,* but decided that this was not a time to strain the crew's credulity.

He repeated the announcement twice, then shut off the blaring alarm that was making him more nervous than he was already.

'End announcement,' he said, and then, 'Communications. Page crewman Alikhan.'

Alikhan's miniature face appeared in the display.

'My lord.'

'I need you at the airlock. There may be a Buena Vista situation coming up.'

'Very good, my lord.'

'End transmission.'

Martinez began reconfiguring his displays to employ more security cameras and see what the Naxids were up to. Hundreds of Naxids were on the concourse, marshalling under their officers and crowding towards the electric Fleet trains that carried personnel and equipment through the Fleet areas of the ring station.

The first of the trains began moving as the door to Command rolled open, and Navigator Trainee Diem entered along with Pilot Second Class Eruken. They looked at Martinez with expressions that appeared to combine annoyance with concern for his mental health.

'May I ask what's happening, my lord?' Eruken ventured.

'Not yet, Pilot. Take your seat.'

Martinez considered alerting the other ships. This would warn the Naxids of his suspicions, but it was too late for them to change their plans now.

'Comm,' Martinez told Vonderheydte. 'Get me the all-ships channel.'

'Yes, my lord.'

There was a moment's pause, and then the shrieks of a huge crowd and the shouts of an overexcited announcer filled the room. Martinez gathered that Goalie Koslowski had just made a brilliant save.

The lanky Cadet Kelly, entering at that moment to take her place at the weapons board, gave a cheer.

'Not the game, Vonderheydte!' Martinez shouted. 'Get me the fucking—!'

'Sorry, my lord!' Vonderheydte had to shout over the cries of the announcer. 'Someone's broadcasting the game on the all-ships channel.'

'Emergency channel, then!'

There was a brief susurrus as the channels were switched, and then the game blared on again.

'Sorry, my lord! It's on the emergency channel, too!'

Martinez clenched his fists. '*Any* channel.'

But he knew by now that Vonderheydte would find the games on every channel. Martinez could try to shout a warning to the other ships over the crowd and the announcer, but who knew if anyone would be listening?

'Ground line, Comm,' he said. Cable data connections to the ring station were still in place.

From behind he heard the soft sound of Vonderheydte's fingertips touching pads on his console.

'Grounds lines are down, my lord.'

'What's going *on*?' Mabumba murmured, just loud enough for everyone to hear.

'Our communications have been cut,' Martinez told him. 'Let's just think for a minute about who might have done that and why.'

The others in the control room exchanged glances, clearly bewildered. At that moment Tracy and Clarke, the two sensor operators, arrived in the sudden silence, and ghosted to their places as if struck by a guilty conscience.

Nervous energy drummed through Martinez. He didn't want to wait, he wanted to be in motion along with his ship. He paged Maheshwari.

'My lord?'

'I wanted you to know that it's begun.'

Maheshwari nodded. 'I heard the alarms, my lord.'

Martinez realized he'd called the master engineer less to alleviate Maheshwari's nervousness than his own. He had been reaching into the engine room for comfort, for someone who understood, who would make him feel less lonely in his moment of command.

It wasn't helping. 'Keep holding at five minutes,' he said, for lack of anything better. 'End transmission.' He then blanked the screen because the first of the computer-guided trains were shooting through the human areas of the ring station.

They didn't stop. They raced on to the Daimong area, where the most powerful ships were concentrated in the heavy squadron, and then began to slow.

Martinez' sleeve button gave a quiet chime. Martinez answered, and the sleeve display shifted to show Alikhan.

'The Naxids are moving past, my lord. I've counted nine trains.'

'I know that. They've jammed or cut all ships' communications, by the way.'

'Shall we move the guard into the ship, my lord?'

Martinez hesitated, and glanced at his screens. The Naxids were disembarking in the Daimong areas and moving for the Daimong ships in columns thirty or forty strong, officers in the lead. They weren't deploying in combat formations, or otherwise looked as if they were going to shoot down the guards and storm the airlocks.

They hadn't showed their hand yet. It all *might* still have a rational explanation. And Martinez, for all the fear and adrenaline that blazed through his veins, still rather hoped it might.

'My lord?' Alikhan reminded.

'Not yet,' Martinez decided. 'When they approach, stall them. Keep everyone calm. Tell them you'll have to speak to the officer of the watch and get into the airlock yourself. But don't come back to the ship, mind the outer hatch instead, and get ready to open it when I signal Buena Vista.'

Now it was Alikhan's turn to hesitate. 'Very well, my lord,' he said finally.

'End transmission,' Martinez said, his eyes riveted to the displays. More trains were loaded in the Naxid areas and sent out, this time to the medium squadron.

The medium squadron, that had *Corona* as its smallest ship.

In the Daimong areas, the first Naxid columns had reached the airlocks. Conversations were going on between the airlock guards and the officers leading the columns.

Martinez felt his nerves coil and tense and flare. *Resist,* he silently urged the Daimong. *Keep them off. Resist.*

At *Bombardment of Kathung,* flagship of the heavy squadron, the guards braced, stood aside, and watched as the Naxids swarmed into the airlock.

'No.' The word forced its way past Martinez' locked throat. 'No, keep them out.'

Two more sets of guards, those on either side of *Kathung,* stood aside as they saw the Naxids enter the flagship.

From the camera above *Corona*'s lock, Martinez saw a train slowing as it prepared to enter the nearest station. The open-topped cars were black with Naxids.

Martinez switched from one camera to the next on the Daimong sections. At least six ships were being boarded. Polite conversations seemed to be going on at the other airlocks. Nowhere did Martinez see any violence.

Martinez zoomed in on one of the Naxid columns. At least half the Naxids were carrying sidearms.

Whatever was happening, it wasn't a surprise inspection. You didn't carry weapons while making an inspection.

His cuff button chimed again. 'Private comm: answer,' he said.

Alikhan. 'They're coming, my lord.'

'Very good. Blank your screen but keep this channel open.'

Martinez configured his own sleeve display so that his words would not be transmitted: this left him free to give other orders without the Naxids overhearing through Alikhan's comm rig.

He called up the airlock display onto his command board and made certain he had the airlock commands ready.

A glance at the displays showed Naxids boarding at least two more ships of the Daimong squadron.

He looked at the first display, that showed the column moving with the usual Naxid scrambling haste towards *Corona*. The column slammed to the equally normal abrupt halt in front of the two airlock guards, and the commanding officer braced briefly to acknowledge the guards' salutes.

Only a lieutenant, Martinez saw. The senior officers were at the games, being seen on camera and maintaining the illusion that all was normal.

'Lieutenant Ondakaal,' the Naxid officer said by way of introduction. 'Fleet Commander Fanaghee requires me to go aboard your vessel and conduct an inspection.'

The words came with remarkable clarity over Alikhan's sleeve comm rig.

'Does the lord lieutenant have a signed order?' Alikhan asked.

'That is hardly necessary.' Arrogance dripped like acid from Ondakaal's words. 'My orders come direct from the fleet commander herself.'

'I beg the lord lieutenant's pardon,' Alikhan said, 'but *you* aren't the fleet commander, and you're not in our chain of command. Can you give me a written order that I can show to the officer of the watch?'

Ondakaal's head bobbed as he scanned Alikhan's sleeve for badges of rank and seeing the red hashmarks of seniority and the badge of the master weaponer. 'Very well, Master Weaponer,' he said. 'If you insist.'

He opened his tunic and produced a letter, which he handed to Alikhan. 'As you can see,' he said, demanding arrogance again in his tone, 'the fleetcom's seal is upon the letter.'

'Indeed, my lord,' Alikhan said. 'Please wait here with your party while I show this to the officer of the watch.'

Alikhan stepped back and opened the airlock before Ondakaal or his group could react. Martinez could see the Naxids quiver with the impulse to hurl themselves at the open door, but Alikhan slid it shut quickly, and the moment passed.

'Shall I open the letter, my lord?' Alikhan's voice seemed a little breathless, as if he'd run a long distance rather than just a few steps.

'Yes, by all means.'

Martinez scanned displays and didn't see a single Daimong ship resisting the Naxid boarders. The entire heavy squadron had fallen to the Naxids without a shot.

Through the camera above the airlock door he could see Ondakaal talking to Dietrich and Hong. Martinez told the display to give him audio as well as video.

'You can see it for yourself!' Ondakaal had grown angry. '*Perigee* is letting the inspectors aboard. You may as well stand aside and let us come aboard.'

'I'm afraid not, my lord.' Martinez wanted to cheer, not at Dietrich's words but at his upright, broad-shouldered stance, betraying no apology or any suggestion that he would cave in to the Naxid's demands.

'I have very strict orders not to let anyone board without the permission of the officer of the watch,' Dietrich explained.

'You are defying the orders of the fleet commander!' Ondakaal said. He brandished an arm, pointing to one side. 'You see for yourself that *Steadfast* is letting the special inspectors aboard!'

Over another channel, Alikhan was reading the contents of Fanaghee's order. It seemed genuine enough.

'No need for that,' Martinez told Alikhan. 'Stand by for Buena Vista.'

Ondakaal was continuing to hector the guards. Martinez

decided he'd better rescue Dietrich and Hong before they were overwhelmed, and he pressed the audio button.

'What is going on out there?' he demanded. 'Who the fuck are you, Lieutenant, and why the fuck are you harassing my people?'

At the tone of command Ondakaal automatically braced into a respectful pose. 'I am Lieutenant Ondakaal, my lord,' he said. 'I am required by Senior Fleet Commander Fanaghee—'

'Can you tell me what's going on?' Martinez continued. 'Communications have been *completely* scrambled. I can't even get a ground line out!'

'My lord, I'm unaware of—'

'The only message I've got,' Martinez interrupted, 'was "Prepare for Buena Vista." Can you tell me what that means, "Prepare for Buena Vista"?'

Ondakaal's surprise and uncertainty kept him from observing the electric glance that passed between Hong and Dietrich, the subtle shifts in their stance as they understood his words and prepared to jump backwards for the airlock.

'My lord, I'm afraid I don't know what those words mean,' Ondakaal said. 'But if you'll let our inspectors aboard, I'll—'

'Buena Vista!' Martinez shouted. 'Buena Vista!' And then, over the comm, he heard Alikhan's voice shouting the words as well.

Dietrich and Hong leaped backwards, out of frame. Ondakaal realized what was happening, but too late: he made a lunge forward, followed in an instant by the warrant officers behind him, but apparently Alikhan got the airlock door shut in time, because Ondakaal soon appeared in the camera frame again, and without the two Terran constables.

Martinez decided to take the offensive. If he kept Ondakaal busy, he might keep the Naxid from doing anything effective.

'What the hell was *that* about?' he demanded. 'Explain yourself, Lieutenant!'

Martinez was suddenly aware that he was enjoying himself.

For once, he wasn't the provincial in the world of the privileged and self-important, or the junior lieutenant deferring to his superiors. He was playing a part, true, but it wasn't a part dictated to him by his seniors, it was one he was inventing for himself. He was the only person within a hundred light-years who knew what was going on, and he was playing Ondakaal for a fool.

And while Ondakaal was blustering about the guards' abrupt withdrawal, Martinez dropped the volume on his outside comm and raised the one on his private channel with Alikhan.

'Alikhan, where are you? Is everyone safe?'

'We are safe, my lord, all three of us. We've shut both lock doors and we're coming down the docking tube elevator.'

'Very good. Once you're aboard, seal *Corona*'s own airlock. Dietrich and Hong are to surrender their firearms to you, unrig the central trunk elevator, then report to their action stations. You are to collect the firearms, then perform the special task I assigned you earlier.'

Safebreaking in the first lieutenant's quarters. A task the nature of which should probably not be spoken aloud, not yet.

'Very good, my lord,' Alikhan said.

Martinez turned to Mabumba, who was watching him with awe and surmise, a combination that triggered in Martinez a pleasurable surge of vanity.

'Engines,' he said, 'resume countdown.'

Mabumba gave a start on being addressed, then turned to his console. 'Countdown resumed,' he said.

Martinez turned to Pilot Second Class Eruken. 'Prepare to depressurize and retract the docking tube as soon as *Corona*'s airlock is shut.'

Eruken busied himself at his console. 'Preparing to depressurize and retract docking tube.'

Martinez raised the volume on the outside comm, in time

to hear Ondakaal again invoke the authority of the fleet commander and demand to be let aboard.

'Lord lieutenant!' Martinez said. 'Explain yourself! Why are you trying to break into *Corona*'s airlock!'

'You withdrew your guards!' Ondakaal shouted 'What is this treachery?'

'Air and water connections withdrawn,' Mabumba reported in a hushed voice, pitched so that Ondakaal couldn't over-hear. 'Outside vents sealed.'

'I withdrew my guards because of your threatening and abusive behaviour,' Martinez said to Ondakaal. 'I shall report this to your superior.'

'Fleet Commander Fanaghee has ordered an inspection of your ship,' Ondakaal said.

'Nonsense!' Martinez said. 'I've heard of no inspection.'

'It's a *surprise* inspection,' Ondakaal said. 'As I was trying to explain this to your master weaponer—'

'Outside airlock door closed,' Eruken said in a near-whisper, in imitation of Mabumba's hushed tones. Martinez put his hand over his microphone to keep Ondakaal from overhearing.

'Depressurize and withdraw boarding tube. Warn crew to secure for zero gravity.'

'Yes, lord lieutenant.'

'All manoeuvring thrusters gimballed,' Mabumba said. 'Pressure at thruster heads nominal.' A warning blast sounded, shrill and sudden, then faded. 'Zero gravity warning sounded.'

'If your master weaponer has shown you the fleetcom's order . . .' Ondakaal was continuing. Martinez took his hand from his microphone.

'Master Alikhan is bringing the order now,' Martinez told him. 'Once I read it, I'm sure there will be no difficulty. Please stand by.'

Ondakaal fell silent, his arms hanging at his sides in an expression of baffled defeat. He had decided to trust that the order from Fanaghee would pry open *Corona*'s airlock, but his posture suggested he very doubted that the order would work its magic.

'Boarding tube withdrawn,' Eruken reported. 'Ship is on one hundred percent internal power. Electrical connections withdrawn. Outside connectors sealed.'

Martinez looked at his own displays. The Daimong ships now had Naxid guards on their airlocks, the Daimong guards withdrawn or under arrest. The displays could tell him nothing, now, that he didn't already know.

He began reconfiguring his displays for engine start and manoeuvre.

'Data connectors withdrawn,' Eruken said. 'Outside data ports sealed.'

Martinez saw Ondakaal start, then began an urgent communication with his sleeve display. Martinez couldn't quite hear the exchange. Then Ondakaal looked up in surprise at the camera above the airlock.

'You have withdrawn air and water connections to your ship!' he said. 'What does this mean?'

Martinez permitted himself a tight smile. 'I am sealing myself from the station,' he said, 'until certain things are explained.'

'You are not authorized!' Ondakaal raged. 'You must open your airlock to our inspectors!'

'Please tell me,' Martinez said, 'why you are bringing armed personnel onto my ship. You don't need guns for an inspection, lieutenant.'

'This is by order of the fleet commander! You are not to question her orders!'

'Main engines gimballed,' Mabumba said. 'Gimbal test successful.' Then, 'Holding at ten seconds.'

'Launch,' Martinez said.

'*Launch?*' demanded Ondakaal. 'What do you mean *launch?*' Martinez cut the Naxid off.

'Engines ready to fire on command,' said Mabumba.

'Clamps withdrawn,' Eruken said. 'Magnetic grapples released.'

Corona was berthed nose-in to the outer rim of Magaria's outer accelerator ring, which was rotating at nine times the speed of the planet below. The rotation of the ring supplied the centrifugal force that provided gravity to the ship. In order to unberth, the ship didn't need to fire manoeuvring thrusters: it merely had to ungrapple and allow the release of centripetal force to hurl the frigate into space.

Which meant that the ship's apparent gravity was gone. Martinez' first indication that *Corona* was clear of the station was the fact that he began to float free of his couch, and discovered that he'd ignored his own zero-gee warning and failed to strap himself in. He busied himself with his harness.

The gimballed acceleration cages creaked slightly as the weight came off them. 'Clear of the ring,' Eruken reported. 'Clear of *Perigee*.' The berths were staggered slightly so that *Corona* wouldn't be swatted out of the sky by the tail of the next ship moored to the ring, but still it was a relief to know that the danger was past.

'Pilot, zero our momentum,' Martinez said. He didn't want *Corona* to keep floating out into space, where it would make a perfect slow-moving target. He presumed that the Naxids wouldn't fire their antimatter missiles, since an antimatter warhead exploding on top of *Corona* would vaporize not only the target, but the dockyards, all the moored warships, and a chunk of the accelerator ring. But the point-defence lasers carried by the warships could be used offensively against *Corona,* and so could the antiproton beams carried by some of the larger ships. Though the lasers probably weren't powerful enough to kill the frigate, Martinez wasn't as confident about the antiproton beams, and any kind of damage might be fatal to Martinez' plans.

Defence against the antiproton beams was the strong magnetic field used in any case by *Corona* to repel radiation. Martinez ordered it turned on, not that it would help against a point–blank strike from one of the enemy beams.

Martinez felt himself nudge gently against his restraining straps, then float free again. Eruken had killed *Corona*'s residual momentum, and the frigate was now hovering with the ring rotating ahead of its nose.

'Pilot, manoeuvring thrusters,' he said. 'Take us directly south of the ring.'

Again that nudge against the straps. 'Manoeuvring due south, my lord.'

Martinez pressed keypads. 'Navigation,' he said, 'I'm sending you a course plot for Wormhole Four. Please load it into your computers.'

'Ah – yes, my lord.' Diem was looking at his displays a little wild–eyed, and Martinez remembered that he was only a trainee, and hadn't yet certified for navigator/2nd.

With himself, that made *two* inexperienced navigators in Command, Martinez realized. Not a good thing under the circumstances.

Vonderheydte's voice came from behind Martinez, and Martinez jumped: he'd forgotten someone was back there.

'I'm hearing complaints from the captain's cook, my lord,' he said. 'Low gravity's making a wreck out of his dinner. He says his sauce anglais is on the ceiling now.'

'Comm, tell the cook to batten everything down and get to an acceleration couch. We're going to be pulling some gees.' He turned to Eruken. 'Pilot, signal crew to secure for hard acceleration.'

Ear-blasting alarms whooped out, wailing up and down the scale. Personnel had been killed for not getting into their acceleration couches in time, and Martinez wanted to give them as much warning as possible.

The alarm faded, leaving a gaping silence in its wake. Diem

was looking over the navigation plot with what looked like growing desperation, while Eruken gazed at his controls and gnawed his lip. Mabumba cast a glance over his shoulder at Martinez, and his gaze seemed to centre on the pistol that lay near-weightless against his thigh.

None of them, Martinez realized, knew what was going on. Nor did anyone else on the ship.

'Comm: general announcement,' he said, and when he spoke again he heard his own voice echo back to him from the ship's public address system.

'This is Lieutenant Martinez in Command,' he said. 'I regret to tell you that a few minutes ago there was a mutiny on Magaria's ring. The mutineers took advantage of the absence of so many of the officers and crews on the Festival of Sport, and they boarded and seized most of the ships on the station.' Martinez licked his lips. 'Probably all ships, aside from our own. It is now our duty to take *Corona* to Zanshaa in order to alert the Fleet and the government to the danger presented by the mutiny, and to aid the Fleet in recapturing the lost ships.'

Well, Martinez thought, that took care of the facts. But somehow he felt the deep inadequacy of his words. A really *great* leader, he thought, would make an inspiring speech at this point, would fire the crew to their utmost exertions and win their undying loyalty through the eloquence of his words. He wondered if he, Gareth Martinez, could ever be such a leader.

What the hell, he thought. It seemed worth finding out.

'One further thought,' he said. 'Because the rebels have seized control of Magaria's ring, they are now in a position to bring overwhelming power onto the planet below. We must therefore consider that Captain Tarafah and the rest of the crew are lost, and can only hope that their captors will treat them decently . . .'

Well *this* is cheerful, he thought in the deep silence that followed. He had better strew a bit of hope in the crew's path before they all committed suicide or vowed to join the mutineers.

'There are only a few of us left on the ship,' Martinez said. 'We are going into extreme danger. We're going to have to stand extra watches and work extra hard for the months it will take us to get to Zanshaa, but I want you to understand that the captain and the other captives will be cheering for us to succeed. Because *we're* the *Corona*'s team now – *we're* the Coronas. And it's up to us to play hard and score the winning goal. End transmission.'

He wanted to cringe into his seat as he brought the transmission to an end, and he felt his skin flush with mortification. Whatever had possessed him to end with that ghastly sports metaphor? This wasn't eloquence, this was some kind of hideous, hackneyed cant that deserved nothing from the crouchbacks but derision. He should have made his announcement about the rebellion and then just shut up.

But as he looked around the control room, he saw that it seemed to have gone all right. Mabumba was looking at his displays with what seemed genuine resolve instead of casting covert glances at Martinez' gun. Eruken had straightened in his chair and was holding the thruster controls with determination. Even Tracy and Clarke – who had little to do, really, but gaze at their radar plots – seemed more intent on their work, and Kelly, who as weapons officer had even less to do, looked positively cheerful.

Only Diem was unhappy, but then Diem was probably transfixed by horror at the navigation plot Martinez had given him and hadn't heard a word.

Perhaps the crew had lower standards for oratory than the Master of Rhetoric at Martinez' old academy.

Martinez' sleeve display chimed, and he answered.

'Alikhan, my lord. I've completed that little errand you send me on.'

The display showed, not Alikhan's face, but the gaping front of Koslowski's safe, with the door removed.

'Yes, Alikhan?' Martinez said.

'Nothing, my lord. Negative.'

Panic began to stroke Martinez' nerves with feathery fingers. The Fleet had wisely made it impossible for a junior lieutenant such as himself to discharge Corona's awesome weaponry on his own initiative. The captain and each of the lieutenants carried keys with codes to unlock the frigate's weapons, but no less than three of the four keys had to be turned at the same moment in order for the weapons to be fired.

Even the defensive weapons, the point-defence lasers, were useless without the three keys. And the odds were that the Naxid ships were going to be firing at him very soon.

'Have you checked everywhere else?' Martinez asked. 'The drawers? Under the mattress?'

'Yes, my lord. Still negative. I can go to the captain's office and repeat the procedure.'

'No, I've got to accelerate.'

'If you can give me two minutes, I can at least get the equipment there. When acceleration starts, I can jump in the captain's rack. It won't be as comfortable as a proper acceleration couch, but it'll serve.'

For the couple hours of life that remains to us, Martinez thought.

'Very good,' he said. 'You've got two minutes.' And broke transmission.

'We've cleared the ring,' Eruken reported.

'Pilot, zero our momentum.'

'Zero our momentum, my lord.'

'Two minutes to acceleration. Mark.'

'Mark two minutes to acceleration,' Mabumba said, but

Diem raised a hand, like a boy at school asking permission to leave the classroom.

'My lord?' he said. 'I've been looking at your plot and – ah—' An exaggerated grimace distorted his thin, pale face, as if he were anticipating being whacked on the head for his presumption. 'It's illegal,' he said. 'You're – we're – flying far too close to the ring for safety.'

Martinez looked at him and tried to don his omnipotent face. 'But am I actually going to *hit* anything?'

'Ah—' In confusion, Diem stared at the plot. 'Not . . . not as such, no. No collisions. Just all sort of . . . of proximity problems.'

'Then we'll stick to the plan, Diem.' He turned to the engineer's station. 'Mabumba, give the crew a one-minute warning.'

'Very good, my lord.' Again the warning wailed, and Mabumba's voice boomed through the ship. 'One minute to acceleration. One minute.'

In one minute, Martinez thought, I am either going to be a hero or the greatest criminal in the Fleet since Taggart of the *Verity*.

'Everyone take their meds.'

He reached for the med injector stowed in a holster below his chair arm, and shot into his carotid a drug that would keep his blood vessels supple and help prevent stroke during high gees. The others in Command did the same.

'Eruken, withdraw radar reflectors.'

'Radar reflectors withdrawn.' The composite, resinous hull of *Corona* wasn't a natural radar reflector, and in order to make navigation and traffic control easier, the frigate carried several radar reflectors. Martinez figured that there was no point in making a target out of himself.

'Twenty seconds to ignition,' said Mabumba.

'Engines, fire on the navplot's mark,' Martinez said.

'Firing on the navplot's mark, my lord.'

'Ten-second warning, pilot.'

Again the warning screeched up and down the scale. Martinez could feel his blood thunder in answer.

'By the way, navigator,' he shouted over the alarm, 'you might as well kill that proximity alarm *now*.'

Then a giant boot kicked him in the spine as the engines fired, and *Corona* was on its way.

Nine

An officer may order the immediate death of a subordinate under which circumstances?

1. On recommendation of a duly appointed Court of Inquiry.
2. When the subordinate is found in arms against the lawful government.
3. When the officer possesses evidence that the subordinate is guilty of a capital crime.
4. Under any circumstances.

Sula touched her writing wand to the fourth and correct answer, then touched the icon that called for the next question. She hadn't felt that military law was her strongest subject, but fortunately for her test scores, military law was so draconian that there was very little room for error or laxity of interpretation.

She also knew that military law was a lot less draconian in practice than in theory. There were relatively few captains who went around offhandedly whacking the heads off their subordinates, because in theory every citizen was the client of a patron Peer whose duty it was to supervise their welfare. While from experience Sula knew that many Peers couldn't be bothered with such duties, it nevertheless remained a possibility that if a Peer felt that one of his clients had been treated unjustly, he could make inquiries and cause trouble, and the result could be a suit in civil law that could drag on for decades. Captains who wanted to punish a subordinate severely would cover their backs by appointing a Court of Inquiry, and though they were not obliged to follow a court's recommendations, they usually did if they wanted to avoid problems later on.

Sula sped through the next few questions secure in the knowledge that she was doing extremely well on the exams. Military law was her weakest subject barring interpretation of the Praxis, and so far the questions weren't difficult.

A first definitely seemed within her grasp.

She tapped the butt end of her wand on the screen as she contemplated the next problem, which had to do with jurisdiction among the various military and paramilitary organizations on a ring station outside the military base proper, and then the door to the exam room banged open.

'*Scuuuuum!*'

Sula could thank years of conditioning for the fact that her mind continued to gnaw on the problem even as she leaped to her feet, chin high, throat bared.

'My lord?' The Daimong proctor seemed more flustered than the cadets. 'Why are you—'

The intruder was Terran, and wore the uniform of a full captain. 'We have an emergency situation,' he said. 'The exams are cancelled. All Fleet personnel are to report to their stations. Those who have no current assignment are to report to Ring Command, Personnel Section.'

'But my lord—' the Daimong protested.

'*Now, scum!*' The captain's order was directed toward the cadets, not the exam proctor.

The cadets crowded for the exit. The problem of jurisdiction slowly faded from Sula's mind, and she looked about her with growing astonishment.

The proctor appeared not to know what to do. She was

making attempts to contact someone on her desk comm, but seemed to be having no success.

Emergency situation, Sula thought, and then ran to the changing room to get out of her robes and into her uniform. Despite the buzzing speculation of the other cadets, Sula's mind was still trapped in the pattern of exam questions.

Examinations for lieutenant, she thought, *have been cancelled for the following reasons:*

1. On the whim of a superior officer.
2. Because we say so.
3. Lieutenants' exams have never been cancelled.

The correct answer, of course, was the third.
Lieutenants' exams have never *been cancelled.*
Which meant that whatever was going on, it was big.

Corona ducked and darted and sped along the southern edge of Magaria's ring, the slim form of the frigate obscured by the brilliance of its blazing tail of annihilated matter. Martinez felt himself pressed deeper and deeper into the acceleration couch, spreading into the supportive gel like a piece of putty pressed into a mould. The weight of the pistol was a fierce pain digging into his right hip.

Martinez may have blacked out as acceleration approached ten gravities, but *Corona* didn't stay at such speed for long, just enough to achieve escape velocity once it was time to dodge out from the ring station and onto a course for Magaria Wormhole Four.

Martinez was using Magaria's ring for cover, knowing that the Naxids would never dare fire at him for fear of hitting the ring. And when it was time to break cover and dash for the wormhole, he kept the rim directly between Corona and the Naxid squadrons.

Corona's acceleration dropped to six gravities, which was

misery for the crew, not because they lost consciousness but because they retained it, and with it the discomfort of the ship's desperate, blazing acceleration.

Eighteen minutes into *Corona*'s escape, Martinez finally heard from the Naxids.

'Urgent message via communications laser, my lord.' Vonderheydte's words came into Martinez' earphones. 'From Ring Command.'

The comm laser was necessary to punch a signal through *Corona*'s hot plasma tail. 'Tell them to stand by, I'll speak in person,' Martinez said.

'Very good, my lord.'

'Are the intership radio channels still jammed?'

'No, my lord. Jamming dropped about two minutes ago, with the Coronas ahead three to one.'

Martinez smiled, and then his smile faded as he realized why the jamming had ceased. Seizure of the non-Naxid squadrons was complete, and it was no longer necessary to prevent the target ships from signalling their distress.

Corona was truly alone now, in a hostile system.

He counted out two minutes – two more minutes in which the inevitable was delayed – and told Vonderheydte to patch Ring Command onto his displays. He waited until the winking light on his console told him he was being recorded.

'This is Martinez,' he said.

His display showed that his interlocutor was a Naxid in the uniform of a senior captain, whose speech was delayed only very slightly by the message crossing the distance between them.

'Lord lieutenant Martinez,' the Naxid said, 'I am Senior Captain Deghbal, commanding Magaria Ring. You have departed the ring without permission, and engaged in reckless manoeuvres that have endangered your ship and the station. You are ordered to return at once.'

'I thought Captain An-Char commanded the ring station,' Martinez said.

'Captain An-Char is unavailable.' The words were spoken after a slight hesitation. 'I am in command of the ring. You are directed to return.'

'Can you can assure me that lord lieutenant Ondakaal is under arrest?' Martinez said. 'He opened fire on my airlock guards and wounded one of them. He said that our ship was to be boarded and we were all to be killed.'

Deghbal reared slightly at this, and Martinez knew that his barefaced lie had caught the Naxid completely by surprise.

Anything to confuse the Naxids and get Ondakaal in trouble, he thought. And more importantly, to delay. *Delay.* Delay had to be his chief object now.

'Everything is now under control,' Deghbal said finally. 'There is no reason to be alarmed. You may return *Corona* to her berth.'

Martinez took a deep breath against the gravities that sat on his chest. 'Lord escap,' he said, 'I have been instructed by my captain not to permit anyone aboard the ship without his express order. Can you get me that order?'

Anger added force Deghbal's reply. 'Your captain's permission is not necessary! My order alone should be sufficient!'

Martinez did his best to look as if he was seriously considering this line of argument. He gave the camera a plaintive look. 'Well, lord escap,' he said, 'I would really like my captain's order on this.'

'I am your superior officer! You must obey my orders! If I am not obeyed there will be unfortunate consequences for both your ship and yourself!'

Martinez wondered if anyone had ever actually disobeyed one of Deghbal's orders before. Probably not. He hoped he could profit by Deghbal's unfamiliarity with disobedience, and again tried to look as if he were pondering the escap's words. Then he hardened his face into what he hoped was a kind of dimwitted, stubborn resolve.

'I want Captain Tarafah's order,' he said. 'I trust him to know what's actually going on.' And then he frowned at the camera. 'End transmission.'

I am enjoying this too much, Martinez thought, but still he pictured Deghbal cursing at the orange *End Transmission* symbol appearing on his displays; and then Martinez wondered if he'd overplayed his hand, if Deghbal would be angry enough simply to order a barrage of missiles to pursue *Corona* until the frigate was destroyed.

He looked towards Tracy and Clarke, who were monitoring the sensor screens, and said, 'Screens, if you see missile tracks, let me know *fast.*'

Pinned by acceleration on their tandem couches, they rolled their heads towards him in wide-eyed surmise – though not related so far as he knew, they looked very much alike, being dark-haired, broad-shouldered young women – and then turned their heads quickly back to their displays.

Martinez paged Alikhan, this time using the ship's system rather than his sleeve display, a convenience that enabled Martinez to use his headset mic rather than having to talk into his sleeve button. Alikhan's own sleeve button showed nothing but the ceiling in Tarafah's cabin, the only view available as Alikhan lay in the captain's bed under six gravities.

'Did you have any luck?'

Alikhan's voice showed the strain of the gravities he was labouring under. 'I got the gear to the captain's cabin, my lord. But all I had time to do was search his desk – no luck there.'

'If I slow our acceleration to two gravities, do you think you could handle the, the gear?'

'I could, my lord.'

'Right. End transmission.' He raised his voice to carry to Eruken. 'Engines. Reduce acceleration to two gravities.'

'Very good, my lord.' Plain relief dripped from Eruken's words. The ferocity of the acceleration eased, and *Corona*'s frame groaned with the release of strain.

'My lord?' Vonderheydte's query came into Martinez' headset. 'May I have permission to use the toilet? I was drinking coffee while I was censoring the mail, and—'

Martinez grinned. The commonplace trumped the dramatic every time.

'Permission given,' he said. 'Transfer the comm displays to my board while you're gone. Be careful.'

Moving under two gravities was like walking with another person on your back, possible but with care. Sprains and breaks were common, though, and Martinez couldn't afford injured personnel. *Corona*'s 'doctor' – actually a pharmacist second class – was also the team doctor, and had been left behind on Magaria.

But he didn't want the crew in Command to pee all over themselves, either.

'Who *else* needs the toilet?' Most of the hands went up. High gees were hard on bladders.

Come to think of it, Martinez thought, he could use the toilet himself. He made a general announcement to the ship's company that people would have some time to make ablutions, again with care.

If *Corona* survived the next few hours, he'd put the crew into vac suits, with the necessary sanitary appliances built in.

Four crewmen had rotated in and out of the toilet before Alikhan reported in. 'I've got the safe open, my lord. No luck.'

Black anger descended on Martinez. This failure had very possibly killed everyone. 'Search the room,' he said. 'Then his office.'

'Very good, my lord. Does he have a safe in his office?'

'I don't know. If there is, you'll know what to do.'

Martinez was last in rotation for the toilet. Stooped with

the weight of gravity, he had just shuffled back into Command when the next transmission came from Ring Command. 'It's the elcap, my lord!' Vonderheydte proclaimed cheerfully, as if proclaiming the belief that Tarafah's mere electronic presence would straighten out all misunderstandings and solve all *Corona*'s problems.

'Stand by,' Martinez said. He lowered himself gently into the couch, released the cage to gimbal to a more comfortable position, then lowered the displays to lock in front of him.

Martinez wondered if he shouted *Where is your captain's key?* at some point in the conversation, if Tarafah would have the chance to answer before the rebels flattened him or switched off. He wondered if Tarafah would even consider giving him the answer to the question.

And he wondered that if he so much as asked the question, he would be confirming Ring Command's worst suspicions and immediately trigger a salvo of missiles aimed in *Corona*'s direction.

He decided he'd better not ask.

'Martinez here,' he answered.

Tarafah glowered at him from the display, which jerked and bobbed a little. It was probably someone else's sleeve camera, since Tarafah was wearing sweats and had no sleeve rig of his own. Martinez heard crowd noises in the background. Tarafah was somewhere indoors, with institutional decor, and his voice echoed off the hard walls – probably he was in one of the rooms or corridors beneath the football stadium.

'What's this I hear about you launching *Corona* and going like a skyrocket all over the ring?' Tarafah demanded.

Delay, Martinez thought.

'I hear the Coronas are ahead three to one, my lord,' he said. 'Congratulations, first of all – your careful planning is bearing fruit.'

'It's four to one now,' Tarafah said. A touch of vanity tinged his anger.

'Sorensen to Villa to Yamana to Sorensen to Digby – and goal. Brilliant, my lord.'

'Thank you,' Tarafah grudged. 'But I've got to get back to the team – we don't want them to get another goal in the final minutes.'

'Yes, my lord. I'm sorry you were asked to leave the game.'

'My ship.' Tarafah's eyes narrowed. 'What about my ship?'

'Armed Naxids tried to board the *Corona,* my lord. I had to get her out of dock.'

Tarafah gave a dismissive look. 'That's been explained. It was a surprise inspection.'

'They were *armed,* my lord,' Martinez said. 'Why do inspectors need guns? And they were storming every ship on the station. Forty of them to every ship. Naxids. *Only* Naxids. With guns.'

Tarafah's eyes cut away, to something or someone out of frame, and then back.

'Was it a Naxid who brought you the information, my lord?' Martinez inquired gently. 'Are there Naxids with you now?'

Tarafah hesitated, and then his look hardened again. 'Of course they're Naxids,' he said finally. 'They're from Fleet Commander Fanaghee's staff.' His tone turned accusing. 'You've got the *fleetcom* involved, Martinez! Do you know how *vast* this is?' A vast cheer roared up from the nearby crowd, and impatience crossed his face. 'I've got to get back to the game. Now you turn *Corona* around and get back to the station – everything will get straightened out once you get back.'

Martinez' heart sank. This, he thought, is the precise moment at which any of this stops being fun.

'You're saying this freely?' he asked. 'Under no duress or compulsion?'

'Of course,' Tarafah snapped. 'Now get *Corona* back to the rim and we'll get everything settled.'

'Yes, my lord.' Tasting the bitterness that striped Martinez' tongue at the knowledge of what he'd have to say next.

Delay, he told himself. Delay was all. Delay would justify everything.

'If you'll just give me the code word,' he told Tarafah, 'I'll swing the ship around and start the deceleration.'

Tarafah had started to turn, ready to return the football pitch, but now he swung back to the camera.

'The what?' he said.

Martinez tried to keep his face earnest. 'The code word,' he said. 'The code word you gave me last night.'

A snarl of frustration crossed Tarafah's face. 'What are you talking about, Martinez?'

'Remember?' Martinez said, sorrow and dread entering his heart even as he tried to keep his face earnest and eager. 'Remember at dinner? When I raised my suspicions about the Naxid movements, you told me that no one was to board *Corona* unless you gave the password.'

'I never gave you a password!' Tarafah said. 'What are you driveling about?'

He seemed genuinely baffled. Sadness weighed on Martinez like the slow, inevitable pressure of gravity. Tarafah didn't yet understand just how seriously Martinez had betrayed him.

'The password that tells me that you're free and uncoerced,' Martinez said. 'You've got to give me the password, my lord, before I can turn *Corona* around.'

'I didn't give you anything—' The camera on Tarafah jiggled. 'Anything of the sort. I—' He hesitated, his eyes cutting out of frame, then back. 'I demand that you turn *Corona* around and return to the ring station!'

'Without the password?' Martinez said, and this time he

allowed his sorrow to show. 'I understand, lord elcap. End transmission.'

He could have kept the dialogue going for another few rounds, but he simply hadn't the heart for it.

He had bought time, and he had bought it with his captain. It would take time for the Naxids to get a password out of Tarafah, the more so because the password did not exist.

For a moment Martinez gave himself up to the images of Tarafah being slashed with stun batons, battered, shackled, shot. He saw Tarafah lying in his blood, insisting through pain-clenched teeth that there was no password.

Delay. Martinez had bought time, that was the important thing.

He paged Alikhan again. 'Anything?'

'There *was* a safe in the elcap's office, my lord. Nothing in it but documents.'

'Have you searched the office?'

'I'm doing so now, my lord.'

'Shall I send you help?'

'Can you trust anyone else for the job, my lord?'

The question brought Martinez up short. Who *could* he trust? The captain's and lieutenants' keys were the most dangerous items on the ship. It was a capital crime – one of those involving flaying and dismemberment – to possess a key that didn't belong to you. Was there anyone on the crew who was truly convinced that it was necessary to get hold of the keys, and actually obey the order?

Martinez considered the matter, then laughed as a possibility occurred to him. He checked the crew manifests to find where the crew action stations were, then paged Zhou and Knadjian. The two stared at him from the displays, surprise plain on their bruised faces.

'I want you to report to Alikhan in the captain's office and follow his instructions,' he told them, to their further surprise.

Corona's merry thugs should have a fine old time tearing the captain's stateroom to bits.

'My lord!' Tracy, the sensor operator, gave a sudden surprised squeak. '*Ferogash* has launched!'

A cruiser, roughly twice *Corona*'s size. 'Do you have a course?' Martinez asked.

'It hasn't fired its torch, my lord. It's just separated from the ring station.'

'Let me know if it goes anywhere.'

'Yes, my lord.'

The Naxids were planning something for *Ferogash,* and Martinez guessed that *Corona* featured in that plan.

He thought a moment, and then paged Saavedra, the captain's secretary.

'Saavedra,' he said, 'you understand our situation.'

Saavedra gave him a careful look, lips pinched beneath his broad mustachios. 'I understand your *explanation* of the situation, lord lieutenant.'

Martinez found growing in himself a distinct lack of enthusiasm for warrant officers who made these sorts of rhetorical distinctions.

'Do you understand that *Corona* is in danger?' he asked. 'That we may be fired on?'

Saavedra gave a terse nod. 'I understand, my lord.'

'In order to activate the defensive weaponry I need the captain's key. Do you know where the captain keeps it?'

Saavedra's eyes hardened. His jaw firmed. 'I do *not*, my lord.'

'Are you certain? The lives of everyone on this ship may be at stake.'

'I don't know where the key is, my lord.'

'You've never come across it? You've never seen him take it off, or take it from a drawer, or from his safe . . . ?'

'On the sole occasions on which I have seen the captain's key, it has been around the captain's neck.'

Martinez decided he didn't like warrant officers who used excessively formal diction, either. He considered visiting Saavedra in whatever compartment he sheltered in and blowing a hole in his knee in hopes a memory might leak out. But the fantasy was only that; he didn't dare leave Command.

Sweet reason would have to prevail.

'I need you to *think,*' Martinez urged. 'Think about where the captain puts his valuables. Where he might hide something precious. Anything you can tell me.'

Saavedra looked imperiously from the display. 'I shall consult my memory, my lord.'

'Consult away.' Disgusted. 'End transmission.'

For the next fourteen minutes *Ferogash* continued to drift away from the ring station without manoeuvring. Alikhan reported no success, even after the two reinforcements arrived and Martinez suggested thumping the panelling for secret compartments and tearing open the captain's pantry. If the office had been carpeted he would have suggested tearing up the rugs.

It was then that another transmission came from Ring Command. 'It's Deghbal, my lord,' Vonderheydte reported.

'Tell him to stand by.'

Martinez counted a minute and a half, as much as he dared, and then answered.

'This is Martinez, my lord.'

Deghbal's black-on-green eyes glimmered in the lights of the ring's command centre. 'Your captain has recalled the password he gave you,' he said. 'The password is "offsides".'

Martinez tried to look relieved, as if the word were the thing he desired most in all the world instead of the first thing Tarafah could think of when the pain finally grew too great to bear.

'Thank you, my lord,' Martinez breathed. 'Now may I hear the word from lord elcap Tarafah himself?'

'Lord Tarafah is unavailable,' Deghbal said. 'Your team has just won a victory, four goals to one. The field is in turmoil. There is much celebration. I don't believe we could locate Captain Tarafah even if we wished to.'

Martinez forced onto his face what he hoped was an ingratiating smile. 'I'd still like to hear it from the captain, if I may.'

'You may not!' Deghbal's response was immediate, and sharp. 'This has gone on long enough. You will return *Corona* to her berth at once.'

'I'd very much like to hear that from my captain.'

'You will return immediately!' Captain Deghbal's voice contained the glottal throb that was the Naxid equivalent of a snarl. *'There have been enough games today!'* Deghbal leaned towards the camera, his black beaded lips drawn back. 'If you fail in your obedience, I will order that your ship be fired upon.'

'Just because I want to speak to my captain?' Martinez said. He widened his eyes in feigned disbelief. 'Just let me hear the word from my captain and everything will be fine.'

'Obey my order or face the consequences.' Deghbal reared back, his black-on-green eyes glaring.

Martinez said nothing, simply leaned back in his couch and looked impassively at the camera. He could think of no other way to delay things. He and Deghbal stared at each other for a long, long moment . . . Martinez counted eight seconds. Then Deghbal gave a contemptuous flick of one hand.

'End transmission.' The orange *end transmission* symbol appeared, and Martinez told the display to vanish.

Now we die, he thought.

But nothing happened right away. *Corona*'s engines burned on for another nine minutes before anything was heard from the ring station.

'*Ferogash* is manoeuvring, my lord!' from Tracy.

'*Ferogash* firing main engines!' echoed Clarke.

Martinez tried to control his suddenly leaping heart. 'What course?'

'Zero-zero-one by zero-zero-one by absolute. Course due north, my lord. Two gravities and accelerating.' The 313-degree Shaa compass had no zero coordinate, but began instead with one, the odd number left over after factoring the prime number. The one, of course, stood for the One True Way of the Praxis.

Ferogash wasn't chasing, it was heading north, the quickest way to clear the ring and open fire.

'Page crewman Saavedra,' Martinez said. The warrant officer's supercilious face appeared promptly.

'We're about to be fired on by a cruiser twice our strength,' Martinez said. 'If you've got any ideas about where the captain keeps his key, it's time to let me know.'

'I have no idea, lord lieutenant,' Saavedra said. 'I had no desire to know where the captain kept his key, and I paid no attention to it.'

'Missile flares!' Clarke called. 'Three, five, six . . . eight missile tracks, my lord!'

'We've got eight missiles coming our way,' Martinez told Saavedra. 'If you've got any ideas about the key, you'd better let me know.'

Saavedra stared stonily at Martinez. 'You could surrender, my lord, and return to base,' he said. 'I'm sure the fleetcom would order the missiles disarmed if you obeyed her command.'

The total, incorruptible bastard, Martinez snarled. Knee-capping was too good for him.

'Fourteen minutes to detonation, my lord,' Tracy said.

'You've got less than fourteen minutes to think of something we haven't tried,' Martinez told Saavedra. 'Then you can die with the rest of the crew.' He signed off and turned to Kelly. 'Weapons. I want you to prepare to launch one of the pinnaces as a decoy.'

'Yes, my lord.' She hesitated, then turned her dark eyes to Martinez. 'My lord, ah – how exactly would I *do* that?'

'We fire the pinnace on the same course, but at a slower speed. We hope the missiles lock onto the pinnace instead of us.'

Without the captain's key, the two pinnaces were the only things Martinez *could* launch. Unfortunately they weren't armed, so they were useless for offence, and the chances of one of the missiles mistaking a pinnace for the frigate were slim to none.

Kelly blinked at her console. 'I think I can do that, my lord.'

'Good. Let me know when you're ready, and I'll check your work.'

She seemed reassured. 'Very good, my lord.'

Martinez called Alikhan. 'Have you tried searching Koslowski's cabin again?'

'We have, my lord.'

'Any new ideas *at all?*'

'Nothing, my lord.'

'Right then. Get your people into the officers' racks. I'm going to kick some gees.' To Mabumba. 'Acceleration warning.'

The wailed cry of the acceleration warning sounded. 'Very good, my lord.'

He increased *Corona*'s acceleration to six gees while he tried desperately to think of a way to escape. The heavy gravity should have wearied him but his mind blazed with ideas – radical manoeuvres, imaginative improvision of decoys, suicide pinnace dives into the ring station – all of them pointless. The only thing he'd succeed at was slowing the rate at which the missiles were closing, and buying his crew a few more minutes' life.

'Twelve minutes, my lord.' *Corona*'s increased acceleration had bought them a few more moments of life.

Martinez realized that his mind was racing too quickly to actually be of any use, and he tried to slow himself down, go through everything he knew step by step.

Garcia had told him that Koslowski never wore his lieutenant's key while playing football. Koslowski was the only one of *Corona*'s officers that Martinez definitely knew wasn't wearing his key, so that meant he should concentrate on Koslowski.

The sensible place for Koslowski to put his key would be in the safe in his cabin, but Koslowski hadn't been that sensible. He hadn't put it in any other obvious place in his cabin, either. So where else could he have gone?

Where else did *officers* go? The wardroom.

The wardroom. It was where the officers ate and relaxed. There was a locked pantry where the officers kept their drinks and delicacies.

But the wardroom was an insecure place, there were people in cleaning, and the wardroom steward and cook both had keys to the pantry. The wardroom seemed highly unlikely.

Perhaps Koslowski gave the key to someone he trusted. But the only likely candidates were on the team.

'Ten minutes, my lord.'

Fine, Martinez went on, but if officers weren't going to be wearing their keys, they were supposed to return them to their captain. So on the assumption that Koslowski did what he was supposed to do, where did Tarafah put it?

Not in either of his safes. Not in his desk. Not in his drawers. Not under his mattress or in a secret compartment in the custom mahogany paneling of his walls.

He put it . . . *around his neck*. Martinez' heart sank. He could picture it happening, picture Tarafah looping the elastic cord around his neck and tucking the key down the front of his sweats, to join his own captain's key nestled against his chest hairs . . .

No. Martinez put the image firmly from his mind. The key had to be somewhere else.

'Nine minutes, my lord.' The words were spoken over a long, groaning shudder from *Corona*'s stressed frame.

Would Fanaghee accept *Corona*'s surrender? Martinez wondered. He could safely assume that she would want the frigate back, certainly. But – perhaps of more vital interest – would Fanaghee accept *Martinez*' surrender?.

Martinez thought not. His blood would probably still be decorating the walls of Command when Fanaghee put her new captain on board. Perhaps it would be easier on everyone if he just took his sidearm and blew out his own brains.

No. Martinez put the thought out of his mind. Where was the *key*?

He pictured Koslowski's cabin, exactly like his own . . . small, the narrow gimbaled bed, the wash stand, the large wardrobe that contained the formidable number of uniforms required, the chests with the grand amount of gear an officer was expected to carry from one posting to the next. The shelves, the small desk with its computer access.

There just wasn't any room to hide something. A cabin was *small*.

He knew that the captain's sleeping cabin was larger, though he'd never been in it, but he couldn't imagine it would be very different.

And then there was the captain's office. The desk, with its computer access. The safe. The shelves, and all the football trophies.

The trophies. The glittering objects, standing in his office and braced against high gee, that meant more to Lieutenant-Captain Tarafah than anything else, including probably his command. The objects that he savoured every day, that he probably caressed in secret.

Martinez was so transfixed by the memory of the trophies that he failed to hear the words that were spoken to him.

'Sorry?' he said absently. 'Repeat, please.'

'I think I've configured the pinnace as you wished,' Kelly said.

'Right. Stand by.'

He paged Alikhan. 'Did you check the *trophies*?' he demanded.

'My lord?'

'Did you look in the trophies? The Home Fleet Trophies are *cups,* aren't they?'

He could hear Alikhan's chagrin even through the strain that six gravities was putting on his voice.

'No, my lord. I didn't think to look.'

'Engines!' Martinez cried. 'Reduce acceleration to one gravity!'

'Reducing acceleration to one gravity, my lord,' Mabumba repeated.

Corona's beams groaned as the oppressive weight eased. Martinez gasped in air, grateful to breathe without labour. He took a half dozen sweet breaths, and then impatience drove him to demand information.

'What are you finding, Alikhan?'

'I'm trying to work the catch to the lid now, my lord. *There* . . . I'm reaching inside . . .'

In the silence that followed, even over the remorseless percussion of his heart, Martinez could hear the metallic scrape of Alikhan's fingernails whispering against the inside of the cup. And then he heard Alikhan's deep sigh, a sigh that to Martinez seemed filled with all the despair in the universe . . .

'Six minutes, my lord.' Tracy's words were leaden.

'I've got them both, Lord Gareth,' said Alikhan in a voice of quiet exultation.

For an instant the hopelessness still clung like a shroud to Martinez' mind, and then it was obliterated by an electric surge of triumph that almost had him whooping aloud.

'Activate the captain's desk display,' he said. 'Insert his key. Prepare to turn on my mark. *Weapons! Kelly! Catch!*'

Cadet Kelly turned as Martinez fished in his pocket for Garcia's key. The expression on her face was luminous, as if with glowing eyes she were seeing Martinez descend from heaven on rainbow clouds. The cadet stretched out her lanky arms, and Martinez tossed her the key.

'Insert and turn on my mark.'

'Very good, my lord!'

Martinez opened his tunic and pulled his own key off over his head. He inserted the key into the silvery metal slot on the command console before him.

'Weapons. Alikhan. Turn on my mark. Three. Two. One. Mark.'

Kelly gave a dazzled smile as the weapons board lit up before her eyes. Another light appeared on Martinez' board, indicating that the weapons were free.

'Alikhan, get to a rack and strap in.'

'Yes my lord.'

And then, as frantic relief poured into his veins, Martinez turned to Kelly. 'Power up point-defence lasers!' he called. 'This is *not* a drill!' Such was his haste that he had to keep himself from screaming the words like a lunatic.

'This is not a drill,' Kelly repeated through a broad, brilliant smile. 'Powering up point-defence lasers.'

'Activate radars aft.'

'Radars activated aft, my lord.'

'This is not a drill. Charge missile battery one with anti-matter.'

'This is not a drill. Charging missiles battery one with antimatter . . . missiles charged, my lord.'

The missiles had been charged with their antimatter fuel, each unit consisting of a solid flake of antihydrogen which had been carefully doped with an excess of positrons that allowed it to be suspended by static electricity inside a tiny etched silicon chip. The configuration was stable and would last for decades, and the chips were so diminutive, well beneath anything that could be seen with a conventional microscope, that the chips as a mass flowed like liquid. The antihydrogen served both as propellant for the missile and as the warhead – any fuel that didn't get used up on the approach would go bang at the end of the journey.

The same antihydrogen fuel was used by *Corona* for its own propulsion, though larger ships used antihydrogen suspended in larger microchips that would provide more power to the engines.

'Screens,' Martinez asked, 'what's the dispersal on that salvo?'

'They're clumped together, my lord,' Tracy responded.

Martinez pulled the radar tracks onto his own display. The oncoming missiles *were* clumped, flying as if in formation. One of *Corona*'s missiles should suffice to knock them out, but perhaps he'd better fire two just to be sure.

He pulled the weapons board into his own displays and began configuring the missiles. 'We'll fire battery one in salvos of two,' he explained to Kelly. 'The first two will take care of the oncoming missiles. The next two will accelerate till they're just short of the enemy missiles, then cut power and drift through the blast, coming out the far side heading for the station but looking on the radars like debris – or so we'll hope. The next pair will burn straight in for the ring station and probably get shot down, but may distract them from the second pair. The fourth pair we'll keep in reserve.'

Kelly looked a little overwhelmed. 'Yes, my lord,' she said finally.

'When you reload, load tube one with a decoy.'

Pressing keypads. 'Yes, my lord.'

On a larger ship, there would be a tactical officer to take care of all these details. But as he spun his plans, as his fingers danced in the displays and tapped console pads,

Martinez found that he was enjoying himself again, relishing the planning and the execution and most of all the little surprise he was planning to spring on the Naxids.

Blow everything. Garcia's words echoed in his mind, and he felt his pleasure fade. It wasn't just rebel Naxids on the ships he planned to destroy, it was their captive crews, and the military installations on the ring were only a small part of the huge structure: millions of civilians lived there as well. All would die if his clever little plan succeeded.

He stared for a moment into a dark, cold imagining: the flash, the fireball, the spray of gamma rays. The ring station rent apart, spinning out of control, parts flung into space, others dragged to flame and impact on the planet's surface by the skyhook cables.

'Three minutes, my lord.' Tracy's words cut through his reverie, and with a deliberate resolve he put aside the horror of his vision.

'This is not a drill,' Martinez said. 'Fire tubes one and two.'

'One and two fired, my lord. This is not a drill.' Then, after a pause in which gauss rails flung the missiles into space and the missiles reoriented and ignited. 'Missiles fired and running normally.'

Martinez watched the missiles fly away through his displays.

'Weapons, this is not a drill. Fire three and four.'

The pair fired, and the next pair, all firing normally. Martinez decided to put more distance between himself and any detonating antimatter.

'Engines, high gravity warning.' The sirens wailed.

'High gee warning, my lord.'

Martinez ordered a resumption of the six-gravity acceleration.

Now, he thought as the leaden weights of gravity were added one by one to his chest, *we'll see how they react.*

The Naxids must have seen his missile launches, and must now know that *Corona* had teeth. They must understand that their dense-packed formation of eight offensive missiles would be obliterated by *Corona*'s counterfire. But it wasn't too late to save their barrage: they could send orders to the individual missiles to diverge, to separate so they couldn't all be knocked out at once.

But they didn't. *Corona*'s first pair of missiles exploded right in the middle of the enemy salvo, destroying them all in the plasma fireball created when the exploding antihydrogen hit the tungsten surrounding the warhead. A wild furious cloud of radiation erupted between *Corona* and Magaria, preventing either *Corona* or the Naxids from seeing what was happening on the other side.

The radiation gradually cooled and faded. The first objects the sensors could detect, through the weakening shroud, were the burning tails of missiles five and six heading for the ring. The second things seen were missile tails as well, the second salvo of eight fired from *Ferogash*.

'Twenty-four minutes till impact, my lord.' That gave Martinez a comfortable amount of time to deal with them.

It wasn't until four of those minutes had passed that *Corona*'s radars finally detected missiles three and four falling towards the enemy with their torches extinguished, speed increasing as they were drawn towards Magaria by the invisible threads of gravity.

'The enemy salvo is still flying bunched up, my lord.'

The Naxids, their attack having failed once, were trying the same thing all over again. Martinez could only hope they'd keep this up.

Martinez realized, as he stared at the displays, that both he and the Naxids were, to an extent, improvising. Standard fleet tactics assumed that both sides would be moving fast, perhaps at a significant fraction of the speed of light, on courses more or less converging. Tactics assumed that the largest problem would be to detect the exact location of enemy ships, since ships could alter their trajectory significantly from the moment of any radar or ranging laser detecting them till the signal returned to the sender. Since the distances involved made ship-killing lasers useless – at $.3c$, it did not take a lot of manoeuvring to evade a beam of light that, however fast, moved only in a straight line – offensive action was taken with intelligent missiles that, with guidance, could chase their targets down. Lasers were relegated to last-ditch point-defence weaponry to be aimed at missiles homing in on a target. Missiles manoeuvred en route to the target, both to anticipate the target's evasions and to avoid countermeasures, and they would manoeuvre behind exploding screens of antimatter that hid them from the enemy, and hid friendly squadrons as well.

No one had ever developed tactics based on one side running away, from a standing start, while the other stood still, firing missiles at what amounted to point-blank range, barely exceeding a light-second. The irony was that the tactical problem was so dead easy that all the sophisticated tactics developed over the centuries were useless. What the situation really called for were those ship-killing lasers, since the range was so short that evasion was impossible, but the big lasers didn't exist. What remained was a slagging match, pure and simple, a giant and a dwarf hammering each other with fists from a range of a few inches.

In order to survive, Martinez thought, the dwarf had better think fast and stay nimble.

Martinez configured two missiles to destroy the enemy salvo, and then hesitated. One missile might be enough to do the job.

He had six reloads for each missile battery, making ninety-six altogether. He'd just burned six. He didn't know how many missiles the enemy squadrons held, but there had to be thousands, with more stored in the huge magazines of Magaria's ring station.

It might be that he couldn't afford to spend more than one missile on the attacking salvo. The Naxids could fire eight missiles to his one and stay well ahead.

He decided to fire only the one missile.

'Two more missile tracks, my lord.'

These, Martinez decided, were aimed at his own fifth and sixth missiles, the ones targeted on the ring. He had anticipated these missiles being targeted and he wasn't upset at losing them. Instead he plotted the intersection points and made sure they could be useful to him. He fired his own missile at the enemy salvo and timed it to intercept the oncoming salvo before the enemy's interceptors would hit his own missiles five and six.

At which point, now concealed from detection by the vast cloud of radiation shooting outwards from the destruction of nine antimatter missiles, he fired his decoy, altered course twenty-three degrees to port, staying within the plane of the ecliptic, and pushed his acceleration to ten gees.

Martinez and everyone else on board lost consciousness. When the concealing cloud began to disperse, the enemy interceptors hit his own missiles five and six, providing two more concealing clouds that masked *Corona* for several more minutes. When the radiation began to disperse, automated systems cut the engines and *Corona* drifted.

What the Naxids saw now on their screens was the decoy, a missile configured to reflect a radar image of approximately the same size as *Corona,* burning at a steady six gees' acceleration on *Corona*'s own course. Their radars would also see *Corona,* of course, but Martinez hoped they wouldn't find him interesting. If he was just a symbol on their screens they might not consider him worthy of investigation, not like the decoy that was so obviously attracting attention to itself. They might think he was a piece of debris, and only if they configured their sensors to show the actual size of the radar blip would they see that *Corona* was the size of a frigate.

And throughout all this, Martinez remembered, missiles three and four were falling, silently, unobtrusively, towards Magaria. Lawn-green projectiles with deadly white footballs painted on the nose.

While he was waiting for the Naxids to respond, he made a general announcement and told everyone to get into their vac suits, only to receive a reply from Maheshwari.

'The engine room crew is already suited, my lord.'

It was the first word he'd had directly from Maheshwari since *Corona* had departed its berth.

'Very good,' Martinez said, for lack of anything better, and then unstrapped to wrestle himself into the suit that had been hanging in Command's suit locker all this time. As he was ripping off his trousers he encountered the pistol belt, and hesitated. He could strap it on over the vac suit, but he decided the weapon was no longer needed.

His crew, his little kingdom of nineteen souls, had followed him on this mad enterprise. Perhaps it was because of the habit of following orders, perhaps it was because of his calm pose of authority in a confusing situation . . . and maybe it was because they were afraid he might use the pistol. But they were all committed now, one way or another, and the pistol was a clumsy thing that had already scored a bruise on Martinez' hip.

He rolled up the pistol belt and stuffed the weapon into the suit locker.

He was partway through attaching the sanitary gear in the lower half of the suit when Clarke, who continued to watch the screens while her partner suited, gave a sudden shout.

'Missile tracks! Lots of them! From *Ferogash,* from *Kashma,* from *Majesty* – they're *all* firing, my lord!'

Martinez kicked himself into the suit and lunged for the

Command cage, then called up the sensor screens. Each ship in the Naxid squadrons had fired a salvo at exactly the same moment.

'Any of them headed for *us*?' Martinez demanded.

'Ahh . . . it's too early to tell, my lord.'

Martinez hung in the cage and continued to attach the sanitary gear while the situation developed, and it was soon obvious that the decoy hadn't worked. Of the hundred and sixty-four missiles that had been fired, too many were heading directly for *Corona,* and too few for the decoy.

But the Naxids had made a mistake in firing so many all at the same moment. Although the weapons directors on the individual ships were taking care to manoeuvre their missiles from the start and not to let them fly in formation as *Ferogash* had done, still they were coming in one broad wave, and Martinez was able to tailor his defence so as to swat large numbers of enemy missiles out of the void with each interceptor he sent.

The Naxids would have done better to have each ship fire a salvo ten seconds apart. Martinez would have had to use up a lot more missiles to intercept them.

Radiation clouds bloomed in the displays as *Corona*'s counterfire wiped out most of the Naxid onslaught. Fourteen enemy missiles survived, all of which were killed by *Corona*'s point-defence lasers. Cadet Kelly proved to have a knack with the lasers, anticipating the missiles' jinks and knocking them down regardless.

By that time the Command crew were suited and *Corona* was under acceleration again, six gees for Wormhole Four. Martinez had eighty-one missiles left.

And he still had the two missiles falling towards Magaria's ring, both of which he watched on the monitors with burning interest. If just one of them got home, the rebellion was over, along with the lives of about four or five million sentient beings.

Apparently the Naxids eventually noticed at least one of the two missile-sized packages falling towards them, because missile four was hit by a defensive laser and destroyed, its antimatter contents spraying out in an uncontrolled fan, never quite managing a large explosion but creating a spectacular radiation cloud. The cloud must have confused enemy sensors, or their operators, because missile three was able to drift closer before it fired its engine and oriented on its target, the Fleet's ring station.

Defensive lasers were tardy in responding and caught the incoming missile only a few seconds from detonation. The missile blew anyway, just north of the ring station, causing a fireball nearly as powerful as if the missile had detonated normally. Martinez watched in knuckle-gnawing suspense as the radiation cloud engulfed the ring station like a wave flinging itself over the shore.

'Fire battery one,' Martinez ordered. Eight missiles leaped from the rails, oriented on the ring, and fired. Martinez sent the missiles their targeting data as they sped on their way.

Martinez again gnawed a knuckle as he watched the radiation cloud slowly disperse from the ring station. The Magaria ring remained intact, a thin, brilliant silver band rolling around the planet without any sign of damage, without any visible fires or gaping holes in its structure.

What failed to occur was retaliation. The Naxids' missile batteries remained silent.

It was the ring's point-defence lasers that blew away Martinez' eight-missile barrage, destroying all missiles before they could endanger the ring.

But through it all no ships fired. Martinez wondered in pure dazzled surprise if somehow he'd killed them.

Hours passed. Without the prospect of imminent death to focus his mind on escape, Martinez remembered his intention to get word out to the rest of the empire. The civilian ships in the system had just witnessed a spectacular combat. Martinez sent messages to each of them via comm laser, explaining that Naxid mutineers had seized the ring station and the fleet, that the wormhole relay stations were also compromised, and asking the ships' captains to inform the nearest Fleet element as soon as they left the Magaria system.

It was fully five hours before Martinez found out the enemy weren't all dead. *Majesty of the Praxis,* Fanaghee's flagship, fired a full twelve-missile salvo, each missile taking a wildly different track towards *Corona.* The different tracks meant they arrived at different times, and provided plenty of time for Kelly and Martinez, working together, to hit them all with the defensive lasers – all save one, which targeted *Corona*'s hitherto useless decoy and blew it up.

The missiles, fired from a standing start, never gained enough speed en route to successfully evade *Corona*'s defences. Knocking them down became sport: Martinez found that he enjoyed the kind of synchrony into which he and Kelly fell as they chose and destroyed the targets; and he enjoyed her broad grin as she aimed and fired, and her little contralto yelp of triumph when she scored a hit.

After the missiles were disposed of, Martinez ordered the acceleration reduced to half a gravity and called the cooks to ask if *Corona*'s victory feast was salvageable. The cooks' opinion was that the captain's and officers' suppers, with their delicate sauces applied liberally to the kitchen walls during the period of zero gee, were probably beyond hope; but that the heartier meal intended for the crew was probably capable of resuscitation. Martinez told them to get busy in the kitchen, and when they reported success told the crew they could take off their vacuum suits and go in shifts to dinner.

He ate on the second shift himself, after appointing Vonderheydte officer of the watch and leaving him strict instructions to call him if anything changed. There were only eight crew eating on the second shift, served by the three cooks, and all ate in the enlisted mess, officers and enlisted together. The few diners made a lot of noise, however, and the mood was exuberant, the crew loudly thankful they'd evaded danger. Martinez noticed only one quiet crewman among the others, the captain's secretary Saavedra, who spoke little, frowned into his meal, and chewed with solemn deliberation.

Martinez found himself sitting opposite Kelly. The lanky cadet was still wearing the broad grin she'd displayed when splashing oncoming missiles, and Martinez found himself reliving the escape with her, missile for missile, shot for shot. Exhilarated with relief and the memory of shared terror, they diagramed shots in the air with their hands and talked in a rush, each sentence tumbling over the one before.

I'm alive! Martinez thought. For the first time he allowed himself to bask in this miracle. *I'm alive!*

'I was terrified you wouldn't use the key when I tossed it to you,' Martinez said. 'I was afraid you'd stand on regulations and refuse.'

'When eight missiles were heading for us?' Kelly laughed. 'I'm as devoted to the regs as anyone, but devotion can only go so far.'

Alive! Martinez thought. Joy bubbled through his blood like champagne.

He joined Kelly in the elevator that took them to Command deck. 'Thanks,' he said. 'Thanks for working so well with me.'

'You're welcome,' she said, and then added, 'my lord.'

The elevator stopped at the command deck. Martinez began to step out, then hesitated. Wild impulse fluttered in his chest.

'I don't mean to offend,' he said, 'but would you like to drop another deck with me and, ah, celebrate our survival?'

The recreation chambers were one bulkhead below their feet. Kelly looked at him in surprise.

'Aren't our tummies a little full right now?' she said.

'You could get on top,' Martinez explained. 'I wouldn't have my weight on you that way.'

She barked a short, incredulous laugh, and gazed out of the elevator to the corridor outside, as if expecting an audience for this surprising comedy routine. 'Well, lord lieutenant,' she said, 'I have a guy on Zanshaa, and it seems *Corona*'s going back there.'

'I understand.'

'And it's a bad idea to get involved with a senior.'

'That's wise,' Martinez nodded.

She looked up at him. Her black eyes glittered, and her broad grin was still plastered to her face. 'You know what?' she said. 'The hell with all that. We've *already* broken all the rules.'

'That's right,' Martinez agreed, 'we have.'

The 'biological recreational chambers' – so infamous outside the Fleet, and the subject of endless jokes both inside the Fleet and out – originated not in the lustful mind of some Fleet holejumper, but as an unstated confession of bewilderment by the Great Masters themselves. The Shaa, after their conquest of Terra, had been perplexed by the varieties of sexuality displayed by their new conquests, and wisely had made no attempt to regulate any of it. Instead they'd insisted, in the most unsentimental, practical way, on minimizing the consequences: every Terran female had to be given a contraceptive implant at some point during her fourteenth year. Any woman having reached twenty-three, the age of maturity, could have the implant removed at any time by a physician, while younger women required the permission of a parent or guardian. The number of unwanted children, though not eliminated altogether, was at least brought within manageable levels.

The Fleet's attitude towards sexuality was even less sentimental, if possible, than that of the Shaa. Though officially the Fleet claimed it didn't care who coupled with whom, customs had developed over the centuries to restrain at least a few of a crew's impulses. Division chiefs were discouraged from relations with their subordinates, because of the danger of coercion or of playing favourites. Relations between officers and enlisted were likewise discouraged, at least if they belonged to the same ship – Martinez' connection with Warrant Officer Taen was well within the Fleet's range of tolerance. And relations between the captain and any of his crew were not only considered a violation of custom, but bad luck as well.

A loophole served the officers, however, as they were allowed servants with whom recreationals were unlimited. But this happened less often than an observer might expect: Martinez suspected that living with a paid companion in the close confines of a warship was too much like the least attractive ingredients of a marriage, all the boredom and constraint of living intimately with a person one simply couldn't escape, and all without the relaxation and charm of getting away from routine to visit a lover in her own place.

Corona had eight recreation tubes, two of them forward and reserved for officers. Martinez properly logged himself into the recreation chamber so that Vonderheydte could page him if he was needed. Martinez was expecting missile launches or some other emergency any second, and there was little time for preliminary caresses or endearments. He was surprised at the desperate quality of his own desires, the unexpected fury of his lust. Kelly mirrored his urgency, lost in explosive pleasure nearly from the start, clutching at him with the little red-knuckled fists at the end of her long, slim forearms. *Alive!* he thought. *Alive!*

Afterwards, with Kelly's head resting on his chest, he wondered how long he dared remain here, how much he should permit himself to relax. He badly wanted to remain in the small tubelike room scented with the odours of clean sheets and the distant undertaste of disinfectant, to close his eyes, and to let the muscles bruised with high gravities relax into the mattress under the light weight of half a gravity. And he wondered how many of the other recreational tubes on the ship were occupied at this moment, with other crew celebrating their escape from death.

It wasn't a call from Command that brought him to full alertness, but a nearby crash, a sound like the contents of an overfull closet spilling out. A crash that was followed immediately afterwards by a long, bellowing laugh.

Well. *This* wasn't supposed to happen.

Martinez dressed, left the tube, and followed the laughter to the captain's cabin, where he found Zhou and Knadjian, along with their partner in crime Ahmet. All three were stinking drunk on the captain's liquor, and Zhou was sprawled on the floor, far beyond speech or movement.

'Hey there, Lieutenant!' Ahmet said, with a wave. 'Come join us!'

Sex wasn't the only form of celebration available, Martinez reminded himself.

At Martinez' orders they'd broken into everything in search of the captain's key, and that apparently included the captain's liquor store. Once released from duty for a meal, they'd made their way back to where they knew they could drink themselves into a coma.

Martinez paged Alikhan. 'Get these people to couches, strap them in, and make sure they're not in a position to touch a single control,' he said. 'Then find every bottle of liquor on this ship, give it to the cooks, and see it's put under lock and key.'

'Very good, my lord.'

'That includes the stuff in my cabin. And in Garcia's.'

'Yes, my lord. I'll be there directly.'

Martinez rejoined Kelly briefly, and found her dressed and pulling on her shoes. He gave her foot a grateful squeeze – leaning into the tube, it was the only part of her he could reach

– and thanked her, with all the sincerity he could muster, for joining him.

'It's not like I didn't have fun,' she said.

Martinez returned to Command, waited the few moments it took Kelly to return, and then ordered everyone into vac suits for some sustained acceleration. It was best to put distance between them while the Naxids were inactive, he thought.

It took ten minutes or so for the three inebriates to be stuffed into their suits and strapped down, and a little longer for the cooks to secure the galley. Then Martinez ordered increased acceleration, to four gees this time – his tummy, he realized, *was* a little full for six gravities to sit on it.

Hours passed. Martinez spent his time obsessively studying the displays, watching Magaria's ring on its slow rotation about its planet, speculating about the Naxids' lack of activity.

'My lord,' Tracy reported from her station. '*Judge Kybiq* has increased acceleration.'

Kybiq was the cruiser that Fanaghee had placed en route to Wormhole One, blocking *Corona*'s escape to Zanshaa.

'Heading for the wormhole?' Martinez asked as he paged through the various displays to try to find the one that showed *Kybiq*.

'No, my lord. Its heading is for Barbas.' Barbas was the planet next out from Magaria, a sort of failed gas giant, huge with a solid core and an atmosphere of furious storms. At the moment its orbit placed it nearly between Magaria and Wormhole One, which led to the most direct route to Zanshaa. For the next several months Barbas would be convenient for a slingshot manoeuvre, by which traffic outbound from Magaria would pick up speed by slinging themselves around Barbas en route to the wormhole.

'Any alteration in course?'

'No, my lord.'

Martinez found the *Judge Kybiq* on his display, and as he stared at it, he found a nervous little suspicion begin to grow in his mind. Why was the Naxid cruiser increasing its speed for the wormhole? Why was it suddenly so urgent to head to Zanshaa?

A few minutes' work with the plotting computer showed Martinez that he had been right to be suspicious. *Kybiq* had been accelerating out of Magaria for three days, and it was travelling faster than *Corona* even though its accelerations hadn't been quite so brutal. It was possible that the cruiser could swing around the near side of Barbas and hurl itself for Wormhole One.

It was equally possible, and a good deal more probable, that *Judge Kybiq* could make a slight, last-minute alteration of course, then slingshot itself around the *far* side of Barbas and head for Wormhole Four and an interception of *Corona*.

The navplot computer did the maths. Depending on how fast *Kybiq* accelerated, it would be three to five days before *Kybiq* could make its slingshot, and then another eight or ten days before the interception. Martinez plotted the worst-case scenario. How hard was his acceleration going to have to be in order to beat the cruiser to the wormhole?

Not bad. To beat the *Kybiq* by half a day even if the cruiser advanced at chest-crushing acceleration, Martinez would only have to average a constant three point eight gees for the next fourteen days. He was exceeding that now, and he'd set the pace before he even knew he was in a race.

He didn't want the Naxids to know he was on to their trick, however, so for the next three days he kept to a regular schedule: accelerating a steady four gees except during mealtimes, when he reduced to a single gravity; with occasional, regular bursts of up to six gees three times a day, for half an hour each time. His body ached, and his ligaments made popping and crackling sounds whenever he moved, but *Corona*'s crew was standing the course, if not precisely thriving.

By the time *Kybiq* screamed through its turn around Barbas, subjecting its suffering crew to accelerations in excess of eleven gravities while it was in the planet's gravity well, *Corona* had a comfortable lead, and Martinez pulled even further ahead by increasing the duration of the six-gravity bursts. *Kybiq* increased its acceleration, but Martinez was able to increase his own proportionally in order to maintain his lead – no matter what the cruiser did, it was going to lose the race, and Martinez took what comfort he could from the knowledge that however much he and his people were suffering, the Naxids were suffering worse.

The acceleration was a dreary grind, however. His body ached and his mind felt dulled. His sleep was uneasy, with suggestive and distasteful dreams, and his waking hours filled with the leaden weight and unwashed stench of his own body.

Martinez knew the Naxids had surrendered the race when they opened fire again. The ships around the ring station fired a hundred and ninety missiles, and then, some time later, *Kybiq* fired two salvos of thirty-two each and then cut its acceleration, giving up the race officially. The barrages were very well planned this time, each missile taking a separate track to converge on *Corona,* from many different angles, within the space of about an hour. By the time they encountered the runaway frigate they'd be travelling much faster than they had been on the first day, and would be much more difficult to hit.

Fortunately Martinez had over two days in which to plan his defences. He, Kelly, Alikhan, and other technical-minded crew conferred, ran simulations, conferred again. Martinez began firing his defensive barrages when the missiles were five hours out, and the results simplified things when it came time to use the lasers.

By this time he was too tired to care much how it all turned out. The wild elation of the first day's escape had faded beneath the relentless crush of gravity, and death would be a release from weariness and the constant struggle simply to breathe. The display filled with a confusing overlay of explosions and clouds of deadly radiation. He and Kelly and anyone who felt qualified each crewed one of the defensive lasers, with the rest turned to automatic: *Corona* was surrounded with its own spiderweb of light, each radial line terminating in an explosion. When in doubt, Martinez launched missiles.

The fight went on for hours while the Naxid missiles vanished one by one in sheets of flame and fountains of angry gamma rays. More missiles flew through the expanding, opaque clouds, had to be located and destroyed. *Corona's* powerful radars hammered out, trying to locate the dodging, weaving parcels of deadly antimatter. The missiles crept closer and closer. Counter-missiles leaped off the rails. Lasers flashed in the darkness. Martinez fired, wiped sweat from his eyes, and sought wildly on the displays for another oncoming warhead, certain that he was missing something – but then he heard a tired whoop from Kelly, who was looking at him with a faded version of her once-brilliant smile, and he realized he'd won, that the missiles were gone and that he and *Corona* were free.

Martinez ordered the ship to decelerate to half a gravity and a meal served. He ordered the spirit locker opened and gave everyone, even his three troublemakers, a shot of their favourite poison. They cheered him. Wearily, but they cheered him. Exhausted pride glowed in his breast at the sound of their massed shouts.

There was no question of a recreational with Kelly: they were both too weary.

Fifteen days and four hours after departing Magaria station, *Corona* entered Magaria Wormhole Four and made an instantaneous transit to the Paswal system. The frigate had twenty crew counting her lieutenant commandant, and thirty-one missiles left. She was travelling just short of two-tenths of the speed of light, and could expect to dock at Zanshaa's ring in about another month, depending on how hard Martinez wanted to press her acceleration and deceleration.

Right now he didn't want to press anything. He sent his report via comm laser to the wormhole relay station on the far side of the system, showered himself clean, reduced gravity still further, to a tenth of a gee, and floated to sleep in his own bed for the first time since he'd stolen *Corona,* fifteen days ago on the Festival of Sport.

Ten

Captain Lord Richard Li was a witness to the moment that saved Zanshaa and the Home Fleet. Fleet Commander Jarlath, trying to get to the bottom of construction delays at the ring dockyard, had called a meeting of dock administrators, civilian contractors, and the officers of ships building and in refit, but his temper rose at the vague answers he received from the administrators and the contractors.

'Do you know your own business or not?' Jarlath finally demanded. The fur on his face stood erect, obscuring his facial features beneath the bristle and making him look like a hairbrush with two huge shaded eyes. The slight lisp, caused by his having to speak around his fangs, became more sinister than comical. 'Why have the estimates been exceeded for *Destiny* and *Recovery*? Why can I receive no firm date for the completion of work on *Dauntless* and *Estimable*?'

No firm dates or answers were given. *All these things sort of depend on other things* was the best answer the commander of the Home Fleet received for completion of work on *Dauntless,* which happened to be the same answer Lord Richard had been getting since his appointment. His ship was full of noise and workmen, the stink of hot metal and the booming rumble of steel wheels on the big slabs of plastic temporary flooring, but nothing seemed to be any closer to completion than the day he'd arrived.

Lord Richard had been receiving hints of impatience from the private firm he'd hired to decorate the officers' suite, to install his new hutch, cabinets, and bar, to lay in his bathroom the lovely rough slate tiles that Terza had chosen for him, and to paint the hull, pinnaces, and missiles in his personal colours, a sublime burgundy red accented subtly with stripes of purple. The firm couldn't start until the rebuild was finished, and now they were making ominous noises to the effect that if these delays continued, they might have to postpone work for months due to other commitments.

This was far too alarming. Lord Richard had thought that perhaps the new fleetcom ought to have some idea how his dockyard was run. 'I simply don't have the seniority to get so much as a single answer from these people,' he'd told Jarlath. 'But they'll have to answer to *you*.'

Now he watched as the commander of the Home Fleet discovered that he didn't have the seniority either.

'I'm calling in the auditors!' Jarlath snarled as he walked down the rim road to the skyhook terminus. 'There's got to be thieving going on. It's only pride in the service that keeps me from calling the Legion of Diligence!'

Jarlath made an eye-catching picture as he stalked down the rubberized roadway. He had bleached his fur white in order to avoid the heat of formal mourning garb, and was dressed only in white trunks and a vest, both piped with service green and heavy with badges of rank. His powerful legs and broad haunches propelled his round-bottomed body with purpose and energy, all now directed towards clearing up the mess in the dockyards.

Lord Richard Li had reason to feel pleased with himself. He was already picturing the bath aboard *Dauntless,* the slate tile, the gleaming fixtures of porcelain and copper, steam rising from the scented water as he lowered himself into the tub . . . and then Jarlath saw Senior Squadron Leader Elkizer, and brought Lord Richard's pleasant fantasy to an end.

The leader of the Naxid heavy cruiser squadron stood with a group of officers and senior enlisted personnel before the massive airlock door that led to Jarlath's own flagship, *The Glory of the Praxis*. Elkizer gestured at the airlock, his chameleon-weave jacket flashing the red-on-black patterns of his beaded scales.

Jarlath saw his subordinate and marched towards him. One of the Naxids saw the fleetcom coming and alerted Elkizer, and Elkizer's four-legged body spun in place, two legs advancing forward, two in retreat, and then braced to attention. One last pattern flashed on the chameleon-weave jacket. Jarlath paused in surprise, and then put his head down and marched to Elkizer again.

'What do you mean, "dupe"?' he asked.

Lord Richard was surprised at Jarlath's words, though Lord Richard's surprise was nothing compared to that of Squadron Leader Elkizer, who swayed backward in astonishment, his back bent like a bow. 'I beg your pardon, lord fleetcom,' he managed. 'I did not use that sign.'

Jarlath bobbed his furry head as he loomed over Elkizer. The bobbing wasn't a nod of affirmation, but a kind of triangulation used by his nocturnal, carnivorous species to fix the precise location of their prey.

'My lord, I spent three years at the Festopath Academy, where Torminel and Naxids shared a dormitory,' Jarlath lisped. 'Believe me when I say that during those three years I learned every disrespectful idiom in the Naxid vocabulary, a fact which aided me greatly when I served as Lord President of the Academy a few years ago.' His lips peeled back from his fangs. 'So kindly explain to me what you meant when you flashed "Silence. The dupe approaches."'

Elkizer was frozen in silence for a long moment before he managed to speak. 'My lord,' he said, 'I must insist. I did not use that sign.'

'What sign *was* it, then?'

There was another long silence while Elkizer searched his mind. 'The sign can also mean "lawn",' he said finally.

'True. So what did you mean by "The *lawn* approaches?"'

Elkizer tried another path. 'I meant no disrespect, my lord.'

Jarlath's tone was savage. 'To me? Or to the *lawn*?'

Lord Richard watched the confrontation in awe, his nerves urging him to fight or fly. The Naxids were descended from predators who ran in packs, but the Torminels had once been solitary, nocturnal hunters of the heavy forest, pugnacious, persistent, and utterly fearless. Lord Richard had thought Jarlath had been angry before, confronting the dockyard superintendent, but now it was clear that Jarlath had barely scratched the surface of his rage.

May I *never* piss this one off, Lord Richard thought.

For the first time Jarlath seemed to notice the crowd of Naxids behind Elkizer, the unusual mixture of high-ranking officers and senior noncoms. 'What are these folk doing here?' he demanded. 'What is your purpose?'

'My lord,' Elkizer said, 'it's an orientation tour. For new personnel.'

Jarlath panned across the party with his huge shaded eyes. 'I see Junior Squadron Commander Farniai, who has been with the Home Fleet for six years. And Captain Tirzit, who was once second officer here at Ring Command. Captain Renzak – you're on your second tour here, are you not?' His huge eyes swung back to Elkizer. 'I'm surprised that these officers require orientation to a ring station they've inhabited for so many years.'

'My lord, it's the others,' Elkizer said quickly. 'We are orienting . . . these others.'

'Petty officers?' Jarlath said. 'Constables?' He did the head-bobbing again, zeroing in on Elkizer's throat. 'Please surrender the impression that I am your dupe – or your *lawn*. What are you *really* doing here, lord commander?'

During the long silence that followed, it became clear to Lord Richard that Elkizer had fired all his ammunition, and had nothing left in the shot locker but rust and scale.

'My lord, we mean no disrespect,' Elkizer finally said. 'We thought you would be in the Commandery.'

All Jarlath's white-bleached fur stood on end, burying once more his facial features, and he *squalled,* the high-pitched yowl his prehistoric ancestors had used to freeze their victims while they pounced. Lord Richard was aware of personnel a hundred paces around turning stumbling with shock at the sound, and turning to stare

'No disrespect!' he screamed. 'By this vile *mendacity*! By this *assembly,* which you refuse to explain! By sneaking around *behind my back,* while you thought I was in my office on Zanshaa!' Jarlath raised an heavy white fist. 'You are up to something, my lord.'

Elkizer's black-on-red eyes rolled. 'My lord, I—'

'I don't *care* for another of your pathetic explanations,' Jarlath said, 'even if this time it's the truth. It is clear to me that you and these other – individuals – are involved in this scheme, whatever it is, because you have too little with which to *occupy your time.* Therefore your squadron – and that of Squadcom Farniai here – will depart the ring station at 17:00 today in order to participate in manoeuvres. Which will *begin* with a six-gravity acceleration toward Vandrith, followed by a slingshot manoeuvre and a full series of wargames between your two squadrons, all of which will be designed by my staff for maximum stress on all ship systems – the crew in particular.'

'My lord!' Elkizer said. 'We have crew on liberty!'

'Recall them! They have four hours to report.' Jarlath bared his fangs again. 'Get moving!'

The Naxids began backpedalling, their booted feet beating at the roadway's rubberized surface while their trunks remained erect.

'My lord,' Elkizer tried again, 'you forget the dinner . . .'

'*Fuck* your dinner!' Jarlath pronounced with satisfaction, and watched as the Naxids turned and sped away as fast as their thrashing feet could carry them.

For the next hour, trapped with Jarlath in the skyhook car as it plunged through the atmosphere to the surface of Zanshaa, Lord Richard and Jarlath's staff had to listen to the fleetcom fume about the reek of dishonesty he smelled in this command, the general rottenness of everything at the dockyards and the way the rot had spread to the Naxid squadrons.

'*Discipline!*' Jarlath said. '*Order! Obedience! These* shall be the watchwords of the Home Fleet from now on!'

'I'll never think of Torminel as cute, furry pudge-pots ever again,' Lord Richard told Terza that evening. 'My dear, the sight of Jarlath in fury was absolutely blood-chilling.'

The two Naxid squadrons, obeying Jarlath's orders, detached from Zanshaa's ring after four hours, oriented themselves towards Vandrith, and began the punishing acceleration that Jarlath had commanded.

Elkizer had no choice. His timetable called for the revolt to begin in four days' time, all Naxids in the Fleet rising at the same moment throughout the empire. If he began early, word might reach other stations, and preparations taken before the Naxids elsewhere could strike.

Plus his instructions had insisted that he take care not to damage Zanshaa or its ring. Zanshaa was the capital of the empire, the place where the Great Masters rested, where the Convocation sat and where the Praxis had been proclaimed. To attack the planet or destroy its ring was unthinkable, near sacrilege. Though firing a barrage of missiles at the Home Fleet in its berths was a tempting prospect, such an attack would destroy the ring and Naxid prestige along with it.

His planning had been systematic. Like every other Naxid party to the plot, Elkizer had no experience at managing a revolution or at fighting a battle, and his lack of experience made him deeply uneasy, and so he strove for a comprehensive plan that left nothing to chance.

Unlike his colleague Fanaghee at Magaria, Elkizer didn't command the fleet at Zanshaa, and he couldn't simply order a Festival of Sport that would take the senior officers and most of the crews away from the ships. Instead Elkizer planned an elaborate dinner for all the senior commanders, captains, and lieutenants, to celebrate the anniversary of the First Proclamation of the Praxis on Sandama. Elkizer planned to hold all the senior officers captive while his Naxids stormed Ring Command and all the berthed warships, after which the lord senior would proclaim the empire's new arrangement to the Convocation. The lords convocate could scarcely be expected to object with the Home Fleet, the ring station, and thousands of antimatter missiles in the hands of the Naxids.

The plan considered that the chief danger would be a security leak, and so Elkizer planned – as had Fanaghee at Magaria – to let people into the secret gradually, as they needed to know. He walked through the ring station several times with his staff, marking each target, planning each assignment. Then he brought in the next group of people, the senior captains and their top noncoms, and it was this group that ran afoul of Fleet Commander Jarlath. If Elkizer's plans hadn't been completely wrecked at that point, each captain would have gradually let others into the secret, the pool of knowledge gradually widening until it encompassed hundreds. Most of the enlisted personnel that composed the boarding parties wouldn't have understood the full implication of their tasks until they had been completed, and Elkizer had made his triumphant announcement.

Comprehensive as the plan was, there was no contingency in case the primary plan failed. The day of rebellion arrived with Elkizer's force out of place. A return to Zanshaa would be suicide, so his squadrons swung past Vandrith, reduced acceleration to a single comfortable gravity, and kept on going, heading in a sedate, determined manner for the Zanshaa Three wormhole, a course that would lead them, after three more wormhole jumps, to rendezvous with Senior Fleet Commander Fanaghee at Magaria.

There was complete astonishment in the Commandery when this became apparent some three hours later. The duty officer decided not to bother Jarlath, but instead queried Elkizer concerning why he had failed to follow the operational plan.

By the time, over six hours later, that it became obvious that Elkizer had no intention of replying or of following orders, rebellion had been proclaimed in the Convocation, and everyone forgot about Elkizer for a while.

The lord senior raised his head and gazed at the convocates ringing the great amphitheatre. 'Although the Convocation is scheduled this afternoon to debate the creation of a uniform tariff structure in regard to the importation of luzhan from Antopone and El-vash, I should like to exercise a point of personal privilege and raise another matter.'

Maurice, Lord Chen looked up from his desk, where he'd been going through the guest list for a reception at the Chen Palace – the limitation of parties to twenty-two guests was both a provocation and annoyance, as it inevitably meant leaving people off the list and running the risk of offending them. No tariffs? he thought vaguely. His clan was involved in the importation of luzhan from El-vash, and he would have been happy to see the Antopone tariffs kept high. Anything that postponed the vote had his favour.

Akzad, the lord senior, rose from his couch. The corners of his stiff brocade cloak dragged on the ground as he moved – as slowly and grandly as Naxid physiology permitted – to the front of the dais, where he held the copper-and-silver wand in both hands, like a spear pointed vaguely at the back of the room.

'I wish to speak on a matter involving the survival of the Praxis itself,' Akzad said. 'For it seems to many of us that the Praxis itself is in danger.'

Surprise rose in Lord Chen. Threat to the Praxis? he wondered.

'When the glory of the Praxis was first revealed,' Akzad said, 'it was clear that not all species were at first able to appreciate its profound truths. The Praxis was first apprehended only by the Shaa, who in their wisdom determined to impose their vision of perfection upon all existence, first upon my own species and then others. For the Praxis is based, above all, on the eternal principle of subordination – on every line of authority and responsibility being absolutely clear, and the Shaa understood this before any of us. The Shaa were above us all, but the Shaa were still beneath the Praxis.'

Lord Chen, nodding at these commonplace observations, observed movement among the Naxid convocates. A dozen or so had left their places and were moving in their bolt-and-halt fashion to the front of the room. The lord senior continued.

'But since the passing of the Great Masters, these perfect arrangements have been replaced by those less perfect. In place of the ideal, in which the species first exposed to the Praxis imposed its will on all others, we now have an equivalence among the species speaking in Convocation.'

More of the Naxids were moving to the front, forming a line in front of the lord senior's dais. Lord Chen looked left and right, seeing puzzled frowns on the faces of his colleagues.

'Where is the critical principle of subordination?' Akzad asked. 'Where are the lines of authority? That is why, when it became clear that the last Shaa would soon pass, there was founded on Naxas the Committee for the Salvation of the Praxis.'

Lord Chen sat bolt upright, his astonished mind reluctant to come to grips with the implications of what he had just heard. Others were faster than he: old Lord Saïd was already on his feet, a fierce scowl on his hawk-nosed, moustached face. The oldest representative of an ancient, deeply conservative clan, he was not about to stand still for any such radical innovations as a self-appointed committee to save the Praxis, not when the Praxis was under the guardianship of Saïd himself and the other lords convocate.

'*Is this treason?*' Saïd demanded, his voice ringing clear in the vast room.

Akzad ignored the interruption. 'In order to save the Praxis, we must restore the principle of subordination! In the place of the Shaa must stand those who have the greatest and longest exposure to the purity of the Praxis!'

'*Treason! Treason!*' Saïd called. Others began to echo him. One of the Torminel delegates leaped onto his desk and waved a furry fist. Fully half the hundred-odd Naxid convocates were now lined up before the dais. The rest seemed bewildered, half on their feet, the rest still prone on their couches.

'You are not recognized!' Akzad countered, pointing the wand at Saïd. He touched one of the wand's silver rings, boosting his own amplification to shout over the disorder.

'Throughout the empire on this day,' he said, 'loyal citizens are acting to save the Praxis in accordance with the instructions of the Committee! Warships, ring stations, and other installations are being seized!' He swept his wand across the arc of the lords convocate. 'It is your clear duty to obey the orders of the Committee for the Salvation of the Praxis! You are commanded to resume your seats and place yourselves under my command!'

'I've heard enough of this!' Saïd's trained rhetorician's voice boomed out over the assembly even without the benefit of amplification. 'I don't know about the rest of you, but I know what to do when I see a traitor!'

And then, despite his eighty-odd years, the grey-maned

convocate picked up his chair and headed for the aisle, brandishing the chair over his head. 'Death to traitors!' he roared.

Lord Senior Akzad had planned to present his demands in the knowledge that they would be enforced by the hundreds of antimatter missiles commanded overhead by squadron leaders Elkizer and Farniai. Akzad and his followers demonstrated enormous courage in following their instructions from the Committee and demanding the surrender of the Convocation even though the two friendly squadrons were four days' hard acceleration away, and headed in the wrong direction, while any missiles remained in the possession of the Fleet.

Lacking military power, Lord Akzad might have considered arming himself or his followers with weapons. But weapons had not been mentioned in his instructions, and a massacre of the convocates was never what the Committee intended. They wanted obedience, and they expected to get it. The thought that the lords convocate might resist them with violence had never entered their minds.

And so, in the end, Akzad faced the Convocation armed only with his courage and a copper-plated wand. When Lord Saïd marched down the aisle and hurled his chair at the lord senior, Akzad lost all control of the situation.

'I demand that you return to your seat!' he called. 'Those who do not submit will be punished!'

But few paid him any heed. More chairs followed the first. Lord Chen himself, though possessed the entire while by a sense of unreality, picked up his chair, marched to the front, and flung it at the Naxid in the brocade robe, the one who stood on the dais, waved his wand, and called uselessly for order. Not even the Naxids who stood before the dais in solidarity with their leader knew how to respond – they stood silent, unmoving, no more able to believe what was happening than anyone else.

The lord senior was giving orders, and they were being disobeyed. None of them had ever seen such a thing before. None knew what to do next.

By sheer chance it was Lord Chen's chair that hit the lord senior, clipping Akzad on the side of the head and knocking him to his knees. A roar of approval went up from many of the convocates, and the loyalists surged forward.

At this threat the Naxids at last responded. Lord Chen, standing at the front of the amphitheatre and staring in wonder at his own success, suddenly found himself flattened by a charging Naxid. He hit the ground and felt the grinding impact of the Naxid's boots as the quadruped trampled him. Pain jolted him as he bit his own tongue.

All sense of unreality vanished. The taste of his own hot blood in his mouth, Lord Chen began to fight for his life.

Even though at least half the convocates either remained in their seats or fled, the Naxids were still outnumbered by the loyalists. Chairs were inefficient weapons, but they were better than the Naxids' bare hands.

Lord Chen nearly gagged on the overwhelming odour of rotting flesh, even though the flesh in question belonged to a chair-swinging Daimong who knocked the Naxid off Lord Chen. There were shouts, screams, thuds, the screech of an outraged Torminel, the agitated chime of Daimong voices. Lord Chen managed to fight his way to his feet, and then the press of bodies threw him up against the dais.

Akzad was on his feet again, shouting and brandishing the wand, oblivious to the blood that poured from his head wound. Everything had gone far beyond his, or anyone's, control. Even the sergeant-at-arms stood perplexed: he was supposed to guard the Convocation against intruders, not take part in a brawl of one group of convocates against another.

'To the terrace!' Lord Chen could still hear Saïd's magnificent baritone carrying over the sound of the riot. 'Take them to the terrace!'

Battered into submission and seized by the angry convocates, the Naxids were dragged through the wide side doors of the amphitheatre. Terrace furniture was knocked and kicked aside as the Naxids were dragged to the stone parapet and tipped over the brink to fall a hundred and fifty paces down the stony cliff. Akzad, in his torn ceremonial cloak, was hurled down with the rest, as were a dozen loyalist convocates, accidentally knocked over by the crowd or dragged to their deaths by Naxids clinging to them in desperation.

Lord Chen, gasping for breath, leaned for support on the parapet. His head swam as he stared at the carnage below, the scatter of centauroid bodies lying broken on the stones. The furious anger that possessed him had faded, and he looked down at his dead colleagues with growing astonishment, not only at what had just happened but at his own part in it.

He was Maurice, Lord Chen, of Clan Chen that had been at the absolute top of imperial society for thousands of years. Chens had served in the Convocation for all of that time, representing themselves and the interests of their clients, all beneath the stabilizing power of the Praxis.

Not one of them had ever participated in a riot in the Convocation chamber. Not one had ever killed a fellow convocate with his bare hands. In all the long history of the empire, nothing like what had happened today had ever occurred. This act was completely unprecedented.

Lord Chen realized that what he was seeing below him, broken on the stones, was not just the bodies of legislators, but the old order itself.

'We must reconvene!' Again Saïd was shouting. 'The Convocation must re-form!'

Lord Chen filed with the others into the Convocation. Smashed and scattered furniture lay on and around the speaker's dais like a scattering of old bones. The convocates retrieved the usable furniture and borrowed more from colleagues who had fled or died. Lord Saïd was proclaimed temporary chairman, though he was forced to conduct the meeting without the lord senior's wand, which had disappeared and was never to be found.

The Convocation immediately passed on a voice vote a measure outlawing the Committee for the Salvation of the Praxis, whoever and wherever they might be. Another vote proclaimed that the penalty for belonging to the organization would be dismembering. Then someone else suggested flaying, and the merits of flaying and dismembering were debated. Then a Terran lady convocate with a torn uniform tunic and a blackened eye rose to suggest that since the first lot had been thrown off a cliff, the rest should be as well.

Of such fascination did the convocates find this debate, and the ten or so laws they passed that day, that it was fully an hour before anyone thought to call the Commandery and inform the Fleet of the menace to the empire. And, once Fleet Commander Jarlath was informed, it was another hour before anyone bothered to tell him of the Naxid squadrons' disobedience.

The empire was as inexperienced at quelling rebellion as Elkizer had been at making it.

Jarlath immediately ordered his three cruiser squadrons in pursuit of Elkizer, leaving the ring and blasting towards Vandrith at over ten gravities' acceleration with only partial crews aboard, but they had been gone for less than an hour before Jarlath realized the pursuit was fruitless and the ships were recalled.

Jarlath was beginning to realize that he might be in a much more dangerous position than he had supposed. A little information about what Akzad had claimed about the Committee for the Salvation of the Praxis was beginning to reach him, and he gathered that large numbers of Naxids were involved. He had also remembered Elkizer's marching around the ring with a group of senior officers and military constables, and with a burst of amazement realized that

Elkizer had been rehearsing the boarding and capture of all non-Naxid ships.

There were 341 warships in the Fleet. Of these, sixty-eight, or nearly twenty percent, were commanded and crewed by Naxids, eight entire squadrons of six to ten ships each plus the odd ship here and there on detached duty. Of these squadrons, two had been stationed at Zanshaa with the Home Fleet, two at Magaria with the Second Fleet, one with the Fourth Fleet at Harzapid, one with the Third Fleet at Felarus, one squadron at the Naxid home world of Naxas, and the last at Comador.

Communications lasers immediately burned with urgent messages directed to fleet and squadron commanders at Harzapid, Felarus, and Comador. Additional messages went to ships at more remote stations. It would take days for some of the answers to come back, even pulsed at the speed of light through the relay stations at the wormhole gates, and Jarlath suspected that when the answers came he wouldn't like them.

He hesitated before sending messages to Fanaghee at Magaria and to the commander at Naxas. But on further consideration, he decided there was nothing to be gained by remaining silent. He queried Naxas as to its status, and sent a message to Fanaghee telling her of the mutiny of his two squadrons, and ordering her to intercept them.

Then he added up the figures in his head again, and didn't like them any better than he had the first time.

Magaria was the key, he decided. If Fanaghee and her force stayed loyal, then the empire would survive what was to come.

If *not* . . . Well, Jarlath would try to maintain confidence.

It was only then, nine hours after Elkizer had disobeyed orders and bypassed Vandrith, that Jarlath remembered that there was one Naxid warship remaining on the station, the brand new light cruiser *Destiny*, which was ten days from completion – or so the dockyard superintendent had maintained for over a month now. *Destiny* had its crew and officers aboard, but had yet to be towed to the Completion Area to receive its missiles, defensive weapons, and to test its propulsion systems with their first charges of antimatter.

Jarlath ordered the military constabulary to seize the ship. They were met with small arms fire from the ship's officers. *Destiny*'s crew ran out of the ship into the dockyard, where they began hurling home-made explosives and incendiaries. It was two hours before they were all rounded up and shot. Eight million zeniths' worth of stores and dockyard equipment had to be written off.

Shortly after making his report on the incident, Jarlath received a reprimand complaining that he had shot the rebels, instead of throwing them off a cliff as prescribed by a new law passed that afternoon by the Convocation.

That was how the first day ended.

Over the next few days information came into the Commandery. The message to Fanaghee at Magaria took twenty hours to arrive and another twenty for the reply to get back to Zanshaa. Fanaghee expressed alarm over the mutiny of Elkizer and Farniai, and announcing that she was despatching the Second Fleet to intercept the rebels.

'Very good, lord commander,' said Lord Convocate Maurice Chen, who, by virtue of the fact that he'd demonstrated martial skill by clouting the chief rebel on the head with a chair, had been deemed worthy of a promotion out of Oceanographic and Forestry and onto the Fleet Control Board. 'It must be a relief to know that Magaria is safe,' he said.

'I *don't* know it,' Jarlath said. His fingers twirled little angry knots into his fur. 'I don't know if I credit Fanaghee's report, or for that matter if I wish to.'

He ordered Fanaghee to provide detailed reports on the status of every ship in her fleet, the reports to be provided in video form and by the captains of the individual ships themselves. Which should make it clear, he thought, whether the captains can speak for themselves.

As he feared, there was no reply to his message. He informed Lord Chen and the rest of the Fleet Control Board that Magaria had fallen to the rebels.

There were five squadrons at Magaria. If the Naxids controlled them all, Fanaghee's force would now equal in numbers the five squadrons remaining in the Home Fleet, and once Elkizer and Farniai joined her, she would have the advantage in numbers.

In which case he may as well surrender hope of recapturing Magaria. It might be all he could do to hold Zanshaa.

The next bulletin came from the Third Fleet at Felarus. Its Naxid squadron had departed the station unexpectedly on what its commander claimed was a training exercise, then opened fire on the rest of the Third Fleet, still moored to the ring station. Antiproton beams, intended as an antimissile defence, had been used offensively, and at point-blank range. Warships were blown apart, along with critical parts of the ring station. The Naxid barrage hadn't been as severe as it could have been, which indicated that they were exercising a degree of restraint, perhaps out of compassion for their fellows, perhaps simply because they intended to return and capture Felarus' ring later. Despite the rebels' self-restraint, half the ships of the Third Fleet were destroyed, and the rest severely damaged. Because of additional damage to the repair facilities of the ring station, it would be many months before any of the Third Fleet's ships could be used against the rebels.

A puzzled message arrived from the commander of the ring station at Comador. The Naxid squadron based there had departed the station and were making their way out of the system, refusing communication. The station commander wished to know if the squadron was flying away on an exercise that he hadn't been told about.

Jarlath also had to presume that the squadron at Naxas was lost.

From Harzapid alone there was good news. The commander of the single Naxid squadron, as inexperienced at staging a rebellion as anyone in the Fleet and far from any advice from the ruling Council on Naxas, had marched his followers into Ring Command and sent forth a public announcement to the effect that he was now in charge. After recovering from her surprise, the commander of the Fourth Fleet organized storming parties and retook Ring Command. Unfortunately this precipitated another point-blank battle with antiproton beams, but this time the loyalists weren't caught unprepared. The Naxid ships were destroyed, at a cost of a third of the loyalists damaged or destroyed. That left enough ships to form two squadrons.

Jarlath ordered that any captured rebels be thrown off a cliff, if one was conveniently at hand, and otherwise be shot.

The victory at Harzapid gave Jarlath two more squadrons, four once damaged ships were repaired, and Jarlath took heart. He counted no more than ninety ships in the enemy fleet, and these included single ships on detached duty and the squadron from Comador, a station so remote that its renegade squadron would take months to arrive near the scene of any prospective action. This total also included the three squadrons captured at Magaria, which were not fitted for Naxid crews and which would take some time to for the special requirements of a centauroid species.

Once Jarlath called in the Daimong squadron from Zerafan, only ten days away if he ordered a brutal, maximum acceleration, that would give Jarlath fifty-four ships in the Home Fleet, which should suffice to hold Zanshaa until further help arrived. Squadron Commander Do-Faq's Lai-own squadron at Preowin could arrive in forty days, necessarily at a much more gentle acceleration due to the less robust Lai-own physique. Individual ships could also be called in, enough to make up in time a squadron of small vessels.

Unfortunately the Fourth Fleet at Harzapid was at least three months away. But after those three months were past and the Fourth Fleet arrived, Jarlath could be reasonably certain that any offensive he launched toward Magaria would stand a good chance of success.

But in the meantime Magaria preyed on his mind. The Magaria ring was an enormous arsenal of missiles, parts, shipyards, and training facilities, a far superior facility to anything else the rebels possessed. Magaria also had the seven wormhole gates that could send an enemy force to much of the empire. If he could retake Magaria, Jarlath could rip the guts out of the rebellion.

Instead he took steps for the defense of Zanshaa. Having put himself aboard his giant flagship, called in all crews and filled all ships with weapons, fuel, and supplies, he launched the remaining squadrons of the Home Fleet five days after Akzad's abortive rebellion, and then began an acceleration towards Vandrith. This was not a pursuit of Elkizer's fleeting squadrons, which by now were well out of reach, but rather an attempt to give the Home Fleet some delta vee so that if an enemy attacked, the defenders wouldn't be sitting ducks and massacred.

For the first few days of the emergency Sula ended up guarding a skyhook terminus again, though this time her party was armed with automatic rifles rather than stun batons, and one moustached petty officer was in charge of a tripod-mounted antimatter gun that would dispose of armoured vehicles, or, indeed, anything at all. Only military personnel with valid identification were permitted on the cars, and Naxids were flatly forbidden to ride the skyhook under any circumstances.

The official stories being broadcast were confused and contradictory, indicating that something had happened that the censors didn't know how to spin. The story they eventually settled on was that the lord senior and a group of his followers had tried to seize the government, and killed a number of convocates, but were promptly flung off a cliff by indignant legislators. Two squadrons of the Home Fleet had rebelled as well, but these were now in flight. Fleet Commander Jarlath and the rest of the Home Fleet would soon depart to take vengeance on behalf of the established order.

Sula supposed that most of this was true, or true enough, except the part about the heroic convocates killing the traitors themselves. The Convocation had never done their own dirty work before, she thought: why start now? But looking at the news reports in more detail, Sula saw that it was possible to draw other conclusions.

Sula knew that the two rebellious squadrons were crewed by Naxids. The list of the traitorous convocates included only Naxids, whereas those convocates martyred by their treachery were all non-Naxids. Sula had been ordered to forbid Naxids to ride the critical skyhook. From all of this, certain conclusions could be drawn.

Sula was quicker at maths than Jarlath, and she didn't like how the numbers were adding up, either.

After two days of standing watch at a mostly-deserted skyhook terminus, Sula received a call on her sleeve display from Captain Lord Richard Li.

'I'm calling to renew my offer of a place on *Dauntless*,' he said. 'We're filling up the crew and I expect we'll be leaving station in a matter of days.' He hesitated, then added, 'I haven't heard officially yet, but the rumour is that your exam results are going to be thrown out. If you want to take the exams again, you'll have to wait months and re-apply.'

Hopeless bitterness filled Sula. 'I understand,' she said. That left her with little option but to accept Lord Richard's offer and get into the war. It was clear that those with experience in combat would have an increased chance of notice and promotion. To miss the war would be to throw her career to the winds.

Lord Richard smiled. 'Before you answer yes or no, I need to tell you the rest of the bad news. I can't take you on as a lieutenant. Lord Commander Jarlath is insisting that all crews be made up with experienced officers – he doesn't want anyone learning on the job, not when so many lives may depend on it. I have to say that I agree with him. So if you come aboard, it will be as a pinnace pilot.' From out of Sula's sleeve display, he gave her what he probably thought was an encouraging look.

'I *will* see that you're promoted as soon as possible,' he said. 'The next time one of my lieutenants is rotated or promoted out of *Dauntless,* you'll have the place.'

That is, of course, if Sula survived her career as a pinnace pilot. Which, in a real shooting war, was not the surest way to lay a wager.

Still, an appointment under a rising young officer, with the promise of promotion to come, was the best offer she was likely to get. It was certainly better than guarding a skyhook while brooding over her lost exam results.

She managed a smile. 'Certainly,' she said. 'Where do I sign?' At least it would get her away from the ongoing Blitsharts trial, which with its appeals might go on for the next decade.

Whatever task the Fleet assigned Sula lately, it assigned her a sidearm to go with it. Her first job aboard *Dauntless* was to enslave the civilian workers. Jarlath, two days into the rebellion, had remembered with fury his experience with the dockyards – had remembered the *discipline! order! obedience!* he had pledged as the watchwords of his administration – and realized he needed *Dauntless* and the captured *Destiny* more than he needed the goodwill of the dockyard staff. He therefore ordered the captains to keep the civilian workers aboard, without allowing them leave or contact with their

friends or families, until the work was done to the captains'
satisfaction.

Lord Richard, nearly overcome with glee at this order,
placed armed guards at the personnel and cargo hatches, and
told the workers that if they didn't complete their tasks before
the fleet commander ordered *Destiny* to leave the station, they
would just have to come along to the war. So Sula spent half of
each day mounting guard inside the cargo hatch, a sidearm on
one hip as she listened to the litany of sad, desperate reasons
why one person or another had to leave the ship. The endless
succession of plaintive excuses wore on her patience and left
her with no pity for the imprisoned workers whatever, and
in the end she gave them a cold, green-eyed stare. 'Odds are
I'm going to die in combat,' she told them. 'Why shouldn't
I take a few of you with me?' After that they avoided her.

Jarlath gave the fleet less than a day's notice before leaving Zanshaa, an announcement that set the workers into
a frenzy. Sula's final task before leaving was to supervise
workers carrying boxes of the captain's slate tiles into storage, where they would remain until such time as *Dauntless*
found another few weeks in dock. Lord Richard seemed
a little wistful as he watched them go by: the last captain's tilework of asteroid material, filled with gaudy splashes
of glittering pyrite, was really not to his taste, and the
panelling in his cabin, in which yellow chesz wood was
accented with trim of scarlet ammana paste, was not his
style either.

It wasn't long before Sula concluded that Lord Richard
was a good captain. He had visited every department on the
ship and had spoken to everyone good-naturedly, displaying
his crinkly-eyed smile. He'd had a knack for distinguishing
what was important from what wasn't, and rarely hounded
his crew over the latter. All unlike her last captain, Kandinski,
who tried to pretend that the crew didn't exist except as
imperfect mechanisms to keep his panelling buffed and his

silver polished, and who never spoke to his crew unless issuing a rebuke.

Dauntless managed to depart Zanshaa ring on schedule, with the rest of the Home fleet. Sula found that she didn't regret leaving Zanshaa. The capital hadn't been lucky for her.

Not that *Dauntless* was shaping up to be any better.

'The Convocation wishes to know when you plan to launch your assault on Magaria.' The speaker was the elderly Senior Fleet Commander Tork, a Daimong whose long, mournful face belied the fervour that added a monotonal harshness to the chimes of his voice. Tork was the chairman of the Fleet Control Board, one of the five active or retired officers who served alongside the Board's four politicians.

Jarlath reclined on his acceleration couch aboard *Glory of the Praxis,* while the Fleet Control Board's holographic images floated before his eyes. Suffering from four days' hard acceleration, his bleached-white fur by now showing its black-and-grey roots, Jarlath knew he hardly presented his best face to his superiors.

'The enemy outnumbers us,' Jarlath said. 'Once the Zerafan squadron joins, I'll have fifty-four ships. Once Elkizer joins Fanaghee she'll have fifty-nine, and we can assume that squadrons from Naxas or Felarus will join as well.'

'You assume that Fanaghee will be able to convert all the captured squadrons to Naxid use by the time you arrive.'

'My lord,' said Jarlath, 'I cannot afford to think otherwise.'

'And you also assume that she'll be able to crew all her captured ships.'

A headache thudded dully behind Jarlath's eyes. He had been over this with his own staff a dozen times.

'Her personnel will be overworked and overstrained, but it can be done,' he said. 'If she strips much of the ring station of its personnel she'll have adequate fighting crews, though her damage control won't be as efficient as ours.'

'But if she strips the ring station personnel, she won't have enough dock workers to refit her captured ships.'

'She can bring workers up from the planet. Most of the inhabitants of Magaria are Naxids, and we have to presume they'll sympathize with the enemy Council.'

'You forget that you have the battleship squadron.'

Jarlath closed his weary eyes. 'I have not forgot.'

'You have six Praxis-class ships to the enemy's one.' A metallic bray of triumph entered Tork's voice. 'Each battleship is the equal of a squadron!'

Then let's send the battleships by themselves and win a glorious victory, Jarlath thought viciously, but he suppressed his anger. His weary muscles dragged his eyelids apart. 'A hit by an antimatter missile will destroy a battleship as easily as it will destroy a frigate,' he said.

'You are being too cautious, my lord commander.'

Jarlath let the two-gravity acceleration drag his lips from his fangs. Enough was enough. 'If the lords commissioners give me a direct order to attack immediately,' he said, 'an order in *writing,* I shall of course obey.'

There was a long silence from the board members. Then Lord Chen spoke.

'I ask you to understand that there is much anxiety in the Convocation. The fall of Magaria has effectively cut us off from a third of the empire. Many of us have friends, clients, and other interests in the area controlled by the rebels.'

Lord Chen looked more than a little anxious himself. Jarlath remembered that Chen owned a shipping company, one that presumably had many ships and cargoes in enemy-controlled space.

'I too have friends on the other side of Magaria,' Jarlath said. 'Throwing away the Home Fleet will do them no good.'

After the meeting came to an end Jarlath wondered if he were wrong and the others right. One great strike at Magaria might well end the rebellion. The Naxids might not be ready. Jarlath *wanted* to make that strike. But the odds gave him caution.

Eight days later, engines burned fire and piled on the gees as Jarlath swung his ships around Vandrith for the return journey to Zanshaa. He was travelling one-fourteenth of the speed of light, and would continue accelerating and performing slingshot manoeuvres around the system's planets until he was travelling at least .5*c*, fast enough to avoid immediate destruction from any of Fanaghee's ships tearing out of Magaria at eighty percent of the speed of light.

It was then that word came from *Corona* and Lieutenant Martinez. Having escaped from Magaria to the Paswal system, Martinez was at last able to send his report through a wormhole relay station that Fanaghee didn't control.

The Convocation responded to the news with raptures. Martinez, *Corona,* and its crew were voted the Thanks of the Convocation. Every crew member would be decorated, and Martinez himself would receive the Golden Orb, the empire's highest military decoration, which was exclusively within the gift of the Convocation and had not been awarded in eight hundred years. Martinez and his descendants were awarded the right to have their ashes entombed in the Couch of Eternity, alongside the Great Masters. A *Corona* monument would be dedicated somewhere in the High City, its location yet to be determined.

The Convocation also reconsidered the matter of Captain Blitsharts' rescue, and decided that Martinez' participation was worthy of the Medal of Merit, First Class. As this decoration was not within their gift, they recommended that the Fleet Control Board award the decoration.

The Convocation also passed on to the Fleet Control Board its recommendation that Lord Gareth Martinez be promoted immediately and given a command commensurate with his new rank.

'Well,' Lord Chen said, 'we can confirm him in *Corona*. There's a vacancy, after all.'

'But have you heard him *talk*?' objected Lord Commander Pezzini, the only other Terran member of the board. 'He sounds like such an unsuitable person for command rank. An accent like that belongs in the engine bays.'

'He is a Peer, however he talks,' pronounced Lord Commander Tork, 'and all Peers are equal beneath the Praxis.'

Pezzini made a sullen face at this, but he had learned not to dispute with Tork on the subject of the Praxis. Tork's ideas of the Praxis were, like the Praxis itself, firm, unchanging, and unyielding, and very much like Tork's ideas about everything else.

'Besides,' Lord Chen said, 'I see from his record that his last superior, Lord Commander Enderby, recommended him in his final testament for promotion. It's the custom of this board, as I understand it, to follow such recommendations whenever possible.'

'It would be awkward,' said another voice, 'if we *don't* promote him. How could anyone employ him then? What captain is going to want a lieutenant who holds the Golden Orb?'

'Let us vote on the recommendations of the Convocation and of the Lord Commander Enderby,' Tork said. 'Let it be moved that Lieutenant Lord Gareth Martinez be promoted to the rank of lieutenant-captain, effective from the date of the rebellion.'

There were no dissenting votes, though Pezzini wearily raised his eyebrows. 'None of his ancestors have ever risen this far in the Fleet,' he said. 'We're setting a precedent here.'

Tork raised a hand, wafting to the board the faint scent of his perpetually rotting flesh. Chen raised a hand meditatively to his chin and surreptitiously inhaled the cologne he'd applied to the inside of his wrist.

'Shall we then vote on whether Lieutenant-Captain Martinez shall be given *Corona*?' Tork asked. 'Or shall there be further discussion?'

'Let's give him the ship, if we must,' said Pezzini. 'But can we station him away from the capital? I don't want to hear that voice again, not if I can avoid it.'

The others ignored this comment and voted in the affirmative.

The Control Board dealt swiftly with other business. Lord Chen tried to vote with the board members who had been in their places the longest, even though he was beginning to develop the suspicion that they, too, didn't quite understand what they were doing.

The suspicion was doubled for Lord Chen, because unlike most of the Fleet officers on the board he sat in Convocation as well. The Convocation had been in almost continual session ever since the day of the rebellion, and significant bills were being passed almost every hour. The Legion of Diligence and the local police forces had been given massive powers of arrest and interrogation. The Antimatter Service and the Exploration Service had both been militarized and placed under the Fleet, which was pleased to increase its administrative heft but hadn't as yet made up its mind what to do with its new departments. Huge sums were being awarded in new military contracts, not only for providing supplies and maintenance to ships, but for building new ships to replace those already lost and the losses that would inevitably follow from battle. The building of so many new ships required expansion and maintenance of old yards, and the building of new, plus creating new facilities for training the crew that would have to be put aboard the new ships. In addition there needed to be new maintenance facilities for the new ships, and workers to maintain the maintenance facilities, and in addition a lot of work formerly done by Naxids now needed to be done by someone else, all of which would result in a lot of new recruitment.

The Fleet had barely begun to cope with all this largesse. Large amounts of money were going *somewhere*, and all Lord Chen could be certain of was that none of it was ending up with *him*. He owned shipbuilding facilities perfectly capable of making warships, but they were all in the part of the empire presumed to be under the control of the Naxids. The world he represented in Convocation was now commanded by rebels, as were most of his clients and property.

If Jarlath didn't get the Home Fleet moving soon and recapture all that was lost, Lord Chen was looking at something like ruin.

'May I raise the matter of the petitions we've been receiving from my clients and constituents?' asked Lady San-torath. She was the sole Lai-own on the board, and represented in Convocation the Lai-own home world of Hone-bar.

'Hone-bar is as close to Magaria as it is to Zanshaa,' San-torath said. 'The inhabitants of Hone-bar are desperate to remain loyal to the Praxis, but fear the enemy. The Fleet has done nothing to protect them – there is only one warship in the Hone-bar system, a light cruiser that is undergoing a rebuild and will not be ready for three months.'

'If we defend Hone-bar, we weaken Zanshaa,' Tork said.

'If Hone-bar falls without a fight,' said the Lai-own, 'the confidence of all the people in the Convocation and its administration – and the confidence of the Lai-owns in particular – will be badly shaken.'

'It's not just Hone-bar,' said Lady Seekin. 'If Hone-bar falls then the Hone Reach is vulnerable.'

Lord Chen felt a chill prickle the skin on his back. Clan Chen had long been invested heavily in the Hone Reach, and he was patron to several of its larger cities.

If the Hone Reach fell, then Clan Chen was in for a huge fall.

'The Reach must be protected,' Lord Chen said automatically. 'We can't let Hone-bar go.'

'We have no indication that the rebels are moving on Hone-bar,' someone pointed out.

'How would we know until it happens?' said Lady San-torath. 'The rebels aren't going to send us a message telling us where they're going next.'

'They could capture Hone-bar with a single ship, and the Reach with a small squadron,' said Lady Seekin. 'Surely we can spare a few ships for its defence, especially since Lord Commander Jarlath isn't doing anything with them.'

It occurred to Lord Chen that Lady Seekin, the Torminel convocate, was from Devajjo, within the Hone Reach itself. He realized that he and she were natural allies, along with Lady San-torath.

Who else? he wondered. Who else can help us defend the Hone Reach?

Lord Commander Pezzini, he realized. The lord commander's nephew, the current Lord Pezzini, was patron to at least one of Devajjo's cities.

'I think we should require Lord Commander Jarlath to defend the Hone Reach,' Lord Chen said. 'Particularly since he's not going to attack Magaria anytime soon.'

Pezzini agreed, loyal to his family, though he brought no more of the board with him. Though four votes wasn't quite enough to carry the nine-member Board, nevertheless Tork agreed to carry the board's concern to Jarlath.

'If the rebels detach ships to the Hone Reach, they weaken themselves at Magaria,' Jarlath pointed out. He spoke to Tork during a meal break, when *Glory*'s acceleration had been reduced to .8 gravities, and relief warred in his body and mind with weariness and pain. He sat in a comfortable chair in his palatial dining room, eating in blessed solitude, a fine meal of lean meat with a side of liver and another of diced kidney, served warmed to body temperature in its own steaming blood.

Tork appeared in holographic form above Jarlath's right shoulder, an annoying little wraith. Even more annoying was the three-minute time lag between Tork's words and his own responses. He got to watch Tork fidget as Tork in turn watched Jarlath gobble raw meat. It wasn't comfortable for either of them.

'The rebels may be weak at Magaria as it is,' Tork said. 'Lieutenant Martinez came within an ace of hitting Fanaghee's whole fleet with a missile. He may have caused critical damage to her.'

'There is no certain evidence of that.'

Tork didn't wait to hear Jarlath's reply before anticipating it and adding his own postscript. 'Fanaghee's force did not reply to Martinez' attack for days. None of the ships undocked.'

'When they finally acted, they fired over two hundred missiles,' Jarlath said. 'That isn't the act of a crippled force.'

'It was only Fanaghee's two original squadrons that fired. The captured ships weren't ready.'

'We can't assume they're not ready *now*.'

By the time Lord Commander Tork's answer came, Jarlath had finished his meal and had gone on to dessert, some meaty marrow bones. He sucked out the contents and crunched the remainder with his back molars. His teeth were still strong, he thought, he had a lot of years left.

'Lord Commander Jarlath.' There was an ominous, discordant chime in Tork's voice. 'You must do *something*. I have served the Fleet for over forty years, and I understand your reasons even if I disagree with them. But the Convocates don't think as we do. They want action *now*, and if you don't provide it, they may *order* it, and who knows what form their orders will take? The vulnerability of Hone-bar has some of them panicked, and I'm afraid that some of the people – even the people on the board – may not be thinking straight. This afternoon they were within a single vote of ordering you to detach part of your fleet to guard Hone-bar.'

Tork leaned towards the camera pickups, his fixed, grey expression mournful, but his voice chiming with suppressed passion.

'Hone-bar may declare for the rebels out of sheer terror, and the Reach will follow if Hone-bar defects. For pity's sake detach a squadron to defend the Reach, or launch the attack on Magaria and trust your *Praxis*-class ships to annihilate the enemy. I would prefer the latter, but I'll leave it up to you.'

Jarlath considered this appeal as his molars crushed a particularly delectable marrow-bone. The blessedly low gravity and fine meal had given him a feeling of well-being, and he thought he might as well leave Tork with the feeling he had accomplished something.

'I want to question Martinez myself about any damage he may have done,' he said. 'In the meantime I'll order a harder acceleration. If I'm going to Magaria, then I'm going to go in *fast*.'

Jarlath gave the orders, unaware that he had just crossed an invisible line, the line between refusing absolutely to go to Magaria and a willingness to contemplate the attack.

Once he had crossed the line, Jarlath found it increasingly difficult to return.

Eleven

Most of *Corona*'s transit to Zanshaa was rather pleasant. There was some suspense right at the start, when Martinez sent his report to the repeating signal station at the far side of the Paswal system, and requested all the recent news. It was many hours before bulletins of the failed revolt at Zanshaa arrived, along with the information that the Home Fleet still stood between the Naxids and the capital.

Corona had a home to return to. Once he knew that, Martinez felt he could enjoy himself in his new command.

He set watches and kept the ship at partial gravity for the first six days, allowing everyone a chance to recover from the exhaustion of fifteen days' desperate acceleration.

Except for the lonely crews of the two wormhole maintenance and relay stations, Paswal was an uninhabited system, dead planets surrounding a bright energetic star in the midst of a globular cluster. It had never been determined exactly where Paswal was in relation to anywhere else in the empire: wormholes could lead anywhere in the universe, and to practically any time. The video views of the outside were spectacular, the cluster's million stars so closely-packed that they looked like a shining wall of diamonds. Paswal didn't experience anything like true darkness, only a kind of twilight, with the near stars great fiery gems amid the background of brilliants. Martinez sometimes slept with a virtual rig projecting the exterior view into his mind, so that falling asleep and waking were both marked by the brilliance of the exterior night, and a million stars walked through his peaceful dreams.

It was three days before he succumbed to the temptation to look at his confidential records. Tarafah's captain's key opened these, as well as those of everyone else, and it occurred to him that if he was to be the captain of *Corona,* then he should be familiar with the records of his crew. So, virtuously, he began with the cadets, then worked his way through the warrant and petty officers and on to the recruits. There were few surprises, though it did startle him to discover that Cadet Vonderheydte had been married and divorced twice in his brief service career, which barely added up to three years.

After this display of rectitude Martinez called up his own records, and discovered that Tarafah had described him as 'an efficient officer, diligent in his duties, though needing more polish in social situations'. The estimate nettled him. When had Martinez *ever* been in a social situation with the captain? he wondered. Where had Tarafah formed that judgment? He thought about erasing the last bit, then decided the action was too dangerous. Someone might look at the time stamp and discover that the report had been modified on a date when Tarafah was in the hands of the enemy.

Vexed, he went on to Enderby's report, which was longer and more detailed. 'An officer of exceptional talent and ability,' it concluded. 'He will have an excellent career if he can restrain his ambition from scheming for awards that would fall to him naturally in the fullness of time.'

Now *that,* Martinez had to admit, was fair.

Martinez glowed, however, when he read Enderby's final testament, in which he requested that the Fleet Control Board promote Martinez as soon as a suitable command became vacant. The old man *had* liked Martinez, had done his best to assure that he'd be promoted . . . *in the fullness of time.* Perhaps even the transfer to the Second Fleet aboard

Corona was aimed at assisting Martinez' chances: vacancies tended to occur more often on the more remote stations. In sudden charity with all the universe, Martinez decided this had to be true.

The glow of pleasure that accompanied this discovery accompanied him through his first few days of command.

On the seventh day he decided the crew's vacation was over. He kicked the acceleration up to a full gravity and started a regular series of inspections, each of the ship's departments in turn. He assigned punishments to Zhou, Ahmet, and Knadjian, the ship's bad lads – they were to repair all the damage that had been done to the quarters of the captain and the premiere lieutenant. As the rooms had been comprehensively destroyed in the search for the command keys, the repairs would take at least till the end of the voyage – and of course Martinez made them stand regular watches as well, so the repair jobs came out of what would have otherwise been their free time. He put Saavedra, the captain's secretary, in charge of this act of rehabilitation, because he knew that the precise and exacting Saavedra was exactly the sort of person whose fastidious ways would most annoy the malefactors.

A few days into the new regime he was informed that the Convocation had awarded him the Golden Orb. Alikhan and Maheshwari slipped away for a few hours to the frigate's machine shop, and at dinner that afternoon made Martinez a presentation.

Martinez had seen a Golden Orb in the Hall of Honour of the Fleet Museum in Zanshaa's Lower Town, and it had been an ornate baton on top of which was mounted a transparent sphere filled with a dense golden liquid that swam and swirled and eddied in reaction to motion, even the motion of a cadet walking past the display. The patterns inside the sphere were fascinating, intricate, the cloud swirls of a gas giant in miniature, patterns wrapped inside patterns clothed inside patterns, an infinite regression of fractals.

The thing about the Orb that had most impressed Martinez, however, was that superior officers – even *convocates* – had to brace and salute a Golden Orb when its recipient walked past. *That* was the sort of power that Martinez suspected he could use, abuse, and enjoy.

'We wished to present this to you, in thanks for saving us and for saving the ship.' So said Maheshwari, offering their homemade Orb on an overstuffed pillow. This wasn't the ornate, magical Orb that Martinez had seen in the Fleet museum, but a plain plated sphere atop a plated stick, but even so Martinez felt a completely unanticipated surge of delight as the crew stood broke into applause.

'I believe it is customary to make a speech on such an occasion, my lord,' Alikhan said, with a disturbingly serene smile that Martinez suspected hid the sadistic impulse beneath.

So Martinez stood and made a speech, at first barely knowing what he was saying. He expressed thanks to the crew for their generous and thoughtful presentation. He told them that even if the genuine article were presented to him by the Convocation in full assembly, it wouldn't mean as much as this. He thanked them also for following his orders when a rational being might have concluded he was mad. 'We *did* think you were mad, my lord,' called out Dietrich. 'But then you had that great big pistol, didn't you?'

There was laughter at that. 'Well,' Martinez said lamely. 'If you can't respect the officer, at least respect his gun.'

More laughter. It was an easy audience, fortunately.

Martinez decided it was time for the compliment direct. He spoke more largely on the qualities of a fighting crew, of which his experience was no less theoretical than his audience, but which he made out to be courage, talent, perseverance, and determination in the face of overwhelming

odds and near-certain death. He implied that the crew of
Corona possessed these qualities in abundance. He said that
he could never have achieved anything without the support
of *Corona*'s crew, that he would never forget any of them,
and that he was proud to call them all his shipmates. 'Even
you,' he told Ahmet, to general laughter.

He finished by saying that he hoped *Corona*'s crew could
stay together long enough to see the end of the war together,
that he hoped they would all return to Magaria, drive the
Naxid rebels from the station, and liberate their captain and
the other Coronas.

More applause as he returned to his seat, and then turned
to Alikhan and ordered the spirit locker store opened again,
so that everyone could toast the return to Magaria.

The next day Martinez received word that he had been
promoted to lieutenant-captain and given *Corona*. Alikhan
acquired shoulder boards from Tarafah's spare uniforms and
put them on one of Martinez' uniform jackets, which he
presented at dinner.

'I believe a speech is customary on these occasions, my
lord,' he said, again with his serene, sinister smile.

I've already *said* everything, Martinez thought, but he
had no choice but to stand and say it again. He made
Corona's crew even more valorous and brilliant than he
had the previous afternoon, their dangers more perilous,
and the return to Magaria even more glorious. And then,
exhausted, he ordered the spirit locker opened.

The next day came word that the Fleet Control Board
had awarded him the Medal of Merit, First Class, for his
part in the rescue of Captain Blitsharts and *Midnight Runner*.
'It is *not* customary to make a speech on these occasions,'
he told Alikhan firmly, and then ordered the spirit locker
opened anyway, to general applause.

Lest anyone feel he was turning *Corona* into a den of
inebriates and slackers he turned out the whole crew next

morning for a muster, inspected their personal quarters, and awarded demerits with a free hand.

Congratulations poured in from family and friends, all relayed by communications laser from the capital. There was a dignified message from Lord Pierre Ngeni, familial greetings from Vipsania, Walpurga, and his brother Roland, a silly video from PJ, and a somewhat warmer greeting from Amanda Taen. Sempronia's video letter had a different tone. 'I was thinking of forgiving you since you turned out to be such a hero,' she said, 'but then I had to spend an hour with PJ and I decided against it.' She raised a hand and waved the tips of her fingers. 'Goodbye!'

Nothing from Caroline Sula. When no message came he found that he'd been expecting one, and he felt its absence with an impact that surprised him.

As a tonic Martinez turned his thoughts to patronage. As a lieutenant-captain he was allowed to promote one cadet or warrant officer each year to the rank of sub-lieutenant. He considered Vonderheydte and Kelly, and realized he didn't know either one of them well enough to promote them, despite having worked alongside one of them for two months, and having been to bed with the other.

Kelly, he realized from a glance at her records, was unsuitable for a lieutenancy. Though she'd shown unexpected talent as a weapons officer, *Corona* was her first posting, and she needed another year or two of seasoning before she'd be able to handle a lieutenant's duties.

Vonderheydte was more qualified. He had served as a pilot/navigator and in the engineering division before taking his turn as Martinez' second in the communications division. When Martinez had been his supervisor, he'd had no complaints against Vonderheydte, and apparently none of his other officers had, either. He was eligible to stand for his exams, and was qualified to stand a watch.

Vonderheydte's only drawback was that he came from a

provincial clan, like Martinez, and one from Comador, so that it was unlikely that Clan Vonderheydte would ever be able to repay Clan Martinez for the favour done their offspring.

And Kelly might resent Vonderheydte's promotion. She might consider that he owed her some special consideration on account of their having been to bed, for sentimental reasons or on account of ambition or . . .

Things had changed so much. When Kelly and Martinez had their recreational, they were outlaws on the run from pursuing annihilation. Now he was a captain and she was his most junior officer.

Martinez' mind was spinning through all these considerations when he realized who he should have been considering all along, summoned Alikhan to his cabin, and offered him the lieutenancy.

'I'm retired, my lord,' Alikhan pointed out. 'I'm a thirty-year man. I'm only acting as your orderly to earn some extra money, and for something to do.'

'My guess is that any retired holejumper without a disability is being called back to the service. So it's not a question of whether or not to serve, but where and at what rank. If you take the lieutenancy, you can really whip *Corona* into shape, and when you decide to retire for once and all you'll be at a higher pay grade.'

Alikhan seemed for a moment to be actually considering the offer, but in the end he shook his head. 'With all respect, lord elcap, I can't see myself at a wardroom table with all those young officers. I wouldn't be comfortable, and neither would they.'

'*Corona* also needs a master weaponer.'

'No, my lord.' Alikhan spoke more firmly this time. 'I spent thirty years in the weapons bays. I'm *retired*.'

'Well.' Martinez rose. 'I hope at least you'll be staying on in your present capacity.'

'Of course, lord elcap.' A ghost of a smile passed beneath Alikhan's mustachios. 'What would I do without my hobbies?'

Martinez, uncertain what to make of being Alikhan's hobby, next offered the lieutenancy to Maheshwari, but the engineer turned down the offer with even less consideration than Alikhan. 'Officers have to put up with too much crap,' he said, his even white teeth biting decisively on the last word.

Which left Martinez with Vonderheydte, assuming of course he was going to promote anyone at all. He called the cadet into his cabin for a talk about Vonderheydte's expectations and abilities. Vonderheydte was expecting to take his exams in the near future, exigencies of the service permitting. Until the rebellion he'd been studying the subjects in which he was weak, but since then had been too busy.

'Do you think there will be exams at all, my lord?' he asked.

'I don't know. But perhaps we'd better assume there will be.'

Martinez offered to help Vonderheydte set up a programme of study and assist him in any subject he felt weak, then dismissed him without having made up his mind about the promotion. Instead he summoned Kelly for much the same conversation, and suggested that she and Vonderheydte try to find time to study together.

Her blinding grin flashed out. 'When? We're standing watches back-to-back.'

'That's true,' Martinez admitted, and then added. 'I'll help when I can.' He hesitated, then said, 'It's unfortunate that with so many vacancies I can't promote you to sub-lieutenant, but you just don't have enough experience.'

'Oh well.' She shrugged. 'Too bad the rebels didn't wait

another year.' Then she looked up at him. 'Are you thinking of giving Vonderheydte a step?'

'I'm not sure I know him well enough. What's your opinion?' She'd been aboard *Corona* since her graduation, and she knew Vonderheydte better than Martinez did.

'Von would make a good lieutenant,' she said. 'He's conscientious enough, and he admires you.'

'Does he?' Martinez felt vanity give a little jerk to his head. And then he thought about Vonderheydte's two ex-wives, and said, 'Do you know anything about his personal life? His marriages?'

'More than one?' Kelly was surprised. 'He only talks about the latest, I guess.' She began to speak, then hesitated. 'I'd rather not repeat anything he told me in confidence,' she said.

'I wouldn't ask you to break a trust,' Martinez said. 'But nothing he's told you would mitigate against his promotion?'

She seemed relieved not to be pressed on the matter. 'No, lord elcap,' she said.

'Right,' he said. 'Thank you.' And then, before he could think too much about it, he added, 'We should probably talk. About the recreational we had some days ago.'

She smiled with her lips pressed together, as if to herself. 'I was wondering if you were — well. Go ahead.'

'If I was what?'

Kelly shook her head. 'You start, my lord.'

He looked at her. 'Well,' he said. 'You want to do it again?'

This time the grin burst out, along with the incredulous bark of a laugh he'd heard when he asked her the first time. Then she composed her face into a solemn expression.

'Well, lord elcap,' she said. 'As I think I've mentioned, I have a guy on Zanshaa. And we're getting closer to him.'

'We are.'

'And you're the captain now, and . . .' She bit her lip. 'That's different, isn't it?'

'It is.'

There was a space of silence. 'Believe me, I'm tempted,' she said. 'But we'd better not.'

Wounded vainglory warred in Martinez' heart with relief. He preferred to think himself irresistible, and disliked evidence to the contrary. He enjoyed Kelly, but having a lover on board was likely to be more complication than he really wanted. 'You win on maturity points, I think,' he said.

Displays great maturity, Martinez wrote later in her file. And – exercising his powers of patronage for the first time – he sent to the Fleet a recommendation that Kelly be decorated for coolness and gallantry in shooting down incoming missiles, and suggested the Award of Valour.

He still made no decision about the lieutenancy. Caroline Sula hovered in his thoughts. She needed promotion and a patron in the service and her record was exemplary.

But it was hard to promote someone who wouldn't talk to you. He considered sending her the offer, but he dreaded her refusal or, worse, her silence.

Eventually the Fleet forced his hand. He received word that they had assigned him a full complement, the enlisted mainly old hardshells called out of retirement and new drafts fresh from the training schools, most of whom had not yet actually graduated. All were assembling now at Zanshaa and would come aboard as soon as he docked. Martinez knew nothing of two of the three lieutenants assigned him, but he knew the third, Sibbaldo, with whom he had served as a cadet. He knew Sibbaldo to be a friendless, sarcastic, bullying man, ignorant of his duties and with a talent for making mistakes and then successfully laying the blame on others.

Martinez sent word to the Fleet that he had just promoted Cadet Vonderheydte into a lieutenancy, and though he would be happy to accept his new first and second officers, he regretted that he would have no place for Lieutenant Sibbaldo. And then he walked to Command, where he informed Vonderheydte of his new status.

That afternoon it was Vonderheydte who had to make a speech. Martinez enjoyed it immensely. He didn't open the spirit locker, but it turned out not to matter.

'I believe Zhou and Ahmet are operating a still, my lord.' Alikhan's report came the next morning, as he was folding Martinez' linen. 'They're buying scraps and leftovers from the cooks and fermenting them.'

'Using the profits from their dice game.' Martinez had already been told about *this* little venture.

'No doubt, my lord.'

'I wonder when they sleep.'

Martinez considered *Corona*'s troublemakers for a moment. 'Unless drunkenness becomes a problem, I'd suggest we don't find the still till near the end of the voyage. Then we mete out punishments and fines with a heavy hand, and the dice game's profits become part of the recreation fund.'

Alikhan's smile seemed approving. 'Very good, my lord.'

'If you find a way to relieve the cooks of *their* illicit earnings, let me know.'

The smile broadened. 'I shall, my lord.'

It was twenty-one days before the sphere of Paswal Wormhole Two engulfed the *Corona,* and the latter part of the trip was spent in deceleration. Martinez was planning a much gentler return to Zanshaa than the departure he'd been forced to make from Magaria, and unless the Fleet ordered otherwise he was going to make a pleasant one-gee deceleration the whole way.

From Paswal *Corona* passed to Loatyn, an inhabited system with eight billion citizens spread out among two planets and three moons. *Corona* was in the system for only the eight days it took to cross between Wormholes Three and Two, and for that brief moment was the only loyalist armed force

in the system since the frigate *Mentor* had left for Zanshaa at
the beginning of the emergency.

It was during the last hour of the transit to Wormhole
Two that *Corona* witnessed the enemy invasion, when eight
warships appeared from Wormhole One. The ships had
actually arrived fourteen hours earlier – the distance from
Wormhole One to Wormhole Two was slightly in excess of
fourteen light-hours – and they were coming on fast, nearly
forty percent of the speed of light. A glance at a wormhole
map showed that the newcomers must be the Naxid squadron
from Felarus, the headquarters of the Third Fleet.

Censors had prevented news of what had happened to the
Third Fleet from spreading, but now that Martinez saw the
Naxid squadron, he felt he could guess.

Their arrival was a nasty shock, but Martinez calculated
that there was no hope of their catching him, not unless
they followed him all the way to Zanshaa, in which case
they'd find themselves in a fight with the Home Fleet, now
building its velocity in frantic burns around the system.
Through the wormhole relay stations he sent word of the
Felarus squadron's arrival to Zanshaa.

Corona dived into Wormhole Two and found itself in
Protipanu, another uninhabited system. Protipanu was a
brown dwarf barely detectible in the visible spectrum,
and in its earlier, bloated red giant stage had gobbled its
inner planets, turned the middle planets to rubble through
gravitational stress, and boiled the frozen atmosphere off the
outer four planets, leaving barren rocks. The result was an
absolutely bare inner system and scattered rings of rocks and
ice in the far system.

The most impressive thing about Protipanu, however,
was the brilliant red cloud, shading into purples and blues,
that occupied fully a third of the sky. This was a supernova
remnant expanding towards Protipanu at about half the speed
of light and scheduled to arrive in another eighty thousand

years. The cloud formed a giant flaming hoop in the sky, like a mouth opening to consume the brown dwarf, and as a result had been named the Maw.

Corona was only in the Protipanu system for four hours, the brief time it took to transit the two wormholes. The personnel on the two wormhole relay stations were warned that the Naxids were coming, though only those at Wormhole Two, at the far end, would have a chance to get out of the system before the Naxids overran them. Martinez didn't actually know what the Naxids were doing with the relay stations, but he presumed they were occupying them when possible, to make use of the communication system that kept the empire together.

From Protipanu *Corona* sped on, spending two days in Seizho before heading through Seizho Wormhole Four to Zanshaa, the Home Fleet, and safety.

Martinez decided it was time to get serious about finding *Corona*'s illicit still.

They will be coming in thirty hours, thought Shushanik Severin. *I have that long to prepare an unpleasant surprise.*

'This is Warrant Officer Severin at Protipanu Two,' he replied via comm laser. 'Thank you for the warning, Captain Martinez. My congratulations to yourself and to *Corona*, and the very best of luck to you all.'

Severin could hardly blame Martinez from flying before an enemy squadron that outnumbered him eight to one. It was a pity, though, that Severin himself was left in the lurch.

Severin was twenty-eight years old and commanded the wormhole relay station at Protipanu Two. He and his staff of six maintained the powerful communications lasers that transmitted messages through the system, these and the giant mass drivers that kept the wormhole stable. They normally spent four months on and four months off, and had just begun their new tour when the rebellion broke out. Now schedules were so disrupted that it was unclear how long they would remain.

The wormhole stations were the domain of the Exploration Service, an organization with a glorious history but which barely explored anything any longer, its budgets slowly reduced over the centuries as the Shaa grew old and died and lost interest in expanding their empire. Maintaining the wormholes and the communications system were now the service's primary tasks, and the two remaining exploration craft were crewed by cadets who built their esprit by reenacting the heroic discoveries of the past.

Severin wouldn't have minded commanding a probe through a newly-discovered wormhole, but his real reason for joining the Exploration Service was because of his aunt, a Commander, and the fact she could guarantee him quick promotion. The pay was good and he could save money easily, since he had no expenses during his four-month stretches in the station. It was a good service, small and efficient, and everyone based at Seizho knew and liked each other.

Severin didn't know how he felt about the service being militarized and annexed to the Fleet for the duration of the emergency. He reckoned he could live with it if he didn't have to take too many idiotic orders from a clutch of useless Peers.

Still, he found himself chafing to do his bit. In earlier days the Exploration Service would have been foremost in any action against rebels. He resented the fact that he'd probably spend the entire war gazing at the round, hollow shape of Protipanu Two.

Protipanu Two was an unusual wormhole in that it was torus-shaped, with a hole in the middle. Most wormholes, those strange remnants left over from the formation of the universe, were spherical, presenting the familiar inverted-starscape-in-a-goldfish-bowl appearance that was the standard

illustration in elementary texts. Other wormholes were tetra-
hedral or octahedral or cylindrical, but Protipanu Two was
the only torus-shaped wormhole that was actually in use.
The famous yachtsman Minh had once repeatedly dived
his yacht through the hole in the centre, threading it like
a giant buttonhole. Severin enjoyed looking through the
broad windows of his command centre at the strange sight,
the weird hoop of another system's stars floating in space.
He took a kind of pride in it, in being custodian of the
most unique wormhole in the empire.

When *Corona*'s signal told him that the Naxids were on
their way and how long he would have before their arrival,
he called a meeting of his staff.

'I think we should strike at the enemy,' he said. 'I think
we should do something worthy of the traditions of the
service.'

'Such as?' Warrant Officer/2nd Gruust was sceptical.

Severin offered Gruust a bite of the spicy garlic sausage
he'd been snacking on when the message came.

'I think we should move the wormhole,' he said.

Part of the task of the wormhole station was to keep the
wormhole stable. Wormholes could be destabilized over
time if more mass went in one direction through the
hole than the other, a problem that hardly existed when
all that passed through them was solar wind and the odd
bit of cosmic dust. Ships, however, were another problem.
If more ships passed through the wormhole in one direction
than the opposite, then the wormhole could deform, drift
away, or even collapse.

Fortunately for the stability of the empire, the remedy
was simple: you simply had to chuck enough matter in the
other direction to balance the equation. Each wormhole
station was equipped with a mass driver that could fire
colossal steel-jacketed chunks of asteroid material through
the hole and into orbit around the other system's star, where

they could be retrieved if necessary and fired the other way. The projectiles were so massive that the driver didn't move them very fast, but speed was hardly necessary – all that was required was a degree of timing, so that a ship heading for the wormhole didn't meet a rock going the other way.

'Move the wormhole?' Gruust asked. 'Can we do that?'

'I expect we can.'

Gruust chewed meditatively on garlic sausage. 'That would really wreck their schedule. They miss the wormhole, there aren't any planets out there to swing around. It would take them months to decelerate and return.'

Severin was already on to the next step. 'Why don't you and the others get the lifeboat packed and I'll warm up the coils?'

The exams that Severin had passed to earn his rank had featured a lot of wormhole theory, and he put it to use now. He began firing his heavy, slow-moving bowling balls toward the great torus, and only then started calculating where they would have to hit in order to skate the wormhole across the sky. He figured the first few shots would just destabilize the wormhole only slightly and make the rest of his task easier.

Once he had his effects calculated and knew where to aim, he began a regular barrage, firing one bolt after another. Only then did he communicate with his superiors in the Seizho system to ask permission for what he was doing.

It took four hours for the Seizho brass to respond, categorically forbidding Severin to destabilize the wormhole. By that time Severin had hurled hundreds of thousands of tonnes of dense matter through the torus, and had begun to detect motion.

The odour of garlic preceded Gruust into the command centre. 'Lifeboat's ready,' he reported. He gazed out of the huge plate windows of the mass driver, as another giant bolt shot off the rails and towards the eerie, hoop-shaped entity in the far distance.

'Why don't you look after the drivers for a while,' Severin said. 'I want to make sure my personal stuff is on the lifeboat.'

The lifeboat wasn't as cramped as its name might suggest: it was designed to keep an entire station's crew comfortable for the journey to and from the station, a journey that might take a month or more. There were a fully-stocked kitchen and exercise facilities, and a full library of videos, books, music, and other entertainments.

What Severin added to all that was a stock of insulated clothing, thermal blankets, and warm socks. He then returned to the command centre.

'The wormhole's moving,' Gruust said.

'I know.'

By the time Severin had fired off all his ammunition, the wormhole had moved seven diameters on a diagonal course from the plane of the ecliptic, and the messages from his superiors, who were detecting the huge freight-train-sized bolts flying into their system, were growing frantic. Eventually their messages trailed away: with the worm-hole moving, the communications lasers were no longer in alignment.

Severin and his crew had a last meal in the station, noodles in a tomato sauce made fiery by dried chiles, and washed down by a dark, toasty beer that one of the crew had made with barley he'd brought onto the station.

The Exploration Service traditionally compensated for their loneliness by eating well.

'You know,' Severin said, 'I'm beginning to think we shouldn't leave the Protipanu system.'

'If we stay here,' Gruust said, 'they'll just take us prisoner.'

'I don't want to stay *here*,' said Severin. 'Not in the station.

I thought we'd take the lifeboat and grapple it to one of those big chunks of rubble orbiting past. That way we could keep the enemy under observation, and if the Fleet returns we can give them the information. And if the rebels leave, we can just reoccupy the station.'

'You're talking *months*,' someone said.

There was some discussion of this. Severin didn't want to live for three or four months with crew who resented the orders that put them there. But in the end he had his way, and without pulling rank: the others were used to spending time together in isolated situations, and agreed that wrecking enemy plans was worth the extra discomfort and time.

'It's going to be cold, unfortunately,' Severin said. 'To avoid detection I'm going to have to power as little of the ship as possible.'

'We should get the thermal blankets aboard,' someone said.

'I already have.'

There was a moment of silence. 'Well, at least we'll have a big pay packet waiting when we return,' Gruust said hopefully.

They moved six months' food supplies into the lifeboat and cast off. Severin already had chosen his rock, an iron asteroid called 302948745AF – the smaller lumps of rock and metal in the Protipanu system were well charted, as they were all potential supplies of reserve ammunition for the mass drivers.

The Naxid flotilla leaped into the system before the lifeboat actually grappled to its new home, but Severin had anticipated this, and made his major deceleration burn before their arrival. He was now drifting gently towards 302948745AF. He should be able to snuggle tight to the asteroid with just his manoeuvring thrusters, and without attracting attention by lighting the antimatter engine.

Floating weightless in the lifeboat's control station, Severin watched the tall antimatter torches race towards the wormhole. The Naxids were coming fast, decelerating but still moving at nearly half the speed of light, and Severin calculated their trajectories and discovered that they were on course . . . for where the wormhole *had been*.

It was perfectly possible for them to find out the wormhole had moved. They could detect it visually or by charting its warp of space-time. But, Severin insisted to himself, they had no reason to. The wormhole had been in the same place since its discovery, and the Naxids had absolutely no reason to suspect it might have crabbed away from its rightful place.

Still, as the minutes ticked by and the blips raced closer, he felt his mouth go dry, and cramp pained his hands as they clamped on the stabilization bars at the control panel. It would require a tiny correction in their course to hit the wormhole, one they might make at any moment . . .

He held his breath. And the Naxid squadron shot past, a clean miss of the wormhole. The little lifeboat's crew broke into cheers. Severin could only imagine the consternation in the rebels' command centres as they realized what had happened to them.

While the Naxids increased the fury of their deceleration burn, Severin knew that he'd delayed their plans, whatever they were, by at least three months, probably a good deal more.

He felt a quiet, certain triumph. He'd done the enemy an injury, done it without having a single weapon to fire at them, and with any luck he'd be in a position to do them another.

In the days that followed his conversation with Tork, Jarlath worked with his staff on plans for a Magaria attack, and the harder he contemplated the possibilities, the less possible he found it to resist them.

Martinez' video report, delivered after a transmission delay of some days, provided little hard information about the damage his missile strike might have done, but it left Jarlath convinced that the missile must have done *something*. Almost all the shielding on a ring station was on its outer rim, facing the sun to protect the inhabitants from solar radiation, and *Corona*'s missile had hit north of the inner rim. The flood of neutrons and highly energetic gamma rays released by the explosion would probably not have done any lasting damage to the ships, but any crew and ring personnel who were not in a hardened shelter had probably got a fatal dose of radiation. Martinez might well have caused a massacre among the enemy, as well as many of the civilian personnel aboard the ring. Casualties to the dockyard workers and other specialists on whom the Fleet depended could have been high. Though hardened military gear would probably have survived well enough, the ordinary electronics on the ring station had probably been slagged, everything from communications to light and power to the electric carts used to haul supplies to and from the ships. Such damage would have interfered severely with the Naxids' attempts to refit their captured ships.

If he came in fast, Jarlath thought, if the Home Fleet roared in so quickly that Fanaghee had no time to alter her own dispositions, Jarlath might well catch her napping. The only way that she could match the abrupt and devastating arrival of the Home Fleet would be to have subjected her own crews to the same merciless accelerations that Jarlath was inflicting on his own personnel. But Jarlath had full crews – his people got at least *some* rest – whereas if Fanaghee had crewed her captured vessels from out of the Naxid ships, *all* her ships would have skeleton crews. By the time Jarlath met them in combat, they'd be beaten into undifferentiated protoplasm by over a month of high gravities and standing continual watches, unable to match his crews in efficiency and combat readiness. They would have no real damage control capability. Three squadrons would consist of ships that had only recently been adapted to their species, and whose controls and capabilities would be unfamiliar.

They would, he considered, have certain advantage of position. Two large planets in Magaria's system, Barbas and Rinconell, happened to have moved on either side of Magaria Wormhole One, with a forty light-minute gap between them. Fanaghee could keep her squadrons involved in perpetual slingshots between the two planets, or between Barbas, Rinconell, Magaria, and Magaria's sun, thus keeping her ships at high speed and in a position to slap at Jarlath's fleet once it emerged from the wormhole.

Jarlath's staff, however, had worked out a series of manoeuvres that would minimize this advantage.

Jarlath's primary worry was that he could still count on being outnumbered. But then he heard – also from Martinez – that the enemy squadron from Felarus wasn't at Magaria, but at Protipanu, and he realized that not every enemy ship was joining Fanaghee. The Naxids seemed to be dispersing, rather than concentrating, their force.

Now it seemed more essential than ever to seize Magaria to prevent the enemy from concentrating.

The appearance of the Felarus squadron at Protipanu sent the Convocation into a paroxysm. If the rebels were dispersing their force, then everywhere was threatened. The Convocation demanded that the Fleet Control Board take steps. ('To protect *everywhere*,' Tork muttered, and followed the remark with an obscenity.)

Accordingly it was decided to send a force to Hone-bar, which would silence at least some of the critics. The Lai-own squadron from Preowin, not yet arrived at Zanshaa, was tasked for this mission, as was the improvised squadron that would be raised by calling in single ships that had been scattered in the capital's vicinity, and which would be led by the captured Naxid cruiser *Destiny*, now being adapted for the Torminel crew that would soon be placed aboard her. It was to this squadron that the *Corona* of the heroic and by now much-decorated Lieutenant-Captain Martinez would be assigned.

Twelve

Martinez stood in the well of the Convocation and let the cheers and applause flood over him. He raised the Golden Orb – the genuine article this time, the heavy baton with the swirling fluid that shimmered and flowed in its glass globe – and the Convocation roared again in answer to his salute.

The Orb had been presented to him, in a glittering jewelled case, by Fleet Commander Lord Tork, chairman of the Fleet Control Board, following a speech of introduction by his family's patron, Lord Pierre Ngeni. Martinez' family, his brother and sisters, stood in the visitors' gallery and applauded with the rest.

Martinez tried not to let his smile, which he hoped radiated confidence and wisdom, turn into a broad, imbecilic grin. He thought he succeeded, mostly.

In time the cheering died away, and Martinez was suddenly aware of how loudly his heart was beating. He took a breath, and then a grip on his courage. He turned to the new lord senior, Lord Saïd.

'I believe a speech is customary on these occasions, my lord,' he said. In his imagination, he could hear *Corona*'s crew whooping at the familiar words.

Lord Saïd seemed surprised by the very existence of this custom, but he acceded with grace. 'Lord Gareth, you are welcome to address this body of Peers.'

Martinez turned to face the audience, the convocates in their wine-coloured uniforms, his family and the Fleet officers in the gallery, the lord senior and Fleet Commander Tork standing expectantly just before him, all turned to dark silhouettes by the brilliant spotlights ranged above the platform. Behind all these, of course, were the obscure billions who would watch this moment on video.

After years of striving, after all the work and the schemes and the danger, Martinez had finally reached his moment of glory. The moment when all the empire waited only for him.

And he couldn't say a word. The fine phrases that had been in his mind a moment ago had vanished, and all he felt was the awesome weight of expectation, the presence of the grand personages of the empire, all waiting for him to make a mistake, to show himself for the rustic nobody that he was.

The silence yawned before him as his heart thundered in his ears. He forced his mouth to open, forced sounds from his throat.

'My lord convocates,' he began, and his eyes desperately sought among the audience to light on Saïd and on Fleet Commander Tork. 'My lord senior,' he managed. 'My lord commander.' His eyes flew to the gallery. 'My friends,' he said.

And then, once he had convinced himself that he could actually speak before this audience, the words broke free in his mind. At first only a few phrases floated to the surface, but once he spoke them others came, and then more. It was fortunate that Martinez had already given the speech twice – that helped him settle into a rhythm. Adopting his sentiments for the Convocation wasn't hard: his audience had fought their own battle, on this very spot, and he could credit them with the same courage, skill, and rare genius with which he'd credited the crew of *Corona*.

By the end the phrases were flying naturally from his lips, as if he'd been addressing the Convocation all his life.

'I know this in my heart,' he concluded. 'With the wisdom and leadership of this body, and with such courage and skill as that demonstrated by the crew of *Corona,* our noble cause cannot fail!'

The room erupted in cheers and applause that lasted longer than it had the first time. Martinez tried to smile his wise, confident smile, and saluted them again with the Orb.

And if you don't like the accent, he thought, *you can lump it.*

There was a reception afterwards in the Ngeni Palace. The place was fragrant with the scent of hundreds of floral bouquets, and brilliant with glowing decorations in the shape of snowflakes, no two alike, that hovered below the high ceiling and cast a silver glow on the assembled throng. Snow, the real thing, dusted the window ledges outside and sparkled brilliantly on the trees in the courtyard. Convocates, high-ranking members of the Fleet, and senior administrators filled the rooms and galleries.

None wore mourning. The Convocation had decided to cancel the mourning period for the last Great Master, and with it the customary restrictions on the size of social engagements. Officially this was because the rebellion took priority over sorrow, though if Martinez were a convocate, he would have wanted mourning cancelled on the grounds of confusion, because it was no longer possible to know whether one was mourning the Great Master, war casualties, dead Naxid rebels, or the stability and peace of the old imperial order.

No longer having to worry about *which* twenty-two to invite to any function, society happily removed its corsets and began to take what pleasure it could from winter and rebellion.

In any case, Martinez was pleased to be wearing viridian again.

'I didn't know you were going to make a speech,' said Lord Roland, Martinez' older brother.

'I'm planning on being a convocate myself some day,' Martinez said. 'I thought I'd let them know that I can speak in public, and can be useful, and that Laredans don't drool or twitch or pitch a fit when they get nervous.'

'Actually *I* was planning on being the first convocate to be co-opted from Laredo,' Roland said. He was a little taller than Martinez, a result of his longer legs. His Laredo accent was pronounced. 'I hope you'll defer to seniority.'

'Maybe,' Martinez said. 'But if I don't, I'll work hard to get you in. Now's the time; there are vacancies.'

Martinez himself didn't know how seriously to take his own words. Lieutenant-Captain Lord Convocate Gareth Martinez? It certainly seemed possible, on such a day as this. The Convocation was in a generous mood. They had already given the Laredo shipyards an order for three frigates, and guaranteed a substantial profit for the Martinez clan and their dependants.

Perhaps, after all this time, Lord Martinez' plans were actually bearing fruit. Martinez' father had been snubbed in the Fleet and on Zanshaa, and had returned to Laredo determined to become so rich that no one would ever dare snub him again. He *had* become ridiculously wealthy, even by the standards of Peers, and his children were elements of his scheme to storm the city and cast down its social walls, but until now Martinez hadn't thought it likely that it was possible to purchase respect, not from the old families like the Ngenis and the Chens.

Until now. Since the rebellion, all sorts of things seemed possible.

Lord Pierre Ngeni arrived, and raised his glass in salute to Martinez of the Golden Orb. Martinez raised the Orb in reply, then noticed a piece of Fleet Commander Tork's flesh hanging from the baton, stripped it away, and let it fall.

'We were discussing,' Martinez said, 'how the first convocate from Laredo should be one of your clients.'

Lord Pierre hesitated. *He,* theoretically, represented Laredo in convocation through his patron/client relationship with the Martinez clan, though of course Lord Pierre had never been to Laredo, and would never go. 'I'm sure,' he said finally.

'You can never have too many allies in Convocation,' Martinez said.

Lord Pierre turned to Roland. 'Now that your ship-yards have got those contracts,' he said, 'you'll be returning home?'

'It will take me three months to get there,' Roland said, 'and by then your frigates will be half finished. There's no need for me to be on site – my father can handle all that. No,' Roland smiled, 'I'll be in the capital for quite a while. Probably a few years.'

Lord Pierre did not seem cheered by this. He turned to Martinez. 'But you, lord captain, you must leave soon.'

'In two days, to make up this new squadron. I've barely met my new officers.' And what he'd seen hadn't encouraged him: a grey-haired lieutenant who hadn't been promoted in sixteen years, and a new-fledged youngster with scarcely any more seniority than Vonderheydte. He clearly had his work cut out for him.

'Do you think Jarlath will strike for Magaria?' asked Lord Pierre. 'Everyone seems to think he will.'

'I don't think he's got the numbers,' Martinez said.

Roland gave a little smile. 'I thought you said we couldn't fail.'

'We can if we *try.*'

Later, as strains of music floated towards the assembly from the orchestra in the ballroom, Martinez found himself with a powerful yearning to have Amanda Taen in his arms. But Warrant Officer Taen was away in her ship, repairing satellites for the next month, and Martinez hadn't the time to make a new connection, not unless he made one now. But, as he walked towards the ballroom, Martinez found himself next to PJ Ngeni. Melancholy seemed to have become a permanent fixture on PJ's long face, and Martinez assumed this to be a consequence of frequent contact with his sisters. Martinez more or less knew how he felt.

'I say, Gareth,' PJ said.

'Yes?'

'Terrific speech you gave this morning.'

'Thank you.'

'It made me want to – to *do* something, if you know what I mean. Do something useful, in the war.'

Martinez looked at him. 'To join the Fleet?'

'I hardly think I—' he hesitated. 'Well, to do *something*.' PJ touched a hand to his collar. 'I wonder if I might ask your advice. On a more personal matter.'

Martinez lifted his eyebrows. 'Of course.'

'I wonder if it's normal for someone for someone from Laredo – a young woman, for example – to maintain, ah, a sort of social and emotional independence.'

Martinez hid a smile. 'Of course,' he said. 'Laredans are renowned for their independence, both of thought and of character.'

'Ah – I wondered. Because, you know—' PJ frowned. 'I hardly ever see her. Sempronia, I mean. Formal occasions, yes, and she gives me a kiss on the cheek and . . .' His voice trailed away, then resumed. 'But she has her own friends, and she spends time with them, and I never . . .' He tried again. 'She's in school, of course, and she says she wants to enjoy her school friends while she can. And I can't object to that, because I've had my friends over the years, and . . .' His brows knitted in puzzlement. 'But so many of her friends are officers. And *they're* not in school.'

For a moment Martinez almost felt a breath of sorrow for PJ Ngeni. And then he remembered who he was talking to, and his sorrow blew away like cherry blossoms in the spring.

'I think you should just have patience,' he said. 'Sempronia's the pet of the family, and she's used to having her own way.' He gave PJ's arm a consoling pat. 'She'll grow to appreciate your virtues in time,' he said. 'And as for the officers – well, I'm sure she just wants to take advantage of their company before they go off to war.'

'Hmm.' These thoughts processed their way across PJ's face. 'Well. I suppose.'

Martinez found out more about at least one of the officers the next morning, after breakfast. He was packing his night case, preparing to leave for a meeting called by his new squadron commander, Captain Farfang of *Destiny,* when he heard a tentative knock on his door.

'Yes?'

'It's me.' Sempronia's voice, muffled by a thumb's length of Shelley Palace teak.

'Come in.'

Sempronia, her expression tentative, swung the thick door open and entered. She saw him in his unbuttoned tunic, and walked up to work the silver tunic buttons, her teeth resting lightly on her lower lip and her hazel eyes comically crossed as she concentrated on the work. She finished the last button, straightened the collar, then stepped back to survey her work.

'Thank you,' Martinez said.

'You're welcome.' She crossed her arms and frowned at him. He went to his dressing table and took from it the gold disc on a ribbon that he could wear if he wasn't going to lug the Golden Orb about.

'You aren't going to carry the Orb with you?'

Martinez placed the disc about his neck. 'To carry the Orb on anything other than a formal occasion would be conceit.'

'But Gareth,' Sempronia protested, 'you *are* conceited.'

Martinez decided that the higher wisdom lay in not answering this charge. He turned to her.

'And the reason you came here, Proney . . . ?'

'Oh.' She hesitated. 'I wanted to talk to you about one of your officers.'

'One of *my* officers?'

'Nikkul Shankaracharya.'

'Ah.' This would be his second officer, who he had met just two days before, and with whom he'd exchanged perhaps three dozen words. A sub-lieutenant of less than six months' seniority, with a faint little moustache and a hesitant manner. At the first meeting Shankaracharya had made little impression, though Martinez had felt a strong sense that this one, perhaps, would take a lot of work.

'A friend of yours, is he?' Martinez asked.

A faint rose colour brightened Sempronia's cheeks. 'Yes. I was hoping that you could, well, look after him.'

'That's my job,' Martinez said. 'But is Shankaracharya likely to need much looking after?'

Sempronia's flush deepened. 'I think he's very talented. But he's shy, and he doesn't put himself forward. You're likely to trample him into the deck without even noticing he's there.'

'Well, I promise not to trample him into the deck.' He cast his mind back, uncovered a memory of Sempronia talking to a dark-haired officer at the family's reception for Caroline Sula.

Her eyes darted from one corner of the room to the next. 'He admires you very much. He pulled strings through his patron Lord Pezzini to get aboard *Corona*.' Her lips twisted into an S-shape. 'Of course, he doesn't know you like I do.'

Martinez approached Sempronia, reached out a hand, and lifted her chin so that he could see her eyes at rest. 'Is Shankaracharya *very* important, Proney?' he asked.

Her lips thinned to a line, and she nodded. He kissed her forehead.

'Very well, then,' he said. 'I'll do my best for him.'

Her arms went around him briefly in a fierce hug.

'Right then,' she said. 'If you look after Nikkul, I *might* forgive you for PJ.'

She dashed from his room, and he finished packing and called for the servants to carry his gear to the cab that would take him to the maglev station. Alikhan wasn't available – Martinez liked to think he was looking after *Corona* in his absence. He threw his winter overcoat over one arm, took the Golden Orb in its travelling case, marched down the broad staircase to the foyer, and said goodbye to his family.

Outside, snow glittered white beneath Zanshaa's dark green sky. The antimatter ring arced overhead, with its dockyards and the improvised squadron of which *Corona* was a part. The squadron would leave tomorrow, on special duty. Martinez didn't know where they were bound, knowing only that they wouldn't be made a part of the Home Fleet – they had been assigned to the Lai-own Do-faq's command, and not Jarlath's. He assumed there would be many long days of acceleration before he found out, unless Captain Farfang chose to inform his captains at the day's meeting.

But it turned out that Captain Farfang couldn't tell him anything, because he was dead.

'*Destiny* was finishing its conversion from a Naxid ship to one crewed by Torminel.' This from Dalkieth, his middle-aged senior lieutenant. Her excited voice was high-pitched and soft, almost lisping, a child's voice that contrasted with her lined face. 'Work was completed on the crew quarters last, so the hardshells had been bunking on the station and only came aboard last night to make final adjustments to the ship's environment. And you know that Torminel prefer a lower temperature than Naxids, because of the fur.'

'So it wasn't sabotage?'

'If it was, the saboteur was on the crew and died with everyone else. Because when they programmed the new temperatures, someone lost a decimal point somewhere, and *Destiny's* environment was cooled to one-tenth what it should be.'

Martinez was puzzled. 'But the temperature change should have been gradual enough to— Oh.'

'Yes.' Dalkieth said. 'Torminel have a hibernation reflex. When it gets cold, they just go into a deeper sleep. But even hibernation doesn't preserve them against an environment below freezing.'

Martinez shivered. 'All of them died?'

'All of them. A hundred and twenty-something, dead in their racks.'

'And the guard on the airlock?'

'*Destiny* wasn't going to be in commission till today. Guards were provided by the Office of the Constabulary, not the ship itself. No one went in or out of *Destiny* till early this morning.'

When they had found ice coating the walls, and frozen Torminel with frost glittering in their fur. Martinez wanted to lean back in his chair and marvel in awe at the horrific, whimsical blow of fate that had deprived the squadron of both its heaviest ship and its commander. But there was too much to do: two-thirds of his crew were strangers, a figure that included the officers. So far as he knew *Corona* and its squadron would still leave the station tomorrow. There was too much to do.

'Who's in command of the squadron?' he asked.

'Kamarullah is the senior captain. Nothing official's been said, though.'

He rose from behind his office desk, conscious of the football trophies that were still bolted to the wall behind him. Tarafah's suite had at last been reassembled, and he'd been moved into it, after insisting on triple-strength locks and bolts on the liquor store.

'Right,' he said, 'department inspections at 26:00.'

'Very good, lord elcap.'

He carried the Golden Orb on his inspection – not the one the Convocation had presented him the day before, but the cruder award that Maheshwari and Alikhan had made in the frigate's machine shop. If the crew drew the conclusion that he appreciated their gift more than that of the Convocation, he would not be disappointed.

The results of the inspection were perhaps a little better than he expected, but he had completed only half of it when Vonderheydte informed him that Comm had just received an urgent, private communication from Squadron Commander Do-faq. Martinez dismissed the crouchbacks, including those he hadn't yet inspected, and took the communication in his office.

Junior Squadron Commander Do-faq commanded the Lai-own cruiser squadron that had been heading towards Zanshaa from Preowin since the rebellion. Hollow Lai-own bones couldn't stand much more than two gravities' acceleration, and he had been accelerating the whole way. Now that Do-faq had arrived at Zanshaa he wasn't about to slow down: he'd continue a wide, eccentric circuit of the system until shooting off towards whatever wormhole the Fleet had assigned him, and in the meantime command his light squadron, which included *Corona*, via remote control.

How Do-faq was going to coordinate his squadrons if he ever had to fight was an open question, given their wildly different performance characteristics. But then Lai-owns were supposed to be diabolically subtle tacticians, as their performance in the Lai-own War had shown, and it wasn't Martinez' job to worry about it anyway.

Martinez used his captain's key to decode the squadron commander's message, which had crossed the six light-minutes that separated Zanshaa from the Lai-own squadron. When the picture resolved on the display, he saw that Do-faq was a youngish Lai-own for his post, as demonstrated by the dark featherlike hair on the sides of his flat-topped head, the hair that Lai-owns lost on full maturity. His wide-set eyes were golden, and his broad mouth, lined with peg teeth, was set in the weary lines that spoke of nearly thirty days of continual acceleration.

'Lord Captain Martinez,' he said. 'Allow me to congratulate you on your promotion and your receipt of the Golden Orb. I hope to have the honour of meeting you in person one day, should the constraints of the service ever permit it.'

Martinez found himself warmed by these civilities. It was always pleasing to discover that your superior officers had a good opinion of you, and were willing to say so. He was more used to his superiors pretending that he didn't exist.

Do-faq slid nictating membranes over his eyes. 'The loss of *Destiny* has forced me to a number of painful decisions. Among them is the reluctant conclusion Lord Captain Kamarullah is unsuited for command of the squadron.'

Martinez stared at the screen in complete surprise, and touched a control. 'Page crew Alikhan to the captain's office.'

Do-faq continued, his voice weary. 'The other captains senior to you would, I am certain, be suitable enough for the task. But they lack combat experience – we *all* lack such experience. All but you.'

The nictating membranes slid away from Do-faq's eyes, and Martinez found himself staring into the lord commander's brilliant gold eyes.

'I am willing to appoint you to command the light squadron, Lord Captain Martinez,' Do-faq said. 'I realize that you may consider this an undue burden, considering the problems you must be facing in *Corona* now, with so many new crew and with the other difficulties of a new command. You may decline the appointment without prejudice . . .'

Martinez paused the message as he heard a knock on the door. He told Alikhan to come in, and as his orderly entered said, 'What's between Do-faq and Kamarullah?'

Alikhan paused for a moment, then silently slid the door shut behind him. 'That would date from the manoeuvres back in seventy-three, my lord,' he said. 'There was a misunderstanding of an order that led to the manoeuvre being spoiled. The Fleet blamed Do-faq, and Do-faq blamed Kamarullah, who was tactical officer on the *Glory* at the time.'

And now I'm in the middle, Martinez thought. The thought failed to depress him.

Nor did the thought of his new and untried crew, the officers he didn't know, the prospect of captains angry at being passed over, and the certain wrath of Kamarullah. He felt instead the onset of exhilaration, the tingle of blood and mind as he began to grapple with the challenges implied by Do-faq's offer.

'Thank you, Alikhan,' he said. And after Alikhan left, he told the comm board, 'Reply, personal to Squadron Commander Do-faq,' and pressed the cipher key.

The light came on that showed he was being recorded, and he gazed into the camera with a face that he hoped broadcast sincerity.

'Though I'm fear you're giving me far too much credit,' he said, 'I am nevertheless honoured to accept the appointment. I and the squadron will await your orders.'

He had almost said *my* squadron, but had stopped himself at the last second.

That, he decided, would be conceit.

The next call came from Lieutenant-Captain Kamarullah. He had a squarish face, a moustache, and the greying temples that suggested Do-faq's wrath must have genuinely harmed his career – lieutenant-captains were generally promoted well before their hair had a chance to go grey.

'You could refuse the command,' Kamarullah said.

'I'm sorry, Captain,' Martinez said, 'but you know that Do-faq would just appoint someone else.'

'You could *all* refuse,' Kamarullah urged. 'If the squadron stood united against him, he'd have no choice.'

'I regret the situation,' Martinez said. 'But I've accepted the lord commander's offer.'

Kamarullah's lips twisted. '*Regret,*' he repeated. 'No doubt.'

Martinez looked at the man coldly. 'Captain's breakfast meeting on *Corona* at 06:00,' he said. 'You may bring your senior lieutenant.'

He'd get the Golden Orb out of its box, he thought, the real one, to demonstrate his authority.

And if *that* didn't work, he'd hit Kamarullah on the head with it.

Two hours before his breakfast meeting, Martinez was awakened by a messenger come to give him his sealed orders from the Fleet Control Board. He put on his dressing gown, signed for the orders, broke the seal, and read his squadron's destination.

Hone-bar. Do-faq was taking two squadrons to Hone-bar, over a month away. That would give him time to work up his ship and his squadron, to have both ready by the time they all arrived.

He paged his steward and ordered coffee.

And then he began to make plans.

The Home Fleet continued its colossal acceleration runs, making circuits of Zanshaa and Vandrith, then swinging wider still to include Shaamah, the system's sun, and other planets. It was joined by the Daimong squadron from Zerafan, which was already at speed when it arrived and was integrated with Jarlath's forces without trouble.

Do-faq's Lai-own squadron from Preowyn arrived, which would serve to protect the capital while the Home Fleet was away. After a month of punishing accelerations mixed with planning sessions with his staff and (by video) with his captains, after endless simulations of the attack, Jarlath no longer even considered holding his armed avengers back. The thought that all the work and pain might go for nothing was too outrageous to contemplate. He asked permission to attack Magaria, and permission was gladly given.

Forty-four days after departing Zanshaa, travelling at .56*c*, the Home Fleet swung around Vandrith for the last time and headed for Zanshaa Wormhole Three en route to Magaria. It would continue accelerating all the way and should be travelling in excess of .7*c* when it first slammed into Fanaghee's fleet.

Jarlath was weary and in pain, but content with his plans. He knew he was in for a hard fight, but all doubts were gone, and he knew that victory would be his.

What he and everyone else privy to his intentions failed to realize was that the Home Fleet's plans counted upon the enemy making mistakes, or having suffered critical personnel or equipment losses, or of being unable to fully crew or refit their ships.

All these were dangerous assumptions to make, particularly when one remembered that the Naxids had obviously been planning their rebellion for a long, long time.

Fanaghee had done well with the time she'd been allotted. Martinez' near miss with his missile had hit her hard, but not fatally. The electromagnetic pulse from the explosion had raced through the communications net on the ring station and slagged it. All ships but *Ferogash* had been in their berths and connected via cables to station communications, and the EMP had burned along the cables and blown the ships' comm rigs, too.

The military communications net was supposed to be hardened against such an attack, and the station *had* been hardened when it was built. But centuries of maintenance shortcuts had bypassed many of the safeguards, and the results left the Naxid command literally speechless.

The secure design of Ring Command had been compromised more recently, in a retrofit that left a coolant pipe connected to the outside without proper safeguards against flash. Though Ring Command was surrounded by slabs of radiation shielding that should have kept everyone safe, the coolant reservoir and radiator was outside Command proper, and had no defences against the wall of neutrons and energetic gamma rays generated by Martinez' antimatter missile. The coolant was instantly vaporized, flashed into Ring Command, and scalded to death every person present, including Senior Captain Deghbal. The catastrophe was only discovered many hours later, when Naxid personnel, unable to raise Ring Command after they had repaired their own comm systems, broke into the hardened facility and discovered Deghbal and her crew sprawled where the erupting poison had caught them.

This was the worst of it, however. The station was on alert, all essential personnel were in hardened shelters either on the station or aboard ship, and none of the other shelters were subject to the same design errors that made Ring Command vulnerable. The radiation casualties consisted of a few stray civilians, prisoners from the captured vessels who had been herded to the base skyhook and were awaiting transport to the surface, and their guards. *Ferogash* lost its sensors but not its communications, though since there was no one to answer, its messages soon took on a plaintive caste.

Fanaghee herself suffered nothing more than humiliation. She was in a skyhook car racing from the planet to the ring when its controls were knocked out, stranding her in Magaria's troposphere without communication for eleven hours.

But communication among the rest of the fleet was restored within hours. Within days the three ships charted by Premiere Axiom of Naxas docked at the ring station, disgorging hundreds of Naxid personnel to crew the captured vessels.

They tended to be young and relatively inexperienced, or seniors drafted out of retirement, and had been told only hours earlier that they now served, not the Commandery or the Convocation, but the Committee for the Salvation of the Praxis.

By the time the recruits arrived gangs were already working at converting the captured ships to Naxid use. This was more than tearing out chairs and replacing them with sofas: the radiation-hardened rooms that would shelter the crew during combat had to be completely redesigned so as to accommodate the Naxid form.

Fanaghee and her original two squadrons separated from the station two days after her reinforcements arrived, and from then on she controlled affairs from her flagship, *Majesty of the Praxis*. She and her squadrons began a series of heavy accelerations between Magaria, Barbas, and Rinconell, intending to provide a bulwark against any retaliation from the Home Fleet at Zanshaa. The two squadrons under Elkizer joined, already travelling fast. And, one by one, the captured squadrons finished their refits and joined Fanaghee in her defensive circle.

The squadrons from Felarus and Comador were committed elsewhere, but Naxas sent half of its ten-ship squadron to Magaria, reserving the others to defend the capital, and some small, individual ships joined from where they had been on detached duty, giving Fanaghee a total of seventy ships. She calculated that Jarlath at Zanshaa probably had fifty-five or so, if he had called in the Daimong from Zarafan, and she considered taking the offensive. The murder of the Naxid convocates had greatly offended her, and she both wanted revenge upon the rioters whom the enemy proclaimed as heroes, and had in mind for their punishment something much more colourful than being thrown off a cliff. The only thing that held her back was the refitted ships, which hadn't had time to match the speed of her other forces –

once she had them all moving at the same rate, she would petition the Committee for permission to seize Zanshaa.

In the meantime she readied her defences. Decoys were fired and echeloned to impersonate entire squadrons – to someone entering the system and gazing at a radar display, the space between Rinconell and Barbas would at first seem to be filled with a fleet three times its actual size. All ships were instructed to proceed without radar – if a newcomer was going to find them, he would have to wait for a radar pulse to reach them and then reflect back, a process that could take hours. Fanaghee arranged her squadrons in their looping trajectories so that any enemy emerging from Wormhole One would find itself sandwiched between two fires, one squadron ahead, another behind.

The captured ships with their new crews gradually built speed. Fanaghee was within a day of petitioning the Committee for permission to launch her strike at the capital when word came, from the relay station on the far side of Wormhole One, that the Home Fleet was on its way, and coming fast.

Scant hours later the Home Fleet had arrived, and Fanaghee's plans were put to the test.

Thirteen

Sula fought her way out of unconsciousness with an urgent tone bleating in her earphones and panic in her heart. For a moment she flailed, feeling the smothering pillow pressed to her face, and then her mind cleared and she realized where she was, in her pinnace with the computer demanding a decision. She clenched jaw muscles, forced blood to her brain, and tried to focus her reviving consciousness on the displays. She'd gone virtual with her primary navigation display, and it looked as if the universe had been painted on the inside of her skull, a curiously empty universe with a single sun and a few planets and asteroids, and little abstract, coloured blips here and there that represented ships, next to packages of floating data representing heading, velocity, mass, and acceleration rate.

To her surprise she floated weightless in the straps. Her boat's engine had shut off. She blinked, shook her head to clear it, tried to make sense out of what the computer was telling her.

Decoys. She and her barrage of twenty-four missiles had been fired at decoys, and her computer, analysing the increasing loads of data pouring in from the sensors, had only just figured that out.

Damn. If she were to die – a highly likely occurrence – she would have liked to take a few of the enemy with her.

Before her hung the flight of missiles, their greater acceleration assuring that they were continuing to fly from her even though their drives had shut off when the deception was discovered. They were querying her for instructions. She scanned the displays and tried to find another target. A bewildering number of possibilities swam before her vision. How many of them were real?

The sour smell of her own body had become a permanent presence in her vacuum suit. Nearly two months of constant acceleration had battered and bruised her, drained her energy and left her listless. The other cadets made jokes about her applying the acceleration drugs via patches, instead of firing them into her neck. 'Patch Girl' they called her. Fortunately Jarlath had decreed two days of near-weightlessness as the end of the long acceleration towards Magaria approached, a chance for Home Fleet personnel to gather wit and strength for the upcoming battle. Sula had alternated between obsessively re-checking the diagnostics of her pinnace and simply, blissfully, floating in her rack, feeling her muscles and ligaments, taut as twisted rope, slowly begin to slacken, a process almost as painful as the accelerations themselves.

They were hardly slack now, not after the hours of acceleration burns that led to the Fleet's leap through the Magaria wormhole, only to be followed by the remorseless, only-slightly-less-than-lethal acceleration that followed her launch from *Dauntless*. Now that weightlessness was sending blood through her body, her limbs were wakening to their pain. She tried to ignore it and instead apply her mind to the displays, but it was difficult to focus on the bewildering swarm of data.

The last time she had been in a pinnace she had been locked for endless days with a dead man. It was hard to forget that even under the present circumstances. It had taken an act of will to enter the pinnace and close the hatch behind her.

She forced her mind to the displays.

Cruiser Squadron Two, nine heavy cruisers that included

Dauntless, led the Home Fleet's assault and was now well clear of the expanding plasma field created by Jarlath's initial covering barrage, missiles fired through the wormhole to explode ahead of the fleet and make a hash of enemy radar screens. The barrage served a dual purpose, both to prevent rebel missiles from locking on and to conceal the last-minute manoeuvring he hoped would catch the Naxids by surprise. Jarlath had wanted firepower in the lead, so the heavy cruisers of Squadron Two were followed by the ten older cruisers of Cruiser Squadron One, just now emerging from the radiation cloud on a slightly diverging course from Squadron Two. And behind them, still in the process of emerging from the expanding plasma cloud, the rest of the Home Fleet, marked by the towers of flame on which stood Battleship Squadron One, the six giant Praxis-class ships with which Jarlath hoped to overwhelm the enemy.

Ahead were the Naxids, a bewildering array of formations cutting across and through each other's paths between Barbas and Rinconell. As yet only a few appeared clearly: the Naxids weren't using active radar themselves, and the Home Fleet loyalists had to wait for their own radar to find the enemy and reflect back before they could get a clear indication of their foe.

And most of those seemed to be decoys, just like those Sula had been sent to chase. Sula paged the sensor images back through time and found that her set of decoys had been manoeuvring just as *Dauntless* and the other cruisers had emerged from the plasma screen, and she and her missile barrage had been fired at what looked like a squadron of small ships setting up to make a run at their flank.

The Home Fleet's radars were slowly revealing formations of the enemy, and Sula calculated trajectories to the nearest of these. But the two lead cruiser divisions were already hurling missile barrages at those enemies, and for Sula to add her own force to these seemed the height of redundancy. She decided to continue her course for the present and wait for an opportunity. The only order she gave was for her pack of missiles to rotate and make a short burn that would drift them towards her instead of away.

From her point of vantage she saw the battle develop, saw more enemy squadrons appear on the displays, saw clouds of hot plasma and blazing gamma ray bursts as missiles began to explode. Saw ships and formations of deadly missiles manoeuvre behind the curtains of expanding radiation. Saw missiles emerge from behind the clouds, saw the flashes as antiproton beams flashed across the intervening distance.

The two heavy cruiser squadrons manoeuvred ponderously nearer the enemy, two Naxid squadrons that Sula's sensors now recognized as the eighteen ships commanded by the Home Fleet defectors, Elkizer and Farniai. The opposing forces were on courses that would intersect, both heading for Barbas to slingshot around the big planet and head for the inner system.

'Starburst,' Sula found herself muttering. 'Starburst *now*.' But the cruisers maintained their formation, only a few light-seconds from each other, and so did the enemy. The space between the converging squadrons was a continual boil of radiation through which the opposing radars sought in vain. The flashes of antiproton and laser beams became a steady pulse of fire, like strings of fireworks flashing in the sky.

'Starburst *now*.' And, as if they heard her, the cruisers began to separate, the ships rotating, engines burning in different directions. Sula didn't see the final missile barrage coming, only the brilliant flashes that burned out all sensors on her boat's starboard side. Most of the symbols on her display faded, replaced by less brightly-coloured symbols representing a purely theoretical position. To Sula it was as shocking as a slap to the face. When part of the schematic universe in her head faded, it was as if half her brain had died.

'Computer: superimpose radiation counter!' she said. She detected a hint of panic in her own voice, and tried to fight it down.

The radiation counter, at least, was still working, and it showed repeated waves of gamma rays, neutrons, and short-lived pi-mesons, the strange fruits of collision between antihydrogen and normal matter. A succession of peaks as missiles exploded, dozens of them altogether.

She waited for the radiation to die back, then switched on alternate detector arrays – the designers of the pinnace *assumed* she'd lose sensors and had provided multiple redundancy in that department. The sensors showed that her pinnace was engulfed by the ferociously hot, expanding cloud of plasma caused by multiple missile strikes. There might be other vessels in the cloud, but if so they were hidden by the electromagnetic storm that surrounded her.

Her pulse throbbed in her ears as she tried to force her senses by sheer willpower to penetrate the cloud. Surely there were survivors. Surely there were friendly ships in the cloud, ships that had perhaps lost their sensors or other electronics but with crew still safe in their hardened shelters . . .

Minutes passed. Sula licked her dry lips with a sandpaper tongue. The expanding plasma cloud lost density and cooled, and Sula's sensor range gradually increased. And then the pinnace burst out of the cloud, and the radar universe suddenly flared in her skull.

Her heart surged as another vessel emerged from the cloud, on track to be one of Cruiser Squadron Two. The vessel was followed by another. Sula shifted from radar display to optics, tried to get as close a view of the two ships as she could. Her hope was strained as taut as her knotted muscles: surely one of these was *Dauntless*.

Recognition eluded her. Optical details were rather vague: the computer was filling in speculative elements where the optics were lacking. There was something strange in the display. Both ships seemed to be *glittering,* as if they were trailing comet-tails of shimmering sparks.

It was only when Sula switched to infrared that all became clear. The two cruisers were *hot*: heat-energy boiled off them, an abrupt contrast to the cold despair that began to chill Sula's veins. She didn't know the melting point of the cruisers' tough, resinous hulls, but she suspected that it had been exceeded. If there were oxygen in space, the hulls would be on fire. Even if the crew were in their shelters, they had probably been baked alive as heat radiated inwards.

Then Sula gave a start as the lead ship blew up, the antimatter fuel spraying out another cloud of gamma rays. Sula got her sensors switched off in time to prevent damage, and when the radiation counter showed the radiation count had dropped she cautiously switched them on again. The first ship had been obliterated, and the second had been hit by a large piece of debris, or perhaps just by the massive sledgehammer of gamma rays and neutrons, because it was now tumbling end-over-end.

Nothing else emerged from the cooling plasma cloud but debris.

No survivors, Sula thought. Nineteen ships of the Home Fleet had just been wiped out. That eighteen rebels had also been destroyed hardly seemed to matter.

Sula floated in her webbing and tried desperately to process this information. She hadn't got to know her shipmates terribly well in the few weeks she'd been aboard, with everyone strapped side-by-side into their acceleration couches and fighting for every breath. She couldn't claim to have lost any friends. But still *Dauntless* was the closest thing she had to a home, and now *Dauntless* was gone, along with its nearly four hundred crew.

And Captain Lord Richard Li was gone. He was the nearest thing she had to a patron, and she could say farewell to the promised lieutenancy.

He put me on my first pony, Sula thought, and then gave a bitter laugh.

Forget about ponies and lieutenancies. None of these would matter if she didn't survive the next few hours.

Even as she made this resolution, a part of her mind was making calculations. The Home Fleet's fifty-four ships were now down to thirty-five. The enemy had started with somewhere between sixty and ninety ships – with radar restricted to the speed of light, not all had yet shown up on the displays – and had now been reduced to somewhere between forty and sixty. Settle on fifty, then, as a mean.

Fifty-four versus seventy were better odds than thirty-five versus fifty. Sula couldn't shake off the feeling that she had just seen the Home Fleet begin its death agonies.

Ahead, beginning its swing around Barbas, was a Naxid heavy squadron, featuring a suspiciously large blip that Sula suspected was the enemy flagship, *Majesty of the Praxis.* They were decelerating now, with the obvious intention of letting the remaining Home Fleet overtake them and bringing on an engagement. Sula considered sending her missiles after them, but she suspected it would be futile. She couldn't attack an entire squadron on her own, and the Home Fleet was somewhere behind her, concealed by the expanding, cooling plasma cloud that marked *Dauntless'* destruction.

Sula programmed in a modest two-gravity burn for both herself and her missiles, intending to close on the Home Fleet while she tried to work out what to do next.

While the burn was going on, two squadrons of small ships, frigates and light cruisers, shot out of the cooling plasma cloud behind her. Her sensors registered the pounding of their radars on her boat's skin. And then a light cruiser hurled missiles into space. Chemical rockets flared and died; the bright antimatter torches ignited. Sula tracked their headings, and saw that one barrage was heading for the decoys at which

Sula had originally been fired. Another barrage was heading for a different set of decoys.

And a third was heading right for Sula.

She gave a startled cry of protest as her heart thundered into overdrive. Without thought she flung the pinnace around its centre of gravity and opened the engine to a constant six gravities. The hull groaned as the engines fought inertia, and her suit clamped gently on her arms and legs. Only then did she send a message, via comm laser, to the firing ship, a light cruiser that was leading a division of frigates.

'This is Cadet Lady Sula of *Dauntless*!' she said. 'You've opened fire on me! Deactivate your missiles!' She tried to keep hysteria out of her voice, but doubted she'd succeeded.

The missiles kept on coming, closely packed in a furious acceleration that the retreating pinnace couldn't match. More missiles flew from the squadron, aimed at anything the sensors could detect, regardless of range. Whoever was acting as tactical control officer had clearly lost his head.

Sula got busy, voice and hands giving orders to her own missiles. Three of her twenty-four began to burn hard to intercept the threat. Whoever was controlling them saw the danger to his barrage and ordered the attacking missiles to spread out. Sula countered, ordered the rest of her missiles to speed away from Home Fleet, then ordered an acceleration that she knew would leave her senseless. As gravity took her by the throat, she could feel her heart flail in panic. She managed to get her sensors off before both she and her terror lost the fight against unconsciousness.

When her programmed acceleration was over, a vestigial memory of fear helped her to claw herself from the velvet black depths of unconsciousness. Her suit gradually released her arms and legs. The radiation counter showed the after-effects of massive explosions, and readings showed that the hull was very hot. Sula could hear the whirring of the cabin cooling system. Because she couldn't view anything, she ordered another furious acceleration, and when she awoke again both the radiation and heat had dropped. At this point she dared to activate some sensors, and behind her saw the vast hot bloom of an explosion that seemed to take up half of space. No missiles seemed to be following her out of the cloud, and the only missiles she could find on her display were her own.

She kept her engine going until the cloud began to dissipate, at which point she shut it down in hopes that a pinnace without acceleration wasn't worth being fired on. She could feel patches of sweat in her armpits and crotch and between her breasts, and her heart still throbbed within her chest as if urging her to run as fast as she could.

The lead elements of the Home Fleet slowly appeared through the dissipating radiation fog. The cruiser flagship had been joined by its entire squadron in flinging out missile barrages, now towards the heavy Naxid squadron ahead. Sula didn't think much of their chance of success, especially as the missiles were taking the long way around Barbas, following in the enemy's wake, instead of cutting the corner, which might actually have made sense.

And then another flight of missiles leaped from the rails and fired.

At Sula. *Again.*

Grim, determined anger sang through Sula's nerves as she again programmed her own missiles to intercept. This time her message was broadcast to every ship in the two light squadrons, sixteen ships altogether.

'*Listen, you fucking moron.*' The words were forced from her diaphragm as gee forces built. 'This is Lady Sula of the *Dauntless*, and you've just fired on me *for the second time!*' She glared into the camera and screamed. '*Do I look like a fucking Naxid, you piece of rodent shit? Stop panicking, get a grip on yourself, and call off your missiles!*' With one hand she thrust a vile gesture at the camera pickup. '*I hope I live long enough for you to court-martial me over this, you bastard!*'

She felt better for having vented the anger, but the missiles were still coming. She programmed a massive acceleration and turned off the sensors. As her head thudded against the padding in the back of her helmet and she felt the miniwaves drumming against her back, she clenched her teeth and fought the smothering blackness that started to creep over her mind . . .

Consciousness returned more slowly this time, a slow rise from an oblivion akin to death. It took Sula a while to focus on the displays even though they were projected onto her visual centres. The radiation count was high, and so was the hull temperature, but neither were as hot as they had been after the first barrage.

Still, Sula was glad for the slabs of radiation shielding that surrounded the cockpit.

When she turned on the sensors she saw the cloud of plasma behind her, again obscuring her view of the fight. No missiles were coming at her, and she had eighteen of her own left. When the clouds finally dissipated, the light squadrons seemed to have lost interest in her: now all sixteen ships were firing on the Naxids ahead. The area on the far side of Barbas was a continual boil as Naxid missiles met those of the loyalists.

Sula programmed her own swing around Barbas, but her wild accelerations away from the oncoming missiles had forced her out of the most efficient route. She swung wide and had to burn hard to get herself onto the line for Magaria's sun, the next step on the loop around the system.

It had been over two hours since Sula had transited the wormhole. She allowed herself a drink of water and ate half a ration bar. It was flavoured with some chemist's idea of strawberry, and the taste didn't encourage her to finish the second half. She had to open the faceplate of her helmet to eat, and the interior of the cabin smelled hot, as if someone had forgotten to turn off a stove burner.

The two light squadrons, taking the inner track around Barbas, had pulled ahead of Sula. Behind them came Jarlath's six huge battleships, and behind them a heavy and a light cruiser division, both of which, to judge by the missile bursts in their rear, were duelling with pursuers.

The light squadrons were firing less regularly now, which argued that they might have finally realized their munitions were not unlimited, but the space between them and Fanaghee's squadron was still opaque with detonations, one blaze of plasma after another.

Disaster happened so quickly that Sula barely had time to register what was happening before the loyalist squadrons were engulfed in flame, a succession of colossal bursts in and among them.

Nothing came out the other side of the expanding plasma spheres. Sixteen ships had just been blown to bits.

Sula's stunned amazement was followed by a burst of rage. She wanted to shriek, to pound a fist against the armoured walls of the cockpit. But instead she forced her mind to work on what had just happened.

Missiles had flown through the plasma screen undetected, she decided. And then decided that wasn't what happened.

The missiles weren't accelerating at all. They had been launched, burned for a short time while their signature was obscured by plasma bursts, and then just lay in wait, drifting towards the oncoming ships. If the light squadrons had seem them at all, they'd seen what looked like debris. The missiles let the light squadrons overrun them and then detonated.

That was how Martinez had hit Magaria ring, Sula thought, let unpowered missiles drift in while no one was looking. Fanaghee had learned a trick from her enemy.

The odds were horribly against the Home Fleet now, nineteen ships against something like fifty, and Jarlath had to know it. The Battleship Squadron broke into two divisions of three ships and began massive accelerations to overtake Fanaghee, whose *Majesty* was supported by eight heavy cruisers. Sula watched in awe as she calculated the growing velocity: everyone aboard the battleships must be unconscious, with the computers doing the steering.

What Jarlath was attempting seemed worthy of Sula's support. The battleship division had to take out the enemy heavy squadron or no one was escaping Magaria alive. Sula programmed her own acceleration and burned an interception course for the Naxid squadron, her missiles spreading out in a wave in front of her. Again, the antimatter engines blazed, flattening her against the couch. Again, she fought against unconsciousness until it spun her into blackness.

She was awakened by a bleating in her ears and a pain in her chest. As she gasped frantically for air, she realized that the pain was caused by trying to breathe against the weight of gravity.

Gradually, awareness of her surroundings came back to her. She looked for the red lights on the displays and saw they were in regard to her own life signs.

Sula sat up with a curse, forgetting that the displays were in her head and she couldn't get a better look at them by leaning forward. She waited for her head to clear, and then read that acceleration had been shut down when her suit had detected a blood pressure spike, well into the dangerous levels even for someone in good health. Her body was failing under the pressure of too many gravities.

She looked at her current readings and found them well within the normal level. Weightlessness had brought the dangerous condition to an end, though she should certainly not press her luck with a high-gravity acceleration anytime soon. Then she checked the situation outside her craft and found her missiles still blazing ahead, towards the enemy.

But Sula's missiles seemed redundant now. Jarlath and the

battleship squadron had already engaged the enemy, and they were hurling out immense waves of missiles. Each Praxis-class ship had over sixty launchers, and they were all firing, all pumping one tremendous salvo after another from their huge magazines.

Fanaghee's ships were shooting back. It was impossible to keep any kind of score of the missile tracks – there had to be hundreds of them, and on a hundred different trajectories, some direct, some looping around to attack from an odd angle.

Sula told her missiles to cease acceleration. She'd reserve them for a final blow against the enemy, if such a thing were needed.

The flanks of Jarlath's ships pulsed with the blaze of antiproton beams, and the ships began to manoeuvre apart from one another. He had learned from the loss of his two squadrons, and anything that looked like debris in his path was getting blown up.

Two of Jarlath's ships died first, and Sula gave a cry of rage and despair as she saw the fireballs erupt around them. But Fanaghee's flagship died next, buried in a wave of missile strikes, and three of the cruisers near her were destroyed in the same fiery salvo.

After that both sides lost the ability to defend themselves against the oncoming attacks. The missiles flooded in. Fury, triumph, sadness, and despair wrenched Sula as antimatter bursts obliterated friend and foe alike.

In the end nothing was left. Battleship Squadron One had ceased to exist, and so had Fanaghee's heavy ships. Only Sula was left, she and her eighteen missiles drifting towards Magaria's sun.

It was clearly time to quit the battle. There were at least forty Naxid ships remaining, and no more than thirteen survivors in the Home Fleet – maybe less, as there was a continual blaze of action behind Sula. She needed to swing around Magaria's sun, then around Rinconell en route for Wormhole One and Zanshaa. Her only contribution to the battle, it seemed, would be to expend six of her missiles defending herself against a useless attack fired at her by an idiot on her own side.

Hatred of her own uselessness stung her throat. She blinked back tears of frustration and rage. All around her was death and ruin, to which she had not been a participant but an angry witness. In a way that was worse than dying. Even annihilation had been denied her.

The long hours went past. Sula ate ration bars to keep up her strength and drank an electrolyte supplement to replace what she'd sweated away. She skated the rim of unconsciousness in her burn around the sun, but managed to hang on, to the bitter knowledge of her own uselessness.

The battle behind her died away. Perhaps everyone concerned was running low on missiles. Her detectors showed six vessels of the Home Fleet surviving, pursued by a swarm of enemy.

Six ships, she thought, out of fifty-four. Whole worlds were ending this day.

Including her own. She had hated the Fleet at least as much as she loved it, but it had provided assurance, stability, continuity, and tradition, in addition to mundane things like meals and a modest salary. All that was gone now. Sula was afloat in the void, surrounded only by a thin shell and preceded by a swarm of eighteen worthless, deadly missiles.

Black despair closed in. She could feel its chill fingers touch her face. All that she had done, all that she had been, and it was only for this.

Death *owed* her, she thought. Death owed her more than this solitary cruise, this lonely circuit around a wilderness of annihilation.

Death and Sula had known one another for a long time. It seemed to her that Death should be a better friend than this.

When Gredel returned from opening her account in Lady Sula's name, she found Caro groping with a shivering hand for her first cup of coffee. After Caro took the coffee to the bathroom for the long bath that would soak away the stale alcohol from her pores, Gredel replaced Caro's wallet, then opened the computer link and transferred some of Caro's money, ten zeniths only, to her new account just to make certain that it worked.

It worked fine.

I have just committed a criminal act, she thought. *A criminal act that can be traced to me.*

Whatever she may have done before, it hadn't been this.

After Caro's bath, she and Gredel went to a café for breakfast, and Gredel told her about Lamey being on the run and she asked if she could move in with Caro so that he would be able to send for her. Caro was thrilled. She had never heard of anything so romantic in her life.

Romantic? Gredel thought. It was sordid beyond belief.

But Caro hadn't been in the sultry little room in the Lai-own quarter, the smell of ammonia in her nostrils while Lamey's sweat rained down on her. Let her keep her illusions.

'Thank you,' she said. But she knew that once she was with Caro, it wouldn't be long before Caro would grow bored with her, or impatient, or angry. Whatever Gredel was going to do, it would have to be soon.

'I don't know how often Lamey's going to send for me,' she said. 'But I hope it's not on your birthday. I'd like you and I to celebrate that together.'

The scowl on Caro's face was immediate, and predictable. 'Birthday? My birthday was last winter.' The scowl deepened. 'That was the last time Sergei and I were together.'

'Birthday?' Gredel said, in her Earth accent. 'I meant *Earth*day.' And when Caro's scowl began to look dangerous, she added quickly, 'Your birthday in Earth years. I do the maths, see, it's a kind of game. And your Earthday is next week – you'll be fifteen.' Gredel smiled. 'The same age as me, I turned fifteen Earth years just before I met you.'

It wasn't true, not exactly – Caro's Earthday was in three months – but Gredel knew that Caro would never do the maths. Might not even know *how* to do it.

There was so much Caro didn't know. The knowledge brought a kind of savage pleasure to Gredel's mind. Caro didn't know *anything,* didn't even know that her best friend hated her. She didn't know that Gredel had stolen her money and her identity only an hour ago, and could do it again whenever she wanted.

The days went by and were even pleasurable in a strange, disconnected way. Gredel thought she finally understood what it was like to be Caro, to have nothing that attached her to anything, to have long hours to fill and nothing to fill them with but whatever impulse drifted into her mind. Gredel felt that way herself – mentally at least she was cutting her own ties free, all of them, floating free of everything she'd known.

To save herself trouble Gredel exerted herself to please Caro, and Caro responded. Caro's mood was sunny, and she laughed and joked and dressed Gredel like a doll, as she always had. Behind her pleasing mask Gredel despised Caro for being so easily manipulated. *You're so stupid,* she thought.

But pleasing Caro brought trouble of its own, because when Lamey's boy called for her Gredel was standing in the rain, in a Torminel neighbourhood, trying to buy Caro a cartridge of endorphin analog – with Lamey's businesses in eclipse, she could no longer get the stuff from Panda.

When Gredel finally connected with her ride and got to the place where Lamey was hiding – he was back in the Terran Fabs, at least – he had been waiting for hours, and his patience was gone. He got her alone in the bedroom and slapped her around for a while, telling her it was her fault, that she had to know that she had to be where he could find her when he needed her.

Gredel lay on her back on the bed, letting him do what he wanted, and she thought, *This is going to be my whole life if I don't get out of here.* She looked at the pistol Lamey had waiting on the bedside table for whoever he thought might kick down the door, and she thought about grabbing the pistol and blowing Lamey's brains out. Or her own brains. Or just walking into the street with the pistol and blowing out brains at random.

No, she thought. Stick to the plan.

Lamey gave her five hundred zeniths afterwards. Maybe that was an apology.

Sitting in the car later, with her bruised cheek swelling and the money crumpled in her hand and Lamey's slime still drooling down her thigh, she thought about calling the Legion of Diligence and letting them know where Lamey was hiding. But instead she told the boy to take her to a pharmacy near Caro's place.

She walked inside and found a box of plasters that would soak up the bruises, and she took it to the drug counter in the back. The older woman behind the counter looked at her face with knowing sympathy. 'Anything else, honey?'

'Yes,' Gredel said. 'Two vials of Phenyldorphin-Zed.'

She was required to sign the Narcotics Book for the endorphin analog, and the name she scrawled was *Sula*.

Caro was outraged by Gredel's bruises. 'Lamey comes round here again, I'll kick him in the balls!' she said. 'I'll hit him with a chair!'

'Forget about it,' Gredel said wearily. She didn't want demonstrations of loyalty from Caro right now. Her feelings were confused enough: she didn't want to start having to like Caro all over again.

Caro pulled Gredel into the bedroom and cleaned her face, and then she cut the plasters to fit Gredel's face and applied them. These did a good enough job at sopping up the bruises and swelling so that the next day, when the plasters were removed, the bruises had mostly disappeared, leaving behind some faint discoloration easily covered with cosmetics. Her whole face hurt, though, and so did her ribs and her solar plexus where Lamey had hit her.

Caro brought Gredel breakfast from the café and hovered around her until Gredel wanted to shriek.

If you want to help, she thought at Caro, *take your appointment to the academy and get us both out of here.*

But Caro didn't answer the mental command. And her solicitude faded by afternoon, when she opened the day's first bottle. It was vodka flavoured with bison grass, which explained the strange fusil-oil overtones Gredel had scented on Caro's skin the last few days. By mid-afternoon Caro had consumed most of the bottle and fallen asleep on the couch.

Gredel felt a small, chill triumph at this. It was good to be reminded why she hated her friend.

Next day was Caro's phoney Earthday. *Last chance,* Gredel thought at her. *Last chance to mention the academy.* But the word never passed Caro's lips.

'I want to pay you back for everything you've done,' Gredel said. 'Your Earthday is on me.' She put her arm around Caro.

'I've got everything planned,' she said.

They started at Godfrey's for the full treatment, massage, facial, hair, the lot. Then lunch at a brass-railed bistro south of the arcades, bubbling grilled cheese on rare vash roast and crusty bread, with a salad of marinated dedger flowers. To Caro's surprise Gredel called for a bottle of wine, and poured some of it into her own glass.

'You're *drinking*,' Caro said, delighted. 'What's got into you?'

'I want to toast your Earthday,' Gredel said.

Being drunk might make it easier, she thought.

Gredel kept refilling Caro's glass while sipping at her own, and so the first bottle went. Gredel took Caro to the arcades then, and bought her a summer dress of silk patterned with rhompé birds and jennifer flowers, a jacket shimmering with gold and green sequins, matching Caro's hair and eyes, and two pairs of shoes. She bought outfits for herself as well.

After taking their treasures to Caro's place, where Caro had a few shots of the bison vodka, they went to dinner at one of Caro's exclusive dining clubs. Caro hadn't been thrown out of this club yet, but the maître d' was on guard and sat them well away from everyone else. Caro ordered cocktails and two bottles of wine and after-dinner drinks. Gredel's head spun even after the careful sips she'd been taking; she couldn't imagine what Caro must be feeling. Caro needed a jolt of benzedrine to get to the dance club Gredel had put next on the agenda, though she had no trouble keeping her feet once she got there.

After dancing a while Gredel said she was tired, and they brushed off the male admirers they'd collected and took a taxi home.

Gredel showered while Caro headed for the bison vodka again. The benzedrine had given her a lot of energy that she put into finishing the bottle. Gredel changed into the silk lounging suit Caro had bought her on their first day together, and she put the two vials of endorphin analog into a pocket.

Caro was on the couch where Gredel had left her. Her eyes were bright, but when she spoke to Gredel her words were slurred.

'I have one more present,' Gredel said. She reached into her pocket and held out the two vials. 'I think this is a kind you like. I really wasn't sure.'

Caro laughed. 'You take care of me all day, and now you help me to sleep!' She reached across and put her arms around Gredel. 'You're my best sister, Earthgirl.' In Caro's embrace Gredel could smell bison grass and sweat and perfume all mingled, and she tried to keep a firm grip on her hatred even as her heart turned over in her chest.

Caro unloaded her med injector and put in one of the vials of Phenyldorphin-Zed and used it right away. Her eyelids fluttered as the endorphin flooded her brain. 'Oh nice,' she murmured. 'Such a good sister.' She gave herself another dose a few minutes later. She spoke a few soft words but her voice kept floating away. She gave herself a third dose and fell asleep, her golden hair fallen across her face as she lay on the pillow.

Gredel took the injector from Caro's limp fingers. She reached out and brushed the hair from Caro's face.

'Want some more?' she asked. 'Want some more, sister Caro?'

Caro gave a little indistinct murmur. Her lips curled up in a smile. When Gredel fired another dose into her carotid the smile broadened, and she shrugged herself into the sofa pillows like a happy puppy.

Gredel turned from her and reached for Caro's portable computer console. She called up Caro's banking files, and prepared a form closing Caro's bank account and transferring its contents to the account Gredel had set up. Then she prepared another message to Caro's trust account on Spannan's ring, instructing any further payments to be sent to the new account as well.

'Caro,' Gredel said. 'Caro, I need your thumbprint here, all right?'

She stroked Caro awake, and managed to get her to lean over the console long enough to press her thumb, twice, to the reader. Then Gredel handed the injector to Caro and watched her give herself another dose.

Now I'm really *a criminal,* she thought. She had left a trail of data that pointed straight to herself.

But even so she could not bring herself to completely commit to this course of action. She left herself a way out. *Caro has to want it,* she thought. *I won't give her any more if she says no.*

Caro sighed, settled herself more deeply into the pillows. 'Would you like some more?' Gredel asked.

'Mmm,' Caro said, and smiled.

Gredel took the injector from her hand and gave her another dose.

After a while she exhausted the first vial and started on the second. Before each dose she shook Caro a little and asked if she wanted more. Caro would sigh, or laugh, or murmur, but never said no. Gredel triggered dose after dose.

After the second vial was exhausted the snoring started, Caro's breath heaving itself past the palate, the lungs pumping hard, sometimes with a kind of wrench. Gredel remembered the sound from when Caro had given herself too much endorphin, and the memory caused her to leap from the sofa and walk very fast around the apartment, rubbing her arms to fight her sudden chill.

The snoring went on. Gredel very much needed something to do, so she went into the kitchen and made coffee. And then the snoring stopped.

Ice shuddered along Gredel's nerves. She went to the kitchen door and stared out into the front room, at the tumbled golden hair that hung off the end of the couch. *It's over,* she thought.

And then Caro's head rolled, and Gredel's heart froze as she saw Caro's hand come up and comb the hair with her fingers. There was a gurgling snort, and the snoring resumed.

Gredel stood in the door as cold terror pulsed through her veins. But she told herself, *No, it can't be long now.*

And then suddenly she couldn't stand still any longer, and

she walked swiftly over the apartment, straightening and
tidying. The new clothes went into the closet, the shoes
on their racks, the empty bottle in the trash. Wherever she
went the snores pursued her. Sometimes they stopped for a
few paralysing seconds, but then resumed.

Abruptly Gredel couldn't bear being in the apartment,
and she put on a pair of shoes and went to the freight
elevator and took it to the basement, where she went in
search of one of the motorized carts they used to move
luggage and furniture. There were a great many objects in
the basement, things that had been discarded or forgotten
about, and Gredel found some strong dedger-fibre rope and
an old compressor, a piece of solid bronzework heavy enough
to anchor a fair-sized boat.

Gredel put these in the cart and pushed it to the elevator.
As she approached Sula's doors she could hear Caro's snores
through the enamelled steel. Gredel's fingers trembled as she
pressed codes into the lock.

Caro was still on the couch, her breath still fighting its way
past her throat. Gredel cast an urgent glance at the clock.
There weren't many hours of darkness left, and darkness was
required for what happened next.

Gredel sat at Caro's feet and hugged a pillow to her chest
and watched her breathe. Caro's skin was pale and looked
clammy. 'Please,' Gredel begged under her breath. 'Please
die now. Please.' But Caro wouldn't die. Her breaths grated
on and on, until Gredel began to hate them with a bitter
resentment. This was so *typical*, she thought. Caro couldn't
even *die* without getting it all wrong.

Gredel looked at the wall clock, and it stared back at her
like the barrel of a gun. Come dawn, she thought, the gun
goes off. Or she could sit in the apartment all day with a
corpse, and that was a thought she couldn't face.

Again Caro's breath hung suspended, and Gredel felt her
own breath cease for the long moment of suspense. Then

Caro dragged in another long rattling gasp, and Gredel felt her heart sink. She knew that her tools had betrayed her. She would have to finish this herself.

All anger was gone by now, all hatred, all emotion except a sick weariness, a desire to get it over. The pillow was already held to her chest, a warm comfort in the room filled only with Caro's racking, tormented snores.

She cast one last look at Caro, thought *Please die* at her one more time, but Caro didn't respond any more than she had responded to any of Gredel's other unexpressed desires.

Gredel suddenly lunged across the sofa, her body moving without any conscious command, the movement seeming to come from pure instinct. She pressed the pillow over Caro's face and put her weight on it.

Please die, she thought.

Caro hardly fought at all. Her body twisted on the couch, and both her hands came up, but the hands didn't fight, they just fell across Gredel's back as if in a halfhearted embrace.

Gredel would have felt better if Caro had fought. It would have given her hatred something to fasten onto.

Instead she felt, though the closeness of their bodies, the urgent kick-kick-kick of Caro's diaphragm as it tried to draw in air, the kick repeated over and over again. Fast, then slow, then fast. Caro's feet shivered. Gredel could feel Caro's hands trembling as they lay on her back. Tears spilled from Gredel's eyes.

The kicking stopped. The trembling stopped.

Gredel leaned on the pillow a while longer just to make sure. The pillow was wet with tears. When she finally took the pillow away, the pale, cold thing beneath seemed to bear no resemblance to Caro at all.

Caro was weight now, not a person. That made what followed a lot easier.

Handling a limp body was much more difficult than Gredel had ever imagined. By the time she got it onto the cart she was panting for breath and her eyes stung with sweat. She covered Caro with a bed sheet, and she added some empty suitcases to the cart as well. She took the cart to the freight elevator, then left by the loading dock at the back of the building.

'I am Caroline, Lady Sula,' she rehearsed her story. 'I'm moving to a new place because my lover beat me.' She would have the identification to prove her claim, and what remained of the bruises, and the suitcases plain to see alongside the covered objects that weren't so plain.

Gredel didn't need to use her story. The streets were deserted as she walked downslope alongside the humming cart, down to the Iola River.

The roads ran high above the river on either side, with ramps that descended to the darkened riverside quay below. Gredel rode the cart down the ramp to the river's edge. This was the good part of Maranic Town and there were no houseboats here, no beggars, no homeless, and – at this hour – no fishermen. The only encounters Gredel feared were lovers sheltering under the bridges, but by now it was so late that even the lovers had gone to bed.

It was as hard getting Caro off the cart as it had been getting her on it, but once she went into the river, tied to the compressor, the dark waters closed over her with barely a ripple. In a video drama Caro would have floated a while, poignantly, saying goodbye to the world, but there was none of that here, just the silent dark submersion and ripples that died swiftly in the current.

Caro had never been one for protracted goodbyes.

Gredel walked alongside the cart back to the Volta. A few cars slowed to look at her but moved on.

In the apartment she tried to sleep, but Caro's scent filled the bed, and sleep was impossible there. Caro had died on the sofa and Gredel didn't want to go near it. She caught a few hours' fitful rest on a chair, and then the woman called Caroline Sula rose and began her day.

The first thing she did was send in the confirmation of her appointment to the Cheng Ho Academy.

The first day she packed two suitcases and took them to Maranic Port and the hovercraft ferry that took her across the Krassow Sea to Vidalia. From there she took the express train up the Hayakh Escarpment to the Quaylah Plateau, where high altitude moderated the subtropical heat of the Equatorial Continent. The planet's antimatter ring arced almost directly overhead.

Paysec was a winter resorts, and the snowfall wouldn't begin here until the monsoon shifted to the northeast, so she found good rates for a small apartment in Lus'trel, and took it for two months. She bought some clothes, not the extravagant garments she would have found in Maranic Town's arcades, but practical country clothes, and boots for walking. She found a tailor and he began to assemble the extensive wardrobe she would need for the academy.

She didn't want Lady Sula's disappearance from Maranic Town to cause any official disturbance, so she sent a message to Caro's official guardian, Jacob Biswas, telling him that she found Maranic too distracting and had come to Lus'trel in order to concentrate on academic preparation for the Academy. She told him she was giving up the Maranic apartment, and that he could collect anything she'd left there.

Because she didn't trust her impersonation of Caro with someone who knew her well, she didn't use video, she typed the message and sent it print only.

Biswas called back almost immediately, but she didn't take his call or any of the other calls that followed. She replied with print messages to the effect that she was sorry she'd been out when he called, but she was spending a lot of time in the library cramming.

That wasn't far from the truth. Requirements for the service academies were posted on the computer net, and most of the courses were available in video files, and she knew she was deeply deficient in almost every subject. She worked hard.

She only answered one call, when she happened to be home, was able to listen to the answerware, and realized the caller was Sergei. She answered and called him every filthy name she could think of, and once her initial anger was a little spent she began to choose words more carefully, flaying him alive with one choice phrase after another. By the end he was weeping, loud gulping honks that grated over the speakers.

Serve him right, she thought.

Lamey had her worried more than Sergei or Jacob Biswas. Every day she half-expected Lamey to burst down the door and demand that she produce Earthgirl. He never turned up.

On her final day on Spannan, Biswas insisted on meeting her, with other members of his family, at the skyhook. She cut her hair severely short, wore Cheng Ho undress uniform, and virtually plated her face with cosmetic. If she looked to Biswas like a different girl, no wonder.

He was kind and warm and asked no questions. He told her she looked very grown up, and he was proud of her. She thanked him for his kindness and for looking after her. She hugged him and the daughters he'd brought with him.

His wife, Sergei's sister, had the sense to stay away.

Later, as the skyhook carried her to Spannan's ring and its steady acceleration pressed her into her seat, she realized it was Caro's Earthday, the real one.

The Earthday that Caro would never see.

Sula jerked awake from a shivering dream, and for a moment Caro's scent seemed to fill the pinnace. There were tears in Sula's eyes, and when she wiped them away she saw something new on her displays.

Five somethings, swinging around from the far side of Barbas. Five ships were burning hard gees there, coming around the big planet at an unusual angle. Sula wondered if they heading for Magaria. No – they burned well past that point.

'Ah. Ha,' she said.

They were looping around Barbas to fly towards Rinconell. They must have done a whole series of wild planet-loops to get where they were. And now Sula saw what they were intending.

They were going to come between Wormhole One and the six survivors of the Home Fleet. There would be a blazing collision as their paths crossed, and the last of the Home Fleet would be annihilated. The five Naxid ships might die as well, if the loyalists had enough missiles remaining, but in any case the last of the Home Fleet would be destroyed.

Frantically Sula began calculating trajectories. Her own missiles were a third of a light-minute ahead of her, and it would take time for her instructions to reach them. She didn't want them to manoeuvre where the enemy could see them, and the only way to do that was to fire their engines when they were behind the huge gas giant Rinconell.

It took Sula almost three hours to calculate the trajectories, triple-check the work, and transmit the missiles' instructions via communications laser. Then she calculated her own trajectory and her own burn. Because she couldn't pull the massive gees of her missiles, she couldn't lay herself on the same track – she'd be a spectator again, whatever happened.

And then she waited. It was nine hours before the tawny gas giant Rinconell became a great crescent on her displays, before her eighteen missiles executed precise pivots and made the furious burn that set them on their new trajectories. And more seconds passed before her own engine punched her and dropped her into nightmare sleep.

But the wait was worth it. On their mad swing around

Barbas, the Naxid ships emerged with a velocity of nearly half the speed of light. The missiles coming at them were travelling in excess of .7c. The closing velocity was so enormous that the Naxids were probably never aware of what was coming at them, and had a few seconds' warning at most, not enough to activate their defences.

Wild, angry joy sang in Sula as she watched the eighteen missiles explode in and among the Naxid ships. Nothing was left of the enemy but stripped ions that glowed fiercely and briefly in the dark.

She reached for the comm unit and punched on the radio, broadcasting on the intership channel to the Naxids, the fleeing Home Fleet survivors, the scattered, cooling atoms that had been *Dauntless* and *Glory of the Praxis* and all the others strewn and lost in the death and fury of Magaria.

'Sula!' she shouted into the transmitter. 'It was Sula who did this! *Remember my name!*'

She programmed her own burn for the wormhole, and escape.

Fourteen

Five hours after transiting Magaria Wormhole One, Sula's pinnace was recovered by the *Bombardment of Delhi*. She pulled herself wearily out of the little boat, and as the riggers helped her climb into the ready room, she saw in the dim emergency lighting that someone waited for her. Her heart surged as she recognized Martinez, and then she realized that a memory had imposed itself on her exhausted mind, a memory of the time Martinez had met her after the *Midnight Runner* rescue.

The person before her stepped forward, and before her she saw a different memory, that of Jeremy Foote.

'*You*,' she said, and began to laugh.

Foote looked at her with impatience. He was considerably less immaculate than when Sula had last seen him, at the party he'd thrown to celebrate his promotion: he was without his uniform jacket, and his shirt was grimy and torn. His cowlick was greasy. His sleeves were rolled up, and there was a smear of something on one forearm, a smear that had an echo on his forehead where he'd wiped away sweat.

The riggers took her helmet and unsealed her gloves.

'I'll need your data foils,' Foote said, his drawl a little more clipped than usual. 'The premiere sent me.'

'I forgot them in the boat,' Sula said. 'Sorry.' She turned to return to the docking tube.

'I'll get them,' Foote said. 'Never mind..'

He dropped into the docking tube and was gone for a few

moments. The riggers shoved Sula's arms over her head and pulled off the upper half of her suit. Sula's nose wrinkled at the acrid odour of her own body, all the stale sweat and terror and burned adrenaline. The riggers began work on the lower half of her vac suit.

Foote popped up from the access tube. 'Turn your back,' Sula told him.

Foote looked resentful. 'I've seen women before,' he said.

'You've never seen me,' Sula said, 'and you're not going to.'

'That's "turn your back, *my lord*",' Foote drawled, but he turned his back anyway. The silent riggers stripped away Sula's suit and handed her a pair of sterile drawers.

'I forgot about your promotion, my lord, sorry.' Sula stepped into the drawers and tied the string waistband. 'It must have been the excitement of seeing you again.'

She was rewarded by a crack in the facade of the riggers' deadpan faces. She winked at the nearest of them, and was further rewarded by a startled grin.

Foote cast an annoyed look over his shoulder, saw she was clothed, and turned to face her.

'The premiere says he's putting you in for a decoration,' he said. 'He says you saved us.'

'Give him my thanks,' Sula said. 'But isn't it the captain who does the recommending?'

'The captain's dead,' Foote said shortly.

The dead captain would have been Captain Foote, the yachtsman, who would have insured young Jeremy's continual promotion.

'Sorry about your uncle, Foote.'

Foote gave a grim nod. 'We're pretty well shot up,' he said. 'You'll be needed on damage control, if you're not hurt.'

'I need some shoes,' Sula said, 'and then I'm with you.'

Bombardment of Delhi had lost its captain, its second and third lieutenants, and everyone else in Command. The forward third of the ship had been decompressed, there were only a dozen missiles left in the magazine, and only one pinnace remained – Sula's.

But *Delhi*, Sula reminded herself, was in better shape than all but five other ships of the Home Fleet.

For two days she worked constantly at patching, refitting, replacing, and testing. Towards the end of the second day, her party succeeded in recompressing the area around Command and in breaking into Command to retrieve the bodies of Captain Foote and the others. They had died due to fire – not from asphyxiation, because they had their helmets on, but due to fierce heat. Nothing in Command was flammable, but even steel will burn if it gets hot enough, and Command had grown very hot indeed. A rain of molten metal had streaked the walls of Command like tears.

The crisped remains of the dead, little husks of carbon each curled like a foetus, were bagged and carried out to the cargo airlock. Sula felt oddly at home amid the dead. She looked at the charcoal on her palms. Take the water out, she thought, and that's all we are.

She found the realization comforting.

'Life is brief, but the Praxis is eternal,' the first lieutenant read from the burial service. 'Let us all take comfort and security in the wisdom that all that is important is known.'

The dead were blown into space. Afterwards, the premiere took Sula aside and told her that the squadron commander had promoted her to sub-lieutenant in order to fill one of *Delhi*'s vacancies.

Really, she thought, I am rewarded for the most extra-ordinary things.

A day later, lying exhausted in her rack, she overheard one of the other cadets talking about test scores. The cadet had done well and was pleased that she'd soon be promoted and no longer had to be envious of Sula.

Sula looked at the woman and thought she remembered her.

'Wait a minute,' she said. 'Didn't you take the exams with me at Zanshaa? The ones they decided didn't signify?'

The cadet looked at her in surprise. 'Didn't you get the announcement? The Board decided the exams would count. They need officers too badly. Instead of the exam on the Praxis they're relying on testaments of loyalty from superiors.'

'Ah. Ha,' Sula said.

She flung herself to the nearest computer display, called up the results, and found out she had achieved her first.

She thought of Caro Sula sliding into the Iola, the cold brown waters rising up about her, choking her nose and mouth, and she wondered if the equation was balanced now. Did an exemplary career and a couple of thousand dead Naxids equal one dead, useless rich girl?

All important things are known. Somehow this didn't seem to be one of them.

Later that day she was supervising a party that was re-reeving bundles of electric cable that had shorted out during the battle. They'd had to pull up a whole corridor of Captain Foote's parquet flooring to get at the utility space underneath, and then they had to be very careful when balanced on the deck beams not to get in contact with the pipe of superheated coolant that ran alongside the cable bundles, the coolant carrying the engines' heat to the compressors and heat exchanger.

Midday came and the job wasn't completed. Sula sent her party to their dinner. And then she lowered herself onto one of the beams. The heat rose from the pipe and brought a prickle of sweat onto her face. She balanced there for a moment and looked at her right hand, at the whorls of Gredel's traitorous, dangerous fingerprints.

Sweat trickled down her cheek. She took a deep breath, bent down, and pressed her right thumb to the pipe.

I tripped on the beams and fell, she rehearsed. *It was an accident.*

She kept her thumb on the pipe until she could smell the burning flesh, and only then did Sula permit herself to scream.

The censors weren't used to adversity, and didn't know how to handle the news from Magaria. Martinez' initial report was that the battle was a glorious triumph in which Magaria had somehow not been captured, and which caused Zanshaa to mobilize to the utmost. He sent a message to the Fleet Control Board telling them that, as a squadron commander engaged in offensive action, he needed to know what really happened.

They told him. After he recovered from his shock, he did some calculations and worked out how long it would take the Naxids to arrive at Zanshaa. They would have to decelerate and dock with Magaria ring to take on new armaments and fuel, then accelerate again.

Three months. Three months, perhaps a little longer, before the Naxid fleet could begin the Battle of Zanshaa.

Corona and its Light Squadron Fourteen was more than halfway to Hone-bar. It would take too long to decelerate and return, so instead Light Squadron Fourteen would swing around Hone-bar's sun and major planets and slingshot its way back to the capital.

And arrive just ahead of the Naxids, apparently. Whose known ships outnumbered the entire loyalist fleet.

He sent a message urging Roland and his sisters to book passage on the next ship for Laredo, and then concentrated on the management of his squadron. He had decreed a whole series of virtual manoeuvres, the crews of each ship simultaneously wired into the same scenario. He matched them against each other, against hypothetical Naxid squadrons. He worked them very hard, hard enough that Kamarullah began complaining about him to the other captains. Perhaps the other captains could take comfort from the fact that *Corona*, with its new crew unused to the ship or their officers, usually failed to distinguish itself in these exercises, performing poorly enough to set Martinez to grinding his teeth. Nor was he the only Corona so affected: he overheard Ahmet complain to Knadjian about the damned newcomers bungling everything and getting in the way and making the ship look bad.

If only Dalkieth were a more driving, ambitious sort of lieutenant. If only Shankaracharya and Vonderheydte had more experience. If only he weren't so torn between managing the ship and bossing the squadron.

Capping it all was Saavedra's discovery that two tons of flour intended for the mess, which Martinez had signed for, was in fact used machine oil badly in need of recycling. Someone was making a nice profit, apparently, selling Fleet supplies, but that person wasn't Martinez.

Martinez briefly lost his mind. His roars of anger, as he marched from his office to the food store and back, sent even hardened crouchbacks dodging out of the way and looking for a place to hide until he stomped past.

When he made his evening entry in the log, he saw the message light blinking and found to his surprise that it was a video from Sula.

She wore a sub-lieutenant's shoulder boards, he saw; she must have passed her exam. One hand was bandaged and cradled in the opposite arm.

Her complexion was lightly flushed, and flawless, and took his breath away. There was a strange intensity in her green eyes, a kind of fever. Perhaps she was in pain.

'So,' she said, 'I lived. I'm the only survivor from my ship. I got picked up by the *Delhi*, and they lost a lot of people, too.' She paused, and with a shock Martinez realized that Sula must have been the pinnace pilot who destroyed an entire enemy squadron. The report he'd received from the Fleet hadn't mentioned any names.

Sula's pointed tongue licked her lips for a second, and then she continued.

'So here's what I've learned: I'm the second luckiest person in the universe. And do you know who's the luckiest?' The intense green eyes glittered. 'You are,' Sula said. 'You are, Gareth Martinez. You. Commander of *Corona,* recipient of the Golden Orb. You.' Her lips tightened in a smile.

She hasn't even heard I'm a squadron commander, it hasn't been announced. Martinez managed this thought through his wonderment.

'When I realized this I decided to make some resolutions,' Sula said. 'So here's the first: *No more whining.* No more complaining about my superiors or my lack of patronage or the fact I don't have much money compared with every other officer in the Fleet. No more whining about,' she hesitated, 'about my past. Why should I complain? I'm the second luckiest person in the empire.'

She leaned a little towards the camera. 'And you shouldn't complain either. You're very entertaining when you do it, and I laugh, but you didn't have any reason before, and you damn well don't have any now. You're the luckiest person in the universe, so what do you have to complain about?'

She leaned back, and the motion must have pained her, because she gave a little wince and cradled her injured hand more carefully. She gave the camera an unreadable look.

'My second resolution,' she said, 'is to come looking for you the second fate and the Fleet permit. Two lucky people like us, what can't we do?' Her eyes turned just a little off-camera, and she said, 'End transmission.'

Slow to master his thoughts, Martinez watched the *end transmission* symbol for a long time. He reached out a hand to re-cue the video and run it again, and then drew the hand back.

Then he thought about replying, but he had no idea what he'd say.

The comm unit bleeped at him. 'This is Martinez,' he said, and looked into Kelly's harassed face.

'It's a complete shambles in the weapons bay, my lord. Chau has totally buggered up one of the robots during a reloading, and now he's under arrest for busting Tippel in the chops, and we still don't know what to do with the robot, it's blocking everything and it's just too big to shove out of the way.'

And what in hell am I supposed to do about it? Martinez wanted to scream.

But then he thought, *No whining,* and rose from his desk and went to his work.

The Maw gaped wide and red, and tinged with a hint of blood the fine lace of the frost that had climbed halfway up the lifeboat's cockpit window. Warrant Officer Severin had got used to the cold, had got used to his breath frosting in front of him and the fact that his nose ran all the time. He had got used to wearing layers of clothing even in bed, and wrapping himself in a thermal blanket whenever he rose so that he looked like an ambulatory tent. He was used to the moisture condensing on the lifeboat's walls, and to the activities of the Naxid squadron in the Protipanu system.

The eight ships had finished their long, long deceleration burn and re-entered the system, swinging in a leisurely orbit about the brown dwarf and its outer planets. They knew where the wormhole was now, but showed no sign of wanting to pass through it. Whatever plans they'd once had were now altered.

The Naxids had been reinforced. Three more warships, and a pair of fat cargo vessels that had chucked large containers into orbit around the sun for the warships to pick up, containers that Severin suspected held food and fuel. The

cargo ships had then gone on to rendezvous with the two
message relay stations and to occupy them. Severin wouldn't
be getting messages out of the system anytime soon.

The Naxids had fired decoys: an elaborate pattern had been
sent in orbit around the Protipanu system. Anyone entering
would have a confusing time sorting real targets from false,
perhaps a fatal time.

The Naxids were up to something. Severin watched everything on his displays and made notes.

The enemy had plans. And Severin was going to work out
what they were, if only he could keep from freezing.

A Note on the Calendar

The Shaa 'year' is, so far as anyone knows, an arbitrary period of time unconnected with the orbit of any planet, or the measurement of anything in the natural world. It consists of .84 Earth years, or 306.6 Earth days. Caroline Sula, 23 in Shaa measure, is 20 by the reckoning of old Earth.

Planets within the empire of the Shaa each have their own local calendar by which they chart the local year and seasons: but all official business is conducted in reference to the imperial calendar rather than the local.

The Shaa year is divided into equally arbitrary units that demonstrate the Shaa love for prime numbers. The Shaa year is divided into 11 months of 27.9 Earth days each, and each month is divided into 23 Shaa days, each 1.21 Earth days. The Shaa day is divided into 29 hours, each of 59.98 minutes; and the hours are divided into 53 minutes, each 67.9 Earth seconds long. Each Shaa minute consists of 101 seconds, each of .67 Earth seconds.

There is no Shaa equivalent of the 'week', though many planets have such a period in their own local calendars.

Measurements of time in this work, unless otherwise noted, are exclusively in Shaa measure. Readers may take comfort in the fact that, though the Shaa day is a little longer than Earth's 24-hour day, the hours and minutes are roughly equivalent.